Resounding praise for
New York Times bestselling author
PATRICK ROBINSON
and his previous
electrifying techno-thriller
BARRACUDA 945

"Patrick Robinson is quickly replacing
Tom Clancy as the pre-eminent writer of
modern naval fiction."
Florida Times-Union

"An edge-of-your-seat terror ride . . .
Patrick Robinson has tapped into our fear . . .
to create a spellbinding novel."
Herald Express

"A gripping tale . . . this techno-thriller . . . may be
just what the book doctor ordered. It is rich with
excitement, suspense and sheer macho fantasy."
Tampa Tribune

"Engrossing . . . An audacious, richly told tale
with action both above sea-level and below."
Publishers Weekly

"If action's your bag, this is mind-blowing."
The Mirror

Books by Patrick Robinson

HUNTER KILLER
SCIMITAR SL-2
BARRACUDA 945
SLIDER
THE SHARK MUTINY
U.S.S. SEAWOLF
H.M.S. UNSEEN
KILO CLASS
NIMITZ CLASS
TRUE BLUE
ONE HUNDRED DAYS
(with Admiral Sir John "Sandy" Woodward)

SCIMITAR SL-2

PATRICK ROBINSON

HarperTorch
An Imprint of HarperCollins*Publishers*

HARPERTORCH
An Imprint of HarperCollins*Publishers*
10 East 53rd Street
New York, New York 10022-5299

Copyright © 2004 by Patrick Robinson
Author's Note copyright © 2005 by Patrick Robinson
ISBN: 0-06-084332-2

HarperCollins books may be purchased for educational, business, or sales promotional use. For information, please write: Special Markets Department, HarperCollins Publishers Inc., 10 East 53rd Street, New York, NY 10022.

First HarperTorch trade paperback printing: June 2005
First HarperTorch paperback printing: May 2005
First HarperCollins hardcover printing: August 2004

HarperCollins®, HarperTorch™, and ❧™ are trademarks of HarperCollins Publishers Inc.

Printed in the United States of America

Visit HarperTorch on the World Wide Web at *www.harpercollins.com*

Library of Congress Cataloging-in-Publication Data

Robinson, Patrick
    Scimitar SL-2 / Patrick Robinson.—1st. ed.
        p.   cm.
        1. Terrorism—Fiction. 2. Volcanoes—Fiction. I. Title.

    PR6068.01959S35 2004
    823'.914—dc22

                                                    2004042897

10 9 8 7 6 5 4 3 2 1

Cast of Principal Characters

Senior Command (Political)

Charles McBride (Democrat, Rhode Island; President of
the United States)
Vice President Paul Bedford (Democrat, Virginia)
Cyrus Romney (National Security Adviser)
Senator Edward Kennedy (Senior Member, Senate Armed
Services Committee)
Bill Hatchard (President McBride's Chief of Staff)
Admiral Arnold Morgan (Supreme Commander Operation
High Tide)

National Security Agency

Rear Adm. George R. Morris (Director)
Lt. Comdr. James Ramshawe (Assistant to the Director)

U.S. Naval and Military Senior Command

Gen. Tim Scannell (Chairman of the Joint Chiefs)
Adm. Alan Dickson (Chief of Naval Operations)
Adm. Dick Greening (Commander in Chief, Pacific Fleet—
CINCPACFLT)
Adm. Frank Doran (Commander in Chief, Atlantic Fleet)
Rear Adm. Freddie Curran (Commander, Submarines Pa-
cific Fleet—COMSUBPAC)

Gen. Kenneth Clark (Commandant, United States Marine
Corps)
Gen. Bart Boyce (Supreme Allied Commander, NATO)

Combat Commanders

Adm. George Gillmore (Search Group Commander, Task
Group 201.1—USS *Coronado*)
Capt. Joe Wickman (CO, USS *Simpson*)
Capt. C. J. Smith (CO, USS *Elrod*)
Capt. Eric Nielsen (CO, USS *Nicholas*)
Capt. Clint Sammons (CO, USS *Klakring*)
Maj. Blake Gill (Commander, Patriot Missile Batteries)

U.S. Navy Seahawk Combat Pilots

Lt. Paul Lubrano
Lt. Ian Holman
Lt. Don Brickle

Middle Eastern High Command

Adm. Mohammed Badr (C in C, Iranian Navy)
Gen. Ravi Rashood (Hamas Supreme Commander Combat)
Lt. Com. Shakira Rashood (Special Navigation and
Targeting—*Barracuda II*)
Adm. Ben Badr (CO, *Barracuda II*)

Ship's Company Barracuda II

Capt. Ali Akbar Mohtaj (Executive Officer)
Comdr. Abbas Shafii (senior submariner, Iranian Navy, and
nuclear specialist)
Comdr. Hamidi Abdolrahim (Chief Nuclear Engineer)
Lt. Ashtari Mohammed (Navigation Officer)
CPO. Ali Zahedi (Chief of Boat)
CPO. Ardeshir Tikku (nuclear computer controls specialist)

Maj. Ahmed Sabah (freedom fighter and personal bodyguard to General Rashood)

Foreign Military

Col. Dae-jung (Commandant, Nuclear Operations,
  Kwanmo-bong Complex, North Korea)
Capt. Habib Abdu Camara (C in C, Navy of Senegal)

Civilian Connections

Professor Paul "Lava" Landon (volcanologist, University of
  London, dec.)
David Gavron (Israeli Ambassador to Washington,
  ex–Mossad Chief)
Mr. Tony Tilton (Seattle Bank President and star witness)
Mrs. Kathy Morgan (wife of Admiral Arnold Morgan, re-
  called to White House)
His Excellency Mark Vollmer (United States Ambassador
  to Dubai)

Author's Note

Scimitar SL-2—that's a medium-range guided missile, submerged launch from a submarine, Mark 2 nuclear warhead. Generally speaking, one of these could knock down a town the size of Brighton.

It ended up the title for this novel. But it was not my first choice. That was *Tsunami*, which had, at the time, raised a near-unanimous objection from my agent, and from my publishers on both sides of the Atlantic: *Japanese word, no one knows what it means*.

Well, everyone knows only too well what that word means now. The horrific events of December 26, 2004, which devastated literally millions of lives, brought the word 'tsunami' into the world's vocabulary. Its literal meaning is "harbor wave," but that doesn't seem an adequate description for what is possibly the greatest geophysical catastrophe that can befall the planet Earth, short of a direct hit by a comet.

And words can barely describe the monstrous events that early morning when a colossal earthquake below the floor of the Indian Ocean caused great waters to rise up and drown, at the time of writing, an estimated 150,000 people on coastlines near and far from the epicenter of the waves' formation.

My research for *Scimitar SL-2* involved months of studing the cause and effect of such mammoth waves. The causes are relatively simple. You need a mighty splash in the ocean, and essentially there are only three ways to get one big enough:

landslide, volcanic eruption, or earthquake. A tsunami can develop a speed of up to 400 knots as it rolls across the ocean floor; a blast in the Hawaiian islands started a tsunami which swept huge rocks thousands of miles, to end up in Sydney Harbor. When the volcanic island of Krakatoa blew off its entire summit in the Sunda Strait in 1883, it was one of the biggest blasts ever witnessed, or heard, for thousands of years. But it was not the blast that killed 36,000 people along the coasts of both Java and Sumatra. Most of them drowned beneath the mega-tsunami that engulfed the entire coastal area. This was the direct result of the splash in the ocean.

For more than a year, I metaphorically lived tsunamis, trying to work out what would happen if the world's most dangerous geohazard—the glowering volcano of Cumbre Vieja in the Canary Islands—should erupt and cause the Atlantic mega-tsunami everyone in the trade believes to be a certainty. The one that would wipe out America's east coast, including Boston, New York, Philadelphia, and Washington.

So when the first person walked up to me on Sunday morning, December 26, 2004, and said "How about that tsunami then?" I experienced one of those cold shudders you're supposed to feel when someone's walking on your grave.

"The Atlantic?" I asked, horrified.

"No, somewhere in the Indian Ocean . . . but a lot of people are feared drowned."

And as the day drew to a close, and I spoke with friends and family and watched on television the devastating effects of this geophysical disaster on the villages and resorts along the coast of the Indian Ocean, devastation that reached as far away as the coast of Somalia, I couldn't help but think of my novel *Scimitar SL-2*, and the imaginary tsunami I had threatened to unleash on a different part of the world: the Atlantic coastlines of the United States, Europe, and Africa. My imaginary scenario is set several years into the future, where a group of high-tech terrorists succeed in exploding one volcano with guided missiles and set out to blow up another in order to trigger a mega-tsunami. I hadn't counted on the natural world providing the scenario for me. Fiction didn't prepare me for the tragic sight of families torn apart, nor the scenes of destruction of homes and businesses in neighborhoods that were already poverty-stricken. And I watched with horror as the death toll rose exponentially hour upon hour.

Thanks to my extensive research for *ScimitarSL-2*, I had a good idea about what had happened. Deep in the Indian Ocean the tectonic plates had shifted, opening up a giant chasm into which the water had cascaded. When the chasm closed again the water was forced back upwards with stupendous force and caused the massive waves of the megatsunami, rolling out in an ever-widening circle.

I went back to my charts of the Indian Ocean and the Bay of Bengal, not used since I wrote *The Shark Mutiny* in the year 2000, and looked at the surrounding coastlines. I knew from these charts that the initial estimate of 15,000 dead was set to rise. There is land at every point of the circle. The tsunami could not miss every town and village along the shore for hundreds of miles.

In the years between 2002 and 2010, it is estimated that more than 200 major volcanic eruptions will occur. But not many will cause a tsunami. Mount St. Helens in Washington State keeps letting out a smoky shout of warning, but the rumble that is the most worrisome is the one beneath the Cumbre Vieja.

The world's foremost authority on volcanoes, Bill McGuire, is professor of Geophysical Hazards at University College, London. Bill McGuire is King of All Disasters, the author of hundreds of papers and books, broadcaster and acknowledged world authority on tsunamis and all that they stand for. He has studied Cumbre Vieja extensively and knows the devastation it could unleash should the worst case scenario happen. Professor McGuire finds an endless frustration with the refusal of governments to heed the warnings of him and his team, and all the other worldwide geohazard reports. And I understand that. For he has the inner sadness of a man who has been crying out for early warnings on tsunamis for many years.

I too have a similar sadness, because I have studied thousands of his words. And, from a plainly removed standpoint, I feel his pain at the apparent suddenness of the Asian tsunami, the absolute shock as it descended into all our television sets and all our newspapers.

But I have also been moved by the incredible generosity of people around the world who have contributed to the charities that have been set up to help those directly affected by the tsunami. In a world where headlines are dominated by the escalating conflict in the Middle East, it is this sort of generosity which shows compassion of the human spirit. Yet the people in the region are going to need help not just in the weeks following the disaster, but in the months and years beyond that while they struggle to rebuild their lives.

You can contribute by donating to Tsunami relief through a number of organizations, all of which are listed on the World Wide Web. They can be found at

http://www.google.com/tsunami_relief.html

Thank you.

Patrick Robinson
January 2005

SCIMITAR SL-2

Prologue

10.30 P.M., Thursday, May 8, 2008
Kensington, London.

PROFESSOR PAUL LANDON, known to an entire generation of
university students as "Lava," hurried through the lower
ground floor doorway of the Royal Geographical Society.
Out into the darkness of wide, tree-lined Exhibition Road
were the capital's highway of enormous museums, running
south from Hyde Park.

He paused on the broad graystone doorstep, a spot where
many another great man had stood before him—the explorers
Captain Scott of the Antarctic and Ernest Shackleton; the first
conquerors of Everest, Sir Edmund Hillary, who made the
summit, and Lord Hunt, who led the historic 1953 expedition.

Like Professor Landon, they were celebrated Fellows of
the Royal Geographical Society, and like him, they had all
delivered a series of stunning Spring Lectures at the lectern
of the auditorium inside the great building. Like him, they
had packed the place, and held their audience spellbound.

The prime difference between the great adventurers of the
twentieth century and Professor Paul "Lava" Landon was
that of subject. Whereas Scott, Shackleton, Hillary, and Hunt
had entertained with breathtaking accounts of human survival in freezing conditions, the Professor had just explained
in dazzling detail the forthcoming end of the world. No firm
dates, of course. Like all masters of global geophysics, Pro-

fessor Landon operated in approximate time slots of 10,000 years.

The upcoming catastrophe would likely occur in around 7,000 years, he concluded. "But then again," he added, "it could just as easily happen next Friday, shortly after lunch."

The typical Royal Geographical crowd, the scholarly, understated, well-heeled English elite, which occupied the auditorium, had loved the lecture. It had been meticulously planned, and flawlessly delivered, with excellent graphics and film clips.

The presentation illuminated the mighty eruptions of volcanoes around the world, the coast-shuddering effects of tidal waves, the ravages of earthquakes. But mostly it focused on the super-eruptions of the past like the one that split Indonesia's Krakatoa apart in 1883, wiping out 36,000 residents of Java and Sumatra.

Landon told them of the staggering eruption of Wyoming's Yellowstone Park volcano, which dumped molten magma and ash into California, Texas, and even onto the seabed of the Caribbean. It actually happened 650,000 years ago but "Lava" Landon made it seem like last summer.

He produced a graphic study of the pulverizing blast of Mount St. Helens in Washington State, in which the north flank swelled into a massive balloon of lava before literally exploding, blowing the mountainside asunder and obliterating nearly 400 square miles of forest.

That happened in 1980, and it led Professor Landon inevitably to the climax of his speech—the possibility of a *tsunami*, a Japanese word describing a series of mountainous waves generated either by an earthquake or, more likely, by a massive volcanic landslide into deep ocean.

Professor Landon's closing focused on the new potential landslide on the southwest coast of La Palma, the northwesternmost of the Canary Islands. (Jutting out from deep Atlantic waters, La Palma stands 375 miles off the southern coast of Morocco.)

The fact was, he explained, that a gigantic hunk of volcanic rock, several miles long and set on a searing fault line in the earth's crust, had slipped in the last forty or fifty years, maybe twelve feet down the steep cliff, detaching from the west flank. And somewhere behind this colossal, unstable chunk of rock lay, potentially, the simmering core of the mighty volcano of Cumbre Vieja.

"That lets rip, and the lot goes," Professor Landon asserted, brightly. "It'd send a staggeringly large rock, several cubic miles of it, crashing off the west flank of the volcano, straight into the Atlantic at more than 200 mph, and surging along the ocean floor, at maybe 400 mph. I'm talking about one of the largest landslides in the past million years. Actually I'm talking about the total collapse of the southwest section of La Palma."

The packed audience of ex–Military and Naval Officers, scientists, academics, and scions of ancient landed families, which had always shown an interest in such scientific matters, had listened, wide-eyed, as the Professor explained the establishment of a gigantic column of waves, ascending from the seabed to the surface, driving forward to reach speeds of 500 mph, and rising to a height of maybe 200 feet into the air as they arrived in shallow coastal waters.

Landon went on to describe how the monstrous tidal surge would wipe out large hunks of coastal southern England, Spain, and West Africa. And then, within nine hours from the moment of the rock's impact on the surface of the Atlantic off southwestern La Palma, the massive wall of water would travel across the Atlantic and obliterate the entire East Coast of the United States.

"If Cumbre Vieja blows, this *will* happen," he confirmed. "A rare and terrible mega-tsunami. Scientific research has estimated a number of intense waves, still perhaps 150 feet high, crashing into the restricted seaways off lower Manhattan, and then flattening the Wall Street area of New York with its very first sweep.

"The opening tidal wave would suck the debris out of the streets and flatten the ground before the next one of the wave series hit, demolishing buildings up to possibly fifteen blocks from the waterfront. And these giant waves—each one more than 100 feet high—would keep coming, progressively, until all of New York City was levelled.

"The biggest tsunami in recorded history. And all because of a single volcano."

Professor Paul Landon was one of the world's preeminent volcanologists, the Benfield Greig Professor of Geophysical Hazards at University College, London, and Director of the University's Hazard Center.

He had worked on the slopes of literally dozens of the world's most dangerous volcanoes, often successfully forecasting powerful eruptions. His nickname was well earned. And his skill in assessing the temperature and intent of the molten magma was matched only by his brilliance behind the lectern.

A bearded man of medium height, with pale blue eyes and the inevitable tweed sports jacket, checkered shirt, and college tie, he was forty-four years old and at the height of his game, his lectures in demand all over the world.

Lava Landon lived outside London in the commuter belt of Buckinghamshire with his wife, a City lawyer named Valerie. Their two sons, age fourteen and fifteen, collectively considered their father to be more or less insane, hearing almost every day of their short lifetimes that the world would probably end next week. Their skepticism didn't faze Professor Landon in the least; like many of his fellow academics he was quite astonishingly self-absorbed and fireproof to criticism.

As he stood now in the hoofprints of the mighty Scott, Shackleton, Hillary, and Hunt, he reflected on an evening's work well done. He knew he had mesmerized the entire audience. But he wasn't aware of one particular listener. Seated among the sea of spellbound faces, at the back of the auditorium, a twenty-three-year-old Palestinian freedom fighter, Ahmed Sabah, was taking notes, intent on every word, every graphic.

After the speech, Sabah slipped out quickly and was now

waiting quietly in the dark southern precincts of Albert Hall, London's spectacular rounded concert hall, situated next door to the Royal Geographical Society.

As Lava Landon walked along Kensington Gore, turning into the courtyard of the great hall of music, named for Queen Victoria's consort Prince Albert, several thousand fans began to flood through the doors, following a live concert celebrating popular bands of the eighties.

It actually took Paul Landon four more minutes to reach the top of the long, wide flight of steps that led down from the hall to the notoriously dark rear-side road. There were hundreds of fans headed the same way and they almost engulfed the great geophysicist on the steps.

Directly below him he could see a black Range Rover, illegally parked, close to the sidewalk, no lights, facing the wrong way, with no one in the driver's seat.

Ahmed Sabah and his two colleagues chose that moment to strike from behind. They expertly rammed a black canvas bag over Paul Landon's head, holding him in an iron grip, and bundled him down the last two steps and into the back of the waiting vehicle.

There was no time to cry out, no time to fight back. An accented voice kept hissing into his ear, urging him to remain quiet unless he wanted to die, and against his left kidney he could feel the unmistakable push of a large knife.

It's curious how the swarm of preoccupied people could have missed entirely what was happening in their midst. It must have been their single-minded determination to get home—searching for cabs, or late buses, hoping to make the London underground station at South Kensington in time for one of the infrequent late-night trains.

No one paid attention to the incident, certainly not the two London policemen on patrol with a large German shepherd named Roger, who were swept along the throng spilling out of the concert hall at the top of the steps, 30 feet above the scene of the kidnapping.

True to the modern ethos of the London police, they

missed the crime, but homed in instantly on the illegal parking, fighting their way down the steps to apprehend the Range Rover's driver, their hands already fumbling, urgently, for their trusty Breathalyzers.

By the time they arrived, the driver's seat was occupied. Seated behind the wheel, his eyes hidden behind dark glasses, was the former SAS Major, Ray Kerman, currently known as Gen. Ravi Rashood, Commander in Chief of the Revolutionary forces of Hamas and, quite possibly, the most dangerous and wanted terrorist in the world.

Right now he was revving the engine impatiently, causing the policemen to unleash the huge dog, who flew at the car in two forward bounds, teeth bared, going for the driver's right arm through the open window.

Big mistake, Roger. From the backseat of the Range Rover, Ahmed Sabah almost blew the dog's head off with a burst from a silenced AK-47. The policeman running in front could not believe what he had seen with his own eyes, and he stopped some three yards from the vehicle, the late attack dog Roger in a heap at his feet.

Ahmed's light machine gun spoke quietly again—three dull muffled thumps—and a short line of bullets through the forehead flung the constable backwards to the ground, dead.

The second policeman, seeing the dog, but not yet his fallen colleague, ran instinctively toward the driver. But he was late. The General was out on the sidewalk, and seized the astonished cop's raised right arm, flinging him down in one fluid motion, his head almost on the seat.

He grabbed him by the throat and rammed his head against the door's recess. One split second later, Ahmed slammed the door shut with stupendous force, cracking the policeman's skull from the bridge of his nose to the hairline. At that moment, that Range Rover became the most expensive nutcracker since Pyotr Ilich Tchaikovsky worked his magic one hundred years before.

Ravi spun the police officer around and, with the butt of

his gloved right hand, thundered a terrible upward punch into his already bleeding nose. The force rammed the bone clean into the brain, the classic unarmed-combat killing blow of the SAS. The London bobby was dead before he slumped back onto the edge of the sidewalk.

The men from Hamas had practiced the "defensive" operation for weeks, and there had been no mistakes. Only the presence of the big German-bred attack dog had surprised them. But not for long. From the moment they first grabbed the Professor, to their quick getaway, only seventeen seconds had passed.

And now the Range Rover made a full turnaround, its lights still dark, and headed for Exhibition Road, the backseat prisoner unaware of the carnage that quickly grew smaller in the rearview mirror.

It took a full five minutes for two or three people among the pop concert crowd to realize that something had happened. No, Roger was not taking a nap. Yes, that was actual blood. No, the policeman lying flat on his back had indeed been shot dead and the holes in his forehead were not birthmarks. And no, the other chap in the blue coat slumped facedown in the gutter was definitely a policeman. And no, he was not drunk. And yes, like Roger and his colleague, he also was dead.

Two London policemen and their guard dog slain at the bottom of the great stone stairway, south of the Albert Hall.

Finally, more than seven minutes after the Range Rover left, someone dialed London's 999 Emergency Service on a cell phone. Within another five minutes, two patrol cars were on the scene. By that time, General Ravi and his men had changed cars and were leisurely driving through West London to a cast-iron safe house owned by a few fellow Muslims in the suburb of Hounslow.

Professor Landon's hands were now bound together with plastic masking tape, and he was still in the bag, in every sense of the phrase. He was sitting between two of the world's most lethal Muslim fundamentalists, and in answer to his frightened pleas to know what was going on—since his captors plainly had the wrong man—he was told softly and firmly, *Keep quiet, Dr. Landon, we wish only to talk to you and then you will be set free.*

The first part was accurate. Almost. The second part was a lie. Lava Landon already knew far too much.

Back at the scene of the crimes, two ambulances were transporting the bodies of the murdered officers to St. Mary's Hospital, Paddington, and a Royal Society for the Prevention of Cruelty to Animals van was loading the carcass of Roger into a box, while the police were desperately looking for witnesses.

But no one had heard gunshots. No one had actually seen either policeman being attacked. No, it was impossible to identify the exact type of four-wheel-drive wagon that may have contained the criminals. No one had seen its license plate.

Someone thought it had driven off with no lights. Someone thought it turned right, down Exhibition Road. Someone else thought it turned left. No one could cast a single ray of light on the physical appearance of its occupants.

It was the most brutal slaying of police officers in London for nearly half a century, since the night when gangsters gunned down three policemen in Shepherd's Bush, a couple of miles to the west of the Albert Hall.

But at that time, the police had been pretty sure who had committed the crime within about five minutes of the shooting. This time they did not have the remotest idea. They had no clues, no witnesses, and absolutely no motives to work on. And of course, they had no notion whatsoever that a celebrity kidnap victim was being held in the back of the getaway vehicle.

* * *

The interrogation of Professor Landon began at one o'clock in the morning. The black bag had been removed from his head, his wrists were unbound, and he was given coffee at a large dining room table in a white room with no windows. Flanking the door were two Middle Eastern–looking guards wearing blue jeans, black boots, and short brown leather jackets. Both were holding AK-47s.

Before him sat a broad-shouldered English army-officer type, more formally dressed, no longer wearing sunglasses. He too was Middle Eastern in appearance, but his voice and tone could have been honed nowhere else on earth but a leading English public school.

The discussion was about volcanoes.

How many genuine eruptions have occurred in the world in recent years?

Probably a hundred since 2002, maybe a few more.

Can you name some?

Certainly . . . Montserrat in the West Indies . . . Karangetang, Indonesia . . . San Cristobal, Nicaragua . . . Tangkubanparahu in Java . . . at least three on the Kamchatka Peninsula, Siberia . . . Fuego in Guatemala . . . Stromboli in Italy . . . Kavachi Seamount, Solomon Islands . . . Chiginagak Island, Alaska . . .

How many in the past twelve months?

You mean serious ones, or just rumblings?

How many explosions?

Well, Colima in Mexico . . . Etna in Sicily . . . Fuego, Guatemala . . . the one in the Solomon Islands, and all three of the big ones on Kamchatka . . . plus Killauea in Hawaii . . . Maman in Papua New Guinea . . . always the Soufriere Hill in Montserrat . . . with a bit of a shout from Mount St. Helens in Washington State. Also some dire rumblings in the Canary Islands—the most serious of all.

Because of the tsunami?
Absolutely.

By 7 A.M. Professor Landon was growing anxious. One hour from now, he was due in his office in the splendid white-pillared Benfield Greig building on Gower Street near Euston Square. As the senior professor in London University's Department of Geological Sciences, his absence from his second-floor lecture room was sure to be noticed. But the questions continued, and he had little choice but to answer them.

What would it take to explode an active rumbling volcano? A big bomb? Maybe a couple of cruise missiles straight down the crater?

Well, the magma is very close to the surface in the Montserrat volcano on the western side of the island. I should think you could bring that one forward with a well-aimed hand grenade. It's never really stopped erupting in the last five years.

How about Mount St. Helens?

More difficult. But there have been small explosions and a lot of rumblings in the past several months. And remember. When St. Helens blew in 1980, it unleashed forces equal to four Hiroshimas every second. But it's very dangerous now and getting worse. I'd say four big cruise-missile explosions bang in the right place on the vulnerable south side would almost certainly unleash its lava again.

And Cumbre Vieja?

You mean to cause the mega-tsunami I was talking about last night? No conventional explosion would prise that huge hunk of rock off the cliffside. The volcano would have to erupt. And you'd need a sizable nuclear blast to make that happen.

You mean a full-blooded nuclear bomb?

*No, no. Not that big. But you mentioned cruise mis-
siles. And if you were thinking short-range, not ballistic, I'd say a medium-sized nuclear warhead would
probably blow a big enough hole to release the
magma.*

*And that starts the landslide into the bottom of the
ocean?*

*No. No. Not on its own. You see, that whole line of
volcanoes in southern La Palma contains a vast
amount of water deep in the mountains. The release of
the magma bursting up to the surface creates stupendous heat inside the rock. In turn this causes several
cubic miles of water to boil rapidly, and then expand,
like a pressure cooker. That's what will blow the mountain to pieces, and will most certainly collapse the
entire southwest section of La Palma into the sea. A
landslide, on a scale not seen on this earth for a million years.*

*So, if you fired a missile at the vulnerable spot on
the volcano of Cumbre Vieja, which you said tonight
was the most active, you'd need it to penetrate the surface and then explode deep below the ground?*

*It would need to hit hard and pierce the rock strata
that guards the lava, before it blew. The released
magma surging up from the core of the earth would
then erupt into the atmosphere, drawing zillions of
tons of incinerating magma right behind it. The
underground lakes would boil, and then flash off into
steam. That's when the whole mountain range would
explode.*

The former Maj. Ray Kerman liked Professor Landon.
This was a man who expertly understood explosions, both
natural and man-made, and who was consumed by his subject. And he did not dwell upon ramifications. He spoke
frankly, as a scientist. Very much to the point. Untroubled by

the obvious innuendoes of the equally obvious terrorist who held him prisoner. The science was what mattered to Professor Landon.

Yes, General Rashood liked him. This whole thing was rather a pity.

"Thank you, Professor," said the Hamas General. "Thank you very much. We'll have some breakfast now, and talk more."

Thursday, January 8, 2009
The White House, Washington, D.C.

THE BRAND-NEW DEMOCRATIC Administration, fresh from a narrow election victory, was moving into the West Wing. With the exception of the President, who knew he was going anyway at the end of his second term, every hour of every day was a trauma for the outgoing Republicans. For the big hitters of the military and government, handing over the reins to what most of them believed to be a bunch of naive, inexperienced, half-assed limousine liberals led by an idealistic young President from Rhode Island, who would have been pushed to hold down a proper executive job—well, anywhere—was appalling.

And today was probably the worst day of all. Adm. Arnold Morgan, the retiring President's National Security Adviser, was about to leave the White House for the last time. His big nineteenth-century Naval desk had already been cleared and removed, and now there were only a few good-byes left. The door to his office was wide open, and the Admiral, accompanied by his alarmingly beautiful secretary Kathy O'Brien, was ready to go. In attendance was the Secretary of State Harcourt Travis; the Chairman of the Joint Chiefs, Gen. Tim Scannell; the Chief of Naval Operations, Adm. Alan Dickson; the Director of the National Security

Agency, Adm. George Morris; and Morris's personal assistant, Lt. Comdr. James Ramshawe, American by birth, with Australian parents.

As the great man took his leave, they all stood in a small "family" huddle, veterans in the last half-dozen years of some of the most brutal secret operations ever conducted by the United States Military. Their devotion to Arnold had grown from the series of great triumphs on the international stage due, almost entirely, to the strengths of the Admiral's intellect.

Like Caesar, Admiral Morgan was not lovable—except to Kathy—but his grasp of international politics, string-pulling, poker-playing, threats and counterthreats, Machiavellian propaganda, and the conduct of restricted, classified military operations was second to none. At all of the above he was a virtuoso, driven by an unbending sense of patriotism. During his reign in the West Wing he intimidated, cajoled, outwitted, and bullied some of the most powerful men on earth. His creed was to fight and fight, and never to lower his blade short of victory. Gen. Douglas MacArthur and Gen. George Patton were his heroes. And now the Admiral was departing, leaving his Washington confidants devastated, convinced that another heaven and another earth must surely pass before such a man could be again.

Many of the high-ranking civilians would themselves go within a few short weeks of the incoming Democrats, but none so utterly ignominiously as Admiral Morgan himself. Called on the telephone by a Miss Betty-Ann Jones, a Southern liberal who had never been to Washington, he was told, "President McBride thinks it would be better if y'all resigned raht now, since he dun't think you and he's gonna get along real well."

Arnold Morgan had needed no second bidding. Five minutes later, he had dictated his short letter of resignation to Kathy, and ten minutes later, they were working on their wedding date, the colossal job of National Security Adviser no longer standing between them.

At Arnold's farewell dinner, at a favorite Georgetown restaurant, Secretary Travis, always the voice of irony and sly humor, had arrived at the table humming theatrically and loudly the tune of "Those Wedding Bells Are Breaking Up That Old Gang of Mine." Shortly he would return to Harvard to take up a professorship.

The military members of Arnold's inner circle would remain at their posts, more or less, under a new Commander in Chief.

And now Admiral Morgan stood at the great oak door to his office. He hesitated briefly, and nodded curtly to the empty room. Then he strode outside to the corridor, where his former colleagues waited. He smiled with some difficulty. "I'd be grateful," he said, "if each one of you would come and take me by the hand."

And so they said their farewells, each consumed by the private sense of trust they all shared with the National Security Chief. The last handshake was with the youngest of them, Lieutenant Commander Ramshawe, with whom Admiral Morgan had a near father-son relationship.

"I'll miss you, Jimmy," he said.

"And I'll miss you, sir," replied the young officer. "I don't suppose you'll ever know how much."

"Thanks, kid," said the Admiral informally. And then he turned on his heel, immaculately tailored in a dark gray suit, gleaming black leather lace-up shoes, blue shirt, and Naval Academy tie.

He walked resolutely, shoulders back, upright, full of dignity, with Kathy, his bride-to-be, at his side. He walked among the portraits of Presidents past, nodding sharply to General Eisenhower, as he always did. He walked like a man not departing but like a young officer recently summoned to the colors. In his mind a lifetime of thoughts, a lifetime of service to his country. The different people he had been . . . the Commanding Officer of a surface ship and then of a nuclear submarine out of Norfolk, Virginia . . . the Intelligence Tsar, head of the National Security Agency in Maryland . . .

and finally the right hand of a faltering Republican President who ended up knowing neither loyalty nor patriotism. That never mattered. Arnold had enough for both of them.

Walking along the familiar corridors, the Admiral heard once more the swish of the waves on a ship's hull heading out of a threatened harbor and into the great rolling swells of the ocean, the metallic scream of the anchor chain, the terse instructions of the COB, and in the deepest recesses of his mind, the shouts and commands of far-lost U.S. Navy SEALs whom he had never seen, never met, obeying his orders. Always obeying. As he himself obeyed his. Mostly.

He heard again the bells of the watch, tolling off the hours. And the smooth slide of his submarine's periscope. Once outside, he knew he would inevitably glance upward in the chill December breeze, and he would see it, snapping so damn proudly, right above him. The flag, always the flag.

He wore no overcoat, though Kathy was cozily engulfed in a light-brown full-length shearling number. And just before they turned left towards the main doors and out onto the West Wing veranda, she stretched out her right hand to take his, confirming once more that he would not be alone, as he left his quarterdeck for the last time and steered their ship into the long years of retirement. Admiral Morgan was sixty-four.

No one who was there would ever forget the departure of Arnold Morgan. Each and every man in the lower corridor felt a sense of control slipping away, as if a giant warship had somehow lost its helm. There had already been reports of civilians replacing the Marine guards at the White House. Patient young men in their early thirties were shaking their heads and sadly talking about the primitive ways of the U.S. Military under a Republican Administration. The new young ideologues came from a different world, the world of the future, where education of the Third World was paramount. Where no one was evil, just ignorant. Where death and destruction were to be replaced by more and more financial aid, where tyrants must be taught the ways of the West, not murdered. And where the poor and the helpless had to be given succor, and trained Americans had to work on their lack of self-esteem. And where absolutely no one could ever be harmed in the interests of revenge, conquest, or the destruction of a rogue regime.

Massive Naval and Military cuts were on the horizon. President Charles McBride was a globalist, certain in his own mind that reason, reason, and mercy would always prevail, however misguided a foe may appear. But like President Clinton, and Carter before him, McBride was a vacillator, a career politician accustomed to compromises, always looking for the middle ground. He was a man of nothing but political conviction, the way forwards for the lifelong lightweight. And he was chronically inexperienced in the harsher reaches of international diplomacy. President-elect McBride could not have recognized a scheming, self-interested statesman at six paces.

The one thing that Charles McBride did know, however, was the futility of spending zillions of dollars on defense, if you weren't planning to fight. No one had yet told him the age-old mantra of the wise—*You want peace, you better prepare for war. And if you don't, you'll end up paying for it in blood, sorrow, and tears.* Or, as Chairman Mao would say— *Real power comes from the barrel of a gun.*

Most of the men still standing in the corridor had a distant idea of the truth of that creed. And most of them believed it was probably true. And that everything would be fine, so long as the U.S.A. held the biggest gun of all. But if ever there was a U.S. President who could have used Arnold Morgan in the next office, it was surely the forty-seven-year-old Charles McBride.

And as Arnold's footsteps faded from the building, General Scannell muttered, "Jesus. I don't know what's gonna happen now."

And Harcourt Travis added, "Neither, General, do I."

A few hours later, Admiral Morris and Lieutenant Commander Ramshawe sat disconsolately in the rear seat of the Navy Staff car driving back to the National Security Agency in Fort Meade, Maryland.

"Hard to believe he's gone, Jimmy," grunted the Agency's Director.

"I just can't seem to accept it."

"Nor I."

"It's not gonna be the same anymore, is it?"

"Nothing is. It's gonna be worse. Because right here we got an incoming President who does not understand what kind of threats this country might face. He thinks we're all crazy."

"I know he does—can you imagine, sir? Getting some secretary to call up and tell Admiral Morgan he's fired. Bloody oath."

"God knows who he'll replace him with."

"Oh, he'll probably come up with some nice little social worker, team leader in the Peace Corps or something . . . Jesus, I can't believe this is happening."

Jimmy Ramshawe shook his head.

"The trouble with Intelligence," said Admiral Morris, "is that you need someone in Government who starts off believing you are not some kind of a dumb ass and who will listen, knowing that you speak from the kind of experience he simply doesn't have. Otherwise there's no point having a vast Intelligence network that costs billions to run. Not if its top operatives are wasting half their time trying to prove the unprovable to guys who are supposed to be on our side."

"I know, sir. That was the best thing about Admiral Morgan. He never dismissed what we said, always took it into consideration at least. He was some kind of a bloke, right? The best I ever met."

"And the best you ever will meet, young James."

The two men rode in companionable but somber silence to the northwestern suburbs of Washington and then out into the country to Fort Meade. Once there, the Director headed to his office, while Lieutenant Commander Ramshawe retreated to the chaos of his own paper-strewn lair for one of his favorite parts of the week.

Thursday afternoons. For thirty-year-old Ramshawe it

represented a couple of hours of pleasurable study. It was the day his personal newspapers arrived: the *Daily Mail* and the *London Telegraph*; *The Age* from Melbourne; the *Sydney Morning Herald;* and the *Toronto Globe*.

All of them were full of snippets of news—diplomatic, military, government, society, finance—stuff you would not necessarily find in the *Washington Post* or even the *Wall Street Journal*.

Curiously, there was one page Jimmy loved above all others. It was the Court and Society page of the *London Telegraph*, a somewhat glorious mishmash of esoteric events, starting with the daily routine of the Queen and the various members of her family who were paid by the British Government's Civil List.

Her appointments were listed, as were those of Prince Philip and Prince Charles. There was reported all manner of obscure educational events and appointments at England's great public schools and the universities of Oxford, Cambridge, and London. There were lists of mourners at important memorial services, lists of medals, awards, and appointments for the Navy, Army, and Air Force, including Commonwealth Services.

There were records of service reunions, announcements of important engagements, weddings, and funerals. An "In Memoriam" column in which service families annually remembered officers who had fallen in action, often as long as sixty years previously.

Jimmy regularly devoured this page, making notes that he would later transfer to his private computer file, say, for a new Flag Officer Submarines, Royal Navy; for example, he would fill in the new man's name and career highlights, just in case Fort Meade needed this information in the future. Quick cross-reference. Instant knowledge. Lieutenant Commander Ramshawe was the consummate Intelligence professional.

In the *Telegraph* of Monday, January 5, there were a few items that amused him, and a few that caused him to scribble hurriedly, but there was one word that almost caused him to spill his coffee.

"Murdered," it said. Right there in the dreariest of Universities sections. A small down-column paragraph announcing the appointment of a new Senior Lecturer at the Benfield Greig Geohazard Research Center at University College, London. Dr. Hillary Betts, a volcanologist, *replacing Professor Paul Landon, who was discovered murdered in West London last May.*

"Murdered! Streuth," said James. "Never saw that bloody word on this page before. Like seeing a stripper illustrating a prayer book."

Instinctively, he went online, looked up the London *Telegraph,* and keyed in a search for Professor Paul Landon. To his surprise, a sizable front-page headline in the edition of Monday, May 12, appeared.

PROFESSOR PAUL LANDON MISSING
World's Top Volcano Expert Vanishes after Royal Geographical Lecture

There followed a detailed story of Professor Landon and his achievements, followed by a police report on his failure to return home to Buckinghamshire after addressing the Royal Geographical Society on the evening of May 8.

There were quotes from the Royal Geographical Society's General Secretary, and from colleagues at University College, and of course from his wife. But no one had the slightest idea what had happened to him.

Three days later Lieutenant Commander Ramshawe found out for himself. The front-page headline over all eight columns on Thursday, May 15, read:

PROFESSOR PAUL LANDON FOUND MURDERED
Washed Up on Thames Island— Two Bullets to the Brain

In the opinion of the police pathologist, Paul Landon had been shot twice in an "execution-style" killing, and then dumped in the river. The coxswain of a London Rowing Club eight had spotted the body washed by the flood tide onto Chiswick Eyot, a small island landmark for racing shells, halfway along the Oxford-Cambridge Boat Race course between Putney and Mortlake.

There were, as yet, no suspects, but there was no doubt in the minds of the Metropolitan Police. This was a cold-blooded murder, though why anyone should want to kill an apparently harmless academic remained a total mystery.

Lieutenant Commander Ramshawe liked mysteries. And for the next hour, he scrolled to and from various editions of the *Telegraph*, spanning the early summer to the fall. He found the inquest, the funeral, a feature on Professor Landon's area of expertise. But he never found a single clue as to why the hell anyone should want to kill him.

He switched to the London *Daily Mail*, a more adventurous downmarket tabloid, which might have come up with a different, more original idea. No such luck. For the week after the professor's disappearance, the *Mail* was totally preoccupied with two murdered London policemen and their dog . . .

GALLANT ROGER KILLED IN ACTION
—BESIDE HIS MASTERS
Police Slaying Baffles Scotland Yard

It beat the hell out of Jimmy Ramshawe too. But the only paragraph that did interest him was one that began: *The Metropolitan Police are believed to have called in the Special Branch, owing to the manner of death of one of the officers, but last night this could not be confirmed.*

So far as Jimmy knew, this probably meant MI5, or even MI6, England's version of the CIA. And although the murder of London cops was not his business and neither, of course, was the killing of a London University professor, he nonetheless logged a full notation about the strange and mysterious death of Paul Landon.

He found it hard to dismiss the incident from his mind. And at the end of the day, he was still puzzling over it on the way to the Australian Embassy in Washington, D.C., where he was dining with his fiancée, Jane Peacock, daughter of the ambassador. It was almost eight o'clock before he arrived, and he gratefully accepted a tall glass of cold Fosters lager from Miss Peacock before joining her parents in the dining room. Jimmy had always gotten along very well with Ambassador John Peacock. Their families had been friends for many years, and indeed, Jimmy's parents, who lived in New York, were due to stay at the embassy two weeks from now.

He waited until they were well into the main course, a superb rib of beef, cooked to perfection and accompanied by a particularly elegant Australian red wine, Clonakilla Shiraz, made up in the Canberra District in the temperate foothills, a couple of hundred miles south of Sydney. John Peacock was a lifelong collector of good wine, and owned an excellent cellar at his home overlooking the harbor in Sydney. As Australian ambassador to the U.S.A., he was expected to serve vintages from his own country, and he rose to the occasion every time.

Jimmy waited until they were all smoothly into a second glass before broaching the subject that had been on his mind for the past six hours.

"You ever read anything about a volcano professor in London who managed to get murdered last May, John?"

"Maybe. What was his name?"

"Professor Paul Landon."

"Now wait a minute. I did notice something about that, because he was coming to speak at two or three universities in Australia—and one of 'em was Monash, in Melbourne, where I went. I think that's the same guy. I remember it because the Sydney newspaper ran quite a story on his death. Why d'you ask?"

"Oh, I just ran into some stuff on the Internet today.

Seemed such a strange murder, no rhyme or reason. No one has ever discovered why he was killed. And no one's ever been charged with anything connected to it."

"No. I remember that. He wasn't just an expert on volcanoes. He was into the whole range of earthly disasters—you know, earthquakes, tidal waves, asteroid collisions, and Christ knows what. As I recall, he was coming particularly to lecture on the effect of a major tidal wave, it's got some bloody Chinese name . . . Let me think . . . chop-sooey, or something. Anyway, it's a lot of water."

Jimmy chuckled. He really liked his future father-in-law, who'd insisted on being called John since Jimmy was a kid at college. "The word we're groping for is *tsunami,*" he said. "Japanese. I've been a bit of an expert since about quarter past two this afternoon."

"Yes, that's it," replied the Ambassador. "It's when a bloody great hunk of rock falls off a mountain and crashes into the sea causing a fantastic upsurge as it rolls along the ocean floor? Right? Expert?"

"Yes, I think that's a fair and thoughtful summation," said Jimmy, frowning, and putting on what he thought might be a learned voice. "Very well put. I think in future, I'll address you as Splash Peacock, tsunami authority."

Everyone laughed at that. But the Ambassador was not finished. "I'll tell you something else I remember about that article. The prof was coming to Australia to talk in particular about these bloody great waves that have happened on Pacific islands north of us. That's the danger spot, right? Your professor, Jimmy, knew a whole lot about one of 'em on New Britain Island off Papua New Guinea. It fell into the ocean and the ole thing developed and drowned about three thousand people on neighboring islands."

"For a bloke who can't say it, you know a whole hell of a lot about tsunamis!" replied Jimmy.

"Gimme a coupla weeks, I'll master the word as well," chuckled John Peacock.

"So why do you think someone murdered the professor?"

"Who knows? Could have been just mistaken identity, I suppose."

"Maybe," replied Jimmy. "But the police think it looked like an execution."

Friday, January 9
The Pentagon, Washington.

The first memorandums were beginning to arrive from the incoming Administration. Clearly, the new President was planning to impose savage defense cuts, particularly on the Navy. He considered the expenditure of billions of dollars on surface warships and submarines to be a lunatic waste of money. And he reasoned, not without just cause, that he had been elected to do precisely that. People did not want to raise armies and battle fleets. They wanted better health care and a better start in life for their kids. The recent election had demonstrated that thoroughly. McBride had not routed the Republicans. In fact he had only narrowly won the White House, and both Houses of Congress were still held by the GOP.

But the people had spoken. They had heard his message of hope and the chance of a better life for their families. They had listened to him rail against their own country, in which people can be bankrupted, their life's savings extinguished, just for being ill. They had listened to Charles McBride swear to God he was going to change all that. Yes, the people had spoken, no doubt about that.

It all struck home, especially in the headquarters of the veteran Chairman of the Joint Chiefs up on the Pentagon's second floor. Gen. Tim Scannell, in the big office directly below that of the outgoing Secretary of Defense, Robert MacPherson, was not a happy man.

"I don't know how long he's likely to last. Hopefully only four years. But this bastard is probably going to inflict more damage on the U.S. fleet than Yamamoto."

Among those sitting opposite the Chairman was Adm. Alan Dickson, and the Chief of Naval Operations was not smiling.

"I've been in the middle of these things before," he said. "And it's not just the big issues. You guys know as well as I do that severe defense cuts have an effect on everything, because all over the place there are people trying to cut costs. And they usually go a step too far—no one *quite* gets the reality. Until it's too late.

"Especially the Navy. You start decommissioning carriers, mothballing amphibious ships, laying up destroyers and frigates, you're punching a major hole in the U.S. Navy's requirements for really top guys. And when they think you don't need 'em, they don't show up at Annapolis."

"Left-wing politicians never understand it," answered Adm. Dick Greening, Commander in Chief, Pacific Fleet. "All those goddamned cities which survive on defense contracts. You stop building warships, you're not just seeing cities going broke, you're watching the unique skills of an area start to vanish. Pretty soon you end up like some Third World harbor, buying technology from abroad."

The room went silent. "Do you guys know what it is that really brasses me off about governments?" said Admiral Dickson. "The stuff no one explains to the people."

No one spoke.

"The fact is that governments don't have any money of their own," continued Admiral Dickson. "Only what they take from the American people and from American corporations. So when they tell the people an aircraft carrier is too expensive, they are talking absolute horseshit. They do not *spend*, in the accepted sense of the word. They only distribute. They take it from whatever source they can get it, without causing outright civil war, and then redistribute it into the economy. They don't *spend*. They only push everyone else's money around."

The Navy Chief paused. Then said, "Half of the money in labor costs goes to the guys building the ships—paychecks to people who *immediately* give a third of it back to the government. They don't tell 'em the rest gets spent in the community, providing other people with jobs, who also hand a third of it back to the government.

"They never mention that a big hunk of the cash goes to U.S. Steel, the electronic companies right here in the U.S.A., the missile systems, shipbuilders in Maine, Connecticut, and Virginia—they're all paying corporate taxes. Some of the money goes to U.S. Navy personnel, who pay their taxes back to the government, just like the people at U.S. Steel. The whole thing is just a roundabout. The goddamned aircraft carrier is not expensive, it's *free*. It's not the government's damned money anyway. They are only moving it around."

"Any clues yet about our cuts?" Rear Admiral Curran asked gravely.

"No one's been specific. But we've been put on a kind of unofficial high alert to start cutting back. I'd say the conversions on those four Ohio Class SSBNs will go on hold."

Admiral Dickson referred to the program to remove the Trident missiles from the old 16,600-ton strategic missile boats, and turn them into guided missile platforms, each carrying 154 Tomahawks. All four submarines were to be upgraded with Acoustic Rapid COTS insertion sonar.

"I wouldn't be sure we'll keep the green light for two more Nimitz Class carriers either. CVN 77 and 78 will probably get canceled."

"Jesus," said the Commander of the Atlantic Fleet, Vice Adm. Brian Ingram. "That would be bad. Some of the big guys are just about getting to the end of their tether. We need new, and we need it now—how about the Arleigh Burke destroyer program?"

"Well, as you know, we're supposed to get thirty-six and we only have twenty-four. I'm just not sure about the final twelve."

"Jeez. I'd just hate to see us run short of missile ships . . . And I'd sure feel better about everything if the Big Man was still in the White House."

By anyone's standards, this was a very worried group of U.S. Navy Execs and the Pentagon boss. Not worried for themselves, but for the future ability of United States warships to continue safeguarding the world's oceans. Whenever necessary.

And the Big Man was far away.

11.30 A.M., Tuesday, January 27
Tenerife, Canary Islands.

Mrs. Arnold Morgan had spent the last hour of her honeymoon on her own. Relaxed on a lounge by the lower pool at the imperious Gran Hotel Bahia del Duque, way down on the southern tip of the island, she was reading quietly.

Behind her, a detail of two security agents was playing cards, and at infrequent intervals a waiter appeared to inquire if she needed more orange juice or coffee. About 100 feet above stood her new husband. Ensconced in an observatory at the top of a tower, he was staring out to sea through a telescope many times more powerful than most people will ever have used.

The Canaries, with their pure Atlantic skies, attracted astronomers from all over the world, and giant telescopes have been built in observatories on every one of the seven islands. The instrument at Gran Hotel Bahia del Duque was constructed mostly with astronomers in mind, and it was generally focused on the heavens. Today, however, it looked out to the surface of the deep blue waters to the south of the Costa Adeje, where the seabed swiftly shelves down to depths of almost a mile.

Kathy wished he'd come make his way back down and talk to her. Isolation did not suit the former goddess of the West Wing. She slipped back into her book, occasionally gazing at the magnificent surroundings of the five-star Gran Hotel, a sprawling waterside complex, half-Venetian, half-Victorian in design, set in a semitropical botanical garden. Her new

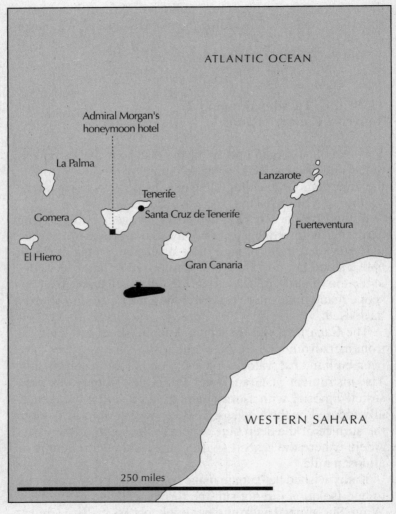

ATLANTIC OCEAN

Admiral Morgan's
honeymoon hotel

La Palma

Lanzarote

Tenerife

Santa Cruz de Tenerife

Gomera

Fuerteventura

El Hierro

Gran Canaria

WESTERN SAHARA

250 miles

THE CANARY ISLANDS; SEVEN VOLCANIC RISES
OFF THE COAST OF NORTH AFRICA

husband adored such grandeur and he had sweetly instructed her, with his usual old world charm, to locate a place and book them in for two weeks— *"Listen, Kathy, just try to stop boring me sideways with goddamned hotel literature, and get us into some goddamned place, Casa Luxurious. And hasta la vista,"* he added, handing her a credit card. *"That's Spanish for on the double."*

He was, of course, utterly beyond redemption and Kathy forgave him only because he treated everyone like that. As his secretary for six years in the White House, she had seen diplomats from the world's most powerful countries quake before his onslaught. 'Specially the Chinese and, almost as often, the Russians.

The whole idea of this tiny cluster of Spanish Islands, set in the sparkling Atlantic off the coast of Africa, had been hers. She had lived in Europe when she was much younger and her sister-in-law, Gayle, who lived in southern Spain, had suggested the Canaries because of the January weather, which was warm, much warmer than mainland Spain, a thousand miles to the northeast. But the most significant reason for Tenerife was that Kathy had wanted to arrange a Catholic Blessing for their marriage, which had thus far been only legally formalized by a U.S. Justice of the Peace in Washington.

Gayle had located the perfect little church on the neighboring island of Gran Canaria, the Iglesia de San Antonio Abad down near the waterfront at Las Palmas, the island's main city. She had arranged for the English-speaking priest to meet Arnold and Kathy on Friday morning and conduct a short private service.

Only after their arrival did Kathy plan to tell her husband that San Antonio, unprepossessing, painted white, and Romanesque in design, was the very church where Christopher Columbus had prayed for divine help before sailing for the Americas.

The Great Modern American Patriot and the Great European Adventurer. Two Naval Commanding Officers somehow united at the same altar, separated by the centuries, but not in spirit. Yes, Kathy thought, Arnold would like that. He'd like that very much, the secret romantic that he ultimately was.

So it was settled. A honeymoon in the Canaries. And even the globally sophisticated Arnold had been taken aback by the sheer opulence of the place, the terra-cotta exteriors, five swimming pools, the perfect alfresco dining area on the terraces looking down to the soft sandy beaches.

"And here he is, up the stupid tower, for the fourth day in a row," thought Kathy. "With the telescope, presumably looking for the enemy."

Just at that moment, the former National Security Adviser to the President of the United States made a timely poolside appearance. "Oh hello, my darling," said Kathy. "I was just thinking this is like being on a honeymoon with Lord Nelson, you up there with that ridiculous telescope."

"It's better, I assure you," grunted Arnold. "Admiral Nelson lost an arm in the battle of Santa Cruz about 40 miles north of here. Right now you'd be sitting in intensive care, waiting to see if he lived or died."

Kathy could not help laughing at his mercurial mind, and encyclopedic knowledge.

"Anyway," added Arnold, "Lord Nelson was not big on honeymoons. Never married Lady Hamilton, did he? Probably trying to avoid a hard time when he was caught using his telescope."

Kathy shook her head. She knew that Arnold Morgan was impossible to joust with because he always won, impossible to reason with because he always had more knowledge, impossible to be angry with because he could find a joke, a shaft of irony, or even slapstick from any set of circumstances. She had been in love with him from the day he had first thundered into her life, instructing her to call the head of the Russian Navy and tell him he was a lying bastard.

Of course he was impossible. Everyone knew that. But he was also more exciting, fun, and challenging than any man she had ever met. He was over twenty years older then she, an inch shorter, and the most confident person in the White House. He cared nothing for rank, only for truth. The former President had plainly been afraid of him, afraid of his absolute devotion to the flag, the country, and its safety.

To the former Kathy O'Brien, when Arnold Morgan pulled himself up to his full five feet, eight and a half inches, he seemed not one inch short of ten feet. In her mind, and in the mind of many others, she had married the world's shortest giant.

It seemed incredible that he was gone from the West Wing. Kathy, a veteran of the White House secretarial staff, simply could not imagine what it would be like without the caged lion in the office of the President's National Security Adviser, taking the flack, taking the strain, and laying down the law about "what's right for this goddamned country."

Whoever the new President decided to appoint in the Admiral's place, he'd need some kind of a hybrid composed of John Wayne, Henry Kissinger, and Douglas MacArthur. And he wasn't going to find one of those. The only one in captivity was, at this moment, sprawled out next to Kathy, holding her hand, and telling her he loved her, that she was the most wonderful person he ever had or ever would meet—

And now, he announced, he was going to take a swim. Four days in Tenerife had already seen him acquire a deepening tan, which contrasted strikingly with his steel-gray close-cut hair. Even as he approached senior citizenship Arnold still had tree-trunk legs, heavily muscled arms, and a waistline only marginally affected by a lifelong devotion to roast-beef sandwiches with mayonnaise and mustard.

He was pretty smooth in the water too. Kathy watched him moving along the pool with a cool, professional-looking crawl, breathing every two strokes, just turning his head slightly into the trough of the slipstream for a steady pull of air. He looked as if he could, if necessary, swim like that for a year.

Kathy decided to join him and dived into the pool as he

went past, surfacing alongside him and slipping into a somewhat labored form of sidestroke. As always, it was difficult to keep up with the Admiral.

When finally they came in to rest on the hotel lounges, Arnold made a further announcement. "I'm taking you to see something tomorrow," he said. "The place where scientists predict there will be the greatest natural disaster the earth has ever seen."

"I thought you said that was due to happen in the White House next month?"

"Well, the second greatest then," he replied, chuckling at his sassy new wife.

"What is it?" she asked absently, turning back to her book.

"It's a volcano," he said, darkly.

"Not another," she murmured. "I just married one of those."

"I suppose it would be slightly too much to ask you to pay attention?"

"No, I'm ready. I'm all ears. Go to it, Admiral."

"Well, just about 60 miles from here, to the northwest, is the active volcanic island of La Palma. It's only about a third of the size of Tenerife, pear-shaped, tapering off narrowly to the south—"

"You sound like a guidebook."

"Well, not quite, but it's an interesting book that I found by the telescope."

"What book?"

"Honey, please. Kathryn Morgan, please pay attention. I have just been reading, rather carefully, a very fascinating account of the neighboring island of La Palma and its likely affect on the future of the world. You may have thought I was just goofing off looking through the telescope. But I actually wasn't—"

"You abandoned the telescope! Then it's surprising Tenerife hasn't come under attack in the last couple of hours. That's all I can say." Mrs. Kathy Morgan was now laughing at her own humor. So, for that matter, was her husband. "If you're not darn careful you'll come under attack," he said. "You want me to tell you about the end of the world or not?"

"Ooh, yes please, my darling. That would be lovely."

"Right. Now listen up." He sounded precisely like the old nuclear submarine commanding officer he once had been. A martinet of the deep. Stern, focused, ready to handle any back talk from anyone. Except Kathy, who always disarmed him.

"The southerly part of La Palma has a kind of backbone," he said. "A high ridge, running due south clean down the middle. This volcanic fault line, about three miles long, takes its name from its main volcano, Cumbre Vieja, which rises four miles up from the seabed, with only the top mile and a half visible. It's had seven eruptions in the last five hundred years. The fault fissure, which runs right along the crest, developed after the eruption of 1949. Basically the goddamned west side of the range is falling into the goddamned sea, from a great height."

Kathy giggled at his endlessly colorful way of describing any event, military, financial, historical, or in this case geophysical.

"Pay attention," said the Admiral. "Now, way to the south is the Volcan San Antonio, a giant black crater. They just completed a new visitors center with amazing close-up views. Then you can drive south to see Volcan Teneguia, that's the last one, which erupted here back in 1971. You can climb right up there and take a look into the crater if you like."

"No, thanks."

"But the main one is Cumbre Vieja itself, about eight miles to the north. That's the big one, and it's been rumbling in recent years. According to the book, if that blew, it would be the single biggest world disaster for a million years . . ."

"Arnold, you are prone, at times, to exaggeration. And because of this, I ask you one simple question. How could a rockfall in this remote and lonely Atlantic island possibly constitute a disaster on the scale you are saying?"

The Admiral prepared his saber. Then, metaphorically,

slashed the air with it. "Tsunami, Kathryn," he said. "Mega-tsunami."

"No kidding?" she said. "Rye or pumpernickel."

"Jesus Christ!" said the President's former National Security Adviser. "Right now, Kathy, I'm at some kind of an intersection, trying to decide whether to leave you here looking sensational in that bikini but overwhelmed by ignorance, or whether to lead you to the sunny uplands of knowledge. Depends a lot on your attitude."

Kathy leaned over and took his hand. "Take me to the uplands," she said. "You know I'm only teasing you. You want some of that orange juice, it's fabulous."

She stood up easily, walked three paces, and poured him a large glass. The Spanish oranges were every bit as good as the crop from Florida, and the Admiral drained the glass before beginning what he called an attempt to educate the unreachable.

"Fresh," he said, approvingly. "A lot like yourself."

The third, and most beautiful, Mrs. Arnold Morgan leaned over again and kissed him.

Christ, he thought. *How the hell did I ever get this lucky?*

"Tsunami," he said again. "Do you know what a tsunami is?"

"Not offhand. What is it?"

"It's the biggest tidal wave in the world. A wall of water that comes rolling in from the ocean, and doesn't break in the shallows like a normal wave—just keeps coming, holding its shape, straight across any damn thing that gets in its way. They can be 50 feet high."

"You mean if one of 'em hit Rehobeth Beach or somewhere near our flat Maryland shore, it would just roll straight over the streets and houses?"

"That's what I mean," he said, pausing. "But there is something worse. It's called a mega-tsunami. And that's what can end life as we know it. Because according to that book up by the telescope, those waves can be 150 feet high. A mega-tsunami could wipe out the entire East Coast of the U.S.A."

Kathy was thoughtful. "How 'bout that?" she said quietly,

feeling somewhat guilty about the lightly frivolous way she had treated Arnold's brand-new knowledge. "I still don't see how a volcano could cause such an uproar—aren't they just big, slow old things with a lot of very slow molten rock running down the slopes?"

"Aha. That's where La Palma comes in . . . Cumbre Vieja last erupted about forty years ago, and the scientists later discerned a massive slippage on the western, seaward flank. Maybe twelve feet downwards."

"That's not much."

"It is, if the rock face is eight miles long, and the whole lot is slipping, at a great height above sea level, sending a billion tons of rock at terrific speed, straight down to the ocean floor. That will be the biggest tsunami the world has ever seen—"

"Are they sure about that?"

"Dead sure. There's a couple of universities in America and I think Germany with entire departments experimenting with the possible outcomes of a mega-tsunami developing in the Canary Islands."

"Did one of them publish the stuff in the book you read?"

"No. That was done by a couple of English Professors at London University. Both of 'em very big deals, by the sound of it. One of 'em's called Day, the other one Sarandon, I think. They sounded like guys who knew what they were saying."

0900, The Following Day.

At the insistence of his two armed agents, the Admiral and his wife chartered a private plane to take them over to La Palma—an elderly ATR-72 turboprop that was only slightly more silent and restful than a train crash. They took off from little Reina Sofia airport, only five miles from their hotel, and shuddered, shook, and rumbled their way up the west coast of Tenerife, past the main resort areas, and along the spectacular coastline. Before the northwest headland of Point Teno they veered out to sea, crossing Atlantic waters almost two miles deep. They touched down at the little airport four miles south of Santa Cruz de La Palma at 9:25 in the morning.

A car and chauffeur awaited them. Actually two cars and one chauffeur. The agents who had accompanied them would follow in the second automobile. A condition of Admiral Morgan's original appointment to the White House had been that he would be provided with round-the-clock protection for a minimum of five years, effective immediately upon his retirement. In the U.S. he had a detail of four agents, working shifts, twenty-four hours a day. Two of them had been designated to accompany the former NSA on his honeymoon.

The Admiral was now a wealthy man. His full Vice Admiral's pension had been accruing since he left the Navy, almost ten years previously. He had no children to educate, no alimony to pay, no mortgage. He had sold his house in Maryland and moved into Kathy's much grander home in Chevy Chase. This too carried no mortgage. Kathy had a liberal trust fund provided by a rich but unfaithful first husband, and she too had been able to bank most of her salary over the last six years while Admiral Morgan took care of regular expenses. Together, Arnold and Kathy had a net worth of several million dollars. Sufficient for the Admiral to have tossed straight into the bin two $5 million offers from New York publishing houses for his memoirs. Neither received even the courtesy of a reply.

Stepping down onto the runway, dressed in a dark blue polo shirt, smartly pressed stone-collared shorts, no socks, tan Gucci loafers, and a white Panama hat, the Admiral was unable to avoid looking precisely what he was—ex-Government, ex-Navy, a powerful man, not to be trifled with. No bullshit.

"The car's over here, sir," said Harry, Arnold's longtime secret service agent. "The front one of those three black Mercedes parked outside the building."

They walked across the already-warm runway under a cloudless blue sky. Harry held open the rear door. The Admi-

ral jumped in first and slid across the backseat. Harry continued to hold the door for Kathy, nodded his head curtly, and
said, "Mrs. Morgan."

Ten years earlier, Agent Harry had once asked the svelte,
newly divorced Kathy O'Brien if she'd care to go out to dinner with him. She had politely declined, and now the memory of that innocent but toe-curling piece of misjudgment
actually gave Harry acute chills on the rare occasions he allowed himself to recall the incident.

With Mrs. Morgan safely on board, the chauffeur moved
slowly out of the airport, while Harry, now at the wheel of the
second Mercedes, fell in behind him, line astern, as the Admiral insisted on putting it. They drove south towards the
very tip of La Palma, all along the coastal highway for
around 10 miles, before arriving at the little town of Los Canarios de Fuencaliente, which used to be a small spa town,
dotted by hot springs. The most recent eruption in 1971 had
buried them, turning them into great lakes deep in the underground caverns of cooled-off lava.

Now the whitewashed outpost of Fuencaliente served as a
kind of volcano mission-control area, with signposts everywhere pointing the way up to the great line of craters and
mountains that patiently guarded the future of the planet earth.

The big white board, which proclaimed Volcan San Antonio above a black painted arrow, instantly caught the Admiral's eye. "Straight up there, Pedro," he told the chauffeur,
checking his stern arcs through the rear window to ensure
Harry was still in strict convoy.

Kathy, who was fiddling with the digital camera Arnold
had just bought her—complete with all bells and whistles,
even a telephoto lens—said distractedly, "How d'you know
he's called Pedro?"

"Well, I'm not dead certain. But many people in Spain are
called Pedro or Miguel, like Peter or Michael in the States."

"God help me," said Kathy. "Darling, you can't go around
making up names for people. It's rude. Like me suddenly
calling you Fred."

"Oh, I agree you couldn't do it with Americans. But the odds are stacked in your favor in Spain. Or anywhere in Arabia. Mohammed, Mustapha, or Abdul. Can't miss."

"Still, it's rude. Just like you shouldn't go around calling every dark-skinned man a towelhead." Admiral Morgan muttered something and, despite herself, Kathy laughed. And she tapped the chauffeur on the shoulder. "Excuse me," she said. "Could you tell me your name?"

"Oh, sure, *señora*. It's Pedro."

"How did you know?" she demanded, smelling a rat, and turning back to Arnold.

"Harry told me," replied the Admiral.

Kathy rolled her eyes heavenwards.

Which was more or less where they were headed. The Mercedes was now revving its way up a very steep escarpment, through the pines, towards the yawning chasm at the peak of the great black cone on the top of the mountain.

Recent rumblings inside this forty-year dormant volcano had caused officials to cordon off the rim of the crater to all visitors. But Harry was already out, talking to the guard and explaining the precise identity of the man in the Panama hat.

The guard waved Admiral Morgan and his wife through and they wandered companionably up to the very edge of the crater, staring down into the abyss. Up ahead of them, they could see another group of four people, all men, taking photographs of the area, and obviously heading north, along the tourist paths, up the great ridge of the mountains. Two large golf carts were parked nearby.

"Can we get a couple of those?" asked the Admiral.

"Lemme check with the guard," said Harry, who returned three minutes later with the good news that one big cart, a four-seater, was on its way up from the Visitors' Center.

"Beautiful," said Arnold. "That way we can ride right up to Cumbre Vieja and then I'd like to take the car down to the coast road to see the cliffs above the ocean."

The excursion in the cart revealed spectacular scenery. All along the lava fields, the Ruta de Los Volcanes, across the rugged range of mountains sometimes redolent with thick light green Canary pines, sometimes just a stone wilderness, the golf cart bumped and lurched across terrain that had been molten rock less than forty years ago. In many places on top of the ridge it was possible to see the Atlantic both to the east and to the west. But they were not sure the battery on the electric-powered golf cart would make it all the way down to the west coast, and they elected to turn back, pick up the car, and drive on down in comfort. Ninety minutes later they found themselves parked at the top of a gigantic cliff of black basalt rock, towering over a strange black sandy beach hundreds of feet below, beaten by the seemingly endless breakers of the Atlantic.

They were parked in a rough, flat clearing and there was only one other car, another black Mercedes, just beyond them. Photographing the cliff were the same four people they had seen on the rim of Volcan San Antonio. They were all swarthy in appearance, with short, curly black hair, but somehow not Spanish. And despite their phalanx of cameras draped around their necks, they were not Japanese either. Arabian, from the looks of them.

"What the hell?" muttered Arnold. "What are they doing up here photographing the landscape and getting in our way?"

"I can't really help you there, my darling," said Kathy. "They never even bothered to leave a copy of their tour plan in the car—"

"Goddamned towelh—" growled the Admiral, but in a gesture of deference to his wife, he checked himself, swallowing the rest of his exclamation.

Two minutes later, the other Mercedes took off, driving swiftly south. And when Pedro finally began to head back south himself, they spotted the other Mercedes up ahead, parked again, its occupants still photographing fiercely, both with cinecameras and stills.

"Pull over, Pedro," said the Admiral. "Let's take another look at the view. Park as close to the other car as you can without crowding 'em."

Sure enough, the photographers had found another prime spot. There was a slight crescent shape to the bay, winding away towards the north, and it offered a spectacular vista from one of the highest points on the western coast.

Arnold didn't really think much of it. It was simply that his job was so deeply engrained in his personality and mind. By sea, the Admiral was paranoid about submarines and on land, since 9/11, he was unable to look at an Arab without thinking, *Goddamned terrorist*. Of course many other operatives in U.S. Intelligence thought much the same, but being Arnold, he had to act upon it in some fashion.

As soon as the car came to a halt Arnold Morgan was out, walking back to Harry and the other agent. His instructions were terse. Get ahold of the camera in the backseat of my car, and then start taking pictures of Kathy and me. Use the telephoto lens, get the guys nice and close."

"Yes, sir."

There were probably 30 yards between the two groups, and Harry did his job admirably. The Arabs seemed to notice that the other visitors' camera was aimed their way, because they quickly looked away. But not quickly enough. Harry had them all clearly, except for one whom he only managed to catch from the side and back. But in one way or the other, all four of them were now sharply recorded in Kathy's digital.

"Could you by any chance tell me what all that was about?" asked Kathy as they began the drive back around the southern headland and on to the airport.

"Well, I don't think those people were really tourists," replied the Admiral. "No wives, no girlfriends. Very serious. Kinda got the impression they had a purpose. You know, stopping and taking a lot of pictures of the cliff."

"Well, they could have been compiling a book. Great Atlantic coastlines," said Kathy. "Or scouting out a location for a movie. Or working for the Canary Islands tourist board, preparing a new brochure. Or working for a hotel or development corporation, looking at new sights with amazing ocean views, anything. After all, we were standing right on the top of one of the great volcano ranges in the world . . ."

"Yeah. I know," he replied. "And I don't think anyone's thinking of building much up there, not with the Cumbre Vieja rumbling away beneath our feet. Fast way to lose your hotel, right?

"I don't know," he mused, slowly. "I just had a feeling about those guys . . . how they kept showing up. And now I got a little record of 'em. And I just might ask young Ramshawe to have a shot at identifying 'em."

"Can he do that?"

"Not if they are entirely obscure. But you never know . . ."

"I'll tell you one thing, though," said Kathy. "If that whole western side of the ridge suddenly collapsed into the ocean, that sure would make a major splash."

"Wouldn't it?" answered the Admiral. "The mother of all splashes."

1500, Wednesday, May 27, 2009
East Coast Highway, North Korea.

THEY WERE JUST NORTH of the seaport city of Wonsan, and the Chinese-built off-road military juggernaut was rumbling up the strangely deserted road. To the right stretched a long expanse of jagged coastline guarded from the great rollers off the Sea of Japan only by a few tiny islands that could be seen in the distance.

This was rugged country, the "highway" cleaving its way north for 200 miles, into the extreme northeast where China, North Korea, and Russia converge, some 80 miles south of Vladivostok.

The Hamas General in the front passenger seat was accompanied by his personal bodyguard, brother-in-law, and veteran Hamas major, Ahmed Sabah, who sat quietly in the rear seat cradling a fully primed AK-47. The General stared through the windshield without speaking. The language was just too damned strange, the people too odd, the country too foreign for any attempt at social chat with the Korean Army driver.

Ravi Rashood was numb with boredom. Here in what might be the world's most secretive country, a police-state throwback to the dark ages of communism, he felt so out of place, so utterly estranged from anything he had ever known,

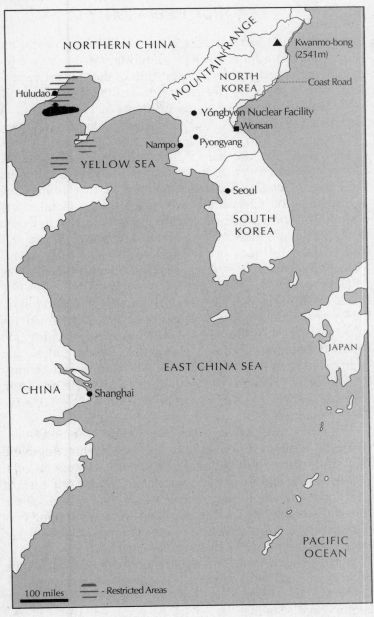

THE "PRIVATE" NUCLEAR MENACE AROUND THE YELLOW SEA;
NORTH KOREA'S WEAPONS FACTORIES; CHINA'S SUBMARINE BASE

that he was at a loss for perspective. He looked over at the driver, whose uniform was without military insignia save for a small metal badge showing a portrait of the "Dear Leader," Kim Jong-il, presumed insane by most of the Western world, but a God-like presence to the residents of North Korea. A red rim surrounded the driver's badge, signifying his military rank.

His father, the late Kim il-Sung, was believed to be the Greatest Leader Ever in the history of the world, including the likes of Genghis Khan, Alexander the Great, Julius Caesar, Washington, Charlemagne, Napoleon, Mao, Gandhi, and Churchill. North Korean children had to learn a hymn to Kim, and sing it daily, "The Greatest Genius the World Has Ever Known." Huge portraits of him littered cities, towns, villages, and parks. His words were still regarded as the Will of Heaven.

Kim's fat little son, Kim Jong-il, quickly matched his father's near immortality, and loudspeakers proclaimed his undisputed family Greatness on the streets, in cities and towns throughout the land. Undisputed, that is, unless you didn't mind jail or even execution. The twenty-first-century regime of Kim Jong-il did not tolerate dissent in any form whatsoever. Which at least simplified the issue—*Love the Dear Leader or else . . .*

The Army truck driver was a true and faithful representative of a terrorized population. And behind his enigmatic half-smile there was the zombified blank expression of a people whose morale had been shattered, whose self-respect was gone, and whose only chance of survival was to toe the line and worship the earthly god Kim—always making certain there was a large portrait of him in the house, ready for inspection, as laid down by the law.

North Korea was an Orwellian nightmare, forever on the borders of outright famine, with hundreds of thousands already dead of malnutrition. This was Russia in winter a half-century ago, Stalinesque in its procedures. And still the populace thronged the streets, cheering the Dear Leader, as the tubby little monster drove past, the living Tsar of one of the worst-run sovereign nations since the Dark Ages. And every day, all day, and all night, if you were listening, the Government of Kim Jong-il broadcasted the "true knowledge" that this country was intrinsically, ethnically superior to any other.

General Ravi was appalled by North Korea. And he really hated doing business with them. But in his game, there were very few places to do business at all. For part of his job made him an international arms dealer, and one of a rare breed: a nuclear arms dealer, an arena near-silent, clandestine, and illegal, in which hardly anyone admitted wanting to buy, and certainly no one admitted wanting to sell.

Aside from a somewhat seedy part of Bosnia, North Korea was very nearly the only game in town. This dastardly, friendless little pariah of a state, trapped between China, Russia, and Japan, had been making the components for nuclear weapons for many, many years, and cared not a jot for the Nuclear Non-Proliferation Treaty (NPT).

For years, since back in 1974, when they first joined the International Atomic Energy Agency (IAEA), Korea had been a clear and obvious problem to the West, constantly trying to produce plutonium, endlessly trying to produce SCUD missiles for sale to the Middle East.

But in 1985, against everyone's most optimistic forecasts, Kim il-Sung signed the Nuclear Non-Proliferation Treaty, promising not to produce a bomb, and to open all nuclear sites to inspection.

That same year, the North Koreans started to build a 200 MWt reactor that could produce enough plutonium to make seven to ten bombs a year. Separately that same year they started to build a large plant to process plutonium into weapon-ready form.

Twelve months later, they had a 30 MWt reactor on line, producing plutonium. In 1987, they missed the first eighteen-month deadline for international inspection. A few months later, they delivered one hundred SCUD-B missiles to Iran.

For the next two years, they refused inspections and continued to build reactors, which would create plutonium. They consistently sold SCUD missiles to Syria and Iran.

By 1992, the IAEA concluded the latest nuclear declarations by North Korea—some 90 grams of plutonium!—were fraudulent, and demanded access to Yongbyon, the ultrasecretive underground nuclear plant that lies 50 miles north of the capital city of Pyongyang. They did not get it.

A year later, both China and Russia had cut off all aid to the Republic of North Korea. And the U.S. demanded that Kim il-Sung come clean and show his nuclear hand like everyone else. North Korea immediately barred all IAEA inspectors, and threatened to drop out of the NPT altogether.

Finally in mid-1994, North Korea quit the IAEA. President Clinton, ever eager for compromise, agreed that the U.S. would provide North Korea with two light-water reactors and 500,000 tons of heavy fuel oil per annum, if only the new Dear Leader, the hideous Kim Jong-il, would rejoin the IAEA and the NPT, and "normalize economic relations" between North Korea and the United States.

It would end up costing the U.S. taxpayer $20 million to $30 million per year, and they called it the "Agreed Framework."

In 1995, less than one year after the Clinton deal, the head of the CIA, John Deutch, estimated that North Korea's new Nodong-1 missile would be deployed within a year, and that the North Koreans were continuing under the most secretive circumstances to work on nuclear, chemical, and biological warheads. The constant warnings of the U.S. Intelligence community were essentially ignored by the Administration.

By the spring of 1997, the situation had deteriorated. It was obvious that Kim Jong-il was producing plutonium.

Evidence was building. A defector, a high-ranking North Korean General, fled to China and published an essay confirming that his former country did have nuclear weapons that could be used against South Korea and Japan. The brilliant U.S. satellite QuickBird picked up sensational pictures of heavy activity in the sprawling Yongbyon nuclear facility, much of which is located underground. The warnings of a new defector, Choon Sun Lee, a senior official in North Korea's giant military infrastructure, of top-secret underground plutonium production and weapons development were almost certainly correct.

In June 1998, Kim Jong-il's government declared it would continue to develop and export nuclear-capable missiles. The U.S. Intelligence community, almost beside itself with concern, issued warning after warning that North Korea had built a huge underground facility that may be either a nuclear reactor or reprocessing plant, and a report from Bill Richardson's Department of Energy claimed evidence that North Korea was undoubtedly working on uranium-enrichment techniques—which meant, broadly, turning that lethal substance into weapons-grade nuclear explosives.

Four months later, the National Security Agency (NSA) in Fort Meade, headed by the aggressive Admiral Arnold Morgan, practically bellowed down the phone to the President that North Korea had between 25 and 30 kilograms of weapons-grade plutonium, enough to make several nuclear warheads.

By the year 2002, things were on their way from moderate to diabolical. It was now clear that Kim Jong-il had already produced a formidable arsenal of SCUD missiles for sale to anyone who needed them.

The writings of Choon Sun Lee came rushing back to haunt everyone involved. Choon had sworn that the great Mount of Chun-Ma had been hollowed out to house a secret uranium processing plant. He described a massive tunnel, extending more than a mile into the mountain, opening into underground facilities housed in chambers carved out of the rock. In one of them there was a plant to turn uranium ore into yellowcake, the first step towards enriching it into weapons-grade material.

U.S. Intelligence considered Choon's observations to be too detailed to be false, and it all stacked up accurately with their own satellite observations of the existence of vast, mysterious excavations, twenty-two of them, in the mountains of North Korea. If you believed Choon, the West was staring quite literally at a nuclear empire operational under the reign of Kim Jong-il.

And Choon was by no means finished. He described every aspect of the ore's removal by truck and helicopter to an underground facility in a hidden valley. A third major defector came forward, announcing in 2002 that the great mountain of Kwanmo-bong, 270 miles to the northwest of Pyongyang—and at almost 8,000 feet the second highest peak in the country—had been hollowed out by an army of thousands, at night, sandbag by sandbag, to house yet another secret nuclear plant.

Everything erupted into an icy standoff in December 2002. The Americans located a Korean freighter near Socotra Island off the coast of Yemen and requested a nearby warship from the Spanish Navy to apprehend it. A few hours later, the Spaniards fired several broadsides over the ship's bows, forcing it to stop, and then boarded. The *So-San*, which flew no flag, contained fifteen SCUD missiles, large as life, carefully hidden under a cargo of 40,000 sacks of North Korean cement. There were, in addition, fifteen conventional warheads, twenty-three tanks of nitric acid (rocket propellant), and eighty-five drums of unspecified chemical. Kim's men had finally been caught red-handed.

But before the U.S. could roar its disapproval, North Korea announced it would immediately restart the nuclear reactors at Yongbyon and resume operations producing electricity. A total lie. They'd never ceased operations, and what the reactors really produced was plutonium—plutonium for nuclear warheads. Kim seemed to think he could best operate his country's economy by becoming an illegal nuclear arms dealer, selling weapons-grade plutonium, medium- and short-range missiles, and warheads. It was hard to imagine a more antagonistic marketing plan, deliberately designed to infuriate the Americans, especially a Republican

Administration that was essentially fed up to the back teeth with rogue states and uncooperative, pain-in-the-ass foreigners.

The international inspectors now claimed they were unable to continue monitoring the North Korean facility. And Kim Jong-il expelled them all within a few more days.

As the first decade of the twenty-first century wore on, the reactors at Yongbyon continued to harvest plutonium, and reports arrived daily at Fort Meade that the big cog in the Korean nuclear wheel had undoubtedly become the great mountain of Kwanmo-bong in the remote northeast, only 25 miles from the Chinese border.

It was to this hidden underground plant that General Ravi Rashood was now headed. Deep inside that mountain, he hoped, was the one weapon that would drive the hated Americans out of the Middle East forever.

He did not even pretend to understand the Oriental mind. All he knew was that North Korea had a reputation for on-time, no-questions-asked delivery. Their product was not cheap, in fact everything carried a risk premium, bumping up the price to compensate the Koreans for any unhappy circumstances that might befall them as a result of their manufacturing policies.

Very few people from the outside world had been permitted to see the North Korean nuclear facilities, certainly not inside the enormous mountain caverns that housed the plant. But the Hamas General, whom the Koreans swiftly identified as a major customer, had insisted on stringent terms for his acceptance of the product.

Yes, he would accept the ex-factory terms. As soon as his order left the plant, it became the property, and its journey to a seaport the responsibility, of Hamas. The Koreans would accept no liability for accident.

General Ravi assumed this meant that if the whole lot accidentally disappeared somewhere on the highway, the Koreans were still owed the money. He told them he would agree only if he and his men watched and supervised the loading, and traveled with the product trans–North Korea to the waiting ship. In the end he accepted that there would be just one Korean driver for the 300-mile journey to the western seaport of Nampo.

He had been told that North Korea, which is about the size of the state of Mississippi, had a population of 24 million, half of whom lived in Pyongyang. But even after driving halfway across the country, miles upon miles through a deserted, rugged landscape, he had no idea where the others lived. Only occasionally were there small fishing villages clustered to his right, on the shores of the Sea of Japan.

Ravi had been allowed no insights or prior knowledge before entering the country. There were no photographs or promotional handouts demonstrating the excellence of Korean manufacturing. He was just given a map of the country showing the main towns and roads, and a driver to take him to the factory inside Kwanmo-bong.

The only other facts the General knew about North Korea were military—that this ridiculous, backward Third World outcast owned the third largest army in the world, with 1.2 million men under arms (as opposed to 650,000 in South Korea). One quarter of Korea's GDP was spent annually on their Armed Forces and yet their Navy was very modest, their air force large but mostly obsolete.

The place gave Ravi the creeps. But he had no time to worry about that. In a couple of hours he would need to be on high alert, and he stared straight ahead, thinking, while the big army truck clattered along the coastal highway.

They came roaring through the towns of Hamhung and Pukchong, and followed the northeastern Korean railroad to Kilju and Chilbosan. Another 20 miles and his driver would veer left off the main road onto what looked like a track— only this one would be a 15-mile track into the foothills of the mountains, and then cleaving a long upward path through the granite range. Wooden guardhouses would stand sentinel on either side, every half-mile. Almost nowhere along this sinister highway was it possible to be out of sight of the armed patrols. It was, without question, the most secret of all roads, befitting this most secretive of all nations.

For General Ravi it meant the end of a long journey, starting essentially in Moscow, although he had not gone there personally. Here, the formal inquiry from the Iranian Navy requesting the purchase of a number of RADUGA SS-N-21 cruise missiles, two of them equipped with 200-kiloton nuclear warheads, had been met with a stony silence, and just one question—*Do you intend to have them fitted into your* Barracuda *submarine?*

The Iranians valued their relationship with the Russian Navy and were not about to tell a flagrant lie. Their affirmative reply had led the Russian Navy to inform them they were unable to supply the RADUGAs under any circumstances whatsoever.

Next stop Beijing. The Iranians asked if they could produce a missile precisely copying the RADUGA. It was a question that elicited an immense amount of hemming and hawing from the Chinese, who finally admitted that after having been so closely involved with the Hamas mission of *Barracuda I* in the U.S.A., the last thing they needed now was for *Barracuda II,* with a boatload of nuclear-capable Chinese-made missiles, to be discovered by the Americans, in brazen conflict with the Non-Proliferation Treaty.

In general terms, the Chinese were not averse to assisting their friends and clients in the Middle East. They had an extremely serious interest in the oil fields around the Gulf, and were prepared to run certain risks while helping the occasional rogue regime. But that did not include arming the second *Barracuda* for these wild men from the Middle East to cause havoc. Too dangerous. No good for business. Americans can get cross with Muslims. Not China. The Chinese did not really have a missile that would be readily adaptable to convert to the RADUGA dimensions anyway. They probably had the guidance and tracking software, cunningly acquired from the Americans in the 1990s, but they were less confident in their own hardware, especially for short-range cruises.

Which left General Ravi with few options, the most unlikely of which was the little state of Bosnia, where Jugoim-
port, a state-owned conglomerate in Belgrade, was reputed to
have been working with Iraq to develop a cruise missile. Ju-
goimport was also reported to be working with the military
operation Orao Arms, located in Bijeljina, the second largest
city in the Bosnian Serb Republic, up in the northeast.

Orao had claimed only to have helped repair Iraqi war-
planes, but the cruise missile evidence was damning, and it
was obvious that Orao (a) knew how to make a guided missile, and (b) how to propel it for fairly long distances. Every
arms dealer in the Middle East knew they had considerable
expertise in the field of warheads. And for that reason, General Ravi had undertaken the journey there from Syria.

But there had been too many gaps. The personnel at Orao
were hardworking and ambitious. They had scientists working night and day trying to perfect nuclear warheads. But
they were not there yet. They were superb in propulsion, and
very competent with the guidance software. But General
Ravi wanted precision, guaranteed workmanship that would
work the first time, every time.

The General demanded massive penalty clauses, should
there be a malfunction. The Bosnians thought long and hard
about the huge income from the Hamas operation, but the
risk was too great. Hamas would clearly have had problems
persuading a court of international law to uphold their delivery contracts. But the Orao executive had an uncanny feeling
that if they failed to make reparations for malfunction, this
cold-eyed Middle Eastern military chief would not hesitate
to have them taken off the map.

They were correct about that, but everyone parted friends.
The last words one of the scientists uttered to General Ravi
before he flew home to Damascus were: *You must go to North
Korea. They can sell you what you want. They have the technology and much more experience than we do.*

And now he was looking for the left turn, the track up

through the foothills of the Hamgyong-Sanmaek range, the one that led to the nuclear complex inside Kwanmo-bong.

And General Ravi looked grim as he considered his awesome checklist—dimensions, fuel requirements, software for the detonation. And, above all, cost. He was about to spend close to $500 million on a magazine of missiles—eighteen cruises with a standard warhead. Two with nuclear warheads, 200 kilotons each of explosives.

Barracuda I had been purchased with a full complement of RADUGA cruises already aboard, so he knew almost to the inch what they should look like. The big Russian shells were gray in color with *SS-N-21 Sampson* (*RK-55 Granat*) painted in small Russian letters on the underside.

They were 26 feet long, 18 inches wide, with a launch weight of almost 1.75 tons. They carried a single nuclear warhead packing a 200-kiloton wallop. RADUGA flies at Mach 0.7, 680 mph, 200 feet above the surface, with a range of 1,620 nautical miles. Launched from a standard 21-inch torpedo tube, the RADUGA's wings, mounted towards the stern, unfold immediately as it blasts clear of the water. The missile is essentially land-attack, and operates on a terrain-following system, guided by a radar altimeter. It's accurate to about 100 yards. Plenty for General Ravi's purposes.

In a world full of big business, nothing was much bigger than his. Nothing was more ruthless. And nothing was more dangerous. He just hoped the North Korean technicians could now justify their low bows, confident smiles, and promises he had seen when he was here last.

As they approached the first gate along the track, he was not looking forward to any part of this visit. Beyond pondering the ability of the North Korean technologists to replicate faithfully the RADUGA missile he was looking for, right now he was a great deal more concerned with their safety procedures in what was obviously a toxic environment inside Kwanmo-bong.

General Ravi was not a nuclear expert. But he knew the

subject, and, above all, the qualities of uranium, its three highly radioactive isotopes with their nuclei of unstable elements, U-238, U-235, and U-234, with the prevalent U-238 forming more than 99 percent of the whole, the weapons-precious U-235 only 0.711 of a percent.

U-235 is the isotope that matters, because it not only has the ability to "fission"—split into two lighter fragments when bombarded with neutrons—it could also sustain a chain reaction, with each fission producing enough neutrons to trigger another, thus eliminating the need for any other source of neutrons. This raging buildup of energy in the bombardment of the neutrons, smashing into and splitting the atoms millions of times over, is, essentially, a nuclear bomb. The U-235 is rare and hard to produce, but it produces an impact that makes regular TNT look childish.

In comparison, though, regular U-238 is no slouch in the weapons industry. It could not produce the deadly chain reaction of U-235, but when converted to plutonium-239 it can. This substance, virtually nonexistent in nature, was the heart of the atomic bomb that destroyed Nagasaki on August 9, 1945.

The General had spent countless hours studying nuclear energy at his home in Damascus and he understood its production to a tee. The mining of uranium—the "milling" process—in which the uranium oxide is extracted from the raw ore to form the yellowcake, that yellow or brown powder almost entirely made up of the oxide. Then there's the huge volume of waste, the "mill tailings," some forms of which are radioactive for 75,000 years.

Ravi had no idea whether any of this stuff had leached into the ground water in the mountain springs around Kwanmo-bong, but he was resolved not to risk it. Any drinkables might be full of radium-226, as well as heavy metals like manganese and molybdenum. He was pretty certain this miscreant communist state would not have the safety measures in place that are enforced by law in the West.

Inside this great mountain there was a vast uranium-enrichment plant that converted the element into a chemical form, uranium hexafluoride, a diabolically toxic and radioactive danger to anyone who gets near it. The "enrichment plants" had suffered a number of accidents, all of them involving hexafluoride, and Ravi was not looking forward to this close proximity with living death.

Shaking himself out of such grim thoughts, he turned around and, grinning encouragingly at young Ahmed Sabah, his own wife's beloved brother, he concentrated instead on the missiles. Could the North Koreans deliver on their promise to use their own technology to convert their one-stage medium-range Nodong-1 missile into a submarine-launched RADUGA? They were approximately the same size and dimension, and had successfully been sold to the Iranians—the *Shahab-3*—but it was open to question whether the North Koreans could engineer the more refined rocket motor, the rocket's automatic wings, and the correct components to affix to a nuclear warhead.

They had sworn they could and had been sufficiently honest to admit their weakness with regard to the software for the automatic guidance system. But Ravi had successfully bargained with the Chinese, who agreed to fit these anonymous but expensive and critical finishing touches to the missile's preprogrammed navigational computers. Most of the technology was American in origin.

So far as Ravi had been informed, the missiles were complete, ready for shipping to the North Korean seaport of Nampo. All he needed to do was conclude the payments, and accept delivery. The Koreans may have been fugitives from the international community, but no one had ever questioned their business methods or their reliability.

The sun was sinking fast behind the mountains now, and it was beginning to rain. Up ahead, Ravi and Ahmed could see lights and what looked like a long, high chain-link fence. They were bumping over a rough and hilly surface, and they could see the big gates folded right across the track, floodlit, the rain glistening off the metal, armed guards standing directly in front of the high steel structure. It would have required a full-blown U.S. M-60 tank to smash its way through there and you would not have put your life savings on its success.

Ravi's driver drew the juggernaut to a halt and wound down the window on the driver's side. The guard, who was obviously expecting the big military truck, held out his hand for papers, stuffed them inside his raincoat, and walked to the front and rear of the vehicle, checking the registration numbers. Then he walked over to the guardhouse and inspected the papers under a light, where it was dry, before walking back out and handing over the documents. The big gates were already being swung back by two other guards. The original man waved them through and the driver continued on up the track in driving rain and pitch-dark.

They passed several more guardhouses on either side of the stony, pitted causeway to Kwanmo-bong and stopped again by another set of high metal gates after about seven miles. The inspection procedures were much the same as before, and again they were waved through, grinding their way up the mountain.

The last five miles were easily the most arduous. The track became steeper, and the rain, if anything, worsened, slashing down out of the northwest, head-on into the windshield of the lurching army truck. You didn't hear many compliments about the cars made in the Qingming Automobile Company in the old Chinese capital of Chongqing. But on the way up Kwanmo-bong, Ravi found a new respect for the Chinese car factory.

"Ahmed," he said in English, "I guess those guys know how to make a mean automobile in Chongqing. This thing has taken some kind of a pounding, and somehow we're still going."

"I didn't even know the Chinese made automobiles," replied Ahmed. "I thought they bought shiploads of them, secondhand, piled on all decks from the U.S.A."

"No, that's the Russians. The Chinese have a huge manufacturing plant in Chongqing."

"Where the hell's that, Ravi?" asked Ahmed.

"It's very deep in the interior. Sichuan. They somehow built this damn great city halfway up a mountain overlooking the valley where the Yangtze and Jialing Rivers meet. It's nowhere near anywhere, 700 miles from Shanghai, 800 from Beijing. Over 15 million people live there, and they make a lot of cars and trucks."

"How do you know all that?"

"I've been there."

"I didn't know you'd been to central China."

"Neither did the Chinese."

Ahmed laughed and shook his head. "You have many surprises no one knows, General Ravi," he said.

"I'm hanging on to 'em as well," replied the Hamas C in C. "Since I plan to go on breathing."

In Ahmed's humble but youthful opinion, the General was without doubt the cleverest, toughest, and most ruthless man he had ever met. He had seen him kill without blinking, destroy without a moment's pity for the dead and suffering. And he had seen him lavish on his own very beautiful Palestinian sister Shakira a devotion and admiration almost unknown in the Arab world.

Ahmed was best man at their wedding. He had acted as Ravi's personal bodyguard throughout several missions against the Israelis and the West. And Ahmed had stood almost dumbfounded when a reckless young Palestinian terrorist had attacked the General before a mission, viciously trying to land the butt of an AK-47 on Ravi's jaw.

The speed with which Ravi had dealt with him was blinding. He had broken the young man's arm into two pieces, and his collarbone, and then rammed his boot into the boy's throat as he lay on the floor, saying quietly, "I've killed men for a great deal less. Take him to a hospital, Ahmed."

On the way, young Sabah had explained that the Iranian-born Hamas C in C had been one of the most feared team leaders in the British Army's SAS, and probably the best exponent of unarmed combat in the Regiment. By some miracle, the former Maj. Ray Kerman had found himself on the wrong side in a bloody battle in the holy city of Hebron, where he had been saved by Shakira.

Shakira had brought him to Hamas. He changed his name back to that of his birth. He converted back to his childhood religion of Islam. And in the process provided the organization with possibly the most important Muslim battle commander since Saladin eight hundred years earlier. At least that's how the High Command of Hamas used his name to inspire new recruits.

And now he fought alongside his Arabian brothers, with whom he shared forefathers. As the most wanted terrorist in the world, he returned to the Muslim religion and married his adored Shakira.

"Allah himself sent him to us," Ahmed had said en route to the hospital. The kid with the broken arm and collarbone was inclined to think Satan himself had also had a hand in it.

The Chongqing-built truck faced the most hazardous part of its journey over the last mile. The gradient looked like Mount Everest, and the engine howled in low gear, the four-wheel-drive tires somehow managing to grip the granite and mud surface, which was slick from a small river gushing out of the mountain.

There were many lights and the final 600 yards were downhill, into a hollow with a tall, steel-topped barbed-wire fence crossing it. "Impregnable" was the only word General Ravi could find to describe it.

To the left and the right of the main gates were high guard posts, each one built on six stilts the size of telegraph poles. They were set 10 feet above the razor-sharp steel spikes ranged along the top of the structure. Inside the post were two searchlights and two armed guards, each one manning a mounted heavy machine gun. General Ravi could not quite work out whether they were trying to stop people getting in or out. Either way, his money was on the guards.

Patrolling the outside was a detail of eight men, split into two groups of four and stationed in the open on either side of the gate, rain or no rain. Through the gate Ravi could see no further light, save for that coming through a regular seven-foot-high doorway. There were no other lights between the huge outside gates and whatever lay beyond. Ravi and Ahmed just sat still and waited.

The guard chief ordered the main gates open and their driver drove forward, headlights on full beam straight at what seemed like a massive wall of rock. It was not until they were quite close up that Ravi saw that the wall was actually solid steel. A small open doorway was set into the steel, and the whole wall suddenly disappeared completely, sliding to the right into the rock face.

Before him was a yawning dark cavern without a semblance of light. It was like driving into a gigantic tomb. The truck moved forward, and silently the great steel doors behind them slid back into place. Ravi sensed them shutting firmly and felt the chill of enclosure by forces way beyond his control.

He and his men had sat for just a few seconds when the entire place was lit up by a near-explosion of electric power. This was no tomb, no cavern. This was Main Street Kwanmo-bong—streetlights, central white lines, and lights from shops, or offices, or laboratories. The street was dead straight, and it stretched through the heart of the mountain as far as he could see.

The General guessed the source of the electricity: nuclear energy gone berserk. North Korea's biggest underground nuclear facility, blasted out of solid rock.

A titanic achievement, to be sure, but at what cost had it been built? Ravi wondered. He stared up at the ceiling, which was still, in places, just barren rock face. But the walls were made of concrete, and even now, through the truck windows, he could feel the soft hum of the generators pervading the entire subterranean structure. Somewhere, behind or beneath this vast reinforced cement cave, there must be a huge nuclear reactor providing the power.

And if anyone wanted to close it down, sealed as it was

from the outside world, beneath the 8,000-foot-high peak of Kwanmo-bong, they'd need, well, an atomic bomb. It was, he thought, entirely possible that the only people who could destroy the nuclear facility inside this mountain were the people who built it.

"Jesus Christ," whispered Ravi.

They drove forwards for about 500 yards, and the truck began an elaborate reverse turn into what appeared to be a loading dock. The driver cut the engine and opened his door, at which point four North Korean officials appeared. Two of them wore white laboratory coats, the others were in that curious military garb of the Far Eastern officer—the olive-drab green trousers, and the open-necked shirt, the same color, with a central zipper instead of buttons, epaulettes, rolled cuffs.

General Rashood and Ahmed joined their driver on the smooth concrete floor and were greeted, in English, by the obvious commandant, who was all business despite the late hour.

"You will see your merchandise?" he said, bowing medium-low, twice. Like a Japanese double-dome. Then he extended his hand and said, "Greetings, General. We welcome you here—hope this first of many visit."

He introduced himself as Colonel Dae-jung, and his colleagues in turn. Then he led the way back around the corner he had come from and into a wide, brightly lit vestibule where two armed guards and a desk clerk were on duty.

Each man stood to attention and saluted the Colonel, who now led the way along a corridor and up a flight of steps into a wide, bright warehouse with overhead cranes, surrounded by cables leading to great, broad, upwards-sliding steel doors. Ahead of them were two gleaming stainless-steel cylinders about 15 feet high and 6 feet in diameter, known as "flasks" in the trade—heavily constructed Western containers whose sole task on earth was to transport radioactive nuclear material. They were actually perfected at British

Nuclear Fuels in England, and were generally considered to be as close to fail-safe as you can get.

Built of one-inch-thick steel, the flasks were heavy with inbuilt shields to reduce radiation, making them at once safer for passersby and also less vulnerable to attack by terrorists.

"Inside there, General," said the Korean Commandant, "are two nuclear warheads you ordered. Each one correctly assembled includes decoys. Both warheads ready for fitting in the new missiles, packed separately—Chinese guidance and navigational engineers may wish work inside the nose cone of missile—this way no encumbrance of nuclear material. Mostly fit warhead at last moment, before missile sealed and loaded into submarine."

Ravi nodded. "May I see the warheads?" he asked.

"Certainly. There is small window, glass four inches thick, but you can see inside." He led Ravi around to the six-inch porthole in the flask and shone a flashlight through it. Ravi peered inside and could just make out the shape of the cone behind the crossbeams and cable that held it secure.

"I assure you, no one disappointed," said the Commandant. "That's 200-kiloton warhead. Detonate properly will make all the damage you intend . . ."

The North Koreans were known for their integrity in these matters, and Ravi did not doubt him. "And the regular missiles?" he asked. "The RADUGA look-alikes."

"Crated over here," said the Commandant, leading the way. "One of them not sealed, so you can see—"

Ravi looked at the long, 30-foot crates, each one weighing two tons. "These conventional warheads are assembled and fitted?" he asked.

"Correct."

"No problem matching the Russians?"

"Absolutely not. We have two Russian RADUGAs here in plant. Reconstruction very straightforward. We have shell casings for certain SCUDs, and for Nodong-1—more or less identical."

"I won't even ask how you got ahold of the RADUGAs," said the General, grinning.

"No. Perhaps not," replied the Commandant, not grinning. "But we fit entirely Korean-made engine for the rocket. We think it's marginally superior to Russian motor, and definitely more reliable. Works on regular nitric-acid rocket propellant."

Ravi nodded. He counted the crates, inspected one of them, leaned over and touched the cold metal casing.

"Are the loading docks at Nampo ready for a heavy cargo like this?"

"Loading docks at Nampo second to none in whole world," replied the Commandant, modestly. "We expert at loading and transporting missile and warhead. Been doing it for very long time now. No mistakes."

"Made one off the coast of Yemen a few years back," said Ravi.

"No mistakes in area of northeast Asia," said the Commandant. "That more important. That's what you need to know."

"You're right there," said Ravi. "That more important."

"Are you satisfied with the shipment?"

"I am. Would you like to conclude the payment details now?"

"Very good, General. Then we have some dinner and then you go. Three of our trucks travel in convoy. Gas tanker inside plant now. Plenty fuel get you to Nampo."

"I appreciate that," said Ravi.

The method of payment had been established several months before—$150 million advance in U.S. dollars; the final balance of $350 million U.S. payable upon completion, ex-factory. Arrangements had been made through the Korea Exchange Bank in downtown Seoul, south of the border, and the money had been deposited direct from Tehran several weeks previously.

The bank in Seoul would receive a code word from General Rashood either by phone, fax, or E-mail. Only when the

Korea Exchange confirmed that with the Bank Melli Iran would the funds be released to a North Korean Government account. Tonight everyone was on standby awaiting the big-money communiqué from the Hamas General.

He sat before an open online computer in the Commandant's office, and tapped in the phrase in Persian, *se-panjah bash-e*—which meant, broadly, *Three-fifty, it's cool*. Moments later the code was transmitted 5,000 miles west and six hours back in time to Bank Melli in downtown Tehran, right on the main commercial avenue, Kheyabun-e Ferdosi, opposite the German Embassy.

The reply was back in Seoul in moments . . . *Release funds to the North* . . . Thus, in less than five minutes, $350 million U.S. changed hands, and the brutal terrorist High Command of Hamas took delivery of its first-ever nuclear weapons.

Dinner with the North Koreans surpassed Ravi's expectations. They provided a superb *sinsollo*—a special national dish of boiled red meat, fish, and vegetables, flavored with *dweonjang* (bean paste) and *gotchu* (red chili), a bit like Japanese *shabu shabu*, but tastier, saltier. Ravi's was served with buckwheat noodles and egg rolls.

They drank only mineral water, which he sincerely hoped had not come out of the ground anywhere near the radioactive environs of Kwanmo-bong.

He declined a tour of the laboratories, but could not help seeing dozens of technicians walking around dressed entirely in white, including low-fitting hats and gloves. He trusted that they were staying well clear of the old hexafluoride, and that the executive of this astounding underground complex had rules and regulations about safety and a secure environment for their noxious raw material.

Before he left, the Commandant informed him, "Remember, we conduct the entire nuclear process right here in Kwanmo-bong. Enrichment, harvesting of plutonium, and refinement of U-235. Right into weapons-grade material.

"Down at far end, nearly one mile away, we make rockets

and missiles. SCUD-B; Hwasong-5 short-range; Hwasong-6 short-range, like SCUD-C; the Nodong medium range; the Taep'o-dong-1, like Soviet SS-4; the NKSL-1/Taep'o-dong-1 intermediate-range satellite launch; and the big long-range ballistic missiles, Taep'o-dong-2 and NKSL-X-2/Taep'o-dong-2—we make Iran's Shahab from that last one—like Soviet SS-5, satellite launch. We make what you want. Two- or three-stage missiles. Big payload. No problem. Very good, ha?"

"Excellent," replied General Ravi. "Most impressive."

They walked on and turned into the bog-loading bay. The Commandant was correct: There were three big North Korean Army trucks in there now, parked between the massive steel girders of the overhead cranes. A team of young soldiers was swarming all over the vehicles, refitting the big waterproof canvas covers over the rear beds into which were now stacked the thirty-foot-long missiles.

Ravi noticed the truck in which he had arrived contained the two stainless-steel flasks with the nuclear warheads. The eighteen missiles were stacked nine on each of the other two—three stacks of three, piled slightly apart, separated with timbers and wooden pallets, but lashed together with bands of sprung steel.

Ravi considered the weight, probably 18 tons per vehicle, and thought again what he had thought on the long journey to the northeast—*They make a hell of a truck in Chongqing.*

He shook hands with the Commandant, and he and Ahmed climbed aboard. The young bodyguard had not removed his AK-47 from the rear seat and it had not been touched. It was still loaded.

The three drivers started their engines, and in convoy, they made their way to the main entrance. The entire place was plunged into darkness immediately before the great doors smoothed their way back into the rock. All three trucks were on dipped headlights now, but no other light came flooding out into the pitch dark of Kwanmo-bong.

They drove straight out into the rain and headed for the

gates, which were open and held back. The duty guards saluted as they rumbled out onto the southward track and drove noisily away from the underground factory.

Despite the presence of two good-sized, utterly illegal nuclear warheads, encased behind him, the General felt quite righteous as they began their journey. He might be planning something diabolical, but his people had a just cause and were prepared to fight and die for their beliefs, for the right to self-government for the ancient peoples of Palestine and other oppressed nations in the Middle East, which were currently forced to march to the beat of an American drum. On the other hand, the North Koreans were just racketeers. They had no plans, no loyalties, no morals, no higher creeds or beliefs, no allies. They just wanted cash for arms—arms of the worst possible type for whoever wanted to commit crimes against humanity.

The great Allah had proved to be on the side of the Hamas warriors. And He had shown it many times. Ravi knew He would accompany them on all of their great missions against the West. Of that he had no doubt.

The three trucks roared and skidded their way downwards, lurching around bends where the track attempted to follow the contours of the mountain. The surface was rough and the gradients uneven, and the rain never let up. Nor would it, all the way to the junction where the forbidden track to Kwanmo-bong joined the east coast highway.

But the gates were open, ready for them at each checkpoint, and they were not stopped by the guards. They just drove straight on through and turned south, where the rain stopped almost immediately. Heading to the capital city of Pyongyang, they swerved around south of the metropolis before picking up the new expressway to the seaport of Nampo, 25 miles to the southwest. General Ravi was disappointed not to see the urban sprawl of Pyongyang, but he understood there was something bizarre about pulling into the tourist area along the Taedong River, with three trucks filled with nuclear warheads and missiles.

Instead, the little convoy kept going, driving through the night towards the shores of the Yellow Sea. It was almost dawn now, and the sun was fighting its way towards the horizon. Daylight came as they passed through the gates into the dockyard at Nampo, the largest port on the west coast. Ravi and Ahmed, tired and hungry, were astounded at the size of the jetties, all occupied by major container ships, moored beneath great overhead cranes. Most of them flew the flags of countries in Southeast Asia and Africa, but there were three from the Middle East and one from Europe. Freighters had no difficulty entering and exiting the port of Nampo, regardless of their size, since the construction of the enormous West Sea Floodgates significantly elevated water levels and dramatically improved berthing capacity.

Ravi's convoy pulled up alongside a much smaller ship, an old 500-tonner, dark blue with rust marks all over the hull. The number 81, just visible beneath the paint, gave little away, but the thirty-six-year-old freighter was in fact a converted ASU-class auxiliary ship originally built for the Japanese Navy, a twin-shafted diesel that now looked to be on its last legs.

The for'ard superstructure was in dire need of a few coats of paint, as was its one broad funnel. The aft area was flat and carried a hefty-looking crane, which had once lifted Japanese Naval helicopters. There had also been a small flight deck, now converted for short-haul freight.

The red-painted hull letters on its port bow were barely legible in either Korean script or English—*Yongdo*. Ravi had no idea what that meant. But she flew the broad maroon stripe and single star of the North Korean flag on her stern, stretched out hard in the gusty morning breeze.

The jetty was staffed entirely by military personnel, and it was not until the three army trucks came to a halt between carefully painted markings, and they all disembarked the trucks, that General Ravi noticed they were in a sealed area. A large iron gate had already been closed behind them.

There was obviously no way out, and there sure as hell was no way in.

Awaiting their arrival was the ship's commanding officer, North Korean Navy Captain Cho Joong Kun.

"Welcome to Nampo," he said in English. "Please come aboard immediately. I have arranged breakfast and cabins. We sail tonight on the tide around midnight. As you know, it's a two-day voyage."

Ravi glanced down at the officer's sleeve insignia—two black stripes on gold, with a downward line of three silver stars. In this Navy you needed to make Commodore to get four stars.

"Good morning, Captain Cho," he said. "I'm glad to see you. We've been driving all night."

"Yes, I was told. You may sleep most of the day if you wish. By the time you awaken we'll be loaded. That crane over there will be ready for us in about three hours. It will take some time. You have a rather delicate cargo."

"Very delicate," replied Ravi. "And expensive."

1900, Thursday, May 28 (Same Day)
27.00N 124.20E, Depth 400, Speed 25.

Barracuda II moved swiftly north, through 460 fathoms of ocean, 80 miles northwest of Okinawa, and now clear of the long chain of the Ryukyu Islands, where the ancient territories of imperial Japan had finally come to an end.

They were running up towards the line of the Japan current, which effectively provides China with a frontier for the Pacific end of the East Sea. The newly promoted Rear Adm. Ben Badr intended to stay out in the deeper water on the Japan side of the current as long as he could. Like most Middle Eastern and Eastern submariners, he preferred to run deep whenever he could, away from the prying eyes of the American satellites.

It was of course unusual for a Rear Admiral to serve as Commanding Officer, but Ben would have a full-fledged Captain on board for their next mission, and his own authority in this ship was tantamount. Anyway, the Hamas were not hidebound by the traditions of other people's navies. They were in the process of establishing their own.

The *Barracuda* had cleared Zhanjiang, headquarters of China's Southern Fleet, on Tuesday evening, on the surface, in full view of anyone who was interested. They went deep just before the Luzon Strait, which separates Taiwan and the Philippines, and were now around halfway through their 2,400-mile journey to the North.

This was the second of the two *Barracuda*s, which the Hamas organization had purchased from Russia in utmost secrecy. And while the Americans may have harbored serious suspicions about who actually owned it, they only knew three things: for one, Russia did not admit to selling this particular *Barracuda* to anyone; two, China did not admit to owning it; and three, neither did anyone else.

The fate of the first *Barracuda,* destroyed in Panama, was known to the Americans, but it was a highly classified subject, and Washington was as close-mouthed as Beijing and Moscow.

Adm. Ben Badr knew that the sight of *Barracuda II*, steaming cheerfully out of Zhanjiang, bound for God knows where, would most certainly have attracted the attention of U.S. Naval Intelligence. And in Fort Meade, the same old question was doubtlessly about to rear its irritating head again: *Who the hell owns this goddamned thing?*

The *Barracuda*, an 8,000-ton, 350-foot-long Russian-built hunter-killer, was on its way to its first mission. Its initial destination was the ultrasecret Chinese Navy Base of Huludao, way up in the Yellow Sea, the cul-de-sac ocean where China prepared and conducted the trials of its biggest Inter-Continental Ballistic Missile submarines.

"Come right 10 degrees," called the CO. *"Steer course three-zero. Make your speed 25, depth 200."*

The Yellow Sea was notoriously shallow, and the last part

of the journey, through China's most forbidden waters, would have to be completed on the surface right below the American satellites.

Admiral Badr wished to conduct the voyage with as little observation as possible, nonetheless, but, in the end, so what? A Russian-built submarine headed for a Chinese base, mostly through international waters—no one was obliged to tell Washington anything. The Pentagon did not, after all, own the oceans of the world. China and Russia were perfectly entitled to move their underwater boats around, visiting each other's ports.

Admiral Badr smiled grimly . . . *Just as long as they don't find out where we're going in the end*, he thought.

Generally, he was pleased with the handling of the big submarine. Her titanium hull, which had originally made her so expensive, helped give her low radiated-noise reduction, but she had proved very costly to complete and would be even more so to run.

Essentially she had never been to sea until a year ago. She'd made one long, unhurried, and uneventful journey halfway around the world, and been in a long and thorough overhaul in the yards of China's Southern Fleet ever since. She handled like a new ship, her nuclear reactor running smoothly, providing all of her power, enabling her to stay underwater for months at a time if necessary.

When armed, the *Barracuda* could pack a terrific bang. She was a guided-missile ship and fired the outstanding Russian "fire and forget" SS-N-21 Granat-type cruises from deep beneath the surface. Right now her missile magazines were empty, a situation that would be rectified as soon as she reached Huludao.

Admiral Badr, Iranian by birth and son of the C in C of the Ayatollah's Navy in Bandar Abbas, was an accomplished handler of a nuclear submarine. And he aimed *Barracuda II* north, crossing the line of the Japan current on the 30th parallel, running into waters around 300 feet deep—friendly waters patrolled by his Chinese buddies.

So far as Ben Badr was concerned, this was a pleasant cruise, among colleagues he knew well, alongside whom he had fought and triumphed in *Barracuda I.* He looked forward to the coming months with immense anticipation. And the words of his father were always fresh in his mind . . . *Stay as deep as possible, as quiet as possible, and when danger threatens, as slow as possible. That way your chances of being detected in that big nuclear boat are close to zero.*

It was almost 2300 hours now on the pitch-dark and rain-swept East China Sea, and the *Barracuda* held to course three-five-zero some 300 miles due east of Shanghai. They were headed more or less directly towards the beautiful sub-tropical island of Jejudo, the 13-mile-long remnant of a long-extinct volcano situated off the southwesternmost tip of South Korea.

Ben Badr intended to leave this sun-kissed tourist para-dise, "Korea's Hawaii," 60 miles off his starboard beam as he continued north into the Yellow Sea, where life would become a great deal more testing and staying alert paramount.

The southern part of the Yellow Sea was a particularly busy spot. A veritable highway for tankers and freighters out of the big westerly ports that serviced Seoul, and the other great seaport of Kunsan, and the heavy tanker and freight traffic in and out of Nampo. In addition, there was constant fishing-boat traffic, also from South Korea, not to mention the ships of the Chinese Navy from both the Eastern and North fleets. The sonar of any submarine commanding officer had to be permanently on high alert through here.

Now, as the four bells of the watch tolled the midnight hour inside the submarine, the Korean freighter *Yongdo* was just clearing the West Sea Floodgates outside Nampo harbor 420 miles to the north, her elderly diesel engines driving her twin shafts in a shudder that might easily have been a protest.

It was a stark contrast to the silk-smooth hum of the *Barracuda*'s turbines, driving the submarine swiftly into the Yellow Sea, now only 100 feet below the rainswept surface of the ocean.

General Ravi and Ahmed had slept much of the day, dined with the CO and his first officer, and were now on the bridge of the *Yongdo* as honored guests. You don't sell a shipload of guided missiles and two hugely expensive nuclear warheads every day. Not even in North Korea.

The *Yongdo*'s journey would be a little more than 400 miles, and somewhere in the northern reaches of this forbidden sea, she would be passed by the *Barracuda*, which was scheduled to dock in Huludao early on Saturday evening. Ravi wondered if he would see her come by, since she would most certainly be on the surface. It was strange to think of his old shipmate and great friend Ben Badr charging up the same piece of ocean as he and Ahmed.

They could see little in the dark, but there was a considerable swell, and the freighter soon began to pitch and yaw. Captain Cho said not to worry, it never got much worse, but General Rashood nevertheless had a fleeting feeling of dread. It would be a real drag if his precious cargo went down. For obvious reasons it could scarcely be insured, and the terms were ex-factory. Those missiles hit the seabed and the losses would be born by the new owners.

They were 240 miles west to the Bohai Haixia—the Yellow Sea Strait—and here navigation was extremely tricky. The narrow seaway between the Provinces of Shandong to the South and the seaward headland of Liaodong Province to the North was guarded by the Chinese, much like the White House is protected by the Americans.

This was the choke point containing two large areas completely prohibited to shipping and the one place where the Chinese Navy can apprehend an intruder with ease. Not even the most daring submarine CO would attempt underwater passage, through the middle, where the water was less than 80 feet deep.

The chart looked like an obstacle course—fishing banned, anchoring banned, oil pipelines, Naval waters. Endless patrol boats. Rocks, wrecks, sandbars, and constant "forbidden entry" signs. Don't even think about it. The Chinese, with a nuclear shipbuilding program in full operation on the distant shores to the north, had much to protect from the West, indeed much to hide.

Even the friendly little North Korean freighter *Yongdo* would have a Navy escort in the small hours of Friday morning. As would the *Barracuda* several hours later.

The *Yongdo* was there first, by midnight on Friday, with the *Barracuda* charging along behind, gaining with every hour. Still underwater, in 26 fathoms, Ben Badr knew he would shortly have to come to periscope depth as the sea shelved up into the Strait and then to the dead-end section of the Yellow Sea.

With every mile they covered, he was more and more pleased with his crew. Everyone had learned an enormous amount in the previous two years—the training with the Russians in Araguba, the endless courses in nuclear physics, nuclear reactors, turbines, propulsion, engineering, electronics, hydrology, weapons and guidance systems.

And alongside him, there were no longer rookies, but seasoned submariners. There was his number two, the Executive Officer, Capt. Ali Akbar Mohtaj, the former reactor room engineer who had commanded this very ship halfway around the world.

There was Commander Abbas Shafii, another engineer, nuclear specialist from General Rashood's home province of Kerman. He would take overall command of the control area. There was the Chief of Boat, Chief Petty Officer (CPD) Ali Zahedi, and CPO Ardeshir Tikku, who would take overall command of the top three computer panels in the reactor control room.

A first-class electronics Lieutenant Commander from Tehran who had three tours of duty in Iran's Kilo-Class diesel-electrics was also onboard; and he was highly valued since he had sailed with Captain Mohtaj from Araguba to Zhanjiang the previous year.

In addition to the always-comforting presence of General Rashood, there was his cheerful personal bodyguard Ahmed

Sabah, who acted as a huge help in crew relations, cheerfully complimenting the men on their work. It was as if his words came from the Hamas military boss himself, and Ben Badr knew it served great purpose towards the general morale of people working under stress, spending weeks on end without laying eyes on the world outside.

And then, of course, the beautiful, slender, steely-eyed Shakira, the General's wife, Ahmed's sister, one of the most trusted operatives in the entire Hamas organization, the Palestinian freedom fighter who had saved the life of Maj. Ray Kerman when he was hopelessly trapped in a murderous shoot-out in the wrong end of Hebron.

In return, General Rashood had allowed free rein to his wife's talent, encouraging her to develop her principal strength—the gathering and ordering of immense detail, mainly in the area of maps, charts, and topology. In Ravi's view, no one could plot and plan with greater detail than Shakira, especially cruise missile navigation. In the end, he had caved in to her demands to be allowed to serve onboard the submarine. And a wise decision it had been.

This lovely, black-haired Arabian woman, now twenty-seven years old, had a mind like a bear trap. And her performance in *Barracuda I* in the missile programming area had been flawless. So flawless that Ravi had almost forgotten her final summing up before he permitted her to become the first woman ever to serve in a submarine—*"Either we both go, or no one goes. You're not dying without me . . ."*

And now she awaited them in the port of Huludao, and Admiral Badr greatly looked forward to seeing her, though perhaps not quite as intensely as North Korea's big customer, sharing the bridge with Ahmed Sabah in comfortable silence, staring at the endless waters of the Yellow Sea, a couple of hundred miles to the north.

For both ships, the journey passed without incident. Escorted through the Strait, no one hit, or even dodged, anything. The *Barracuda* docked at around 1900 on Saturday evening. The *Yongdo* came in twelve hours later on Sunday morning.

Chinese customs, all in Naval uniform, boarded her before anyone was permitted to leave the ship. And they insisted on inspecting at least two of the new missiles and having them identified with the full paperwork provided by the owner, General Rashood.

Two of the crates were unbolted, one of them containing the missile that would include one of the nuclear warheads sealed in the bright stainless-steel flasks lashed down for'ard of the freight deck.

General Ravi knew they were looking at one of the two nuclear cruises, because he could see the lettering near the stern, in English, denoting it was a Mark-2 Submarine-Launched weapon, custom-built for a designated submarine.

The missile had been named by Shakira, in honor of the ancient curved blade of the Muslims, the sword forged in Damascus and carried by Saladin himself when he faced the Lionheart's Christians at the gates of Jerusalem in the twelfth century.

The name was clear, painted at Shakira's request in letters of gold. They stood stark against the gunmetal-gray curve of the missile's casing—*SCIMITAR SL-2.*

1130, June 4, 2009
National Security Agency
Fort Meade, Maryland.

THE LIEUTENANT COMMANDER'S OFFICE looked as if it had been ransacked. There were sheets of paper covering literally every square inch of the area—on the desk, on the "research table" next to the printer, on the printer, and all over the floor. There were big piles, little piles, and single pieces. There was colored paper and plain. There was stuff in files, stuff wrapped in rubber bands. Stuff crammed between the pages of books. There was SECRET, TOP SECRET, CLASSIFIED, HIGHLY CLASSIFIED. The last pile was the largest.

Contrary to first impression, however, the place had not been ransacked—merely Ramshawed. Every office space he had ever occupied looked the same. His boss, the National Security Director, Rear Adm. George Morris, put it down to an active mind. Ramshawe mostly operated on around seventeen fronts. Damned efficiently.

"I try," he once said, "to keep tabs on important matters, plus a few others that might become significant."

Right now he was into one highly significant matter, and another that had elbowed its way forward from the back burner. The "highly significant" item required attention today as it involved a potential enemy's nuclear submarine.

The envelope from the "back burner" required action yesterday, because it had just arrived from Adm. Arnold Morgan.

The very name of the now-retired National Security Adviser
still sent a tremor through the entire Fort Meade complex.

Jimmy Ramshawe had just sliced open the envelope with a
wide-bladed hunting knife with a bound kangaroo-hide handle that would have raised the pulse of Crocodile Dundee.

Inside the outer envelope was a plain white file containing
six 10 x 8 black-and-white photographs. Attached was a
brief note from the Admiral—*Four towelheads photographed on top of a volcano in the Canary Islands. When
you've got a moment, try to identify them. I think it might be
useful—A.M.*

Jimmy studied the pictures. There were four men in each
frame. The pictures had been taken high on a cliff top with
the ocean in the background. Three of the men were very
clear, one was less so. But even this fourth image was well focused and showed the man in stark profile, from either side.
The last one was snapped from his "seven o'clock," as the
Admiral might have said, *right on his portside quarter*.

If the request had come from anywhere else, Jimmy
Ramshawe would have put it in the nether regions of all back
burners. But requests from Admiral Morgan, though rare, did
not even count as requests. These were orders.

Jimmy picked up the envelope and headed to the office of
his immediate boss, Admiral Morris, who was alone at his
desk reading one of the endless stacks of field reports.

"G'day, chief," said the Lieutenant Commander. "Just got
an envelope from the Big Man, thought you might like to see
it . . ."

Admiral Morris was instantly on alert. "What does he
need?" he asked, already pulling the pictures from the file.

"Only the impossible," replied Jimmy. " 'Please identify
four towelheads out of a world population of about seven billion, spread through nineteen countries of their own, and
about five hundred belonging to other nations.' "

"Hmmmm," said the Admiral. "I guess he thinks they may

be prominent, or at least a couple of them may be. He wouldn't ask us to identify a group of camel drovers, would he?"

George Morris studied the pictures for a moment and nodded. "Well, they're good-quality shots, which means that Arnie didn't take 'em himself. With something like a modern camera, he'd have an attention span of about five and a half seconds . . . Right. These would be the work of Harry. Remember the ones from the Admiral's farewell party?"

"Yeah. Couldn't forget 'em. There was one Jane said made me look like a bloody swag man, hair floppy, shirt out, holding a pint of Fosters, asking Mrs. Morgan for a dance."

"Yes. I saw that one. And here's four more guys who look like they didn't want to be photographed. Again in very sharp focus. More dignified than you, of course, but very finely focused."

They both chuckled. But Admiral Morris was not taking this lightly. "Okay, Jimmy," he said. "Get these copied. Let's have fifty sets. Then draft a note and we'll send them through the regular mail to places we might get some feedback."

"Like where?" said Lt. Comdr. Ramshawe.

"Well, we could start with our embassies in Iran, Iraq, Syria, Egypt, all the Arab Emirates, Saudi Arabia, Jordan, Lebanon, Israel. Then we'll get the Pentagon to make some more copies and check out the commanding officers in all our Military and Naval Bases around the Middle East. We'll get the FBI on the case, and the CIA. We'll ask the Brits, MI5, MI6, Scotland Yard . . ."

"Christ, that's a lot of trouble to go to, sir."

"Happily we are assisted by a very large staff. I suggest we avoid putting anything on the networks. No Internet, no computers or E-mails, other than internal secure. The pictures are, after all, taken by a private citizen. And there is no suggestion of urgency. Arnold's honeymoon was five months ago. It's taken him that long to send them. But if the Big Man wants a check, we give him that check. As well as we can."

"Okay, sir. I'll take care of it right away." And Jimmy Ramshawe retreated to his paper-strewn lair, muttering,

"Some bloody private citizen. Takes a few holiday snaps, sticks 'em in the mail, and half the world goes into free fall."

He picked his way through the piles of paper, and studied the photographs again in a thoroughly Ramshavian way . . . *Well, they were taken on top of a volcano, but we can't see it . . . We can only see the top of this cliff . . . a very high one . . . right on the shoreline of the Canary Islands . . . So the volcano must be behind the photographer . . . Wonder what it looks like . . . Suppose it's dormant . . . They wouldn't be standing around on top of it, not if the bastard was chucking molten lava all over the place . . . I didn't even know they had volcanoes in the Canary Islands.*

But he had no time for reveries. He called for someone to come and make copies and for someone else to draw up a list of all the U.S. Embassies in the Middle East. He buzzed U.S. Army Capt. Scott Wade down in the Military Intelligence Division and asked him how to circulate the pictures to the U.S. Middle East Bases. Then he summoned Lt. Jim Perry and asked him to put the whole thing into action.

He drafted the letter of request himself, E-mailed it to Jim, and told him to download, print, and distribute it, together with the pictures, as soon as they were ready tomorrow morning. Then he turned his attention to something he thought might really matter.

Fresh from the National Surveillance Office there was a satellite shot of a Russian-built *Barracuda* nuclear submarine making its way north through the Yellow Sea, presumably to the Chinese naval base at Huludao, because there's not much else at the dead end of the Yellow Sea to interest anyone.

He also had a three-day-old picture of the *Barracuda* clearing the breakwater outside the base at Zhanjiang, headquarters of China's Southern Fleet.

The satellite had taken two shots of the submarine, the second one about 25 miles out of the base, just before she dived. The next snapshots of that stretch of ocean showed absolutely nothing, and Jimmy had wondered where the hell the ship was going.

There was only one operational *Barracuda* in all the world, and the new photograph of the submarine cruising north on the surface meant this one in the Yellow Sea was the same that had cleared Zhanjiang four days ago.

He still did not know who owned it. The Russians had been evasive, claiming they had sold it to the Chinese, and the Chinese flatly refused to reveal anything about their submarine fleet to a Western power, even to the U.S.A. whose money they so coveted.

Thus, there were unlikely to be any definitive answers. Jimmy Ramshawe would write a brief report and keep a sharp eye on the photographs from northeast Asia, ready for the moment the *Barracuda* sailed south again heading for God knows where.

Again he pondered the mystery of the *Barracuda*. Why the hell's the damn thing going to Huludao anyway . . . *That's their nuclear missile base, where they built their two over-sized, primarily useless* Xia-Class *ICBM boats. Beats the shit out of me. The ole 'Cuda's too small for an ICBM. Maybe the Russians are really selling her this time.*

But then, they could just as easily have sold her in Zhan-jiang. Why take her north for 2,500 miles? What's in Huludao that the Barracuda *might need . . . Maybe specialist engineering for her nuclear reactor . . . Maybe, and more likely, missiles. The Chinese make cruises up there . . . I don't know . . . but I'd better watch out for her if she leaves port . . .*

He scanned the photographs again, pulling up a close-up of Huludao and its docks and jetties. It was a busy place, full of merchant ships in a seaport geared to handle well over a million tons of cargo per year. The place was groaning with tankers and merchant freighters.

He tracked the activity at the Huludao base for the next two days, and was pleased with the NSO's very clear photograph of the *Barracuda* arriving, and heading straight into a covered dock.

The next set of prints showed the unusual sight of a civilian freighter, with a longish flat cargo deck parked bang on the submarine jetties. *Must be bringing in spare parts,* he thought, not knowing that the *Yongdo*'s lethal illegal cargo had been unloaded in another covered dock, two hours before the satellite passed.

He fired in a request, purely routine, for the CIA to identify that ship, but did not have much luck. Langley said it was a pretty old vessel, probably Japanese Navy in origin, but converted like so many old warships in the Far East for civilian freight. They were uncertain of the owners, but guessed it was either still Japanese, if not, North Korean.

Probably bringing in a couple of fucking atom bombs for onward shipment to the Arabs, he thought, sardonically. *Nothing serious. Only the end of the bloody world.*

Another week went by without event. The *Barracuda* had not been seen since, and no one had been able to identify the Japanese-built freighter in the submarine yards at Huludao. And then something fascinating happened. The United States ambassador in Dubai, who had previously served in the embassy in Tehran, sent a note to say that he recognized *two* of the four men in Admiral Morgan's photograph.

His Excellency Mark Vollmer, a career diplomat from Marblehead, Massachusetts, was absolutely certain. According to his note: *During my tenure in Iran I was personally asked to process the visa applications from two extremely eminent professors from the Department of Earth Physics at the University of Tehran. One of them was Fatahi Mohammed Reza, the other was Hatami Jamshid, both natives of Tehran.*

Ambassador Vollmer recalled that they had each accepted a one-year degree course at the University of California in Santa Cruz. Both men were specialists in volcanology and in the ensuing landslides that could devastate areas in the immediate vicinity after an eruption. He had thoughtfully marked on the photographs which prof was which. Jimmy Ramshawe guessed from the men's body language that Professor Hatami was the senior man, and the serious, frowning look of Professor Fatahi suggested he too was an expert in his field.

Ambassador Vollmer's phone call to the University of Tehran confirmed that they were both back in Iran, members of the faculty, and lecturing at the Department of Earth Physics. Both were resident in Tehran, and traveled widely, observing and researching the behavior of the subterranean forces that occasionally change the shape of the planet.

"Wow," said Jimmy. "That Vollmer ought to be working here, not scratching around in the bloody desert with a bunch of nomads."

He was both relieved and amazed that the matter had been so easily cleared up, and with some slight feeling of pride, he drafted a note to the Big Man.

His E-mail ended with a flourish . . . *A couple of volcano professors doing their thing . . . here endeth the mystery of the Arabs on the mountain.*

Kathy picked up the E-mail, as she always did. Her new husband was always threatening to hurl the expensive laptop computer into the Potomac—*It was so goddamned slow.*

Arnold read the note with great interest and thanked Jimmy, asking him to keep a careful watch for any information on the other two anonymous figures in Harry's cliff-top snaps.

"Typical Admiral Arnie," Jimmy reported to George Morris later in the day. "He gets a ten-million-to-one triumph, and *still* wants to know more. You'da thought the two professors would be plenty. Cleared it all up. Just four volcano academics having a careful look at their subject."

"You know him nearly as well as I do," said George. "It's not his fault. It's his brain. The damn thing is unable to relax while there are questions to be answered. And he wants to know who those other two guys are . . . Can't help himself."

"He'll be lucky," replied Jimmy.

Prophetic words indeed.

Four days later an encrypted signal from the CIA landed

on Lieutenant Commander Ramshawe's desk. It was the cyber note heard round the world . . . *MI5 London passed on your request of June 5 to British Army Special Forces. Colonel Russell Makin, Commanding Officer 22 SAS, says the figure on the far right, not facing the camera, is the missing SAS Maj. Ray Kerman. Four other SAS personnel confirm. Mr. and Mrs. Richard Kerman driving to Stirling Lines tomorrow. Please forward date, time, and place of photographs soonest.*

Lieutenant Commander Ramshawe nearly jumped out of his skin.

He strode along the corridor, knocked and barged into the office of Rear Adm. George Morris. The room was empty, so he stormed out again and found the Admiral's secretary.

"He's around somewhere, sir. You want me to have him call you?"

"Tell him to come to my office. I have something which will shrink his balls to the size of a jackrabbit's . . ." James Ramshawe could hardly contain his excitement, never mind his language.

Ten minutes later, George Morris picked his way through the piles of paper on the floor, sat down, and read the note.

He nodded sagely. "Well, Jimmy," he said, "we just proved what we already knew. One—Major Kerman was definitely alive five months ago, and two—we all ignore the instincts of Arnold Morgan at our peril. I am sure you have considered the fact that it was he who first felt uneasy about those guys, he who had them photographed, and he who suggested we find out who they were."

"I have, sir. That's really all I've been doing for the past fifteen minutes."

"You haven't told him yet?"

"No, sir."

"Well, don't. I'm gonna give him a call, and suggest you and I take a run over there this evening. With a bit of luck, Kathy'll ask us to dinner."

"I agree with all that, sir. I think a chat with the Admiral right now would be a very good exercise. He might come up with something else."

"Meanwhile, find out anything more you can about those two professors. If they're working with Major Kerman, there's got to be a plot. And if he's in it, that plot's likely to be big. And you know Arnie's likely to fire a lot of questions."

"Okay, sir. I'll get right on it."

And for the next four hours, he scanned the Internet ceaselessly, starting with the University of California. He discovered a substantial department of geophysics and, to his surprise, a special area devoted entirely to the phenomenon he'd been discussing with his future father-in-law a few weeks back. Tsunamis. There were several world-renowned computer models of great volcano-induced tsunamis of the past, and a number of highly detailed research studies of those that could happen in the future.

Several of them pinpointed the hot spots in the South Pacific, especially around the Hawaiian Islands. Interestingly enough, an entire section dealt with what could potentially be one of the biggest landslides in the entire history of the world: the southwest corner of the island of La Palma in the Canaries.

One of the most renowned professors in the United States had published a thesis in which he stated flatly that because of the initial size and shape of the unstable flank of the Cumbre Vieja, the waves would most likely retain a significant proportion of their energy as they propagated outwards from the Canaries, heading for the U.S.A., Europe, and northern Brazil. The initial wave heights would be approximately one kilometer and as the tsunami traveled westwards at high speed—as fast as a passenger jet aircraft—it would slow down and pile up, increasing its height as it entered shallower water. Those waves could be 50 meters high—approximately 160 feet, considering the evidence of massive undersea boulders and other deposits off the coast of the Bahamas, from the last tsunami that developed in the Canary Islands several thousand years ago.

The irrevocable conclusion of this computer model, perfected over years of study, was the same that Arnold Morgan had outlined for Kathy: some six to nine hours after the initial landslide from La Palma, the collapse of the Cumbre Vieja would cause devastation on the Eastern Seaboard of the United States.

The Web site provided brilliant modern graphics, particularly in reference to wave heights, red bands, blue bands, and yellow dots. Jimmy Ramshawe's eyes were on stalks.

"One hundred and sixty feet," he breathed. "Christ, there wouldn't be a coastal city left standing, from Boston to Miami. No wonder the bloody Arabs were checking it out. But I dunno what Major Kerman was doing there . . . unless he's planning to wipe out half the U.S.A. in one fell swoop—"

But then he gathered himself up. *No, he couldn't be doing that . . . he might be all right having a whack at a power station or a refinery that basically blew themselves up . . . but this stuff is different. This is the giant power from the core of the bloody earth. This is God, and Christ knows what. This is a greater power than the human race has ever seen. Right here we're talking the fist of the Almighty, not a bunch of half-assed terrorists . . . I think.*

Other than his find on the University of California Web site, there was little hard copy on the two Iranian professors, and nothing about Major Kerman, who hadn't been seen in the West since his defection five years previously. There were a few reluctant statements from the Ministry of Defence in London, but nothing casting any light on his whereabouts and certainly not his future plans.

Mrs. Kathy Morgan came through in precisely the way Admiral Morris had hoped, and invited them both for dinner at their house in Chevy Chase. And both men looked forward to it, since neither of them had seen the Big Man for several months.

They arrived at eight o'clock sharp in the Morgans' somewhat grand Maryland residence, which had been a part of Kathy's divorce settlement. The Admiral came to the front door and greeted them with great warmth, hustling them inside and announcing he was personally cooking dinner outside on the barbecue.

He'd fix drinks and then they could lay the bombshell on him that Admiral Morris had promised earlier in the afternoon. All three of them went for a long Scotch and soda on the rocks, and stepped out into the warm early summer night for the first highlight of the evening.

"Okay, Arnie," said Admiral Morris. "Prepare for a shock. The guy on the right-hand side of your photograph, the one Harry never snapped face-on, is Maj. Ray Kerman, late of the British Army's SAS. How about that?"

"Are you kidding me?" said Arnold. "That little bastard, standing not 30 feet from me on top of the goddamned cliff. Hell, if I'd known that, I'd have killed him with my bare hands!"

"If he'd known who you were, he'd probably have killed you first," said Jimmy, laughing, with no idea how close to home his words were. Then he explained to Morgan how they'd confirmed the identification of the most wanted terrorist in the world.

"Now that, George, is really something," said Admiral Morgan. "But, more important, what the hell's he doing on the top of the volcano with the Arabs?"

"Well, I guess that's the question," said George. "And it's very tricky, because there's no evidence anywhere that these men are actually Islamic Fundamentalists . . . they're academics whose life study is volcanoes."

"If you ask me," said Jimmy, "the question is, why La Palma? Of all the volcanoes in the world, why is the most vicious terrorist leader in the world having a fucking powwow with a couple of scientists on the slopes of the most potentially dangerous volcano on earth."

Arnold Morgan grinned wryly. "How do you know it is?" he said.

"Oh, I just became a world volcano expert around five o'clock this afternoon . . . checked out the old Cumbre Vieja on the Net . . . on the University of California Web site. That's the school out in Santa Cruz, where those Iranian professors went for post-grad courses."

"Goddamned Internet," said Arnie. "I had to travel halfway around the world at vast expense to get my knowledge of the La Palma range. You get the same thing in about five minutes at a cost of about five bucks—"

"Five cents," replied Jimmy. "Not including the print-out paper."

Just then Kathy came out of the house with a large serving plate containing four New York sirloin steaks—one-pounders, aged and primed.

"Hello, George," she said, handing the platter to her husband. "Jimmy—will these do?"

"Oh, g'day, Mrs. Morgan," replied the Lt. Commander. "I'd say they'll do just great."

Kathy, as always, looked nothing short of striking. Her red hair was loose, cut shoulder length, her makeup consisted of lipstick and little else. She wore a ruby-red silk blouse with white matador pants. Around her neck hung a pendant—two golden dolphins, stylized as though from Greek mythology, but nonetheless an adapted emblem of the United States Navy's submarine service.

Arnold pronged the steaks with a long fork and placed them on the grill, eliciting four loud, encouraging sizzles—the national anthem of his home state of Texas.

"Git along, little doggies," muttered the old submarine trail boss, maneuvering the steaks into position—bow, stern, port, and starboard. He declined to close the lid, keeping the gas heat on the grill high. "Way to cook 'em, boy," he said to Jimmy. "Just like my daddy taught me. Big heat, keen eye, and fast reactions. That's what you need with barbecued steak."

"And life," replied Jimmy, grinning. "Turn your back and you'll probably get burned."

"Hopefully not by a goddamned volcano," said Arnold. "I just wonder what those bastards are up to."

"Maybe nothing," said George Morris. "Maybe this Kerman character just has an interest in the subject. Maybe he just went on a field trip with the two professors. Maybe he's on a world volcano tour."

"I don't think so," said Arnold, somewhat predictably. "Guys like that don't have hobbies. They're fanatics, consumed every waking hour of every day with their own agenda. I just don't trust those bastards . . . especially this Kerman character . . . I mean, if he's done half of what we think he's done, he's getting up there with Attila the Hun, and he's a lot worse than Colonel Gadhafi."

"I was looking at the Cumbre Vieja problem this afternoon," said Jimmy. "There's no explosion in this world big enough to blow a four-cubic-kilometer hunk of mountain into the ocean."

"I know that, Jimmy," said the Admiral. "But it's not the eruption of the volcano that's the catalyst. It's the rush of molten lava to the surface, heating the underground lakes and causing a massive steam explosion."

"I've seen an old picture of a locomotive boiler blowing up," said Jimmy. "It knocked down the entire station, and it was a big railroad terminus. But it would surely have to be an unbelievable force to set off that kind of chain reaction," mused Jimmy. "One professor said, thankfully, the entire scenario would have to be an act of God, and the Almighty hasn't bothered with anything that big for centuries."

"Hope he's right," gritted Arnold, flipping the steaks deftly. "Just don't trust any Arabs on the goddamned mountain, that's all. They're up to no good. They always fucking well are."

They sipped their drinks amiably. But there was a tension in the air that summer night. George Morris knew that Arnold was not happy about the arch-terrorist Ray Kerman consorting with the volcano men. And Arnold's roaming mind was scanning the problem, wondering what to do and what might lie in store for the future.

The man was out of the White House, essentially a civilian. The cares and worries of high office should have been behind him. He and his new wife ought to have been planning vacations, world trips, visiting friends. And indeed they were. But Arnold Morgan had always treated the problems of the United States as if they were his own, and it was an old habit that was hard to break.

Kathy was quiet too. She hated it when her husband acted as if he were still the President's National Security Adviser. But she knew that nothing she could say or do was going to make much of a difference. So she just hoped the mood would pass. She tried to distract him instead, asking solicitously if he felt the wine they were serving was sufficiently close to room temperature.

It was a question that almost always did the trick. The Admiral hurried inside to taste the rich 1998 Pomerol, Château de Valois, and a few moments later he seemed to have forgotten about Major Kerman, briefing his guests instead on the superb red Bordeaux they were about to drink.

"Right bank for the 1998s, eh, Jimmy?" said Arnold.

"What's that?" said Jimmy.

"Nineteen ninety-eight was an excellent year for Bordeaux, but was only reliable on one side of the Gironde Estuary."

"Where's that?"

"Oh, where the Gironde and Dordogne Rivers flow out into the Bay of Biscay in western France—and on the left-hand side of that estuary are most of the great French châteaux. On the other side you have the other great Bordeaux vineyards, Saint-Emilion and Pomerol. And in 1998, there was a lot of rain, just before the harvest—swept down off the Pyrenees, up the left-hand shores of the estuary and soaked the Medoc. But somehow it missed Saint-Emilion and Pomerol, which had a wonderful harvest. I've opened a couple of bottles for tonight. After George called, I asked your future father-in-law to join us, but I believe the whole family's out of town?"

"Yes. They're with my folks in New York. Pity John's not here . . . he'd have loved to try the wine." Jimmy paused. He could see Morgan's mind whirring. "Sir, I'm not sure when you last read up on the subject, but I gave it a good go this afternoon," said Jimmy. "I know the scientists do have dire warnings about La Palma, but in fairness, most of 'em think the big bang is about 100,000 years away . . ."

"So they might," said Admiral Morgan. "But I'd sure as hell prefer it if this Kerman character were dead."

0500 (Local), Monday, July 5
Submarine Jetties, Huludao.

One month in the huge dry dock at the Chinese Naval Base had the *Barracuda*'s full complement of North Korean guided missiles in perfect order. The Chinese electronic engineers had tested every system in every missile, and fitted the nuclear warheads into two of them.

The guidance and navigation "brain" in the nose cone of the most deadly of the Danmo-gang cruises was checked and rechecked. It would blast clear of the water, and then set off on the course plotted and preset by Lt. Comdr. Shakira Kerman.

All eighteen of the missiles were correctly loaded into the magazine of *Barracuda II*. The Chinese would now present an outrageous bill for the work to the Iranian Navy, as agents, but not owners—$8 million U.S. No one ever said the Chinese were confused about making a buck. Of course, their expertise was very nearly priceless in this part of the world. And their scruples were few.

Scimitar SL-2 was ready to roll.

They had begun pulling the rods the previous evening, and the turbines had been declared ready at 0300 by the chief engineering officer, Commander Abdolrahim, the top nuclear specialist on board. The veteran Iranian submariner had been on duty all night, monitoring the slim Hafnium shafts being withdrawn in groups from the potentially lethal uranium heart of the reactor. Every few minutes, the neutrons were thus given greater freedom to split and cause further fission, heating the system, creating that self-sustaining critical mass, the basis of nuclear energy.

Commander Abdolrahim was in total control, regulating the heat through the pressurized circuit to its phenomenal operational norm of 2,500 lbs. per square inch—in contrast to the 15 lbs. per square inch that humans are accustomed to living in.

With the water temperature high enough, the 47,000 hp (horsepower) turbines were ready to run—powered from the colossal energy contained inside the impenetrable stainless-steel cylinder covering the seething uranium-235 core that, when suitably enriched, forms the business end of a nuclear bomb. The dome was essentially sealed inside the reactor room's 8-inch-thick walls of solid lead. Here, Lt. Comdr. Hamidi Abdolrahim, the chief nuclear engineer, headed a team of fellow Iranian personnel, five strong.

Two hours before dawn, the Hamas underwater boat had been towed out of the covered dock behind two Chinese tugs. The ships' entire company was either ex–Iranian Navy or Hamas professional, trained in Bandar Abbas, China, and/or Russia.

They had cleared the outer breakwater now and were operating under their own steam. The Executive Officer, Capt. Ali Akbar Mohtaj, had the ship, and CPO Ardeshir Tikku was standing behind his principal operators in the separate reactor control room.

They watched as the *Barracuda* accelerated to eight knots—staring at the three critical computer panels: propulsion, reactor, and auxiliary.

The Chief of Boat (COB), CPO Ali Zahedi, was with Captain Mohtaj, and the Navigation area was occupied by Lieutenant Ashtari Mohammed, a British-born Iraqi whose family had fled the brutal dictator Saddam Hussein in the

1990s. Ashtari was a revolutionary at heart, and he in turn had fled the UK to join Hamas and ended up at staff college in Bandar Abbas.

His skills in the navigation room in a nuclear submarine had been honed at the Chinese Naval training college at Qingdao, 230 miles to the south along the western shore of the Yellow Sea. He had worked on the *Barracuda I* mission and had been commissioned for this operation because of his outstanding work in the past.

Up on the *Barracuda*'s bridge, as they ran fair down the channel in dredged but close to alarmingly shallow water, Admiral Ben Badr stood with General Rashood and Lieu-tenant Commander Shakira. Dead ahead, the eastern sky was colored a deep rosy pink, as the rising sun tried to fight its way over the horizon. The sea was flat, oily, with a distant ruby-red cast in the early minutes of the dawn.

The Chinese tugs, escorting the 8,000-ton nuclear boat out into the Yellow Sea, slowed and turned away to starboard, their officers giving a friendly wave of farewell. The *Bar-racuda* was entirely alone now. But the men on board had faced danger together before, and each was confident in the task that lay ahead. Only Shakira, clutching Ravi's arm in the warm morning air, shuddered involuntarily, as they steered an easterly course, making 12 knots on the surface of waters that were only about 50 feet deep.

They were in the strictly prohibited area of Liaodong Bay, an 80-mile-long by 60-mile-wide cordoned-off zone strin-gently patrolled by Chinese Navy ships, way up on the north-west corner of the Yellow Sea.

Shortly before 0730, Admiral Badr went below and or-dered a course change to the south, back down towards the choke point 120 miles away. It was too shallow to even go to periscope depth out here. And they were constantly un-der the observation of their protectors in the Chinese Navy.

But the North Sea Fleet of the People's Liberation

Army/Navy were not the only eyes upon them. At 0745, almost immediately after they made their turn, Big Bird, the U.S. military satellite, snapped off several shots of the *Barracuda*, noting at once its speed and direction. It was almost six o'clock the previous evening in Washington. The photographs from the National Surveillance Office would be on Lieutenant Commander Ramshawe's desk by eight o'clock his time.

By then, of course, the *Barracuda* would be well into the Bohai Haixia, the Chinese obstacle course that guards the business end of the Yellow Sea. And from there she would dive, running free, just below the surface in depths of around 150 feet, not quite invisible, but close.

Meanwhile, Ravi and Shakira stayed on the bridge as the day grew warmer. Ahmed Sabah brought them coffee, while the rest of the crew carried out their customary daily equipment checks. Admiral Badr huddled in the navigation area with Ashtari Mohammed, poring over the sprawling Navy charts, plotting their way through the myriad islands around the southeast coastline of Japan, their route to the North Pacific.

0800 (Local), Monday, July 5
Fort Meade, Maryland.

Lieutenant Commander Ramshawe stared at the photographs of *Barracuda II* running south down the Yellow Sea. "And where the fuck do you think you're going?" he muttered to no one in particular.

He was looking at a map reference of 40.42N 121.20E. The NSO had helpfully identified the submarine as the only *Barracuda*-class boat in existence, exiting the Chinese Naval Base.

This is unbelievable, said Jimmy to himself. *We still don't know who actually owns this damn thing. The Russians re-*fuse *to admit selling it to the Chinese, on account of it's none* *of our damn business. And the Chinese decline to say any-thing, presumably for the same reason.*

He pulled up a chart of the Yellow Sea and Japan on his computer and gazed at the screen. *Sometime in the next couple of days, that bloody ship is going to go deep once she's clear of the Bo Hai Strait, and we're not going to see her again for Christ knows how long.*

She could run north up through the Korean Strait and into the Sea of Japan. She could run right around the east of Japan and into the Pacific, where she could run north, south, or east. Or she could continue and dive back to Zhanjiang where she came from—that would begin to look suspiciously like China was the owner. She could do anything, and we will not know for sure until she resurfaces, which could be six months. Fuck.

Lieutenant Commander Ramshawe did not like dead ends. His dislikes especially included the Yellow Sea and everything to do with it. And here was the *Barracuda* in the West's least accessible waters, running cheerfully along the sunlit surface, plainly with Chinese help and protection, if not actual crew.

He requested blowups of the very clearly focused pictures, and an hour later, he could see three figures on the bridge. But all of them wore hats, and the photographs were shot mainly from directly overhead, making it impossible to identify any of them, even with regard to rank or nationality.

There's nothing we can bloody do, he grumbled. *I better show them to the boss, but I can't progress this any further except to keep watching the satellite shots until she dives . . . but I still have a feeling that China bought this damn submarine for someone else . . . Middle East, Pakistan, North Korea? Who the hell knows?*

He stood up and walked to the door, stepping out into the corridor, which led along to the Director's office on the eighth floor of the OPS-2B building, with its massive one-way glass walls and twenty-four-hour heavily armed guard patrols.

"I just hope," he murmured, as he walked, "that we haven't inadvertently shot another photograph of Major Ray fucking Kerman, right out there, large as life, on the bridge of the damned *Barracuda*. Because if we have, that's big trouble right around the corner, and this new President's going to hate us worse than he does already."

1400, Wednesday, July 7
32.50N 125.28E, Yellow Sea (South)
Speed 12, Course 112.

They were due southeast of Jejudo, the big holiday island off the southernmost tip of South Korea. The *Barracuda* was about to run into deeper water, 400 feet in the rough, wide reaches where the Yellow Sea meets China's East Sea. Right here they would dive, making a hard southeast course, straight towards the scattered islands that stretch hundreds of miles off the end of the Japanese mainland at Kyushu.

It was somewhat tricky coming through the archipelago, but there were wide deep-water routes that would permit the *Barracuda* to stay well out of reach of the American satellites. Once those islands had been negotiated, it was a straight run into the two-mile-deep western Pacific, where they would become invisible.

Selection of this particular route had occupied hours of their time in the week before departure. General Ravi had very much wanted to swerve northeast and up through the tight, shallow Korea Strait into the almost landlocked Sea of Japan. His broad plan was to exit the Sea 600 miles later through La Perouse Strait, then head up through Russia's Sea of Okhotsk, and make a dash through the Kuril Islands into the open waters of the Pacific. Sheltered, protected water all the way.

But Ben Badr had objected, strenuously, on about ten different fronts. Worse, Shakira agreed with him. So did Captain Mohtaj.

The crux of the matter was that Ben Badr had become a very serious submarine officer in the past couple of years, constantly operating under the same sense of danger that affects all submarine commanding officers.

"Just look at this Sea of Japan," he said. "I know it's big, and I know it's 480 miles wide and 1,000 miles long, and I know it's very deep right across the Yamato Basin. But it's a death trap. If we got in there and ran into an American warship, we simply could not use our speed to get away. They'd pick us up and we'd be like rats in a trap, because we could not get into open ocean. We'd either have to turn around and get back to the Korea Strait, or head for La Perouse, a classic choke point, way north of Sapporo at the end of Hokkaido Island.

"Ravi, they'd sink us. And if we tried to sink them, they'd send more ships from their base at Okinawa, and we *still* could not get away. We really do not want to go in there."

"Well, I understand the remote possibility of being detected by the U.S.A.," said the General. "But if we did creep through quietly and made La Perouse Strait, we could move quietly into the Sea of Okhotsk, which is huge, and slide through one of those gaps between the Kuril Islands on the right, and into open ocean."

"Ravi, I actually regard the Sea of Okhotsk with even more dread than the Sea of Japan, mostly because it's considered by the Russians as their private ocean. And it's full of their warships and submarines. I don't know if the Americans are in there or not, but if they are, and they pick us up, we'd be in an ocean bounded by land, Russian, on three sides, with a line of Russian islands barring our only escape route into the Pacific.

"If the Americans are watching anywhere in this part of the world, it's got to be the passes between the Kuril Islands.

In my view, it would be potential suicide to try and escape that way. It's a bit longer, but we have time, and I say we head straight for the Pacific. Forget the Sea of Japan, and Okhotsk. Let's just get clear of these communist nutcases, into open ocean, and make our own way to our destinations. We're in a very fast boat, and I just hate to see us squander that advantage in landlocked oceans."

General Rashood saw the sense of the argument but continued to believe that Ben Badr was being somewhat overly cautious. Shakira was equally adamant, though.

"Don't we have enough risk?" she said. "What's the point of taking more when we don't need to. Also, I would not want our operational Commanding Officer to be making an underwater journey entirely against his will. I know my husband is in overall command, but surely we don't want to put more pressure on Ben. After all, if we do get caught, he's the one who has to get us out."

"I think the inland seas would be a big mistake, Ravi," emphasized Admiral Badr. "But I accept that the final word is yours. And I will abide by your decision."

The General smiled and said, "Let's go, Ben, all ahead . . ."

"Which way, sir?"

"Straight into the North Pacific."

"Aye, sir."

And so they accelerated to the southeast, taking a route south of the bigger islands of Yaku-shima and Tanega-shima. They crossed the line that marks the Japan Current and held their depth at 150 feet. They left the ocean rises of Gaja-shima and Yakana-shima to starboard, twice coming to periscope depth, just short of the 130 degree line of longitude. They picked up the flashing light on Gaja and then the more southerly warning off Yakana.

And after that it was much simpler. The ocean shelved down to depths of more than two miles, and there was relief in the voice of Admiral Badr when he made his course change.

*"Come left 40 degrees, steer course zero-seven-zero . . .
bow down 10 and make your depth 600. Make your speed
12 . . ."*

They held a course inshore, some 60 miles off the jutting
headlands of Ahizuri, Stiono, and Nojima Beach, the latter of
which lies 50 miles south of Tokyo. The seabed rose and fell
along here, and the water was famously "noisy," never less
than a mile deep, and full of crisscrossing currents. Captain
Mohtaj had the ship where he wanted it, in deep, turbulent
sea, full of fish and undersea caverns where the mysterious
sounds of the deep echo and re-echo, causing mass confusion to all sonar operators.

The *Barracuda* continued to run northeast, 600 feet below
the surface, the sonar room constantly on high alert for fishing boats and their deep trawl nets. Right off Nojima Saki,
Admiral Badr ordered another course change:

*"Come right 70 degrees, steer course three-six-zero, retain
600 feet . . . speed 12."*

They were still 60 miles offshore, 1,440 miles and five
days out from Huludao, when they made their turn up towards Japan's big triangular northern island of Hokkaido,
north of the 40th parallel. From here they would begin to
edge out to starboard to the east, away from the Russian patrols along the Kurils. Ravi insisted on ensuring a good distance between themselves and the Kamchatka Peninsula,
when eventually they reached that far northern outpost of the
old Soviet Navy's Pacific Fleet.

The first landfall they would record would be the Alaskan
Island of Attu, which sits at the very end of the Aleutians,
bang in the middle of the North Pacific, dead opposite, and
due east of, the Russian Navy Base of Petropavlovsk, less
than 500 miles of ocean between them.

The Aleutians stretch in a narrow 1,000-mile crescent
from the seaward tip of the great southwestern panhandle of
Alaska, more than halfway across the Pacific, dividing the
world's largest ocean from the Bering Sea, which lies to the

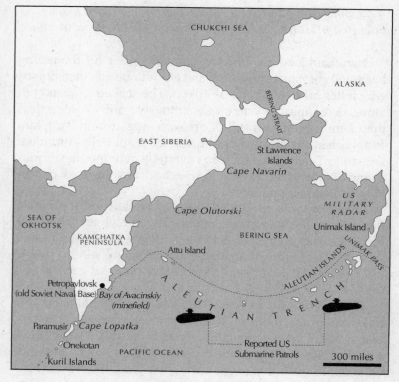

ROUTE OF *BARRACUDA II* FROM RUSSIA'S NORTHERN
FLEET BASE TO NORTH AMERICA

north of the islands. The weather, all along the Aleutian chain, is mostly diabolical, a freezing, storm-lashed hell for eight months of the year.

Not that this worried General Ravi and his men, who would make the journey past the islands in the warm comfort of their underwater hotel, way below the gales and thunderous ocean.

For 1,500 miles they ran northeast from the Japanese coast south of Tokyo. They stayed deep, leaving the little cluster of Russia's Komandorskiye Islands 120 miles to the north, off their port beam. These remotest of islands stand 140 miles off Kamchatka, with their southeasterly point only 180 miles from the outer Alaskan Island of Attu.

The Commanding Officer of *Barracuda II* elected to take the western side of the freak ocean rise of Stalemate Bank, where the near-bottomless North Pacific steadily rises up from *four miles* deep to a mere 100 feet—no problem for surface ships; a brick wall for a deep submarine. It only just fell short of being the real outermost island of the Aleutians, and perhaps once had been.

Admiral Badr knew the Stalemate required a wide berth, but he considered its eastward side too close to Attu Island. To transit the 230-fathom channel between the two would take them far too close to known American ocean surveillance. Attu was a very sensitive listening station for the U.S. Navy, having stood as the first line of defense against ships from Soviet Russia for many, many years.

In Shakira's opinion, they needed to make a slow sweep around to the north and then begin their 1,000-mile journey along the island chain. It was Friday, July 16, shortly after noon, and they were moving very slightly north of the 53rd parallel, heading due east across the two-mile-deep Bowers Basin, which lies to the north of Attu.

There is a long, near-deserted seaway between the Attu group and the next little cluster of Rat Islands, and according to all the data Shakira had amassed, the U.S. Navy surveillance, both radar and sonar, were extremely active all through these waters. She had spoken at some length to Admiral Badr and they agreed they should give Attu a wide berth to the north and to stay out there for 540 miles, deep at 600 feet, making no more than 7 knots.

That ought to take them past the next major U.S. listening station on Atka Island somewhere to the north of Nazan Bay. Thereafter, the Aleutians comprised the much larger, yet still long, narrow islands, Unmak, Unalaska, and Unimak, all three of which Shakira claimed would have intense U.S. surveillance in place.

They had of course accepted Shakira's assessment of the southern route, which she had deemed impossible, since she was stone-cold certain there would be at least one, and possibly two, Los Angeles–class nuclear submarines patrolling the Aleutian Trench 24/7, the long, deep ditch that lay between the sensitive U.S. Navy SOSUS wires to the south and the southern shores of the Aleutian Islands.

On the previous mission Lieutenant Commander Shakira had claimed she would rather see the whole operation abandoned than risk being fired upon in the Aleutian Trench by a U.S. submarine, which would unleash deadly accurate torpedoes, fatal to any intruder.

They crept past Attu Island at slow speed, 600 feet below the surface, the great black titanium hull of the *Barracuda* muffling the revs of its turbines. At the 175th line of longitude east from Greenwich, Ben Badr risked a slight acceleration—not much, just from 5 knots to 8. At that moment, the hydraulic system on the after planes jammed, angled down.

Immediately the bow went down and the *Barracuda* headed on a steep trajectory towards the seabed. Alarms in the control room flashed, the depth was increasing, the angle of the entire boat was wrong, and the aft plane refused to move.

The CPO Ali Zahedi had an instant vision of the submarine heading all the way to the bottom, and shouted . . . *"ALL REVERSE . . . ALL REVERSE!"*

The 47,000 hp turbines slowed and then churned furiously in the water, pounding the wash over the hull the wrong way and causing the nearest thing to underwater commotion a big, quiet nuclear boat can manage.

The huge prop thrashed, arresting the forward speed, then hauling the 8,000-tonner backwards. But the angle was still wrong.

"BLOW FOR'ARD BALLAST TANKS!" There was urgency but no panic in the voice of Chief Zahedi. Ben Badr came hurrying into the control room, just in time to hear

the propulsion engineer reporting . . . *"Aft plane still jammed, sir. Hydraulic problem, probably a blown seal . . . Switching to secondary system right away, sir. Thirty seconds."*

Everyone heard the for'ard tanks blow their ballast, much more loudly than Admiral Badr would have wished. The submarine righted itself. And moments later the secondary system came on line and the jammed plane moved correctly. There were already two engineers working on the seal change, trying desperately not to make a noise, hanging on carefully to the rubber-coated wrenches, knowing the crash of anything on the metal deck could be heard miles away. Everyone in the boat was aware of the continued, unbreakable rule of silence, the need to tiptoe through the ocean, making certain that no one, anywhere, could hear anything, ever.

Unfortunately, luck was against them. The U.S. listening and processing station at the easternmost point of Attu picked up the sound, at 45 miles. And it was a strong signal, more than just a fleeting "paint" on the sonar. The young American operator nearly fell off his stool, so stark were the marks of the *Barracuda*'s turbines being flung into reverse. Then he saw the nearly unmistakable signature of big ballast tanks being blown.

"Christ!" he snapped. *"This is a goddamned submarine . . . and it sounds like it's sinking or in collision!"*

The underwater sounds continued on and off for about a minute. The operator summoned his supervisor in time to see the submarine's ballast. But just as suddenly, everything went quiet again. Making only five knots, the *Barracuda* vanished, humming through the pitch-black, ice-cold depths of the Bering Sea.

"That was a transient, sir. Don't know who the hell it was, but it was a submarine, and not American. We got nothing up here . . . with luck we'll hear it again."

They did not. The *Barracuda*, holding its five-knot speed as it moved away from Attu Island, was careful not to accelerate.

Nonetheless, the Americans were suspicious, and they posted the information on the nets . . . *"161750JUL09 Transient contact north of Attu Island station western Aleutians approximately 175.01E 53.51N . . . Nuclear turbine, possibly Russian Delta. Contact included ballast blowing and high engine revs for one minute. Not regained . . . No submarine correlation on friendly nets.*

The signal was relayed through the normal U.S. Navy channels and would be read that afternoon in the National Security Agency in Maryland. Meanwhile Admiral Badr kept moving slowly east north of the islands towards the mainland of America's largest state.

They were not detected again, all along their 720-mile route to the gateway to the Unimak Pass, through which they would try to make safe passage behind a freighter to the southern side of the Aleutians and then turn left into the Gulf of Alaska. The journey to the Pass took them until midnight on Wednesday night, July 21, by which time the surface weather was brutal, with a northeasterly gale and driving rain, plus a blanket of fog that refused to move despite the wind. They took up the same safe position they had occupied the previous year, 10 miles off the flashing beacon on the northern headland of Akutan Island.

Visibility on the surface was less than 300 yards, and they faced a long and frustrating wait, trying to locate a sufficiently large merchant ship or tanker, astern of which they could follow at periscope depth, their mast obscured by the wake of the leading ship, the typical sneaky submariner's trick.

That Wednesday night was quiet. They finally detected two medium-sized freighters moving towards the Pass, but they were not big enough, and they were heavily laden, going slowly, hardly leaving a wake. Ben Badr wanted a major container ship or a giant tanker in a hurry to cross to the Gulf of Alaska.

But traffic remained light all night. The watches slipped by, sailors slept and ate, and the reactor ran smoothly. Ravi and Shakira retired to their little cabin at 0200, after two fruitless hours of waiting. The General ordered the COB CPO Ali Zahedi to call him instantly if anything was sighted, but nothing was, and the *Barracuda* continued in a slow race-track pattern, occasionally coming to PD for a GPS check, observation, then back under the surface.

The weather, if anything, worsened. The fog had cleared, but the rain was still lashing down, visibility at maybe only a couple of miles. At 0915, sonar reported a likely contact approaching from the northwest. Taking a swift look through the periscope, Ali Zahedi spotted a serious crude oil tanker churning down into the Pass, the great 10-mile-wide seaway between the islands.

"Here he is, sir," he called. *"A real possible . . . three-zero-zero . . . but it's close . . . only 3,000 yards . . . I'm 35 on his starboard bow . . ."*

"PERISCOPE DOWN!"

Admiral Badr moved in. "Lemme look, Ali—"

"PERISCOPE UP!"

"Three-three-five," he called.

"Now bearing that . . . range that on 24 meters. . . . What are we, 2,500 yards? . . . Put me 25 on his starboard bow . . . target course . . . one-two-zero."

"DOWN PERISCOPE!"

"Come right to zero-six-zero . . . dead slow . . ."

"Here she comes, sir . . ."

"UP PERISCOPE!"

And for the next three minutes, they worked the mast up and down, finally accelerating in behind the freighter, with a burst of 12-knot speed, before slowing down to the freighter's nine knots and becoming invisible in her wake.

"She's Russian, sir," called Ali Zahedi. "Siberian crude, I imagine."

Over in the U.S. listening station at Cape Sarichef, the seaward northwesterly point of Unimak Island overlooking the approaches to the Pass, the American radar picked up the periscope mast of the accelerating *Barracuda*, 18 miles away to the west.

But just as quickly, the "paint" vanished after only three sweeps, leaving behind a mystery. Had they picked up the periscope of a submarine? Or was it just flotsam in the water? And if it was a periscope, did it belong to the same submarine the Attu Station had heard and reported last Friday night?

In the normal course of events, the Unimak Station would not have reported any of the random radar paints picked up on a commercial thruway like the Pass. But there was something about this contact, the stark clarity of the paint, its sudden appearance from nowhere, and its equally sudden disappearance. Plus the report from Attu last Friday.

They decided to put the information on the nets . . . *221127JUL09 Possible transient radar contact detected Unimak Station. Five seconds, three sweeps on screen. Further to Attu Station submarine contact 161750JUL09 . . . Unimak detection consistent with slow five-knot submarine progress from Attu to Unimak Pass.*

It was a signal that would, in a very few hours, send off alarm bells inside the head of Lieutenant Commander Ramshawe in Fort Meade. And it would cause his mind to whirl in hopeless search for the missing *Barracuda*. Though even he would have to admit that he couldn't say, even within 10,000 miles, where it might be. But it would not be the first time he had wondered about a clandestine submarine passage along the route north of the Aleutian Islands. And right now, he would have given almost anything to know the precise whereabouts of that mysterious underwater ship and who its owners were.

Meanwhile, Admiral Badr had his ship perfectly ranged behind the Russian tanker, the whole operation one of geometry rather than navigation. They were separated by about 100 yards of swirling white water, and they had a beam ranged on the mast light of the merchant ship.

The correct angle was around 13 degrees. If it decreased, they were falling behind, out of the wake that protected them from the U.S. radar. If the angle increased, it meant they were getting too close. And the tanker, blissful in its ignorance of the nuclear arsenal following in its wake, kept steaming forwards. Captain Mohtaj, the XO, personally took the helm during this most intricate part of their journey, and steered them dead astern of their leader.

"Ninety-five revolutions . . . speed over the ground 9.2 by GPS . . . 8.6 through the water, sir. . ."

When they reached the GPS position, 54.15N 165.30W, they no longer needed to be a shadow. They broke away and went deep to 300 feet, heading for a point 60 miles southeast of Sanak Island, where Ben Badr ordered a course change to due east. They had turned away at last from the long sweeping arc of the Aleutians and were making 8 knots along the 54th line of latitude, straight into the Gulf of Alaska.

Down in the navigation area, General Rashood was sharing a pot of coffee with Shakira and Ashtari Mohammed. The Arabian Lieutenant Commander and the Navigator were poring over the big charts, trying, as always, to second-guess the United States' defenses.

General Ravi was sitting at a high desk with a pile of notes illuminated by an adjustable reading light. In great detail, sectioned off in colors, numbered and bound, they contained details of geological strata, depths of rock, likely weak points in certain areas of the earth's crust. Lists of volcanic activity. Lists of "modern" volcanoes likely to erupt. There were detailed maps of great mountains that could develop interior lava in the next five years. There were estimates of potential damage, endangered areas, and a special section on inland volcanoes, plus two entire eighteen-page chapters on seaward volcanoes.

Ravi had compiled the document himself; he had typed up, filed, and cataloged every specific section, cross-referenced each and every volcano that might interest him. It was a precious project, representing the very bedrock of his plan to drive the Great Satan out of the Middle East forever.

Every aspect, every detail, was gleaned from the personal knowledge and research of the world's foremost authority on geophysical hazards—Professor Paul Landon. Ravi Rashood regretted that their friendship in London had been so very brief.

0300, July 23, 2009
53.30N 161.48W, Depth 500
Speed 5, Course 080.

THE *BARRACUDA* crept east nor'east across the steep underwater cliff faces at the eastern end of the Aleutian Trench, where the gigantic Pacific "ditch" that guards the southern approaches to the islands finally shelves up, close inshore, into the Gulf of Alaska.

Here, despite the colossal depths of more than two miles, the ocean steadily grew shallower, angling up towards the coastal islands of mainland Alaska. In this, the more friendly U.S. end, enemies are just about unknown, unlike its other side, out towards the western Aleutians towards Russia and China, where American submarine COs stay on top of the game at all times.

Ravi and Ben considered their slow expedition into the quiet section of the Trench not much of a risk; it was simply not a place where the U.S. Navy would be looking for trouble, mainly because of the serious difficulties of getting there . . . either straight through the patrolled waters of the Trench (*Out of the question, unless contemplating suicide*); through the Unimak or Samalga Passes (*Impossible under U.S. radar*); or across the Pacific Basin and through the Gulf itself, passing over the lethal, constant electronic trip wires of SOSUS—again suicidal.

Both Ravi and Ben considered the *Barracuda* safe in the eastern waters of the Trench, and at this dead-slow speed they would hear any U.S. submarine a long time before it detected them.

At first, it had seemed logical to cross the 1,000-mile-wide Gulf of Alaska, straight through the middle, in water never much less than two and a half miles deep. But Ben Badr was nerve-wracked, thinking about the U.S. Navy's deadly Sound Surveillance System, and in answer to every one of General Rashood's questions weighing the possibilities of the much shorter straight-line route, he just said, "Forget it, Ravi. They'll hear us."

And then he added the inevitable: "We have to stay inshore, along the coast, in noisy water, where there's massive shoals of fish, rough ocean, island surf, changing depths, and that north-running current. That's where we're safe, out there with the commercial traffic—freighters, tankers, and fishing boats, all kicking up a hell of a racket while we creep along 500 feet below the surface."

Ravi had been staring at the chart. "You mean right up here, through this Shelikof Strait between Kodiak Island and the mainland coast?"

"I wish," said Ben. "And I expect you've noticed we'd have 600 feet almost all the way along that island for about 130 miles. However, you'll see that the Strait ends right at the gateway to the Cook Inlet, which leads up to Anchorage. Afraid that's not for us. Shakira says it's bristling with radar, busier traffic than Tehran, and only a couple of hundred feet deep."

"That's not for us," agreed Ravi. "What do we do? Go outside Kodiak?"

"Absolutely," said Ben, staring at the chart. "Even wider than that. We need to get outside the 200-meter line . . . See? Right here . . . we'll get in the Alaska Current and head zero-seven-zero."

Ravi looked at the chart. "We stay 50 to 60 miles offshore all the way up that coast, we'll be in water that's two miles deep. As far as Prince William Sound. What does Shakira say about U.S. surveillance up there?"

"She thinks they will have plenty of shore-based radar, which won't affect us because we'll be deep. And she thinks there'll be surface patrols in that big bay beyond the Sound, which also won't affect us. But she has seen no sign of increased submarine patrols up there.

"And knowing the huge expense of mobile underwater surveillance, I'd be surprised if they put a couple of nuclear boats in there to protect essentially foreign tankers. Submarines operating in defensive mode in a nonwar area like Alaska really only protect against other submarines. And let's face it, the chances of a foreign strike submarine getting into those waters with intent to attack are zero."

Ravi smiled. "Not even us?" he said.

"Not even us," answered Admiral Badr. "We're just passing through, very quietly, very unobtrusively. There's no U.S. submarine patrols and a lot of noise. We'll be fine."

And so they set off up the Gulf, steering a northeasterly course, deep. It took them four days to reach the old Russian colony of Kodiak, and they left it 50 miles to port. They moved slowly past the rugged, mountainous island that held more than 2,000 three-quarter-ton Kodiak brown bears—the largest bear on earth, on the largest island in Alaska.

The frigid waters that surged around Kodiak were home not only to a 2,000-strong fishing fleet, but also to the giant king crab. Vast legions of these iron-shelled 15-pound monsters, which sometimes have a leg-span measuring four feet across, occasionally made the city of Kodiak the top commercial fishing port in the United States.

And the Alaskans guard their precious stocks assiduously. The biggest U.S. Coast Guard station in the state operates four large cutters, with fully armed crews, out of the old U.S. Naval Base on Kodiak. They patrol these waters night and day, ruthlessly seizing any unauthorized fishing boat. As Shakira Rashood warned her Commanding Officers, *"They*

*may not be looking for submarines, but they'd sure as hell
blow a very loud whistle if they thought they'd heard one."*

By midnight on Tuesday, July 28, way below the bears, but
several hundred feet above the clunking armor of the King
Crabs, the *Barracuda* was dawdling silently northeast at only
six knots. Occasionally they heard the deep overhead rumble
of a laden tanker moving west towards Anchorage from the
new terminal in Takutat; occasionally, the State ferry, *Tustu-
mena*, from Seward on the Kenai Peninsula; less often, the
growl of the powerful coast-guard diesels.

Three hours before dawn, Lieutenant Commander Shakira
came into the control room and brought Ben and Ravi hot
coffee and toast, announcing they were 90 miles southeast of
the port of Kodiak, steaming with the Alaskan Current in 550
fathoms, staying west of the shallow Kodiak Seamount.

She also brought with her a snippet of knowledge to dazzle
the two senior officers on board. "Did either of you know that
the port of Kodiak was practically leveled as recently as
1964?"

"Not me," confessed Ravi.

"Nor me," said Ben.

"The whole downtown area," she confirmed, "the entire
fishing fleet, the processing plants, and 160 houses. The
Good Friday Earthquake, they called it, shook the entire island from end to end."

"How come an earthquake wrecked the fishing fleet?"
asked the ever-probing, practical General Rashood. "Why
didn't they just head out into the bay like every other ship
does when an earthquake starts?"

"Because it wasn't the earthquake that got them," said
Shakira. "It was the tsunami, the huge tidal wave that developed when half a mountain fell hundreds of feet into the
sea . . . There you are, darling, your very favorite subject, delivered personally."

Ravi grinned. "I'm telling you," he said, "those tidal
waves, when they get going, they're a real killer—"

"According to my notes on this area," said Shakira, "this

tsunami developed with great speed. When the wave surged into the port of Kodiak, it just picked up all the ships and dumped them from a great height into the streets, flattened every building . . . turned everything—ships, boat sheds, and shops—into matchwood. Most people luckily had just enough time to get out and drive to high ground. Anyone who didn't was never heard of again."

"Allah," said Ben Badr. "I suppose that's the only good thing about a tsunami. It takes just that little bit longer to get organized. There's warning. And the wave inshore is making only 30 or 40 knots. Probably gives everyone a half hour to get out."

"In some cases, much longer," said Ravi, thoughtfully. "Some of those Pacific surges that started with earthquakes or volcanoes in the Hawaiian Islands took hours to reach very distant shores . . . where they inflicted their worst damage."

"If you want to know about tsunamis, ask my oh-so-clever husband," laughed Shakira. "He knows everything. Or thinks he does."

"Unlike you two, I have been given expert tuition, instruction, and knowledge from a great master," said Ravi. "Professor Paul Landon, the world's leading authority on volcanoes, earthquakes, and tidal waves, took me under his wing for a few days," said the General. "Brought my knowledge right up to scratch."

"Excellent," said Admiral Badr. "Not too long now."

They ran on past Kodiak, crossed the sea-lanes leading up to the Cook Inlet and to the port of Anchorage. A day later, they were creeping through 1,200 fathoms of water south of Prince William Sound, 500 feet below the surface.

Following the big sweep of the Gulf, they changed course there, making a gradual turn to the southeast, staying in the Alaska Current, outside the 200-meter line, tiptoeing warily past the Yakutat Roads, on down to the Dixon Entrance, north of Graham Island. These were waters where both senior Commanders had worked before.

The sheltered, noisy expanse of the Hecate Strait looked

tempting, lying as it did between the 160-mile-long Graham Island and the Canadian mainland. But the depths were treacherous. Right here the ocean runs hard south past the great archipelago of islands—hundreds of them—on the rough, violent coast where the Rocky Mountains sweep down to the sea. It's noisy, it's damn near paradise, except for the outstanding opportunities to rip the hull wide open in 30 feet of granite-bottomed seabed.

"Outside the island, I'm afraid," said Ben Badr. "It's deep, and according to Shakira, almost certainly shuddering with SOSUS wires. It's our usual story—very slow, very careful, right down 800 miles of Canadian coastline, past the Queen Charlotte Islands, past Vancouver Island, then past the great American state of Washington. Should reach our op area on August 6. Then it's more or less up to Shakira."

And no one knew that better than the beautiful Lieutenant Commander, who worked tirelessly at her desk in the navigation room. Occasionally, Admiral Badr took the *Barracuda* to the surface for a satellite fix and to suck messages swiftly off the comms center in the sky, reporting course and position to Bandar Abbas via the Chinese Naval Command Center in Zhanjiang.

They were in the risk-reduction business, and their modus operandi did not include providing the slightest glimmer of information, even on Chinese military satellites, to sharp-eyed Fort Meade detectives like Lt. Comdr. Jimmy Ramshawe. Ravi and Ben wouldn't know Jimmy's favorite exclamation—*Christ, here's the ole Shanghai Electrician.*

This somewhat esoteric description had evolved from the more usual phrase of "casting a chink of light" on a problem, and George Morris had found Ramshawe's linguistic ingenuity so amusing that he spread it all over the eighth floor of OPS-2B. For most people, it contained a touch more panache than a mere "chink of light," the same kind of espionage flourish as *The Tailor of Panama*.

Ravi and Ben were not willing to give one thin amp of

credibility to the Shanghai Electrician. They accessed the satellite only every four or even five days, averaging 24 seconds of mast exposure per twenty-four hours. They stayed deep and slow, all the way along their southern voyage, past the Canadian coastline. They slipped down to 600-foot depth as they crossed the unseen frontier, west of the Strait of Juan de Fuca, into North American waters off the coast of Washington State.

Out where the *Barracuda* ran, 45 miles offshore, the waters were not officially American, but in the world of international terrorism, those great Pacific swells far off the coast of the Evergreen State were about as American as Fifth Avenue; patrolled ruthlessly by U.S. warships working out of the sprawling Navy Bases of Everett and Bremerton, deep in Puget Sound, which guards the great northwestern city of Seattle.

Shakira's view was to stay well clear of the vast seascape that washes onto the shores of Washington State. She regarded it as the most dangerous part of their long journey, a place where there might well be U.S. submarine patrols, and many more highly sensitive surface warships, all carrying state-of-the-art detection and surveillance ASW equipment.

In her opinion, they should stay deep until they were well south of the fast and lethal predators from the Bremerton and Everett U.S. Navy Bases. Those predators would show not the slightest mercy to an intruder, especially an unannounced Russian-built nuclear they had been puzzling over for several weeks. And there was no doubt, certainly in the mind of General Rashood, that the Americans were most definitely wondering about them.

Admiral Badr kept in touch with Shakira's heavily marked charts all the way, unfailingly agreeing with her and her sense of caution. They moved on slowly, the big, lightly used reactor running steadily, all systems operating flawlessly throughout the submarine. Ravi and Shakira would have liked a bigger cabin, but there was no chance of that. They worked and slept exhausted, welded together by the fire of love and revenge upon the Great Satan and its Israeli devils.

They crossed the 48th parallel, which bisects the northern timberland of Washington State, then the 47th, which took half a day. On August 5, they were due west of the estuary of the mighty Columbia River, the great 1,200-mile-long waterway that rises in a snow- and rain-filled torrent in the mountains of British Columbia, surges south, and then swerves west to form much of the border between Washington State and Oregon.

The Columbia was the most powerful river in the United States, generating one third of all the hydroelectric energy in the entire country. The Chief Joseph, the Grand Coulee, the John Day, and the Bonneville were the biggest of eleven massive mainstream dams. And the names of the latter two had been marked carefully on Shakira's charts and circled in red, her personal code for potential danger.

In Shakira's view, these two hydro giants, set upstream from Oregon's commercial hub of Portland, would be heavily protected from terrorist attack, and the chances of high radar sweeping the skies above the dam were excellent. What Shakira wished to avoid especially was a missile detection from U.S. radar defenses, mainly because she considered that to be an unnecessary hazard, and most certainly avoidable.

The preprogrammed data inside the computer of the Scimitar SL-Mark 1s (plain TNT, *not* the nuclear warheads of the Mark 2s) would guide the rockets downstream of the big protected dams, crossing the Columbia in lonely, practically deserted countryside.

But the entire project made her nervous, and she found it difficult to sleep, often pacing the navigation room at all hours of the night, pulling up the charts of coastal Oregon on the screens of the satellite navigation computers.

Ravi too understood the scale of the project they were undertaking, but he was consumed with the minutiae of the target area. He combed through the notes provided by the late

Professor Landon and longed each day for the luxury of a satellite communication that would detail the ever-changing situation among the high volcanoes within the mountain ranges of America's vast northwestern coastal states.

He had pages of data on Mount St. Helens, the Fuji of the United States, which was almost identical in its symmetrical shape to the legendary Japanese volcano. At least it was before it finally blew with stupendous force on May 18, 1980, sending a shudder across the entire southwestern corner of the state of Washington, and literally shot a tremor straight through the gigantic Cascade Mountains.

The blast flattened fully grown Douglas fir trees up to 14 miles away from the volcano, and obliterated 400 square miles of prime forest. Fifty-seven people died. Raging mudflows thundered into the rivers. Volcanic ash showered from the darkened skies all the way to Montana, 650 miles to the east.

The colossal eruption blew the entire snowcapped glory of the summit clean away from one of the most spectacular mountain peaks in the United States. Before May 18, Mount St. Helens rose thousands of feet above every hill and mountain that surrounded it, dominating the landscape. It stood, serenely peaceful, 9,677 feet high. After the blast, it stood less proudly, at only 8,364 feet. Its great shining white crest was entirely missing, like a spent firework.

A broad, tilted circular crater more than two miles across was embedded into the pinnacle of the mountain. From its lower edge, carved into the north side, the crater's rim was cut into a giant *V*, through which had thundered the pyroclastic flow. The molten lava was now set into a grotesque black basalt highway down the mountain, splitting into a wide fork as it reached the six-mile-wide base. The western surge had rumbled into the clear and refreshing waters of Spirit Lake. The rest had barreled down the beautiful snowy valley of the Toutle River. It was like an open-cast coal mine set in the garden of Santa's Workshop.

Ravi knew the facts verbatim. But the part that captivated him most was one particular detail of the blast. The central "chimney" of Mount St. Helens was blocked with hundreds of tons of lava from the previous eruption, and the surging new magma, climbing into the volcano, had nowhere to go. It ultimately forced its way higher into the north flank, pushing outwards and forming a giant swelling, a dome of rock, volcanic ash, and general debris.

These great carbuncles are not unique to Mount St. Helens. They happen often with active volcanoes. But shortly before the eruption, this one had developed into a fair size—a mile across and probably 120 feet high. And it was not the rising magma that finally smashed the great bulge asunder, but a relatively small earthquake that completely destabilized the north face of the mountain.

The dome, cracking on all sides, blew outward within minutes of the quake, and crashed down the mountainside in a landslide. The mammoth weight of a half-million cubic yards of rock was now removed from the upward flow of the lava, and the gases decompressed instantly, detonating out like a bomb, leveling every tree in sight.

It was the carbuncle that Ravi now focused on. According to Professor Landon, another one was forming on the same gutted north face of Mount St. Helens, right in the old crater, 46.20N 122.18W on the GPS, to be absolutely precise.

There had been strong, steaming activity inside the volcano for several years, since the early 1990s—occasional eruptions of steam and ash, less frequent pyroclastic flows, with intermittent swellings on the northern rock face of the mountain. A much more violent blast of steam and ash on July 1, 1998, had frightened the life out of the locals before it had seemed to subside again. The new mile-long carbuncle had begun to develop in 2006, right in the middle of that massive, sinister crater that scarred the once-beautiful north face.

As they crossed the 46.20N line of latitude, Shakira knew

they were dead-level with their target, dead-level with the four-mile-wide estuary of the Columbia River. They were 200 miles offshore, 600 feet below the surface, steering one-eight-zero, straight down the 127-degree line of longitude. Mount St. Helens lay 75 miles due east of the estuary. Right now, moving slowly, they were exactly 195 miles from their target, a mere formality for the North Korean–built Scimitar SL-1 missiles currently resting malevolently in the magazine room of *Barracuda II*.

The Pacific was a little less than a mile deep here, the seabed a flat, scarcely undulating plain. On the surface, the swells were long, rising 10 feet, but here in the quiet depths of the cold, gloomy ocean, there was nothing, save for the stark network of the U.S. Navy's SOSUS wires, resting like angry black cobras in military formation on the ocean floor, ready to spit venomous, fatal betrayal on any unsuspecting intruder.

Admiral Badr recommended running south for another 100 miles, a position that would put them in easy range of the great scarred mountain in southwestern Washington. Shakira's missile course was plotted and agreed upon. General Ravi had decreed there was no reason to move too far away. His overall strategy had been something of a surprise: He was ordering a daytime firing, rather than using the hours of darkness, which they all felt to be much safer, although when cocooned in their boat at 600 feet, there was not the slightest difference between night or day, summer or winter, or the days of the week.

When Shakira wanted to know why, Ravi's explanation was succinct. "Because a big cruise missile trails a large fiery tail when it leaves the water. It can be seen literally for miles, especially in the dark. If we do it in the day it will be much, much less visible."

"But before we fired at night."

"That was because we did not want the missiles to be seen by security guards at the target end. This is different. We are firing into a void. Into the open wild, where there are no guards, no surveillance, no people."

"Hmmmm," mumbled Shakira, irritated that she had not thought of that herself.

"Our only danger on this mission," said her husband, "is being detected by a passing warship, out there in the night, with the ocean lit up like a bloody amusement park by our rocket motors."

"The missile could still be seen during the day," said Shakira, "if there were passing ships."

"There won't be," replied Ravi.

"How do you know?"

"Because I intend to fire when there is fog on the ocean surface. And I intend to use passive sonar and my own eyes to ensure there is nothing around."

"But even you cannot just order fog."

"No, but this part of northwestern America is well known for the rain that sweeps up the Pacific. And where there's rain and cool temperatures interrupted by warm air currents, there's fog."

"But there may not be any, not exactly when we want it," said Shakira.

"We'll wait."

Shakira Rashood asked him if he would like some tea, and her husband replied that he considered that an excellent idea, briefly toying with the temptation to remark how thrilled he was that she had decided to return to what she was good at. But he quickly rejected it, not wishing to have the entire contents of the teapot poured over his head.

Instead he looked up and smiled. "I'm very grateful, my darling," he said, "the way you force people to explain themselves."

"You're too clever," she said, affecting a mock pout. "Always too clever. I like being on your side."

"You're a good officer, Shakira. Ready to challenge when you do not quite understand. But in the end, respectful of your Commanding Officer. As we all must be."

"I am a good officer," she said seriously, but smiling. "But

I hope you think I'm a better wife. Because I expect to be that for much longer."

"If you go on doing as I tell you—at least while we're in this ship on Allah's mission—you will be my wife for a long time. I usually know what to do, and how to keep us safe."

"You see," she laughed, "you don't even have a Commanding Officer. You make your own rules."

"I have a Commanding Officer," he replied. "And I hope He's watching over both of us."

Shakira looked at him with undisguised adoration—this powerfully built ex–British Army Major, the toughest man she had ever met, with the polish of a Sandhurst-trained officer and the strategic brilliance of an SAS commander. And yet he was an Arab still, with his dark tanned skin, the softest brown eyes, and the inborn fortitude of his Bedouin forebears.

And she thanked Allah for the day she had fled with him, terrified, through the rubble of shattered Hebron, while all around them there was only the blast of shells and the whine of bullets and the cries of the wounded. She thanked Allah for the strength she had found to take him into hiding with the Hamas freedom fighters.

Looking back, when she dared, to the devastation of that blasted cement house in the Palestinian district, she could still see her slain children, and the blood from the wounds of the dead SAS sergeants, blood pouring down Ravi's combat uniform, blood on her children, on her own hands and dress. And she remembered how her own little Ravi had lain so still in the dust, next to his tiny dead sister, and how Ray had saved her life by committing two savage murders.

There was nothing, she thought, that could have been worth all that. But the former Maj. Ray Kerman had made it almost so. She could not imagine anyone loving another person more. She would have followed him into the mouth of hell.

As it happened, Ray followed her into the mouth of the

galley, where the cooks were not working, and he kissed her longingly behind the shelves of canned fruit.

"You said this is why girls are not allowed in submarines," she giggled, twisting away, in case anyone discovered them.

"People are only required to do as I say," he said, cheerfully. "Not as I do."

"You see—I'm always telling you—you do just as you like, because you have no Commanding Officer."

Ravi looked admiringly at his wife, her beauty undiminished even in her standard dark navy-blue sweater, and he said simply, "I don't think Allah would desert any of us on this mission. He has given us the power of the false gods of the ancient world, and He will guide us to victory. We are doing His work."

"And to think," said Shakira, shaking her head in sham disbelief, "you used to be an infidel . . . one sugar or two?"

General Rashood chuckled, quietly thankful at the talent Shakira had for diminishing the tensions of his great mission, if only for a few moments.

They made their way to the navigation room, Shakira carrying the teapot and three little silver holders containing glass mugs already with sugar, in case Lt. Ashtari Mohammed was working. It was almost midnight now.

They found Ashtari hunched over the chart of the eastern Pacific, plotting their southern course. He stood up and stretched, grateful for the tea. "Admiral Badr thinks we should run for another day, maybe less, and then turn east towards our target."

Ravi nodded in agreement, and glanced down at Shakira's chart. It contained so many notes, it was almost incomprehensible. But the line she had drawn from the 127th western line of longitude had four definite course changes at various points of contact, from the 47th parallel to 46.20N at 122.18W.

Ravi had managed only two sips of his bitter hot tea when a quiet voice came down the ship's intercom . . . *"General Rashood to the control room . . . General Rashood to the control room. . . ."*

He took his tea with him and headed for the area directly below the bridge, where Ben Badr was waiting.

"At which point do you want to begin searching the area for surface ships? We're about 100 miles north of the datum right now . . . I was thinking maybe 50 would be right . . . I presume we don't want to surface?"

"No, we don't want to do that. But we should get up as high as we can, maybe to periscope depth every couple of hours, just for an all-around look. Meanwhile we can use passive sonar as our main lookout. We cannot risk detection. There are no suspects for a mission such as this—it would seem ridiculous to alert *anyone* to our presence—"

"I agree, Ravi. So 50 miles from our firing position is okay?"

"Yes, good. If there's anything around, we may want to track it for a couple of days . . . make sure it's well clear. Meanwhile we'll just hope for fog."

The *Barracuda* pushed on, running quietly all through the night until midafternoon on Thursday, August 6. At 1630, Admiral Badr ordered the planesmen to angle the bow up 10, sending them smoothly to periscope depth. The Admiral himself took a look all around, and Lieutenant Ashtari called out the numbers—43 north, 127 west.

Lieutenant Commander Shakira wrote them down on her chart, marked the spot where the line of latitude bisected the longitude, checked her distances with dividers, and wrote in blue marker pen, *290 miles to Target.*

In seconds, Ben Badr ordered them deep, *bow down 10 to 600.* There was no communication on the satellite, no ships anywhere nearby. Their part of the Pacific was a sunlit wilderness, devoid of engines, lacking in fog. Their only danger was the ever-present "black cobras" on the seabed who must not be disturbed. Admiral Badr ordered a racetrack pattern, speed 5, banking on the fact that the "cobras" were deaf to such low revolutions in a boat as quiet as the *Barracuda.*

And so they waited for two days and two nights until at 0300 on Sunday morning, a gusting summer rain squall swept eastwards across the ocean, right out of the northwest. They picked it up on sonar and moved silently upward, through the black depths to PD for a firsthand look. They stayed there for only seven seconds, sufficient time for the Chief of Boat, CPO Ali Zahedi, to report a slashing rainstorm on the surface, very low visibility, at no more than 100 yards.

General Rashood considered the possibility of firing there and then. But he knew it could still be clear on the shore, and he did not relish sending missiles with fiery tails over inhabited land, even at three o'clock in the morning. No, he would wait for a large-scale spell of fog, which he was sure would happen as soon as the regular warm summer air currents ran into the cold, squally Pacific gusts surrounding the storm.

At dawn, they checked again, moving slowly to periscope depth. Ravi had been correct. A great bank of fog hung over the ocean, visibility at no more than 50 yards. Ravi guessed it would probably extend all the way inshore, with the clammy white blanket hanging heavily against the mountains of Oregon's coastal range.

"This is it, old boy," he said to Ben Badr.

"Aye, sir," replied the young Iranian Admiral.

"Prepare Tubes 1-4 . . . missile director and Lieutenant Commander Shakira to the missile room . . . Planesman, bow up 10 to 200 feet . . . Put me on course zero-three-zero . . . speed 5 . . . Sonar room, check no contacts . . . Missile Director, final check prefiring routines and settings."

They all felt the submarine angle up slightly, and they heard Ravi summon the crew to prayer. Those not hurrying to the missile room knelt on the steel decks in the Muslim fashion. Men clambered out of bunks, engineers laid down their tools, and everyone heard the Mission Commander's warning of the coming turmoil, urging them to be prepared to hear the Angels sound the trumpet three times. At the sound of the trumpets, he said, only the righteous would cross the bridge into the arms of Allah. They were engaged in the work of Allah, they were His children, and they dwelt today in this great weapon of war on behalf of Allah. It was built for Him and they were born to serve Him.

He read from the Koran—

"'*From Thee alone do we ask for help . . .*

Guide us to the straight path,

The path of those whom you blessed.'"

General Rashood ended as he often did with undying praise of Allah. "'*I have turned my face only towards the Supreme Being who originated the skies and the earth . . . To You be the glory . . . Yours is the most auspicious name. You are exalted and none other than You is worthy of worship'*"

They prayed silently for a few seconds and then returned to their tasks. Shakira reported to the Missile Director and checked once more the Scimitar's preset guidance programs—"*Zero-three-zero from blastoff to latitude 46.05N degrees. Then course change to zero-nine-zero to longitude 127W . . . Then course change to three-six-zero for 30 nautical miles . . . Then final course change to two-one-zero 15 miles to the precise position of the target.*"

It was 0630 when General Rashood gave the order . . . "*STAND BY TUBES ONE TO FOUR!*"

Then, seconds later, "*TUBE ONE LAUNCH!!*"

And at long last, the 26-foot steel guided missile, driven in an army truck from the bowels of Kwanmo-bong last May, was on its way. *Barracuda II* shuddered gently as it blew out of the launcher, lanced up to the surface, and split the Pacific swells asunder, its engines igniting, the searing light of the fiery tail obscured by the fog.

It blasted upwards, crackling into the morning sky, adjusting course and leveling out at 200 meters above the surface. At 600 knots, the gas turbines kicked in, removing the giveaway trail in the sky, steady on its northeasterly course, its flawless precision a tribute to the craftsmen of Kwanmo-bong.

As they prepared to launch Tube Two, the senior command felt safe in the knowledge that the Koreans had sworn to make a true and faithful replica of the old Russian RADUGA, and that the Scimitar would match its perfor-

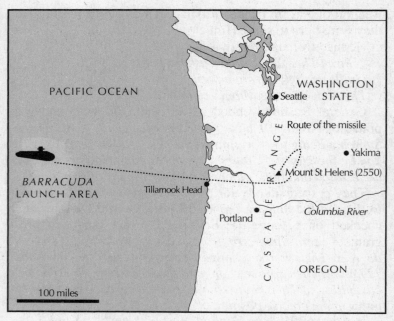

BARRACUDA STANDS OFF THE OREGON/WASHINGTON COAST;
DRAWING A BEAD ON MOUNT ST. HELENS

mance in every way. The refined new rocket motor would be
no problem, and the automatic rear wings would spread immediately when the missile was airborne.

At this very moment, the North Koreans were batting
1,000, and the cruise missile they had created was hurtling
diagonally towards the distant northern shores of the American state of Oregon. It was 220 miles to its landfall, and it
would cross the coastline in twenty-one minutes, by which
time three other identical missiles, already under the control
of the *Barracuda*'s launch sequencer, would be streaking
line astern right behind it. Same course. Through the fog.
Destination: the fractured, haunted north face of Mount St.
Helens.

Missile One screamed in over the high, rugged coast, just
north of Tillamook Head, at 1654. It thundered on across the

3,000-foot peak of Saddle Mountain, rising and falling with the contours of the earth. It passed Clatsop State Park and into Columbia County, making 600 knots as it crossed the wide river, then the state frontier, 20 miles downstream of the city of Portland.

This was high country, deep in the towering southern uplands of the Cascade Range. The Scimitar's preset computer brain, reading the sonar altimeter, was working overtime dealing with the dramatically changing ground levels. But the Chinese technicians had served General Rashood well.

The big Mark-1 missile ripped across Interstate 5, and shrieked through the peaks of Cowlitz County, heading along the Kalama River Valley to the Swift Creek Dam, where it swerved north, right on schedule. By now, the mighty tower of Mount St. Helens was just a dozen miles to port, and the missile swept right past, still heading north. It flew swiftly over the great forests of the Cascades, and just after the little town of Gifford, it made its turn, wheeling left in a great semicircle.

The wilderness below was silent, but from the high peaks you might have heard the *W-H-O-O-O-O-SHHHHHH!* of disturbed air, as the Scimitar turned to the southwest. It held course two-one-zero, drawing a bead on the giant, unstable carbuncle, which grew on the floor of the volcano crater, near the pinnacle of the mountain.

It came in fast, gathering speed as it lost height, almost 700 knots as it cleaved through the morning air above the foothills of Mount Hughes, where the Green River rises, east of Coldwater Creek. Moments later, it hurtled into the skies high above the fog-shrouded blue waters of Spirit Lake.

It rocketed through the thick, damp mist and crossed the north shore, still making over 600 knots, and then angled up sharply to follow the steep slopes of Mount St. Helens. It scythed through the air, taking just under nine seconds to make the one-and-a-half-mile ascent to the summit, where it banked wickedly downwards, and hammered its way straight into the middle of the crater.

Programmed to detonate two seconds after impact, the missile's sharp reinforced steel nose lasered into the crater's unstable base of loose rock and ash, burying 15 feet below the surface before exploding with a booming impact. Rock and shale flew 100 feet into the air.

The Scimitar's warhead sent cracks like lightning bolts deep into the crust of the earth, splitting open the already shifting strata, way down where the magma seethed and churned, ever seeking an outlet. By itself, the Scimitar could not have caused Mount St. Helens to erupt. But there were three more where that came from, and the great volcano, had it known, would have braced itself for the incoming man-made thunder.

As it was, a great belch of steam did shoot skywards, but local residents did not see the warning; not even those driving trucks through the morning mist along local routes 503, or 90, or south on 25 from Gifford. Even in clear conditions, it was not always easy to see the mountain peak from the tree-lined roads, and almost everyone had seen gouts of steam up there before, even the occasional fiery burst of ash.

Fifty-five seconds later, Missile Two hit, in exactly the same spot, 46.20N 122.18W. It drove deep into the brand-new hole, not 10 feet from Missile One. It slammed into the lava rubble, detonating with staggering force into a part of the mountain that was rotten to the core—a shifting, sliding heap of black fragmented rock debris.

The fury of the explosion, though muffled to traffic five miles away, was enough to send long fissures deep into the upper conduit of the lava chimney. White-hot magma now came seething up through the black shale, as yet only eking its way out of the relatively slender gaps, but moving steadily higher.

Less than a minute later, there was a breakthrough. Missile Three came screaming in with sufficient force to knock down three skyscrapers. More burning magma came searing up through the underground channels—not yet a blast but close. The lava began to spill into the crater; steam and fire burst into the foggy skies.

And then came Missile Four, arrowing straight down into the molten lava and exploding instantly, with the same force as the others, the same place, the same effect. The metal casing melted, but the warhead's TNT did its work. It blew the crevice wide open, releasing a zillion cubic feet of compressed gases. At 0706 on Sunday morning, August 9, 2009, Mount St. Helens erupted with savage force for the second time in less than thirty years.

The explosion leveled thousands of Douglas fir trees within roughly a 12-mile half-circle to the north. The crater, which contained the unstable carbuncle, was already tilted that way, and when the eruption came, it exploded northwards, leaving the area behind it, to the south and west, more or less unharmed, except for a rainstorm of ash.

Again, as in 1980, the massive pyroclastic flow of molten lava surged down the upper slopes of the mountain, creating a terrifying nine-foot-high white-hot river of molten rock from the very core of the earth. It seemed to move slowly, but it was making 40 mph as it crackled and growled its way into Spirit Lake, burning everything in its path, wiping out the lake's vegetation, boiling the water, sending hot steam up into the fog.

Of the campers on the north side of the lake and on the lower slopes of the mountain's pine forest—mostly kids and college students—none had a chance. A handful of burnt dust buried deep in volcanic rock would be all that remained of the soldiers, in a cruel and sadistic war no one even knew was being fought.

The fog had cleared now around the little towns of Glenoma, Morton, and Mossyrock up on Route 12 and 508, and the pinnacle of Mount St. Helens could just be seen jutting up through the summit's mist, belching fire and spewing thousands of tons of rock and red-hot ash hundreds of feet into the air.

It looked awesome, like many displays of nature too frightening to contemplate. But every man, woman, or child in those picturesque little Washington townships knew they were witnessing havoc, pitiless destruction, and heartbreaking loss of lives. Everyone who stood helplessly watching knew there would be many, many empty places at dinner tables tonight, all over the American Northwest.

The lava rolled over a total of fifteen cars parked around the lake's perimeter, and the burning hot deposits of avalanche debris cascaded into the north fork of the Toutle River, almost damming it in some places. It completely blocked Coldwater Creek. A vast area of lateral blast deposits, thousands of tons of ash, spread over a distance of 200 square miles, choking rivers, burying forest and remote farmhouses.

The warm, sleepy Sunday morning of August 9 would be remembered forever throughout this lonely rural corner of the 42nd State, as Mount St. Helens, the towering snow-capped sentinel of the Gifford Pinchot National Forest, suddenly, without warning, reared and destroyed the very land that gave it grace.

On that Sunday morning, those who had not witnessed the shocking 1980 eruption saw the real nature of the mountain. And it had little to do with grandeur or with the great silent peak that had dominated this southern part of the Washington State mountains—the bastion of strength, Queen of the Cascades.

This was the real St. Helens—a colossal 8,000-foot-high black, unstable pile of rotten volcanic rubble, spewing forth dark-gray burning ash, white-hot rock, black smoke, and lava, vomited up from the basement of Hell. And it was bent on burning everything it could reach.

Within minutes of the first major eruption, right after Scimitar-4, the fires began. Great hunks of molten rock and dense showers of red-hot ash were landing in the pine forests.

The dead tinder-dry needles on the forest floor practically exploded into flame, and the trees took only moments longer to ignite. The inflammable resin inside the needles, boughs, and trunks of the Douglas firs popped and crackled into a giant, highly audible bonfire. From a distance, the blaze sounded like the eerie murmur of a battlefield.

Thousands of acres burned ferociously, spreading with terrifying swiftness before the west wind that billowed gently off the Pacific, dispersing the fog, fanning the flames. Every five minutes, there was another grim and furious roar from the summit, and another plume of fire and ash ripped into the powder-blue sky, and another obscene surge of magma rolled over the crater and on down the mountainside.

By 0830, every household, every car full of tourists, every truckload of outdoor sportsmen inside a 25-mile radius knew that Mount St. Helens had erupted. The radio stations were cobbling together news bulletins based on almost nothing except the incontrovertible fact that the damn mountain just blew its goddamned head off. Again.

Volcano experts from all over the area were being rounded up, electronically, and interviewed. All of them admitted to absolute bewilderment, and by 0900, radio and television newsrooms were desperate for information. The State Police had placed a ban on media helicopters, and it was impossible to get near the mountain.

The "experts" who were permanently monitoring the volcano were impossible to find, and the university study groups, collecting data in the foothills below the crater, were dead. Most of the observation posts to the north of the mountain were devastated, the buildings on the high ridges reduced to burned-out hulks, the low ones swept away by the incinerating magma.

Trees smashed by the blast leaned at ridiculous angles against the others that had withstood the explosion. These now formed enclosed, towering pyramids of volatile, combustible dry pine branches lit from within, as the fire raced across the dead needles on the forest floor.

From above, they looked like scattered furnaces, burning to red-hot flash points and instantly setting fire to anything made of wood and resin within spitting distance.

By lunchtime, the President had declared southwest Washington State a disaster zone and Federal help was on its way. The trouble with volcanoes, however, is that there are no half-measures, no wounded, no traumatized persons—and no witnesses. The fury of this type of assault on the planet is too formidable.

If you're near enough to cast light on the actual event from a close-up position, your chances of survival are close to zero. It was no different at the base of Mount St. Helens on that Sunday morning . . . except for one big four-wheel-drive-vehicle that had been parked all night on the northwest shore of Spirit Lake. This contained a selection of sporting rifles, fishing rods, and four sportsmen, three of them local—one from Virginia.

The leader of the little expedition was Tony Tilton, a former attorney from Worcester, Massachusetts, currently President of the Seattle National Bank. Accompanying him was the legendary East Coast dealer of marine art Alan Granby, who had moved west with his wife, Janice, after a money-grabbing private corporation threatened to build a massive wind farm opposite their backyard on the shores of Nantucket Sound.

The third member of the party was another East Coast native, the eminent broadcaster and political observer Don McKeag, who had finally abandoned his show on a local Cape Cod radio station for a huge network contract that required him to live and work out of Seattle—the "Voice of the Northwest."

The fourth serious sportsman in that accomplished little group was the big-game fisherman, duck hunter, and car racer Jim Mills from Middleburg, Virginia. They were on a weeklong hunting, shooting, and fishing trip, and they'd been camped by the lake all night, ready for an assault on the superb trout that made Spirit Lake their home.

There was one prime difference between these four and the rest of the sportsmen scattered around the lake in the warm summer months. Tony Tilton and his wife, Martha, had been cruising in the eastern Caribbean when the Montserrat volcano exploded in 1997, burying two towns, wrecking the entire south side of the island, and showering everything within 40 miles with thick, choking volcanic ash. Tony Tilton had stood on the foredeck of his chartered yacht and watched the towering inferno belch fire from the Soufriere Hills.

Etched in Tony's memory was the speed with which the mountain unleashed its wrath upon the island. He had seen the blast, watched the roaring plume of burning ash and smoke burst upwards, hundreds of feet into the sky. Almost simultaneously, he had seen the great glowing evil of the magma begin its fatal roll down three sides of the mountain. A trained attorney, he had the lawyer's grasp of facts, and the banker's eye for the minutiae. In Tony's opinion you had approximately fourteen minutes to get the hell away from that mountain or perish.

And now, twelve years later, on that early Sunday morning on the shores of Spirit Lake, Tony heard a strange and sudden wind, a *wh-o-o-o-o-sssh* through the dense foggy air above the water. Instinctively he had glanced up but seen nothing.

Less than twelve seconds later, he heard a dull, muffled roar from way up on the mountain, but again he could see nothing up the slopes through the fog. He heard the wind again, and another shuddering distant thump from the summit of the mountain. It was louder this time, but perhaps only because Tony was already on high alert.

That did it for the Seattle Bank President. He turned to Don McKeag and said sharply, "Get in the wagon, Donnie. And don't speak. Just get in." Then he yelled towards the tent *"ALAN, JIMMY. . . . GET UP AND GET IN THE WAGON . . . RIGHT NOW . . . WE'RE IN BIG TROUBLE."*

Alan Granby, a big man, but as light on his feet as the late, great Jackie Gleason, understood immediately. He and Jimmy had slept fully dressed and they both came scrambling out of their tents, alerted by the obvious tension in Tony Tilton's voice.

The engine of the wagon was already running, and they both jumped into the rear seats. Tony hit the gas pedal and they burned rubber on the warm shores of the lake, heading west, through the short forest trail that led to Route 504. The trail was straight and relatively smooth and the wagon was moving at almost 70 mph when they heard the third explosion right behind them, followed quickly by another.

"What in the name of hell was that?" asked Don McKeag.

"Nothing much," said Tony. "Except I think Mount St. Helens just erupted." By now they were on the country road, which would lead north up to the town of Glenoma and the much faster Route 25. And all around them were strange glowing lights falling into the trees like a meteor shower.

But the brightness had gone out of the day. Alan Granby glanced at the sky. "If I had to guess," he said, "I'd say this was the start of a partial eclipse of the sun."

At that moment, they felt an earth-shuddering rumble beneath the wheels of the wagon, and a howling wind screamed through the forest, like a hurricane. Tony hammered the wagon up deserted Route 12, heading north and conscious of the burning debris beginning to litter the road.

"Let's hope I don't get into reverse by mistake," he muttered. "I got a feeling anyone left back there might not make it."

The miles whipped away beneath their wheels, and now the sky was darkening into a thick, high gunmetal-gray cloud above them. Yet through the rear window they could discern a terrible glow in the sky. In eleven minutes, they had put twelve miles between themselves and the lower slopes of Mount St. Helens. Up ahead it looked slightly brighter, and Don, ever the journalist, suggested they pull over after another couple of miles and take a look back at the mountain, and the fires, and the scorched earth they had somehow escaped.

"Any of you guys fancy a short hunting-fishing trip next year to Indonesia?" asked Tony. "You know . . . a nice little base camp on the slopes of Krakatoa . . . I'm getting to be a real pro at volcano escape . . ."

Three Hours Later.

"Good morning, everyone, this is Don McKeag, reporting firsthand from the front line of our statewide catastrophe. During the sudden and devastating eruption of Mount St. Helens, I was in a hunting camp right in the foothills of the volcano as it was about to detonate.

"I think I can say honestly, it is nothing short of a miracle that I am here talking to you this morning . . . because I was spared from certain death by the quick thinking of my friend Tony Tilton who somehow drove us to safety . . . through the fires and the volcanic ash . . . out in front of the molten lava . . . away from the cataclysmic explosion.

"For my regular weekday morning program, you know I always take calls and discuss the politics of this great state . . . Today I'm changing the formula . . . I just want to sit here, catch my breath, and try to explain what it's like, literally, to escape from the jaws of hell. . . . So far, we're getting reports of perhaps a hundred of our fellow citizens who never made it . . . To their families I want to express my deepest, most profound sorrow and sympathy . . . I might very easily have been one of them. . . ."

As Donnie spoke in measured, yet inevitably dramatic, tones, every fireman in southwest Washington State was engaged in fighting the fires along the periphery of the central blaze. It was pointless to even think about entering the interior zone below the north face of the mountain or about running a fleet of ambulances into the inferno. There would be no injured.

The only thing that could be done now was to try and stem

the blazing forest, to stop it spreading outwards to wreak havoc and misery upon unsuspecting home owners. Soon they would have crop sprayers in the skies dumping hundreds of tons of water on the parts of the forests that remained intact. Others were out there, pumping and spraying great tracts of forest, trying to stop the searing heat from evaporating the water before the fires even arrived.

By mid-Sunday afternoon, the disaster was big national news. CNN had pictures, as did Fox News and most of the networks. By Sunday evening, all of the twenty-four-hour news channels were struggling with the story. They were without any fresh information, new facts, or revelatory opinions. Yes, Mount St. Helens had made a titanic eruption early on Sunday morning. Yes, there was a lot of fire and fury, ash, molten rock, and lava. And yes, anyone trapped in the immediate vicinity of the mountain was most certainly dead. And yes, there were God knows how many forest fires raging all around the northern territories beyond the volcano. Eyewitnesses from close up: zero, except for Don McKeag and his three friends.

Volcanoes traditionally do anything they damn well please, ruling out the possibilities of indignant editorials proclaiming in time-honored cliché, *WHY THIS MUST NEVER HAPPEN AGAIN.* Or, *DID THEY DIE IN VAIN?* Or, *WAS THIS AN ACCIDENT WAITING TO HAPPEN?* Or even that cringe-making old favorite, *HEADS MUST ROLL!* Instead, the news and feature rooms turned, admittedly with a mixture of reluctance and relief, to the "experts," many of whom had died on the mountain, but some who were ready to cast a light on an occurrence about which they had not the remotest clue.

Yes, there had been steam and even some gases leaking from the crater on the summit in recent weeks. Yes, there had been signs of fire, ashes, and black smoke bursting into the atmosphere. And no, it would not have been a tremendous surprise if Mount St. Helens had erupted in the next five years. The giant carbuncle was indeed a significant factor.

What baffled the professors was the sheer speed of the eruption, so sudden, so unexpected, so utterly without warning. This was a new concept for volcanologists all over the world. No angry early blasts, no torrents of high sparks and sinister rumbles, not even the sight of molten lava creeping out over the rim of the crater. Nothing. This was the Whispering Death of Mount St. Helens. Unseen. Unsuspected. Unannounced.

CNN rustled up a young volcanologist from the University of California in Santa Cruz. He had never even seen Mount St. Helens, and had not been born when it erupted in 1980. His father was not born when Lassen Peak, the only other comparable volcanic eruption in the U.S., let fly in 1914. But the recently qualified Simon Lyons from Orange County spoke with the unwavering authority of those sufficiently youthful still to have the answers to everything.

"Any halfway decent student of geohazardous situations must have known this volcano could have erupted at any time," he said. "That carbuncle was growing at a very fast rate, maybe a half-mile across in the last two years. That's the sign we're all looking for. That's the sign of the encroaching magma, surging up from the core of the earth. You see a carbuncle being force-fed with lava from below, right there, you're looking at a volcano fixing to blow."

"Then you blame those study groups based on the mountain, supposedly monitoring it for the benefit of us all . . . using Federal funds?"

"Yes, sir. I most certainly do. Incompetence. Ignorance of the value of the data. Ought to be anathema to a real scientist."

Professor Charles Delmar, of the University of Colorado, was older, more experienced, and more circumspect. Fox News got ahold of him, and he was the first to admit he could throw little light on the eruption.

He said the photographs he had been shown suggested the Sunday morning blowout on the summit of the mountain had been aimed to the north, which suggested the carbuncle itself had given way to the pressure of the magma below. Professor Delmar found that "most unusual" simply because there were no other reported symptoms of eruptions from that precise location. There had been evidence of steam gouts and some smoke, but that was reportedly emanating from the mountain peak, not from cracks in the carbuncle, which would have been an indication of pressure underneath the dome of lava rock.

Therefore, Professor Delmar considered it "most odd" that it should suddenly have obliterated itself, and "even more odd" that it should have given way so comprehensively, so quickly, that the third biggest volcano eruption in the U.S.A. in a hundred years should have happened, literally, within moments.

The *Barracuda II* moved slowly south down the Pacific, following the 127th western line of longitude for another 100 miles. It was almost 0300 when the great submarine moved stealthily to the surface, ran up an ESM mast, and transmitted a one-word message to their command headquarters, via the satellite, to faraway Bandar Abbas on the Strait of Hormuz.

Saladin was the word. And the transmission was forwarded on by E-mail to a computer based on Via Dolorosa, in the Muslim section of Jerusalem, the very street down which Jesus is said to have carried his cross en route to Calvary.

Within moments, a stamped, sealed letter with airmail stamps already affixed was in the hands of a messenger, running swiftly through the old city to the central post office on Schlomzion Street.

It was addressed to *Vice Admiral Arnold Morgan, The White House, 1600 Pennsylvania Avenue, Washington, DC,*

U.S.A. PRIVATE AND CONFIDENTIAL. General Rashood knew the Admiral no longer worked in the West Wing, but he was confident the U.S. Administration's gigantic 50,000-letters-a-week mail room would find a way to forward the letter to the Admiral's private home address.

5

Friday, August 14
Chevy Chase, Maryland.

HARRY, CHIEF SECURITY AGENT to Admiral Arnold Morgan, signed for the four letters delivered by the White House courier. Then he walked to the mailbox especially fitted inside the porch, emptied it, and walked around to the high gate that guarded the entrance to the swimming pool area of the house, the large dark-blue rectangular body of water.

Three of the high surrounding stone walls were in a light Spanish-style salmon pink. Giant terra-cotta pots overflowing with green shrubs were planted all around. The fourth wall was a high wooden fence into which was set a small cabana with a polished teakwood bar and four stools.

"*Sir!*" Harry called. "Would you like me to bring the mail through?"

"I guess if you must persist in ruining my entire day with goddamned trivia, then you better do it," came the rasping voice over the top of the fence.

"Yes, sir," said Harry, who let himself in and walked across to the wide glass-topped table, where Admiral Morgan sat in a director's chair, frowning, as he mostly did, at the political views of the *New York Times*. As were many of America's daily publications, the paper was currently enjoying a gleeful period, congratulating the wonderful new Democratic President Charles McBride.

"Jesus Christ," growled Arnold. "I didn't realize you could get that many total assholes under one editorial roof. Except possibly in the *Washington Post* . . . which I haven't read yet, since I'm trying to keep my blood pressure steady."

"Yes, sir," said Harry, putting the Admiral's mail on his table next to the coffeepot. "See the Orioles won again last night?"

"I did," replied the Admiral. "*And* they made two errors. Same spot as usual. Straight up the goddamned middle. I'm telling you, they've needed a top shortstop ever since Bordick retired. And until they get one, they'll never make the play-offs . . ."

"You watch the game, sir?"

"Just the last coupla innings, after dinner. Missed all the runs, though. Only saw the errors. For a minute, I thought the Yanks might catch us."

"Yeah. So did I. Good closer, though, that kid from Japan. Saved our ass, right, sir?"

"He did too . . . now, what's all this bullshit you've brought me? Hop inside and bring me out a plastic bag, will you? I've a feeling this consignment is about 99 percent rubbish."

"Okay, sir . . . be right back."

The Admiral looked at the top four letters, the ones from the White House. One was from the pensions department, two were invitations, the fourth was from someone in the Middle East, judging from the portrait of a sheikh on the stamp.

Arnold rarely looked at a photograph or painting of an elderly Arabian without remembering, automatically, the towers of the World Trade Center eight years previously. He took the letter and tore open the cream-colored envelope impatiently. The single sheet of writing paper inside was not headed by a printed address. It was plain. No date. Across the middle were three typed lines, plus a one-word printed signature. Nothing personal.

> *Admiral Morgan, you do not suppose for one moment that the eruption of Mount St. Helens was an accident, do you?*
>
> *—Hamas.*

Arnold gaped. He turned the sheet over, checked the envelope. There was not another clue, anywhere. Just this barefaced inquiry, full of menace. Could it be a hoax?

In the old days, he would have instantly summoned Admiral Morris, and then gone straight to the Oval Office, without knocking.

Today, however, sitting by the pool at eleven o'clock on a warm morning, a civilian in every sense of the word, things were very different. What were his duties? What should he decide? Well, nothing, was the answer on both counts. He was not required to decide a damn thing, and he found this almost impossible to accept.

Kathy was out at the hairdresser. He absentmindedly watched Harry bring out the plastic bag in which he would deposit most of the mail. But the letter from Hamas was burning his hand like a hot coal. He watched Harry wander out of the pool gate, poured himself a cup of coffee, and ruminated.

Finally, he decided the correct thing to do was to take the correspondence, place it in an envelope, tell Harry to whistle up the White House courier, and send the little package around to the man who had replaced him in the office of the President's National Security Adviser.

Let him worry about the damn thing. It was no longer his—Arnold's—concern. So he went inside, carefully made a couple of copies, and did exactly what he had decided. After placing the letter into a plastic bag, he added a little note to his successor, Cyrus Romney, former professor of Liberal Arts at Berkeley, and for all Arnold knew, marcher *in almost every misguided, half-assed, goddamned demonstration for peace the West Coast had seen in living memory.*

If Arnold Morgan had had his way, Cyrus Romney would have been instructed to march his way to Outer Mongolia and stay there. Arnold Morgan did not at all believe the Californian to be an ideal choice to occupy the great office of the Department of State, which, by all accounts, he owed mainly to a lifelong friendship with fellow peacenik Charles McBride.

Arnold's letter was cool:

Dear Cyrus . . . This came to me, mistakenly, today, possibly from people who did not know of the changes in the U.S. Government this year. Make of it what you will.

Sincerely,
Arnold Morgan.

The personal note from the old Lion of the West Wing would, Arnold knew, probably get short shrift from both Cyrus and his boss. Did he care what either of them thought? Not a jot.

Did he care what the implied Hamas threat might mean to the United States of America? On a scale of 1 to 1,000, Admiral Morgan was somewhere in the high fractions above 999. He walked back to the pool, picked up his mobile phone, and made a call to the private line of Admiral George Morris at Fort Meade.

"George . . . Arnie . . . got time for a brief private chat?"

A half hour later, he was on his way around the beltway, Harry at the wheel of the Admiral's new automobile, General Motors' state-of-the-art four-wheel-drive masterpiece, the 2009 Hummer-H2A. A polished city ride, at home on Fifth Avenue or downtown Washington, this broad-shouldered, off-road vehicle is a direct descendant of the military's old desert warhorse, the Humvee. The new Hummer can go through streams twenty inches deep and climb over rocks sixteen inches high. Mud, deep sand, no problem. Admiral Morgan's great friend Jack Smith, the Energy Secretary in the last Republican Administration and former President of General Motors, had told him: "This thing is made for you, mainly because Kathy could drive it easily, and you could go to war in it."

Arnold replied, "Would General Patton have liked it?"

"General Patton would probably have lived in it!" replied Jack.

Two other armed agents in a private White House car followed hard astern. They too had bulletproof glass.

They swung north up the parkway and drove quickly through the sprawling countryside surrounding the National Security Agency. At the main gates, a security guard walked to the driver's side and asked for passes. He was hardly able to finish his sentence.

"Get in, and escort me immediately to the office of the Director, in OPS-2B."

The guard recognized the former Tsar of Fort Meade, and understood that he might be working out the last three minutes of his career if he was not careful.

"SIR, YES, SIR!" snapped the former U.S. Army Master Chief, and hopped right into the backseat. Harry knew the way, and the guard jumped out and hissed to the next guard on the main doors. "Chuck, it's the Big Man—I'm taking him up to Admiral Morris."

"Rightaway, sir," he replied and opened the door while Arnold was disembarking. He and his escort went up to the eighth floor in the Director's private elevator.

"Tell Harry to take you back, then to wait right outside for me . . . and thanks, soldier."

"You're welcome, sir," he replied holding the door open and waiting to hear Admiral Morris greet the Big Man, as he knew he would.

"Arnie, great to see you . . . come and sit down. It's been too long."

Actually it had been about two months. Too long, for both of the old seafarers. And for the first time, Admiral Morgan did not walk around to the big chair, which he had once occupied himself. He accepted an offer of coffee, declined lunch, and parked himself in a large wooden captain's chair in front of the Director's desk.

Solemnly, he reached into his inside jacket pocket and handed over a copy of the letter he had received a couple of hours previously. George Morris stared at it, his bushy eyebrows raised.

"Jesus," he said. "When did this arrive?"

"This morning."

"How?"

"Regular mail."

"From where?"

"The Middle East. All the postmarks were very smudged. But I think the stamp was Palestinian, the special ones issued in parts of Israel. Had a picture of some sheikh on it."

"Have you told anyone?"

"Oh, sure. I sent the original over to the White House, to my successor. Told him the letter had come to me by mistake."

Admiral Morris nodded. "You did not elaborate about our previous discussions on the subject of Arab terrorists and volcanoes?"

"Hell, no. They would have loved an opportunity to imply that I was a paranoid old relic from the Cold War . . . and anyway, I don't have the energy to argue with jerks."

"Yes, you do."

"I know. But I don't feel like it."

George Morris looked again at the message from Hamas. And he recalled their evening together with Jimmy Ramshawe in Chevy Chase a couple of months before.

"Of course I know what you're thinking, Arnie . . . your honeymoon mountain in the Canaries last January, right?

One of them almost certainly a Hamas assault commander? And we have your photograph of him, in company with two volcanologists from Tehran? And now this—eight months later, Hamas sends a note . . . implies they blew Mount St. Helens. Kinda fits together."

"Well, the coincidence is a little striking. Although I understand you can't just go around blowing up volcanoes. So far as I recall, no one's ever done such a thing. Not in all of history, and volcanoes have a lot of that—thousands of years."

"Yeah, but the last sixty are the only ones that count," said George. "No one had a big enough explosive before that."

"You read anything about nuclear fallout in the Mount St. Helens area?"

"Well, I haven't looked. But we would have been informed if there was any such thing. I'd guess that mountain is still a lot too hot for anyone to make any checks."

"I don't get it," pondered Admiral Morgan. "I cannot believe anyone just planted a bomb in the crater. And anyway, a bomb probably would not have done the job. They don't explode downwards. Surely to blow a volcano, you'd have to burrow down into the ground, way down, and then detonate."

"Christ," said George. "Imagine doing that. Excavating the main lava chimney of a volcano, probably several hundred feet, knowing the damn thing could erupt any moment and fry you."

"How about a missile?" said Arnold suddenly. "How about a missile coming in at high speed with a sharp front end, designed to bang its way into the rock on the floor of the crater?"

"Well, who knows? It would take a pretty wide investigation to find out if such a thing was possible—like how thick was the floor of the crater . . . You know, it might have been impenetrable. And, anyway, where could the missile have come from—I imagine you're not talking ICBM, are you?"

"Well, not from Hamas. God help us if they've got one of those. But I'm thinking maybe a cruise aimed at the crater. Or two. Or three. Or more."

"Fired from?"

"Usual place, George. Possibly that second *Barracuda*, which appears to have vanished off the face of the earth."

"Well, I suppose that's all possible. But with this Administration, we cannot spend a lot of time chasing up theories like that. They're already asking us to downsize every department. There's going to be enormous budget cuts, and they have their own agendas, mostly to do with calling off our worldwide hunt for imaginary terrorists."

"Hmmmm," said Arnie. "Do you think they're going to react in any way to the letter from Hamas?"

"Romney will dismiss it as a hoax. And the President will agree with him. My guess is, it will never get as far as here. Though they might just forward a copy to the CIA."

"How about it isn't a hoax. How about they did hit Mount St. Helens? How about they are in that fucking nuclear submarine, loaded to the gunwales with missiles, planning God knows what? How about they really did send a letter of warning?"

"I guess we'll know soon enough," said George.

"How'dya mean?"

"Well, that letter was unfinished," said George. "'*You don't think Mount St. Helens was an accident,' because it wasn't . . . We did it . . . and what's more . . .*"

George's voice trailed off. "That's what it really said, right?"

"Absolutely. And if the letter has any substance whatsoever, we'll hear again, correct?"

"That's my take on it, Arnie, old buddy."

"Okay. But meanwhile I would like you to ask young Ramshawe to do a bit of sleuthing, check a few things up for me . . . I want to show him the letter, if that's okay by you."

"No problem. I'll walk you down to his office. He's less busy these days. We all are."

The two Admirals finished their coffee and walked down to the office of the Director's assistant. Lieutenant Commander Ramshawe was hunched over a pile of papers, his office much less like a rubbish tip than usual, the clear and obvious sign of a workload reduction.

Everything had changed in the world of international Intelligence. Where once people in the White House and the Pentagon jumped when a single word of warning emanated from Fort Meade, nowadays there was only cynicism. NSA suspicions were dismissed curtly. The new Administration's significant operations staff followed their President's lead—that is, the CIA, the FBI, the Military, and the National Security Agency were comprised of a group of old-fashioned spooks, out of touch with reality, living in a somewhat murky past of Cold Wars, Hot Wars, and random terrorism.

The modern world, at the conclusion of the first decade of the new millennium, was a completely different place. What mattered here was friendship, cooperation, not military buildups, witch-hunts for allegedly corrupt dictators, and truly ferocious attacks by America's Special Forces against those who displeased or ran foul of the United States.

People like old Arnold Morgan, even General Scannell, Admiral Dickson, and certainly Admirals John Bergstrom (SPECWARCOM) and George Morris, were regarded as dinosaurs. Young White House execs had taken to using Jurassic Park as a kind of insider's code name for the great Fort Meade Intelligence complex. The Pentagon's high command were The Psychopaths. And President McBride had served notice that he did not like being surrounded by the Military, not inside his own White House. And this despite the fact that the Navy practically ran the place, the Army providing the cars and drivers, the Defense Department the communications, the Air Force all aircraft, and the Navy the helicopters.

Yes, a President could marginalize the military. And yes, he could dismiss them as irrelevant to his programs. But, as Commander in Chief, he would upset the Admirals and Generals at his own peril. No President of the United States had ever gone quite as far as losing the confidence of the Pentagon.

So far, Charles McBride was only tinkering. But he was already having an effect, and soon young officers like Lt. Comdr. Jimmy Ramshawe might decide the civilian world was beckoning. But not yet.

"G'day, gentlemen," he greeted the two Admirals. And he stood up to shake hands with Admiral Morgan. "Peaceful retirement, sir? Not missing the factory yet?"

Arnold chuckled, amused that Jimmy still remembered he traditionally referred to the White House as "the factory."

Admiral Morris took his leave, saying, "Jimmy, the Admiral wants to have a chat with you. I have to go to that meeting. You needn't bother about it. Stay here and talk to Arnold. He's got some interesting stuff to show you."

"As ever," replied the Lt. Commander, grinning his lopsided Aussie grin. "See you later, sir. Okay, Admiral, I'm all ears."

Arnold Morgan took out the copy of the Hamas letter and handed it over, watching while Jimmy read. "Streuth," he said softly. "That looks to me like these bastards just blew up Mount St. Helens?"

"Maybe," said Arnold, cautiously.

"Well, if they didn't, what's this then?"

"Good question, James. Good question. Although we shouldn't dismiss the straightforward answer that it's just an ordinary hoax, the kind we get from all manner of fucking lunatics, all the time."

"Yeah. But this is a bit subtle for a lunatic, sir. They're apt to write more on the lines of . . . *'Listen to me, assholes. I just blew up the goddamned volcano, and I'm planning to do it again. God's telling me to clean up the planet. Ha Ha Ha.'*"

"I know. That's true. And I'm glad you're getting a feeling of authenticity from this note. Like I am. It's just the way it's phrased. And George jumped on the fact that it seemed like unfinished business . . . *'You thought it was an accident . . . well, it wasn't . . . it was us . . . and we'll be in touch. . . .'* That's its tone. It doesn't say so, but it might as well have ended by stating . . . *'We'll be in touch.'*"

"That's my feeling. No doubt," replied Jimmy.

"Well, to short-circuit a lot of chat," said Arnold, "let's assume they did blow Mount St. Helens. A bomb could not have done it. Which leaves a missile, or missiles.

"As ever, they seemed to come from nowhere. As ever, they must have come from a submarine. You know, specially made cruises, big, sharp-pointed nose cones that would pierce the floor of the crater. So far as I can see, that's the only possibility. So . . . where, Jimmy, is the second *Barracuda*?"

"Hold it, sir. Lemme just jump into the ole computer." He hit several keys, the screen flashed a few times and settled into the file he requested. "Sir, I'll read this stuff off, just the important bits . . . You might want to make a couple of notations while I do it. Here's a notepad and a pen . . . ready?"

"Fire at will," replied the Admiral, easing into the spirit of things.

"July 5, spotted the *Barracuda* making a southerly passage down the Yellow Sea out of Huludao, where she'd been for one month in a covered dock. We got her at 40.42 North 121.20 East heading for the Bo Hai Strait. After that, it's anyone's guess.

"She could have gone through the Korean Strait, or around the outside of Japan, and headed north, south, east, or west. Or even back to Zhanjiang, where she'd been for many months. The satellite shots showed three tiny figures on the bridge. I made a note, hope to Christ one of 'em wasn't Major Ray Kerman, or we're in real trouble!

"She dived as soon as the water was deep enough off South Korea, then vanished. But I have two more notes here . . . on July 16, our SOSUS Station on the island of Attu, far west end of the Aleutians, reported a transient contact to the north, 53.51–175.01 East. They thought it was a nuclear turbine. They also thought it was Russian. Heard a lot of noise, ballast blowing, high revs for one minute. Then nothing.

"But we picked up something on July 22, six days later, precisely consistent with a submarine making a very slow 5-knot passage for 720 miles to the Unimak Pass. It was just a

radar contact . . . five seconds . . . three sweeps on the
screen.

"Then it disappeared. Tell you the truth, sir, I would not
have bothered much. It was just the length of passage, 120
miles a day for six days, average 5 knots, just the exact numbers you would expect from a sneaky little son of a bitch,
right?"

"Running north of the Aleutians, eh?" said the Admiral.
"How about its passage from the Yellow Sea to Attu? Does
that fit a pattern?"

"Hell yes, sir. Ten days, no trouble. I should think they
were moving pretty carefully. It could have been the *Barracuda*. Plus, I checked the boards and there's not another
bloody submarine within a thousand miles, except our own
patrol in the Aleutian Trench."

"I wonder," said Arnold Morgan. "I really wonder. Could
these little bastards really have exploded a massive volcano?
You've got to doubt that. But with this Ray fucking Kerman,
who knows? And he was checking out the most dangerous
volcano in the world when I last saw him!

"Jimmy, I think we want to get in touch with a top volcano
guy and find out once and for all whether it was *possible* to
have exploded Mount St. Helens. Then we want to find out if
there was anything remotely suspicious about that eruption.
Maybe check out the local police and FBI. Then we want to
cast a long look over any major volcano story that appeared
anywhere in the past year. Anything that might show that the
guys we seek are active in the field . . ."

"Sir, we'll have to settle for *one of the top* volcanologists,
rather than *the top* volcanologist."

"We will? Why's that?"

"Because the top man was found murdered in London last
May. He was called Prof. Paul Landon. Washed up in the
middle of the River Thames, some island halfway along the
University Boat Race course according to the *London Daily
Telegraph* . . ."

"Christ," said Arnold. "That sounds bad. Must have been

Chiswick Eyot, just upstream from Hammersmith Bridge—
that's really the only island around there."

Arnold chortled, always pleased to have bamboozled the
young. "I know the river pretty well. A long time ago, I pulled
the bow oar for Annapolis at the Henley Regatta in the
Thames Cup. And a few years later, I did a couple of stints
helping coach the eight."

"Ah, well, Landon was the main man in his field. I don't
believe the police ever did find out who or why. They seemed
to write it off as mistaken identity of some kind. I wouldn't
have been so sure myself. The Professor was executed, two
bullets in the back of his head. Doesn't sound much like an
accident to me."

"Jimmy, have another look at that, will you? Talk to someone about the feasibility of blowing Mount St. Helens. And
find out if anyone had any suspicion whatsoever about the
eruption . . . meanwhile I've gotta go . . . tell George g'bye
and keep him well posted."

"Okay, sir, I'll walk you downstairs."

"No need, kid. I was finding my way in and out of this
place while you were throwing toy tanks across the room."

They both laughed, shook hands, and Admiral Morgan
was gone. Four hours later, a copy of the letter from Hamas
arrived on George Morris's desk. It was direct from the
White House, headed "FYI," and signed by Cyrus Romney.
At the bottom was a note scrawled by hand informing the Admiral that both Cyrus and the President regarded it as an obvious hoax and no action would be necessary, nor should
time be wasted upon investigation.

Admiral Morris, who had been sequestered with Lieutenant Commander Ramshawe for the past two hours, just
muttered, "Oh, I see, Mr. Romney. And that's with the benefit of your entire five months' experience of international terrorism? Asshole."

Meanwhile, down the corridor, Ramshawe was in full cry.
He tackled the London murder first, because they were five

hours ahead and if he needed to call anyone today, he'd have to be quick.

He keyed into the Internet and searched diligently for anything more on the Professor. Found nothing after the report of the body being washed up, and an account in the *Telegraph* about the subsequent Memorial Service in London, attended by Great Britain's heaviest academics. But he'd read that already in the Court and Society Page, a couple of months ago.

He scrolled down into a Web site that pulled up front pages of the *Telegraph*, the *Daily Mail*, the London *Times*, and the *Financial Times*. He'd found it useful before, and he went into each day from May 9, when Professor Landon was first missing.

Jimmy had checked out the *Daily Mail* and the *Telegraph* before, but that was three months ago, when no one else was interested. He was much more thorough now. Whereas last May he had only persisted for a week after the Professor's disappearance, he now went further. And he checked those front pages assiduously.

It was the edition of the *Daily Mail* for May 18 that caught his eye. There was a splash front-page strapline, which read: SCOTLAND YARD BAFFLED BY THE ALBERT HALL MASSACRE.

Beneath this, in three decks of huge end-of-the-world type, set left, it demanded:

WHO KILLED THESE
MEN ON THE NIGHT
OF MAY 8TH?

To the right were three photographs showing Police Constables Peter Higgins and Jack Marlow, and then Professor Paul Landon. A photograph of Roger, the dead German shepherd attack dog, was set much smaller in the center of the page. "GUNNED DOWN: A CRUEL END FOR BRAVE ROGER," was the caption.

Lieutenant Commander Ramshawe almost had a seizure.

The *Daily Mail* had skipped over one highly significant fact: that the Special Branch had been called in to investigate one of the police murders. Jimmy knew there must have been some suspicion of terrorism.

The *Daily Mail* knew something really important, however, of which James Ramshawe had been utterly unaware so far. All three murders may have been committed within a few yards of each other at precisely the same time.

Jimmy sat back and regained his composure. He poured himself a cup of cold coffee and settled down to read every word of the newspaper account.

And slowly, as he read the story, the indisputable facts became clear. On the night of May 8, Professor Landon had delivered his speech at London's Royal Geographical Society, and then headed southwest, towards his car. The vehicle was later found nearby, parked in the precincts of Imperial College off Queens Gate. The Professor had been seen by a member of his audience hurrying through to the wide steps at the rear of the Albert Hall.

That was the last time Lava Landon was seen alive. He never returned home that night, and his body was found in the river six days later on the afternoon of May 14. The police pathologist said he was uncertain of the time or even the day of death, because the body had been in the river for some time.

That same night of the lecture, the two policemen were murdered in the area directly behind the Albert Hall, on the precise route of Professor Landon's walk to his car, at the precise time Professor Landon was there on the wide steps. The *Daily Mail* had shrewdly connected the two and, taking a leaf out of Roger's book, bounded eagerly into the fray, announcing THE ALBERT HALL MASSACRE. There were, after all, three dead bodies. Plus Roger.

Of course, an Intelligence officer would instantly ask the crucial question: Who said the Professor was murdered, like the policemen, on the back steps of the Albert Hall? Plainly the Professor could have been kidnapped and *taken* anywhere, and in the end, *been shot* anywhere. There was not one lick of evidence to suggest he too had died on the steps of the Albert Hall.

Indeed, if he had, the killers would probably have left his body there, together with the policemen.

In Jimmy's opinion, the *Daily Mail* was essentially on the right track. The devastating coincidence of the place and time of the crimes was simply too great. There must have been a connection of some kind, and the big London newspaper had made it, even though Scotland Yard had not been able to come up with a motive.

But, Jimmy thought, chances were that the Professor had been taken alive, and the two cops had been killed for interfering. The question now was: What the hell were the Special Branch doing, involved in a civilian crime?

"Well, it wasn't a bloody kidnap as such, was it," mused Jimmy. "Otherwise there'd have been a ransom demand. Whoever grabbed Landon wanted him for something else. They took him away alive, then killed him later. I'd be bloody certain of that."

He pondered the problem, called someone, and inquired what precisely one had to do to get a hot cup of coffee around here? And was there anyone in residence who cared one way or another whether he carried on trying to save the world, or instead died of thirst. The resident eighth-floor manager of the twenty-four-hour-a-day executive kitchen had a very soft spot for the affable Aussie Lt. Commander, although he secretly believed that Jimmy was becoming more and more like the terrifying Admiral Arnold Morgan every day.

"Be right over, sir . . . Want some cookies or anything?"

"Those are the words of a bloody Christian," replied Jimmy, in his best Aussie accent. "Ship 'em in."

And he put the phone down slowly, still wondering what exactly the New Scotland Yard's Special Branch was doing in the investigation into the London murders.

Not for the first time, he decided to call an old Navy buddy, Rob Hackett, over in the CIA at Langley, just to check if they had anything on the murders. The answer was sharp. Nothing. It was a purely British domestic crime and the CIA had made no inquiries.

Jimmy's pal couldn't help with the question of the Special Branch, but he immediately agreed to make a few calls. Within forty-five minutes, Rob was back.

"Ve-e-e-e-ry eeeenteresting," said the CIA man slowly, impersonating Hercule Poirot, or some other European gumshoe. "The Special Branch were in there because of the manner of death inflicted on one of the policemen . . . Not the one who was shot, like the woofer. The other one whose skull was split."

"Yeah?" said Jimmy. "I didn't even know his skull was split."

"And how," said Rob. "Straight down the middle of his forehead, like he'd been hit with a fucking ax. And then we have the e-e-e-e-nteresting part. What killed him was a terrific punch under his nose, which drove the bone directly into his brain. It was a blow, according to my guy in London, that could *only* have been delivered by a trained Special Forces expert in unarmed combat. That's why the Special Branch was in there. Plus four antiterrorist guys. Scotland Yard never announced one word of this."

Jimmy Ramshawe froze in his chair. "Have we been here before, Rob?"

"We surely have. Last year. That Member of Parliament, Rupert someone, was killed in exactly the same way. Though with less of a long fracture of the forehead."

"No wonder the antiterrorist guys were in there," said Jimmy. "Hey, Rob, thanks a million . . ."

"Okay, Jim," chuckled the CIA man. "Now don't go rushing in there and adding up two and two to make six."

"Not me, old mate. I'm about to add things up to at least four hundred, maybe more." He slowly replaced the receiver, blew out his cheeks, and expelled the air noisily—the universal sound of utter amazement.

"Holy shit," he said to the otherwise empty room. "That

fucking Lava Landon was grabbed by Major Ray Kerman. I think. Told him how to blow up a volcano. And he's just bloody done it. And what's more, he's just *TOLD* us he's bloody done it. *H-O-L-Y SHI-I-I-T!! . . ."*

He steadied himself, cooled down his excitement. Thoughts rampaged through his mind . . . *What do I do first? Call George? Call Admiral Morgan? Write a report? Stand on my fucking head? Have another cup of coffee? How urgent is this? Hold it, Jim . . . get into control . . .*

He'd been given three tasks by Admiral Morgan, and he'd done two of them—checked out the volcano stories and checked out the Special Branch involvement. Scored a bull's-eye both times.

Conclusion: Professor Paul Landon, the world's leading volcanologist, was snatched in London by Major Kerman and his men. In the course of this operation, they had to kill two interfering policemen and one attack dog. Kerman then grilled and subsequently executed the Professor. Three months later, on behalf of Hamas, the ex–SAS Major calmly informed the U.S. he had blown up Mount St. Helens.

The third, and only, outstanding task Jimmy had left was to check with the Washington State police whether there was anything to suggest a missile had been fired into the bloody crater near the top of the mountain.

With the West Coast three hours back, he picked up the phone and asked the operator to connect him to someone in the State Police HQ who had firsthand knowledge of the Mount St. Helens dossier. It took a while to make the call, because the highly trained Fort Meade operator went from person to person until he found a trooper likely to satisfy a high-level investigator from the National Security Agency. Then they had to call back to verify the validity of the call from the NSA.

When Jimmy picked up the phone, a voice said, "Sir, this is Officer Ray Suplee speaking. How can I help?"

"Officer, this is Lt. Comdr. Jimmy Ramshawe, assistant to

the Director of the National Security Agency at Fort Meade, Maryland. May I assume you were involved in the immediate report on the Mount St. Helens disaster?"

"Yes, sir. I was on patrol along Route 12 heading south towards the mountain when it erupted. It happened pretty quick, and I could see it from a high point in the road. I heard it too. Huge blast, followed by wind, and the sky seemed full of ashes, blocked the sun right out."

"Did you get in close?"

"No, sir. No one could. It was too hot. We realized real soon that anyone caught close to the mountain could not have survived the blast, and the heat, and, 10 minutes later, the molten lava. Our task became one of containment . . . leading in the fire trucks to douse the forest . . . getting people to evacuate their homes where we thought the forest fire was spreading. Almost no one who was anywhere near the actual eruption could possibly have lived to talk about it."

"I understand, Officer. I guess there was more time to get clear in 1980?"

"Oh, definitely. They were working on an evacuation program for several days before it finally erupted. This time there wasn't a New York minute. Damn thing just blew. Without warning . . ."

"Officer, you said *almost* no one who was in close lived. Did you mean that? Or did you mean *absolutely* no one?"

"Sir, I meant *almost*. Because there was a wagonload of outdoor sportsmen who somehow did get clear. Four of them, three of them local. But I never heard tell of anyone else."

"Did you interview them?"

"No, sir. I heard it on the radio, 'bout four hours after the blast. One of them was a well-known broadcaster, Don McKeag, 'Voice of the Northwest.' Everyone listens to him, but not usually on Sundays. He's a weekday guy, you know, the eight-in-the-morning slot to eleven, regular news and politics."

"Did he have much to say?"

"Plenty. Described in big detail how they got away, racing through the burning forest, trying to stay ahead of the fires . . . It was like listening to a thriller."

"Did these guys actually hear the first eruption?"

"Oh sure. They were camped in the foothills of the summit. They said about a mile and quarter from the peak."

"Did Don mention how they made such a fast break for safety?"

"He did. One of the four was a pretty well known Washington State finance guy. Mr. Tilton, President of the Seattle National Bank. Tony Tilton. Apparently he'd been on a yacht in the Caribbean when that volcano blew up and damn nearly destroyed the entire island, maybe ten, twelve, years ago?"

"Montserrat?"

"That's it, sir. Mr. Tilton was watching that from a few miles offshore. Boat got covered in ash, he was washing it down with a hose. Anyway, he knew better than anyone how darned quick you have to be to get away from an erupting volcano."

"Sounds like a big scoop for Don."

"Hell, yes. But there was one thing I heard Mr. Tilton mention on the program that I thought was a little offbeat. He said he heard the mountain erupt three times, way up there in the crater. But before the first one, he heard a strange gust of wind, above the lake, kinda through the mist.

"I don't know. Didn't seem to connect to me. A high wind doesn't set off a volcano, does it? And he wouldn't have made anything like that up, not Mr. Tilton. He's a very well-respected guy in Washington. Some folks say he might run for governor."

"Officer, could you arrange for me to speak to Mr. Tilton?"

"Certainly, sir. I'll get on to the bank right away and get back to you with a time."

"Thanks for that," said Jimmy. "You've been a real help."

"Okay, sir. I'll be right back on the line."

Lieutenant Commander Ramshawe replaced the telephone thoughtfully. Had Tony Tilton actually heard a couple of low-flying cruise missiles heading for the fractured crater of Mount St. Helens?

It did not take long to find out. Five minutes later, State Trooper Ray Suplee was back. "Twenty minutes, sir. Mr. Tilton will be waiting on this line—"

Jimmy jotted down the number and decided to wait until he had completed his three-part investigation before he told Admiral Morris what he suspected. He took his watch off and propped it up in front of him—a habit he'd copied from his father—then carefully wrote up his notes.

At precisely 6:10 P.M., he punched in the number and was instantly connected to an ivory-colored telephone 2,800 miles away, in a spacious air-conditioned office tower in downtown Seattle, where it was only 3:10 in the afternoon.

"Tilton," said a voice, at the end of a private line.

"G'day, Mr. Tilton. This is Lieutenant Commander Ramshawe. I'm assistant to the Director of the National Security Agency at Fort Meade, Maryland. I believe you were expecting my call . . ."

"I was. Heard from the State Police about twenty minutes ago. What can I tell you?—It has to be about the volcano; there's never been so many people wanting to chat to me, all on the same subject."

Then the Lieutenant Commander got down to the heart of the matter. "The state trooper told me you'd given a radio interview and you mentioned a high wind just before the blast?"

"Almost. What I heard, in sequence, was this strange, sudden whoosh of air, right above the lake, in the mist. It was the kind of sound you get in an old house in the middle of a rainstorm . . . You know, when a strong wind suddenly rises and makes that kinda creepy wailing noise. Except there was hardly a breath of wind on the lake that morning. Just that sudden rush of air."

"Anyone else hear it?"

"No. I was the only one who heard it. I actually looked up, out over the water, it was such an unusual noise."

"Then what?"

"Seconds later, I'm talking maybe ten seconds, there was this dull, muffled thumping sound from way up the mountain. That really got my attention, and Donnie's. As you know, I'm jumpy about volcanoes, after Montserrat, and we got the other two out of the tents. Then I heard it again, 'bout a minute later . . . that wind. Followed by another more obvious explosion. Way high up."

"Did you hear a fourth explosion?"

"No. But we sure felt it. The whole area kinda shuddered. And then the sky became overcast . . . and all this burning stuff was falling into the trees. The first fire we saw, out on the right, was way up ahead, maybe a half mile. That's how far the debris was being blasted. We were on the road by then . . . I'd say a good six miles away from the mountain . . ."

"Mr. Tilton," Jimmy said, "I can't thank you enough. You've been a real help."

"No problem, Lieutenant Commander," replied the bank President. "But tell me, why is the National Security Agency interested in a plain act of God?"

"Oh, just a routine checkup. We always take a look at these things. You know, earthquakes, major fires, tidal waves . . . Thanks for your help, Mr. Tilton."

1130, Tuesday, August 18
The White House.

President McBride, a slim, lanky man, with receding curly gray-brown hair, was irritated. A few moments earlier, he had been looking forward to his salad, and now this. A detailed three-page memorandum direct from Jurassic Park—copy to Cyrus Romney—outlining the possibility that a person or persons unknown had blown up Mount St. Helens from a submarine apparently parked several hundred miles away, on the bottom of the goddamned Pacific Ocean.

Absurd, and precisely the kind of harebrained, quasimilitary scare-mongering the President had vowed to eradicate. *Years and years wasted on lunatic military adventures, billions of dollars of taxpayers' money, chasing shadows, witch-hunting spies, Reagan and Bush, threatening people, bombing people . . . and for what?*

President McBride's views were well known. He considered the prospect of war, any war, unthinkable. He'd been known to say, "If we've got to fight in order to retain our place in the modern world, we ought to opt out and become isolationist."

The President held up the memorandum he had just skimmed through, shook his head, and resisted the temptation to toss it in the bin. Cyrus had even told Fort Meade to waste no time on it. Of course they'd done the exact opposite, and now this. He hit the button requesting his National Security Adviser to come in and discuss the matter. He always felt better when he was chatting with Cyrus. Old friends, they had marched shoulder to shoulder in Washington protesting Middle Eastern wars. They were both "enlightened," not stuck in the gloomy, antagonistic past.

Cyrus tapped lightly on the door, and entered. "Hi, Mr. President," he said, cheerfully. "And what awful turmoil has this uncaring world visited upon you today?" Cyrus wrote poetry in his spare time.

"This, old buddy," replied the man in the Big Chair. "This deranged bullshit from Jurassic Park. They think there's some kind of monster from *Waterworld* groping about on the bottom of the Pacific Ocean, pushing buttons and letting off our American volcanoes. Can you believe this crap?"

"To be honest, I've only just got to my mail. I assume they copied me?"

"Yes. They have. It's based on that hoax letter about Mount St. Helens. Admiral Morris seems to think that there might be someone out there firing cruise missiles at Washington State."

"Jesus Christ," said Cyrus. "Those guys! They should've been novelists."

"All I know is there are two gigantic U.S. Navy bases in Washington State, and now these clowns at Fort Meade are telling me that despite several trillion dollars of surveillance equipment sweeping Puget Sound and all points west—on the water, above the water, and under the water—there's a damn great nuclear submarine prowling around underneath our ships, firing stuff at volcanoes. Now, am I missing something, or is this a load of horseshit on an almost unprecedented scale?"

"Well, I haven't read it yet, Charlie. But it does sound kind of far-fetched."

"The gist of the thing is that some terrorist organization snatched a volcanologist in the street in London last May, and then murdered him. They think he told Hamas how to erupt dormant volcanoes, and they may have done it a couple of weeks ago, right here in the U.S.A."

"Did they catch the murderers? Any charges? Evidence?"

"Hell, no. The Brits never caught anyone. But Fort Meade seems to think that there was some Middle East connection."

"Well, what do they want us to do about it?"

"They want the entire U.S. Navy on high alert, and they want their theories to be taken seriously. They want us to believe these guys are for real, and that they do know how to blow up volcanoes."

"Those guys at Ford Meade are nuts. You do know that, don't you? You want me to draft a reply to them?"

"That's more or less what I had in mind. And, Cy . . . for Christ's sake, tell them to avoid these rabble-rousing scare stories. They don't do a lick of good to anyone."

"Okay, Chief. I'll read this and get it done."

Cyrus left, and later that afternoon, Admiral George Mor-

ris received his sardonic reply to the threatening scenario
he'd presented to them that morning.

*Dear Admiral Morris—I am sorry you chose to ignore
my advice about that hoax Hamas letter sent to Arnold
Morgan. As you know, my judgment was then, and remains now, that it was simply a ludicrous declaration
involving the power of God. I expect you have noticed,
those who are truly deranged typically invoke the
power of the Almighty, especially when laying claim to
global disasters.*

*I have conferred with the President on this matter,
and his view reflects mine, mainly that there is not one
shred of hard evidence connecting any Middle Eastern
Terrorist with those London murders. And it is difficult
to see how you manage then to conclude that before he
died, Professor Landon wrote out some kind of a world
volcano-eruption guide and handed it over to a bunch
of Arab freedom fighters.*

*Certainly there is not enough serious evidence here
to accept the implications of what is nothing but a
crank letter.*

*Sorry, Admiral. The President is adamant. We are
unconvinced.*

*Remember, always, we are spending the taxpayers'
money, and they voted President McBride in, precisely
to avoid the obvious financial excesses of the Armed
Services. Today, in the Third Millennium, people want
a say in how their money is spent.*

Sincerely—Cyrus Romney.

Lieutenant Commander Ramshawe looked up at his boss
in disbelief.

"We're up against it here, old son," Admiral Morris said.

"Right up against it. They're against us before they start,
before they even read our opinions and advice."

"Do we let the Big Man know the state of the battle?"

"Absolutely. We tell him the full details of our investigation. And we also tell General Scannell. I don't mind being ridiculed by the President and his know-nothing National Security Adviser. But if I happen to believe that President is willfully putting our country in danger, then it is my duty to blow a few whistles. He might be the President, but he's only a goddamned politician. And he's not here for long.

"We belong to a permanent organization that is here specifically to keep the United States of America safe. Mostly, we do what the President wishes. But there is a line, and he steps across that line only at grave peril to himself."

"You think he just did?" asked Jimmy.

"I read your report, Lieutenant Commander. I *know* he just did."

Admiral Morris and his assistant got lucky again. Jimmy Ramshawe called Arnold Morgan at home and requested a private meeting as soon as possible on a matter that Admiral Morris regarded as a "supreme priority."

"Can't it wait until tomorrow?" asked the ex–National Security Adviser.

"Yes. It could. But Admiral Morris believes we should meet NOW, and you know he doesn't get overexcited on a regular basis."

Admiral Morgan did know that. And he paused for a moment before saying, "Look, Jimmy. I'm taking Kathy out this evening to her favorite little restaurant in Georgetown. I can't cancel at this late hour, so I suppose you and your boss better join us."

"Are you sure, sir?" said an utterly delighted Jimmy Ramshawe.

"No, I'm not. But you've cornered me. Le Bec Fin. I expect you know where it is. I've seen John Peacock there a few times."

"Yes, sir," replied Jimmy. "Went there for Jane's birthday. What time would you like to see us?"

"Eight bells. End of the Last Dog Watch, and don't be late."

"No, sir," said Jimmy, laughing to himself at the old submariner's unending sense of humor, so often disguised as a growling commanding officer's impatience.

At 8 P.M. precisely, the staff car from Fort Meade pulled up outside the restaurant. They found Arnold and Kathy sitting opposite each other in a wide, comfortable private booth towards the rear of the main dining room. George was placed next to the Admiral, Jimmy next to Kathy.

"I'm really sorry, about this," said the young Lieutenant Commander, "but I have to give a short document to Admiral Morgan to read before we can talk. It's about three pages long, and it's not my fault—the culprit for this awkwardness is sitting right opposite me, and he's too big a cheese to argue with."

That rather skillfully broke any ice that might have been hanging around after the enforced invitation. Arnold and Kathy both laughed, and the Admiral poured four glasses of white Burgundy for them. He never was much for asking people what they wanted to drink. As with most things, he felt he knew best. And, as with most things, he was usually right. The pale-gold Burgundy was excellent, from the Domaine Chandon de Briailles, a 1998 Pernand-Vergelesses blanc. Jimmy Ramshawe knew what he inelegantly described as a real "snorto deluxe" when he tasted it.

"My oath, this is a great glass of wine, sir," he ventured.

"Silence, Ramshawe. I'm reading."

"Yes, sir."

It took the Admiral about five minutes to finish the report on the eruption of Mount St. Helens. And when he did so, he took a Navy-sized gulp of his wine. "Mother of God," he breathed. "Our old friend Major Kerman again. And by the sound of this, he's only just started. The volcano was just a sideshow, or he wouldn't have sent that self-congratulatory letter to me, would he?"

"No, he would not," said George Morris. "In my opinion, we'll be hearing from him again."

"And mine," said Arnold. "But meantime, where the hell is he? Because I agree with Jimmy, I think we heard that damn creeping *Barracuda*, twice, north of the Aleutians. And a few days later, what sounds like a very reliable man hears a couple of guided missiles bearing down on Mount St. Helens, seconds before the entire thing explodes. That'll do for me, it's Kerman, and he's out there, under the water, planning God knows what."

"That'll do for me as well," replied George. "However, it will not do for our President and his main adviser." At which point he handed Arnold a copy of the letter he had received from Cyrus Romney.

Again Arnold read, in obvious alarm. "Everything I ever feared about a soft, left-wing President," he said. "All on one page, written by one of the greatest assholes on this planet. Jesus Christ. Romney's a goddamned flower child dressed up in a suit. The *New York Times* published one of his godawful poems last month. Goddamnit, we've got the Wordsworth of the White House guiding the defenses of the United States against one of the most dangerous terrorists we've ever encountered . . . *A host of golden daffodils . . . Season of mists and mellow fruitfulness . . .*"

"Darling, those happen to be the lines of two different poets," interjected Kathy.

"Excellent," said the Admiral. "I happen to be dealing with two different assholes."

Lieutenant Commander Ramshawe came remarkably close to shooting 1998 Pernand-Vergelesses down his nose, but the waiter arrived at that precipitous moment and deflected everyone's attention to the menu.

"I think we need another five minutes," said Arnold, and immediately returned to the subject at hand. "George," he said. "First I want to congratulate Jimmy on an outstanding example of detective work. And secondly, I want to tell you that I have never been more nervous of the men who occupy the key Administration seats in the White House.

"The letter to you from this Romney character is, in my

view, nothing short of a disgrace. The head of our National Security Agency, an Admiral and former Commander of a United States Navy Carrier Battle Group? I'm absolutely shocked. But all that pales before the real problem. And that's the reluctance of this Administration to act in the true interests of this nation.

"Even if the President does not believe it personally, he has to face up to the truth that these terrorists may already have killed maybe a hundred of our citizens up in Washington State. And that dismissal of the facts may mean that Charles McBride is in serious breach of his oaths of office."

"So what do we do?"

"For the moment, we keep very quiet. But I do want to alert General Scannell and Admiral Dickson. If something as serious as this is really happening, I want to ensure that the proper authorities are up to speed. We probably should tell 'em to keep a weather eye out for a slow Russian nuclear, anywhere along our West Coast waters."

"Arnie, what would you recommend we do if we locate that *Barracuda* somewhere in the Pacific offshore, but maybe not strictly in our national waters?"

"Sink it, George," replied the Admiral. "Sink that son of a bitch, hopefully in damn deep water. No questions asked. Deny all knowledge."

"Right on, sir," said Jimmy, grinning. "That's the spirit." And all three of them, at that moment, wished to high heaven that Admiral Morgan was still in his old office in the West Wing.

Midday, Tuesday, August 18 (Local)
The Pacific Ocean, 24.30N 113.00W.

The *Barracuda* cruised slowly south-southwest, following the coastline of the U.S.A. and then Mexico, about 500 miles offshore, 600 feet below the surface. She had stayed farther west while they ran the gauntlet of the huge U.S. Naval Base in San Diego, then angled left, moving inshore.

There was apparently no one searching for her. They heard no transmissions and made none themselves. They had not surfaced for more than a week, and were now running parallel with the great 800-mile-long Mexican peninsula of Baja California. Indeed, they were heading in the direction of the Tropic of Cancer, just about opposite the most southerly headland of the peninsula.

Ahead of them was an 8,000-mile-long haul, all down the west coast of South America, around Cape Horn and up the Atlantic. At their current speed of only five knots, this would take more than two months. But the ocean ahead of them was lonely, largely unpatrolled by the U.S. Navy, and not heavily photographed by the U.S. satellites.

Down there, along the wild and woolly coastline of Peru and then Chile, they could make much better speed. They could wind those big turbines up to perhaps 15 knots in very, very deep water, where the southern Pacific shelves down steeply west of the colossal mountain range of the high, craggy Andes.

General Rashood spent the day, along with everyone else, in a watchful but relaxed mood. He and Shakira dined together quite late in the evening, while Ben Badr had the ship. And Shakira went to bed at around midnight.

It was almost two o'clock in the morning when Ravi ordered the *Barracuda* to periscope depth. They came sliding up out of the black depths and immediately raised their ESM mast.

They made no report to the satellite. They just sent a fast signal of a couple of words in the six seconds their mast remained visible.

Saladin Two.

6

0130, Wednesday, August 19
Bandar Abbas Naval Base
Hormuz Strait, Iran.

THE SATELLITE SIGNAL from General Rashood arrived exactly on time. And Admiral Mohammed Badr received it with some relief. They were still operational. And his beloved son, Ben, was safe.

The sealed documents in the package next to the telephone were almost burning a hole through his desk. The Admiral rose swiftly and stepped out into the night. A staff car drove him out of the base on the north road, and then swung sharply west down to the airport, less than two miles from his office.

Already on the runway, its engines howling, was a small private jet from Syrian Arab Airlines. Admiral Badr's car took him right up to the aircraft and he handed the package personally to the pilot.

Then he stood and watched the little jet scream into the dark, hot skies, banking northwest for the 1,200-mile journey across the Gulf, along the Saudi–Iraqi border to Jordan, and then north up to Damascus.

A Lieutenant Commander from the Iranian Navy would be awaiting it, and he would drive the package personally to the Saudi Embassy on Al-Jala'a Avenue. From there it would be placed in the Kingdom's Diplomatic Bag to the Syrian Embassy at 2215 Wyoming Avenue NW, Washington, D.C.

One way or the other, that's a package just about impossible to trace. It would arrive in the White House mail room delivered by the Special Diplomatic Courier Service, addressed to the President of the United States. Official. Very Official. But origins unknown.

Admiral Badr was rather proud—and rightly so—of the circuitous route he had planned for its arrival in the Oval Office.

1100, Friday, August 21
The White House.

President McBride's Chief of Staff, "Big" Bill Hatchard, former underachieving defensive lineman for Yale University, tapped lightly on the door of the Oval Office. The President was on the phone, but Bill was used to waiting for the former Rhode Island Congressman, having served him on the Hill, driven him, written for him, protected him, and finally headed up his campaign for the Presidency. Charlie McBride treated him like a brother.

Finally, he heard the old familiar call, "C'mon in, Bill, what's going on?"

Bill entered, clutching the package from the Navy Base at Bandar Abbas, which he had opened and skipped through. Only packages that the President's aides deemed of unusual importance went directly to the White House Chief of Staff. And this one looked highly important, having arrived by diplomatic courier, marked for the specific attention of the President: PRIVATE AND CONFIDENTIAL.

Nothing, however, got past Big Bill Hatchard en route to the Chief Executive. As opposed to his fairly disastrous football career, he could stop anything or anyone from his West Wing office. "Safe Hands" Hatchard, that was Bill.

But this morning, a worried frown clouded his big, broad,

usually cheery face. It was an expression mightily familiar to all his colleagues on the Yale bench, but it was seen much less in the White House. Part of Bill's Presidential brief was to keep morale high throughout the building, to jolly people along, to play down the stress, to make light of any problems.

"Whatever you've got in your hand, young William, is giving you cause for grave concern," said the Chief. "If it's anything less than a direct death threat, I'm going to find it necessary to lighten your mood."

Bill laughed, thinly. "Sir, it might be a whole lot worse than a death threat. And I would like you at least to read through it—it's only two pages. Mind if I have a splash of this coffee?"

"Help yourself, buddy, and get one for me too, will you? Meanwhile, I'll take a glance at the ill tidings you bring me."

> *Mr. President:*
> *You will by now have realized that the eruption of Mount St. Helens was not an accident. It was indeed perpetrated by the freedom fighters of Hamas, as I intimated in my communiqué to Admiral Morgan. I am now ready to lay out my demands, which you must obey, in order to prevent us from destroying the entire Eastern Seaboard of the United States of America, including Boston, New York, and Washington.*
>
> *We intend to do this by causing the greatest tidal wave this world has seen in living memory.*
>
> *We estimate the wave will be approximately 150 feet high when it rolls through New York Harbor and straight through Wall Street, until it engulfs Manhattan. It will almost certainly keep going for 20 miles inland across New Jersey, before finally breaking and sucking back over the land towards the coast. However, it will be followed by another wave similar in height and then another. Possibly a total of fifteen in all, each of them more than 80 feet in height.*
>
> *No city could possibly withstand such an impact from*

the ocean, and I fear there will be little left of your eastern seaboard when this mega-tsunami is finally over.

You may be doubting our capability to cause such havoc. But it is quite simple, it has happened several times in the history of our planet.

There are various places where such an effect on the ocean could be caused, but we have chosen one which could not fail. I am sure you will agree that if we can explode the biggest volcano in the United States, we can probably arrange a large rockfall into the deserted ocean. Have no doubt, Mr. President.

Which brings me to the objective of this letter. In order to prevent us from carrying out this threat, you will undertake the following actions:

1) You will evacuate all U.S. military personnel, and remove all stockpiled artillery, bombs, missiles, ammunitions, and other materials of war from your illegal bases in Kuwait, Saudi Arabia, Qatar, Oman, United Arab Emirates, and Djibouti. All warships and aircraft will leave Bahrain and the British-owned base at Diego Garcia. All three of your Carrier Battle Groups, and all other Naval forces afloat in the Gulf of Iran and neighboring seas, will depart the area immediately. You will remove aircraft and support equipment from the Turkish Air Base at Incirlik.

Our time frame is not flexible. We expect to see immediate movement of troops, ships, and aircraft within seven days. We expect final withdrawal to be complete within six weeks, even if this means abandoning matériel.

2) There will be immediate recognition by the Israeli Government of an Independent, Democratic, and Sovereign State of Palestine, based in the territories of the West Bank and the Gaza Strip, occupied by Israeli forces on and since June 4, 1967. There will also be agreement to take immediate steps to withdraw all Is-

raeli troops from the occupied territories. We also require an immediate undertaking from the Government of the United States to make Israel comply with the Hamas demands without delay.

Failure to comply with the above conditions will mean the certain destruction of your great cities of Boston, New York, and Washington, D.C., as well as the remainder of the East Coast of the United States.

We are assuming you receive this document on August 21. You have until midnight, Thursday, October 8, to enter the final stages of your total evacuation from the Middle East. Unless we see clear signs that this is happening, we shall cause the tsunami within twenty-four hours of that date.

I am certain your experts will confirm for you the absolute feasibility of our intentions. We are perfectly capable of causing a landslide, sometime on October 9, 2009.

Do not delay. With the great Allah fighting with us, we wish you out of the Middle East forever. Only He can grant us victory. We will stop at nothing to achieve our objectives.

—Hamas

President McBride sighed. "Bob," he said, "this letter is from a nutcase. He came up with the bright idea of claiming to have exploded Mount St. Helens—after the fact, of course. Which anyone could have done.

"Then he used the absurd notion that someone might have believed him, in order to press home these outrageous demands. But I doubt even he is crazy enough to think we might start evacuating the entire military force of the United States from the most volatile part of the world. Just because he has threatened to drown New York City."

"I guess so, sir," replied Hatchard. "But, Christ . . . you don't suppose this guy *could* be for real, do you?"

"Hell, no. Let me tell you something. Anytime there is a natural disaster—volcano, earthquake, flood, fire, or famine—you get a spate of letters from deranged people claiming to have caused it, started it, inspired it, or forecast it.

"Billy, no one takes notice of these crank communications. It's not as if someone called the day before and announced, *I'm going to blow Mount St. Helens tomorrow at around 7:30 in the morning*. And then did it. Because that might prove pretty difficult. Nutcases like this wait till something happens, and then say, *Oh, right, that was me.*"

"Okay, sir. If that's your decision. Meantime, you want me to have this letter copied and sent around to various interested parties in the military and in Intelligence, maybe the Defense Secretary, Secretary of State, perhaps?"

"I don't think that's necessary, Bob."

"Okay, sir. But a word of caution. In the million-to-one chance that someone actually did explode Mount St. Helens, and is now planning to drown the East Coast, how about I just circulate this document, with a short cover letter? You know, informing people you are inclined to dismiss the entire thing as a hoax? But you are open to guidance? That way, we've covered our asses. I know it's not going to happen, but if it should, well, then, it won't be your fault. It's the useless military for not taking care of it in the early stages . . . In politics, always cover your ass . . . right, sir? You stick that document in a file, and then it happens, there's no one to blame but you. Why take that chance? Trust me, sir, let's cover our ass . . ."

"Okay, buddy. But if we suddenly have the entire office filled with raging Admirals and Generals champing at the goddamned bit to attack Arabs, I'll blame you."

"Fine, sir. You can do that."

Bob Hatchard retreated and had copies made of the Bandar Abbas letter. He dictated a short memo to each recipient that read:

The President believes this to be either a hoax, or from a straightforward crank. He notes the writer's claim to have erupted Mount St. Helens did not come until a few days AFTER *the event, and has asked me to inform you that, at this time, as Commander in Chief, he has no intention of evacuating our entire military presence from the Middle East as requested.*

Nonetheless, he wanted you to see this, for what it's worth, and he will keep you informed, should there be a further communiqué.

Sincerely,
Bill Hatchard, Chief of Staff.

The document was sent to the Secretary of Defense and the Secretary of State, who both agreed entirely with their leader. It was also sent to Admiral Morris, who did not; to General Tim Scannell, who had read Lt. Comdr. Jimmy Ramshawe's brief, and to Adm. Alan Dickson, the Chief of Naval Operations, who, in agreement with Scannell, most definitely did not go along with the President's assessment.

Adm. Arnold Morgan was not on Bill Hatchard's circulation list. But he received a copy by courier from George Morris. Alan Dickson sent a copy to Adm. Dick Greening (Commander in Chief, Pacific Fleet, CINCPACFLT), to Rear Adm. Freddie Curran (Commander, Submarines, Pacific Fleet, COMSUBPAC), and to Rear Adm. John Bergstrom (Commander Special War Command, SPECWARCOM).

By midafternoon (EDT), all high-ranking U.S. Navy personnel with major responsibilities in the Pacific operational area had been instructed to read the Ramshawe brief, *before* reading the latest communiqué from Hamas.

To a man, they considered the coincidences to be too great. There was, no doubt, ample evidence for linking the assumed Hamas terrorist leader Major Ray Kerman to the current volcano problem. According to Ramshawe, Admiral Morgan had actually photographed Kerman in company with leading Iranian volcanologists, on top of Cumbre Vieja, which most realized after reading Ramshawe's brief was the most likely target for the kind of event threatened in the letter.

Meanwhile, it did seem likely that the second *Barracuda* might be creeping, at that moment, quietly through the eastern Pacific right off America's West Coast. Or, alternatively, beating a rapid path around Cape Horn into the Atlantic, making straight for the towering, unstable southwest coast of La Palma in the Canaries. If a collective response had been possible from the concerned military, it would have undoubtedly been along the lines of *H-O-L-Y S-H-I-I-I-T!!!*

President or no President, General Scannell, Chairman of the Joint Chiefs, called an emergency conference in the Pentagon for Monday morning, August 24, at 1030. This was strictly military, highly classified, and the General also invited Admirals Morgan and Morris, plus the young "Sherlock Holmes of Fort Meade," Lt. Comdr. Jimmy Ramshawe.

The task was fivefold: one, to examine the letter from Hamas and call in an expert to judge the psychological condition of the writer; two, to appreciate the situation and discuss a possible plan of defense against an attack on the volcano of Cumbre Vieja; three, to discuss the possibility of the terrorists going for any target other than Cumbre Vieja; four, to hold preliminary discussions on the possible evacuation of New York City, Boston, and Washington; and five, to make recommendations to the President of the United States for immediate civilian action in those cities.

General Scannell called Admiral Morris and requested he bring data with him outlining the basic requirements a terrorist might need for knocking down a high, four-mile-long granite cliff. Also, it would be useful to have an American expert from one of the universities to explain the ramifications of such a landslide, perhaps to offer expert opinion on the real-time chances of a mega-tsunami developing.

He booked lunch tomorrow, Saturday, with Arnold Morgan, Admiral Dickson, and the visiting Rear Admiral Curran, to try to assess a Navy operational plan in the eastern Atlantic, almost certainly to surround the west coast of La

Palma with a U.S. battle group with state-of-the-art surface-to-air missile capability.

General Scannell broke with long-standing Pentagon tradition by inviting the retired Admiral Morgan to chair the lunchtime meeting on the basis of his considerable experience as a strategist and a Commanding Officer, and by virtue of his months-long involvement with the terrorist volcano threat.

Admiral Morgan accepted, pretending to be put out, protesting that he was supposed to be retired, enjoying himself hugely.

"Aren't you?" asked Admiral Dickson, handing over a preliminary chart of the deep waters around La Palma.

"You bet I am," replied Arnold, glaring at the detailed map of the ocean depths. "Now where we gonna find these fucking underwater towelheads?"

The great man hadn't lost his touch, no doubt of that, and the three senior officers who sat at the table with him, in General Scannell's private conference room, all felt a stab of nostalgia for the old days, of not so long ago, when the world was a simpler place.

As recently as one year previous, this meeting would not have taken place privately, on a Saturday. It would have happened in the West Wing's Situation Room in the White House, with the full backing and probably the attendance of a President who believed in these men. This was different. The meeting was on the verge of being subversive. The current President did not trust their judgment.

"I think we all accept that if Mount St. Helens was deliberately exploded, it was hit probably by a broadside of cruise missiles coming through the early morning fog. Correct?" Admiral Morgan was swiftly arranging his ducks in a line.

Everyone nodded.

"Those missiles must have been fired from a submarine, which we photographed leaving the Yellow Sea, and was picked up twice, north of the Aleutians. No other submarine in the entire world fits the pattern, and every one of them is accounted for. The dates fit. The speed fits. And the possible attack on Mount St. Helens fits.

"Also, we have the perfect witness—a highly reliable, highly respected Seattle Bank President standing at the foot of the mountain. He's a banker and a lawyer, paid to have suspicions, but not reckless imagination."

Admiral Morgan paused. "Gentlemen, that's not 100 percent, cast-iron fact. But it is way, way too strong to be dismissed. Agreed?"

Everyone nodded again.

"And therefore," continued the Admiral, "in light of the letter received from Hamas, we must face the possibility that there is a boatload of Middle Eastern terrorists determined to bang a big hole in the face of a cliff of La Palma. Militarily, any other line of thought is childish. That's what we're for, goddamnit. To keep this country safe. And we have no right to go around making half-assed assumptions that it might not happen. And I think it will happen, unless we can get between their fucking missile and that cliff."

"Correct," said General Scannell. "I hope we are all agreed on that . . . gentlemen?" Once more, Admirals Dickson and Curran nodded their agreement.

"And for the purposes of this meeting," said General Scannell, "we should concentrate on how we catch 'em. Which is unlikely to be easy. We learned that the hard way."

"Essentially, we're looking for a submarine-launched cruise missile," said Admiral Dickson. "I suspect not a big ICBM that we would pick up a long way out. I'd say it's a cruise, probably to be fired at around a 500-mile range. You can fire 'em from 1,000 miles, but that would give us too long to locate it. They'll want to be in closer than that, maybe only 250 miles . . . 25 minutes up range from the target. No nearer. Freddie?"

The Pacific Fleet submarine chief was frowning. "That's likely to add up to one hell of a lot of water, sir," he said. "If we take a best-case distance of a 500-mile north–south line, up and down the La Palma coast . . . forming a box out into the Atlantic from both ends . . . with the Cumbre Vieja volcano in the middle . . . then take a spot 500 miles due west of the mountain, we're talking probably 200,000 square miles of ocean. If the *Barracuda* stands any farther offshore, it's a whole lot more. But that way, we'd have more time to locate an incoming cruise . . ."

He paused for a moment, then added, "If I were trying to launch and get away, I'd probably go for around 300 miles up range of my target . . . So if we placed a cordon up to 500 miles out, we'd kind of have him trapped . . . Except the little son of a bitch could creep right out underneath us, dead slow in very deep water, and vanish. As he has done a few times before."

"How many ships would we need?" asked the Chairman.

"Well, if we had a hundred in all—twenty submarines, plus frigates, destroyers, and cruisers—they'd each have to look after 2,000 square miles—roughly a 45-mile square each."

"Jesus, Freddie . . . we didn't have that many ships in the South Pacific in 1944," said Arnold Morgan.

"And our enemy didn't have nuclear submarines that could go as deep, stay there indefinitely, and run so quietly as this bastard," replied the COMSUBPAC. "And I'll tell you something else. Even then, with that big a fleet, we still might not catch him. With any less than a hundred ships, I'd say we were almost guaranteed to miss him."

"Even if we caught him, chances are he'd get one of his missiles away," pondered Admiral Morgan.

"I'm not too bothered about that," replied Admiral Curran. "Because I think we'd nail that missile. But I'm sure, sir, as ever, you'd rather nail the archer than the arrow."

That was an old favorite policy of Admiral Morgan's, and Arnold smiled wryly. "You got that right, Freddie," he said. "But hunting submarines in a big pack is very difficult . . ."

"We'd have to use a box system," said Admiral Curran. "You know, give each U.S. submarine an area in which he must stick . . . otherwise we'll have 'em shooting at each other . . ."

"And there's always a problem with that," replied Arnold. "You pick the enemy up and track him to the edge of your box, then you've either got to break the rules and pursue him into somebody else's box or let him go and hope your nearest colleague will pick him up as well."

"Actually, sir, I was thinking of a search box only. I suggest our submarine COs will have orders to open fire and sink the enemy instantly."

"Freddie, I think that's exactly correct," said Arnold. "Which means we can't have our guys rampaging all over each other's designated areas. In the final reckoning, the box system is usually best. Though I did once hear the Royal Navy's High Command was somewhat less than thrilled when one of their submarines picked up the Argentinian submarine somewhere north of the Falklands and then let him go because they'd reached the end of the patrol box."

"I guess that's always the downside," said Admiral Curran, thoughtfully. "But generally speaking, the worst-case scenario would be one of our nuclear boats hitting another."

"Well," said General Scannell. "I'd be more than happy for you guys to work on some kind of a fleet plan for Monday's meeting . . . but I would like to know if we have enough ships!"

"No problem," replied Admiral Dickson. "Right now we have Carrier Groups patrolling the northern Gulf, the east end of the Strait of Hormuz, the northern Arabian Gulf, and one in readiness at Diego Garcia. There's a fifth preparing to leave Pearl Harbor. All of them could be in the mid-Atlantic in well under three weeks. That's fifty-five ships."

"Okay. The rest, I presume, are already in the Atlantic, or in Norfolk, or New London, or somewhere else on the East Coast?"

"Correct, sir. We do not have a problem getting a full complement of ships into the operational area."

"As for the *Barracuda*, of course we have no idea where that might be?" asked the CJC.

"Hell, yes, we got a hundred ideas," said Arnold Morgan.

"None of 'em reliable. But it seems to me, if this bastard un-leashed a battery of submarine-launched cruise missiles at Mount St. Helens, somewhere off Washington State, or even Oregon, earlier this month, he's got to be on his way to the eastern Atlantic by now.

"He will not want to go the longest way around. Not the way he came, all the way back north of the Aleutians, way down the coast of Asia, and then all the way across the Indian Ocean. That's too far. Twenty thousand miles plus, most of it at slow speed. It'd take him nearly three months."

Arnold Morgan let that rest for a few moments, and then he continued, speaking quietly to three very senior men who found it impossible to accept that he was no longer their spiritual leader.

"And this clever little son of a bitch certainly will not want to take the shorter route across the Pacific Basin," said the Admiral. "As you know, it's literally trembling with our SO-SUS wires. No, sir. He'll know that. And he'll avoid that.

"And he plainly cannot use the Panama Canal. Which means his most likely route will be down the west coast of South America, which is not heavily patrolled, nor surveyed, by our ships and satellites.

"It's shorter, safer, and much, much quieter, if he's trying to get into the Atlantic . . . Remember, he hit Mount St. Helens on Sunday morning, August 9. Today's the twenty-second. That's thirteen days, and he was probably making only seven knots for ten of them, but now he could probably be making fifteen in deserted waters. Which means he's put nearly 3,000 miles between himself and the datum.

"Way down at the southern end of Chile, he'll be moving even quicker. That damned *Barracuda* will be around Cape Horn in a couple of weeks, minimum."

"Any point putting a submarine trap down there some-where . . . try and stop him entering the Atlantic?" General Scannell was wracking his brains.

"Sir, it's such a vast, deep seascape," said Admiral Curran. "We'd need a lot of ships, and if we missed him, which we probably would, we'd be involved in some kind of race back to the Canary Islands . . . and we might lose that race. And that *Barracuda* could fire its missiles at the cliff face real quick. Sir, I think we'd be much better to get ourselves in line of battle, right where it counts—west of La Palma. We *know* he's going there."

"I'd go with that," said Admiral Dickson. "This seems like no place to be taking any chances whatsoever."

"I understand," said the CJC. "And I have one last point to make before I hand over to the Admirals . . . We have just one credibility gap in my view. That's the actual existence of the cruise missiles.

"But we do have one cast-iron witness, and we're not making the most of him. Gentlemen, I recommend we bring Mr. Tilton in from Seattle for Monday's meeting. Just so he can demonstrate to every one of us that what he heard was the genuine sound of an incoming missile."

"I agree with that," said Arnold Morgan. "You know the President and his half-witted advisers are going to pour scorn on our missile theory. I would even consider filming Mr. Tilton so his evidence can be locked in, and if necessary, shown to the President."

"No problem with that either," replied General Scannell. "Now we'll go and find some lunch, and decide an approximate formation of ships, and whatever security we need on the southwest side of La Palma. Who's going to track down Mr. Tilton on a Saturday morning out in Seattle?"

"I'll take care of that," said Admiral Morgan. "Have someone call Fort Meade and get Lieutenant Commander Ramshawe to call me on this private line, fast. He'll be on inside ten minutes."

That was way too big an estimate. The Admiral had just embarked on an alarming account of how he had been in the middle of his honeymoon, *"standing on the same volcano as the world's most wanted man and . . ."*

The phone rang. General Scannell answered.

"Good morning, sir. This is Lieutenant Commander

Ramshawe of the National Security Agency returning a call . . ."

"Just a moment . . . Arnie . . . it's your man . . ."

"Hi, Jimmy. You remember that bank president you spoke with about the missiles at Mount St. Helens?"

"Yes, sir, Tony Tilton. Seattle National."

"That's him. Can you get him on the line? This line. I mean I'd like to have him at our Monday morning meeting here."

"Might take a while, sir. The bank's closed this morning, I guess. But I'll find him."

"You in the office?"

"Yes, sir."

"Okay. Let's bring him in Sunday night. Leave Seattle around 0900, his time. Straight to Andrews."

"How's he to travel, sir?"

"Military aircraft, what d'you think? The fucking space shuttle?"

"Er, no, sir."

The Admiral chuckled. "Jimmy, get him on standby, then call us back and we'll give you his travel details. He can stay at our house."

"Okay, sir. I'll get right back."

Lieutenant Commander Ramshawe hit what he called the "obvious buttons" first. Directory assistance. He found a Tony and Martha Tilton in Magnolia, and dialed the number himself, sparing everyone the hang-up of yet another third party tuning in to a classified subject.

No one answered. It was 8:56 on this Saturday morning. And Jimmy left a message, knowing the phrase "National Security Agency, Fort Meade," was *likely to put a rocket under anyone's ass.*

This was a three-minute rocket. Tony Tilton was on the line, agreeing to travel to Washington the next day for a Monday morning meeting at the Pentagon, but to discuss it with no one. Jimmy told him he'd be right back with travel details, and hit the wire to the office of the Chairman of the Joint Chiefs.

"He's coming, sir. Let me have the travel plans. He's waiting by the phone."

This took another twenty minutes, but one day later, at
8:30 A.M. on Sunday, the Bank President drove to work at his
regular high-rise off Union Street at 6th Avenue. Waiting in
the lobby were two uniformed Naval officers who escorted
him to the wide flat roof of the building, thirty floors above
street level. And there, its rotors running, was a big Navy helicopter, a Bell AH-1Z Super Cobra, which in less peaceful
time carries eight Hellfire missiles for regular strike/assault,
and in air warfare is equipped with two killer AIM-9L heat-
seeking guided missiles.

This morning, the air was clear, the helicopter was unarmed, and it was already hot. Tony Tilton was the only passenger, aside from the three-man crew. They lifted off almost
vertically, then clattered their way north up Puget Sound,
about 3,000 feet above the water, for the ten-minute journey.

They descended gently through windless skies and put
down on the helicopter pad at the Whidbey Island Naval Air
Station, around 30 miles north of the Seattle downtown area,
the same distance from the sprawling U.S. Naval Base at
Everett.

One crew member disembarked immediately and assisted
their civilian passenger down the steps to the area beside the
runway. Less than 30 yards away stood a Lockheed EP-3E
Aries Naval jet, its engines running, steps down, ready for
Mr. Tilton's arrival.

He climbed aboard, a young officer came back to ensure
that he was strapped in, and they moved forward to the takeoff area immediately. One half-minute later, they were in the
air, screaming off the runway, scything into the hot, muggy
air above the calm U.S. Navy waters of the Juan de Fuca
Strait.

Fourteen minutes earlier, Tony had been standing on the
sidewalk on 6th Avenue, right outside the National Bank
Building.

"Christ, I've waited up longer than this in Boston just for a shuttle ticket," remarked Tony, as the aircraft made a steep left-hand turn, and, still climbing, headed resolutely inland, east, making 450 mph over the rapidly disappearing ground.

The Navy Lieutenant sitting next to him laughed. "Guess so, sir," he said. "It's just that in our game, we don't usually have a lot of time to fuck about. We're very big on speed. Would you like some coffee?"

The Bank President gratefully accepted, as they set off over the high peaks of the Cascade Range. Their route would take them southeast across Montana and Wyoming, over the Rockies, along the Nebraska-Kansas border, then due east, south of Cincinnati, into Washington, D.C.

During the six-hour journey, the Navy Lieutenant came up with more coffee and a beef sandwich, and they touched down at Andrews Air Force Base, southeast of the capital, at 6 P.M. local.

A black Navy staff car awaited them and the driver took Tony's bag, slung it on the front seat, and opened the rear door for the man who had escaped the wrath of Mount St. Helens.

Moments later, they were headed fast up to Route 95, and on to the beltway. They drove all around the north side of the city, got off at Exit 33, and into the tony suburb of Chevy Chase. The remainder of the journey took five minutes, and Admiral Morgan's agents met them inside the gateway of the grand Colonial-style house where the former National Security Adviser lived with his new(ish) wife, Kathy.

It was just 6:45 on a hot summer evening, and the Admiral was dressed in white Bermudas with a dark blue polo shirt and straw panama. He greeted Tony Tilton warmly and thanked him for coming. Harry came over and volunteered to take the visitor upstairs to his room, and Arnold told Tony to come back down right away so they could have a couple of drinks.

Tilton changed out of his blazer and tie, put on a dark green polo shirt, and headed back out to the wide patio by the pool.

The Admiral was sitting in a big, comfortable chair and he

motioned for Tony to join him. The drinks were on a table between them, and both men took a man-sized swig at the cool, relaxing Scotch whisky.

"I expect Lieutenant Commander Ramshawe filled you in on why we wanted you in Washington?"

"He did . . . the meeting tomorrow morning in the Pentagon, I believe."

"Correct. But I should give you some more info . . . and first I better know, if you don't mind . . . May I presume you're a Republican?"

"You may."

"Thought so. West Coast banker. Capitalist. Red in tooth and claw. Would you say you're rightish, or leftish?"

"Rightish. We have a very Republican State these days. Full of independent people, entrepreneurs and dyed-in-the-wool, self-sufficient country boys wary of Washington, paranoid about the present Administration. East Coast liberals don't play well out where I live. No sir."

"That's awful good to hear," replied the Admiral. "You can imagine what it's like in the Pentagon right now?"

"Sure can."

"Which brings us right back to Mount St. Helens. Can I call you 'Tony'?"

"Of course."

"I'm a civilian now. So that'll be Arnie to you . . . anyway, Lt. Comdr. Jimmy Ramshawe tells me you understand perfectly well we have the gravest suspicion about that particular eruption."

"Well, he was on the line from one of the most important government agencies in the country, asking me in great detail about those two blasts of wind on that still morning by the lake . . . I mean, there must be suspicion . . . It's difficult to arrive at any other conclusion . . ."

"Not if you work in the Oval Office," growled the Admiral.

Tony Tilton chuckled. "I should tell you, Lieutenant Commander Ramshawe did not reveal anything else about his investigation. I merely surmised what he was getting at."

"I understand," said the Admiral. "But because I believe you're someone we can trust, I'll give you a little more background, and then have you explain to me, all over again, exactly what you observed on that Sunday morning. Then I shall request you tell precisely the same thing to the meeting tomorrow morning."

"No problem."

"Okay, Tony Tilton. Have another slug of that Dewars and pay attention . . ."

"Lay it on me, Admiral."

"Arnie."

"Oh, I'm sorry," said Tony, shaking his head. "These habits of formality . . . hard to shake in my trade . . . May I have your account number . . . ?"

This was too much for the Admiral, who burst into laughter, and then had another slug of Dewars himself. A few minutes later, Morgan finished by concluding:

"A submarine. Do you follow me?"

"I surely do, Arnie. And you think what I heard were those missiles?"

"Yes, I do, Tony. That's precisely what I think."

"Can you launch them from below the surface? More than one at a time?"

"Oh, sure. They're called SLCMs—submarine-launched cruise missiles. You can get 'em away one at a time, but close together, separated by perhaps less than a minute. They make a heck of a speed, well over 600 knots, flying maybe 500 feet above the ground."

"How come they didn't crash into the mountains up there?"

"They self-adjust to the contours of the earth, rising and falling on the instructions of their own altimeter."

"And you think I heard them come in?"

"I think you heard the first two . . ."

"If it'd been the last two, I don't think we'd have made it out of there."

"Can you tell me exactly what you heard?"

"I'm afraid it can't be much more than I told Don McKeag or Lt. Comdr. Jimmy Ramshawe . . ."

And just then the French doors slid open, and Mrs. Kathy Morgan made her entrance, walking briskly, wearing a pink floral Italian cotton skirt with a pink summer shirt, no shoes, and a gold anchor pendant on a chain around her neck. Her lustrous red hair was worn loosely and she carried a large platter that, still marinating boldly, held a large butterflied leg of lamb.

This was, unaccountably, her husband's favorite—Texans, of course, are supposed to demonstrate the cattleman's traditional devotion to beef, harboring at all times the cowboy's general derision of the efforts of sheep farmers.

But Arnold loved butterflied leg of lamb and, much to Tony Tilton's good fortune, liked it especially on Sunday nights, when he gleefully opened a couple of bottles of outstanding château-bottled Bordeaux, as carefully recommended by his Chief Adviser, the former Secretary of State Harcourt Travis, now lecturing modern political history, somewhat loftily, to students at Harvard University.

Admiral Morgan introduced his wife to the star witness for the prosecution, and poured her a glass of cold white Burgundy.

"Arnold's been telling me, Tony, how you got away from the volcano," she said. "That must have been very scary . . . I think I would probably have fainted with terror."

"Kathy, when you're as scared as I was, it's amazing what you can do," replied her guest. "The morning was very quiet. No wind, just a few people camping around the lake, not more than a half dozen tents. Nearly everyone was asleep. There was a mist across the water, a high mist, not just a seafret. You could see neither upwards nor across the lake. It was one of those soft, silent times you can get out in the wilderness in the early morning. So quiet, you found yourself talking softly, even my buddy Don, and he's trained to lambaste the world with his opinions."

Arnold Morgan chortled and took another sip of Dewars. "Keep going, Tony," he said. "I'm enjoying this."

"Anyway, I heard this sudden wind. Not quite a howl, you know, nothing theatrical. But a real creepy wailing sound, more like that rise in sound you get in an old house when there's a storm outside.

"It was about as weird as a sound can be . . . *wh-o-o-o-o-sh!* On a dead-still morning. And it was not a sound that was static where we were, it was passing us by, as if heading into the mountain. I found myself looking upwards towards the peak, and then there was this deep thumping sound from way up there, like an underground explosion . . . Moments later I heard the goddamned noise again."

"How long, Tony?"

"Not as long as a minute. But close. And I heard it sweep past. Same sound. In a split second, I was looking up over the lake, but there was nothing, not even a movement in the mist. But the sound was identical. And ten seconds later there was another explosion from Mount St. Helens. This one was a much more open sound, a real crash . . . you know . . . *KER-RRR-BAM!* Like you'd imagine a bomb, although I've never heard one."

"And then?"

"I started up the wagon and we took off. That's when we heard the third explosion. That one was real loud, and suddenly there was fire and ash raining into the forest around us. Trees were on fire and God knows what. We just kept going, driving faster than I've ever driven in my life.

"The fourth explosion was bigger than all the other three put together—we didn't see it, but the road shook. And then it began to get dark . . . tons and tons of ash and debris flung into the atmosphere, I suppose. Kind of blotted out the sun. If I hadn't seen that sucker blow all those years ago, I guess I'd still have been standing gawping at Mount St. Helens when the lava started down the mountain. It just swallows everything."

"Including the half-gallon of Dewars, according to your man McKeag," chuckled Arnold.

"Yeah. Just imagine . . . one small section of volcanic rock, amber in color, in the middle of all that gray . . . Dewar's Rock. Now that's a landmark."

"According to Don McKeag's program, you might be running for state governor in a couple of years," said Arnold. "Could be your first major act on environmental issues . . . renaming the rock at the foot of Mount St. Helens."

1030, Monday, August 24
Second Floor, The Pentagon.

One by one, they filed into the private conference room of the Chairman of the Joint Chiefs. There was Adm. George Morris and Lt. Comdr. Jimmy Ramshawe. Adm. Alan Dickson; Rear Adm. Freddie Curran; Admiral Morgan; and Tony Tilton. Gen. Scannell had invited the Air Force Chief, Gen. Cale Carter, plus Maj. Gen. Bart Boyce, NATO's Supreme Allied Commander, and Gen. Stanford Hudson (Readiness Command, U.S. Army).

No politicians were present. But as military brainpower goes, this was a solid roomful, deep in the most secretive inner sanctum of Pentagon planning, directly above the office of President McBride's dovish Secretary of State for Defense, Milt Schlemmer, formerly of the International Atomic Energy Agency and the Campaign for Nuclear Disarmament. The man's name alone brought Arnold Morgan out in hives.

There were only two men from outside the U.S. Military's High Command—an Air Force colonel from U.S. Aerospace Command HQ, who waited in the reception area with Tony Tilton. Positioned outside the office were two Marine Corps guards, with four others on extra duty in Corridor Seven, which leads directly to E-Ring, the great circular outer thruway of the Pentagon.

The ten men sat at the large conference table, and General Scannell called the meeting to order by informing everyone this was a gathering of the most highly classified nature, and that no one—repeat, no one—was to be informed that it had even been convened.

For reasons that would become obvious, he declared that Admiral Morgan would chair the meeting, and he cited Arnold's long and detailed involvement in the subject. He also explained that Adm. George Morris had been "on the case" for several months, and that Lt. Comdr. Jimmy Ramshawe, the Fort Meade Director's assistant, had "essentially made the running throughout the unofficial investigation."

General Scannell had issued only the most cursory briefing by coded E-mail to the senior officers around the table. But each man sufficiently understood the grave suspicion that now surrounded the eruption of Mount St. Helens, and each man had been furnished with a copy of the letter from Hamas, demanding the United States' formal evacuation from the Middle East.

"Each of you understands," said General Scannell, "the distinct likelihood that the crater, high on Mount St. Helens, was hit by four oncoming cruise missiles on the morning of August 9. Only one man was near enough to bear any kind of witness to this event, at least only one man who survived. And he is with us this morning—Mr. Tony Tilton, the President of the Seattle National Bank.

"Now, because I would like to fly him home as soon as possible, I am inviting him to speak to us and explain exactly what he witnessed in the foothills of Mount St. Helens on that morning. Mr. Tilton has already debriefed Admiral Morgan, so I invite Arnold to steer our visitor through his account of the incident."

Admiral Morgan introduced Tony formally to the group, and then invited him to recount, in precise detail, everything he had told him on the previous evening. And he did so with a lawyer's clarity. At the conclusion of his story, Admiral Morgan asked if anyone would like to ask Mr. Tilton any further questions, but there were none. The bank chief and the former National Security Adviser had, between them, delivered a detailed, virtuosic performance.

They formally thanked Tilton for coming, and then Admiral Morgan stood up and escorted him from the room. Two young Naval officers were waiting to walk him out to the helicopter pad for the five-minute journey to Andrews, and the flight back to Puget Sound.

Back on the second floor of the Pentagon, the group was listening to the summing up of the Air Force psychiatrist who had been examining the long letter from Hamas. His conclusions were very clear . . . "While the demands of the letter are plainly outrageous, I detect no sign of hysteria or dementia of any kind. This letter was not written by a disturbed person. It was written by an educated man, whose natural language was most certainly English.

"I do not detect one instance of difficulty or confusion in writing past and present tenses—the classic sign of a foreigner trying to write in another language. Nor, indeed, one instance of a discordant word, nor a colloquialism that we would not use. Or even the slightest distortion of a common colloquialism. Also, there is no sign of heightened excitement anywhere in the writing. The language is straightforward, even in its demands . . . *'immediate steps'* . . . *'immediate undertakings.'* He talks of *'entering the final stage.'* He wants to see *'clear signs.'*

"There is one sentence in which he points out that if he and his men can explode *'the biggest volcano in the United States, we can probably arrange a large rockfall into the deserted ocean.'*

"The key word here, gentlemen, is 'probably.' Because it represents *irony*, perhaps the most elusive of thought patterns, the ability to understate, yet have equal effect. People think Americans sometimes lack this subtlety. The educated British seem to practically live on it.

"And I would remind you of the phrase *'intimated in my*

communiqué'—those are the words of a trained military officer or even a diplomat. That sentence could have been written by anyone in this room.

"Gentlemen, this letter was written by a very serious person. Very sane. Very cold-blooded. I suggest we ignore this guy at our peril. And for what it's worth, if the writer of this letter told me he just blew up Mount St. Helens, I'd have no reason to disbelieve him."

The psychiatrist was followed by Lieutenant Commander Ramshawe, who outlined the problem of the missing *Barracuda*, then pointed out the most recent sightings and detections, and gave his conclusion that the boat was probably on its way down the west coast of South America.

General Scannell then steered the meeting towards the demands of the terrorists, and he requested General Hudson of Readiness Command to outline the deployment of personnel, plus stockpiles of equipment and munitions in the Gulf.

The General immediately distributed a single sheet of paper to each man around the table, and read from his own, for everyone's benefit:

"Bahrain. Headquarters of the U.S. Fifth Fleet, and 4,500 personnel. This is the nerve center for all U.S. warships deployed in the Red Sea, the Persian Gulf, and the Arabian Sea.

"Kuwait. U.S. Army Command, approximately 12,000 military personnel. We have a large training base at Camp Doha, which is now our top-favored desert-training area. We're building another near-identical facility at Arifjan. The U.S. Air Force flies from Ali Al Salem and Ahmed Al Jabar air bases.

"Saudi Arabia. Reopened. U.S. Air Force Command, approximately 10,000 personnel. Combat aircraft, including fighter and reconnaissance. We have E3-AWACs and air-refueling aircraft based at Prince Sultan air base, protected by two Patriot missiles batteries.

"Qatar. Around 4,000 personnel. Al Udeid air base, which has the region's longest runway, is available to us. We've built aircraft shelters there, and we operate the KC-10 and KC135 air-to-air refueling aircraft. Central Command (CENTCOM) of all forces in the Gulf has been established at Camp Sayliyah.

"Oman. We use the docks and Al-Seeb International Airport as transit points for onwards movement, either to Afghanistan or to the Gulf. Approximately 3,000 personnel are based there.

"United Arab Emirates. We have 500, mostly Air Force personnel, based here.

"Djibouti. Way down there on the Gulf of Aden. Up to 3,000 U.S. Special Forces, Marines, and Air Force personnel, all part of the counterterrorism task force. This is the base for the CIA unmanned Predator aircraft.

"Diego Garcia. There's around 1,500 U.S. personnel there. It's our base for the upgraded B-52 heavy bombers and the B-2 stealth bombers.

"In addition, we've always got three Carrier Battle Groups in the area, on a rotation basis, depending on the political climate."

General Scannell interjected, "Which adds up to one hell of a lot of people and equipment to move out of the area on the sole demand of one Middle Eastern freedom fighter."

"Unless," added Admiral Morgan, "that freedom fighter really does have the capability of destroying the entire East Coast of the United States. Then, of course, the evacuation of our military in the Middle East would be a very small price to pay."

"It cannot be possible. It simply cannot," said General Boyce.

"*'If we can explode the biggest volcano in the United States, we can probably arrange a large rockfall into the deserted ocean,'*" intoned Admiral Morgan.

And for just a few seconds, the entire table went silent. Then Admiral Morgan spoke again. "Gentlemen, let's face it, we have to start from the basis that this guy is not joking. And our options are very limited. Priority number one is to catch and destroy the fucker. Right?"

He glared around the table. No one dissented. "Therefore, number two is to produce a fleet deployment plan. Number three is to appoint a Commander in Chief to that fleet. Number four is to try to get the President, the Commander in Chief of all U.S. Armed Forces, to agree to such a deployment. The last one is the most difficult, by a very long way."

"You want an educated forecast?" asked Admiral Morris.

"Always," replied Arnold Morgan.

"He is not going to agree, now or ever, to put this country essentially on a war footing to deal with what he believes is a crank letter. And he will not listen to us. Now or ever."

A silence enveloped the table. "Then we may," said General Scannell, "have to go without him."

"Which would be a bit unorthodox," said Admiral Dickson.

"Maybe," replied the CJC. "But we cannot, knowingly, let the people of this nation down, when we all believe there is a real danger someone could wipe out the East Coast of the United States. I believe Lieutenant Commander Ramshawe has issued everyone with a short and concise report on the experts' assessment of the volcano on the island of La Palma."

"I guess there's no stopping the tidal wave once it develops?" asked General Boyce.

"Apparently not," replied Arnold Morgan. "Because when that develops, we're looking at probably the greatest force on earth, traveling along the seabed at the speed of a jet aircraft. Less than nine hours to New York, the waves building all the way."

"Jesus Christ," replied the General.

"So far as I can see," said the Admiral, "we have two

chances. The first one slim, the second one better, but not fool-proof. We set sail for the Canary Islands with a 100-strong fleet and search for the missing *Barracuda*, which we proba-bly won't find. Not if the driver's as smart as I think he is.

"Secondly, we position a defensive screen of surface war-ships to the west of La Palma, primed to hit and destroy the missile, or missiles, in mid-flight. It would help, of course, if we knew roughly where they're going to fire it from. But we don't."

"Well, regardless, we'll have to move the entire East Coast fleet the hell out of all our Navy bases," said Admiral Curran. "A wave like that would wipe us out. We can't leave any ship in port. We have drafted a rough plan that I think Admiral Dickson would like everyone to see . . . that is, if we are unanimous about the reality of the threat. And are we unani-mously agreed that we must go ahead with a fleet plan to counteract that threat, regardless of the opinions of our polit-ical masters? Right hands please."

Nine right hands were solemnly raised high.

"No choice," said General Scannell. "Absolutely no choice."

"Okay. Now today's the twenty-fourth," said Arnold Mor-gan. "That means we have forty-seven days to get things into line. I suggest we invent some forthcoming fleet exercises in the Atlantic and start getting ships at least on standby for de-ployment. I presume the Middle East is sufficiently quiet for us to move the Carrier Groups into the Atlantic without caus-ing a huge amount of fuss? Alan?"

"No problem."

"Good. Now perhaps we should hear the preliminary plan I understand Alan and Freddie have been developing for the past couple of days . . ."

Admiral Curran handed out a single sheet of paper to each man. Then he told them, "As a submariner, I have been asked to explain the first part of the plan before I turn things over to Admiral Dickson. I am sure you know there are innate diffi-culties in conducting underwater hunts with submarines because of how they are apt to shoot each other if we're not damned careful.

"My recommendation is we take a 'box' 500 miles north to south, running up and down the La Palma coastline, by 500 miles west out into the Atlantic. That's a colossal area of 250,000 square miles, and from somewhere in there, we expect the *Barracuda* to fire her missiles at the cliff.

"It is not impossible that she could fire from even farther west, perhaps up to 1,000 miles out from La Palma. But I personally doubt that. Her Commanding Officer will know we're out there in force looking for her, and will probably be keenly aware of our excellent surface-to-air missile defense systems and probably will not want to have his birds in the air for too long.

"If I had to guess I'd say he'll launch from under 300 miles from the La Palma coast. But we cannot take that chance. We need to cover the outer limits of his range."

"How many missiles do you think, Freddie?" asked Arnold Morgan.

"Possibly twenty SLCMs, to be sure of knocking the cliff down. Unless he goes nuclear. Then he'll only want two."

"Can he go nuclear?"

"I don't think so," interrupted Admiral Morris. "Simply because I can't imagine where he'd get 'em. They have to be especially fitted for the *Barracuda*, and the Russians are not about to help him to that extent. They won't even admit selling the *Barracuda* to anyone except China. And the Chinese will not even admit to owning it.

"Certainly they are unlikely to admit compliance with a bunch of terrorists trying to wreck the East Coast of the United States of America. The Chinese might be cunning and they might be devious, but they're not stupid."

"They might be able to buy 'em at that place in Bosnia," said Arnold Morgan. "But I'd be surprised if a European country would agree to that, especially one in NATO, or the EU."

"How about North Korea?" said Admiral Morris.

"Possible. Though I'm not sure if they have developed the sophistication to build a nuclear-headed missile that would fit into a big Russian submarine."

"Let's hope not," said Admiral Dickson. "But I guess in the end it doesn't matter where they got the warhead. We have to stop it, whether it was made in Korea, Belgrade, or Macy's."

"Okay," said Arnold, "let's hear that outline from Freddie on the deployment of the fleet."

"We'll definitely need to use a 'box' system for our submarine force," said Admiral Curran. "And my recommendation is, we form a screen from the 500-mile mark moving inshore to perhaps 300. Each one of fifteen boats taking a square of around 40 miles by 40 miles, each of them with a towed array, trying to pick up every sound in the water. Altogether, that should take care of an area of 24,000 square miles.

"My personal view is that the *Barracuda* will not hang around in the ocean west of La Palma, firstly because he'll guess we're in there, thick and fast, and secondly, because he'll be coming in from farther south and may have a great distance to cover at a slow speed. Our best chance is to catch him coming in, though I have no real confidence he'll make the kind of mistake we need to detect him.

"I then recommend we take five more submarines and position them in boxes 40 miles long, right inshore. The water's very deep, and there is just a chance the *Barracuda* will move in quietly at night in order to launch with a visual look as well as the GPS.

"I do not say this is any more likely a scenario than any other. But it would be ridiculous to have our defensive screens way offshore, while our enemy creeps underneath us, in two-mile-deep ocean, and opens fire from close range, giving us restricted time to set up for the intercept."

General Hudson apologized but requested permission to interrupt, reminding the group that there plainly had to be a Patriot missile-shield positioned at the top of the cliff, and around the rim of the volcanoes. "We can only hope he launches something that flies high, rather than a sea skimmer," he said. "Just to give us a real shot at it."

Admiral Curran nodded in agreement. He suggested the submarine force should answer directly to SUBLANT headquarters, wherever that might be. It was becoming ominously certain that they were looking at a general evacuation of all Naval and Military command posts on the East Coast of the U.S.A., as the October 9 deadline approached.

Adm. Alan Dickson very briefly discussed the deployment of the surface fleet, recommending that another eighty ships would be required for the offshore vigil that might save the East Coast. "We're looking at a force of maybe forty frigates—modern missile ships with towed arrays—listening in the water throughout that central area between the two submarine forces.

"We're talking maybe a 200,000-square-mile patrol area with eighty ships—that's 2,500 square miles each, a 50-mile-square box—and they'll search it end to end, night and day, waiting for the intruder. If he's good, we may never hear him. If he's careless, just once, near any of our ships, he's rubble.

"If the meeting agrees, we'll begin work on the defensive layout right away, and we better start moving ships into the area from the Middle and Far East."

"I agree with that," said Arnold Morgan. "But I remain concerned about the time frame, and I remain concerned about Hamas watching our activities at the bases around the Gulf over the next couple of weeks.

"If they see we are doing absolutely nothing in response to their evacuation demand, they might just get frustrated and whack the cliff, or somehow up the ante. I'd like to try and avoid that."

"You mean, start moving stuff as if we're obeying them?"

"So far as I can see," said Arnold, "that's the only chance we have of buying time. If they see we're reacting to their threats, they may be happy to give us more time. And we need time. A defensive operation like this needs all the time it can get."

"Sir," said Lieutenant Commander Ramshawe. "I wonder if I may ask a question?"

"Sure, Jimmy, go right ahead."

"Do you think these jokers will attempt to bang some high ordnance straight into the cliff and knock it into the sea, or do you think they'll try to bang a couple of big nuclear warheads straight into the Cumbre Vieja volcano, blow it wide open, and let nature take its course with the steam blast?"

"Good question," replied the Admiral. "In the normal way, I'd say any terrorist in that situation would want to fire in a missile, hit the cliff, and bolt for freedom, from maybe 300 miles offshore.

"But this bastard's different. We believe he's an expert on volcanoes. Option two—hitting the crater—will take much longer to develop, and it is more difficult to execute, but it's also more deadly. Altogether a more awesome and terrifying project. I think he'll go for Option Two. He's not afraid of difficulty, and he'll try for maximum effect."

"Just like he did at Mount St. Helens," replied the Lieutenant Commander, thoughtfully.

"Exactly so," said Admiral Morgan.

"Which brings us back to the business of time," said General Scannell. "Does everyone think we should stage some kind of an unobtrusive departure from the bases in the Gulf?"

"I don't think we can, not so long as President McBride thinks we're all crazy." General Boyce, the Supreme NATO Allied Commander, was visibly unhappy. He shook his head and said twice, "I just don't know."

General Tim Scannell was braver. "Bart," he said, "I think I mentioned it before. On this one, we may just have to go without him."

And the eight men sitting around the big table in the CJC's conference room felt the chill of a potential mutiny, led, unthinkably, by the Highest Command of the United States Military.

0800, Friday, September 4
56.18S 67.00W, Speed 15, Depth 300.

ADM. BEN BADR held the *Barracuda* steady on course, two-seven-zero, 25 miles south of Cape Horn, beneath rough, turbulent seas swept by a force-eight gale out of the Antarctic. They were moving through the Drake Passage in 2,500 fathoms of water, having finally concluded their southward journey down past the hundreds of islands and fiords that guard mainland Chile from the thundering Pacific breakers.

They had made good speed across the southeast Pacific Basin, and the Mornington Abyssal Plain, and were now headed east, running north of the South Shetland Islands in the cold, treacherous waters where the Antarctic Peninsula comes lancing out of the southern ice floes.

Ben Badr was making for the near end of the awesome underwater cliffs of the Scotia Ridge. At the same time, he was staying in the eastern flows of the powerful Falkland Islands current. His next course adjustment would take him past the notoriously shallow Burdwood Bank, and well east of the Falkland Islands themselves.

These were lonely waters, scarcely patrolled by the Argentinian Navy, and even more rarely by the Royal Navy, which was still obliged to guard the approaches to the islands for which 253 British servicemen had fought and died in 1982.

It was midwinter this far south, and despite not having seen daylight for almost two months, Ben Badr assured the crew that they did not want to break the habit right now. Not with an Antarctic blizzard raging above them, and a mighty southern ocean demonstrating once more that Cape Horn's murderous reputation was well earned.

Submarines dislike the surface of the water under almost any conditions. They are not built to roll around with the ocean's swells. But 300 feet below the waves, the *Barracuda* was in its correct element, moving swiftly and easily through the depths, a smooth, malevolent jet-black tube of pending destruction, but the soul of comfort for all who sailed with her.

That 47,500 hp nuclear system had been running sweetly for eight weeks now, which was not massively demanding for a power source that would run, if necessary, for eight years. The Russian-built VM-5 Pressurized Water Reactor would provide every vestige of the submarine's propulsion, heat, fresh water, and electronics on an indefinite basis. Barring accident, the only factor that could drive the *Barracuda* to the surface was if they ran out of food.

Their VM-5 reactor was identical to the one the Russians used on their gigantic Typhoon-class ballistic missile boats. The world's biggest underwater warships, which displace 26,000 tons of water submerged, required two of them, but the reactors were the same state-of-the-art nuclear pressurized water systems.

The *Barracuda*, with its titanium hull, was a submariner's dream. It could strike with missiles unexpectedly, from an unknown position. It was incredibly quiet—as quiet as the U.S. Navy's latest Los Angeles–class boats, silent under seven knots, undetectable, barring a mistake by her commanding officer. A true phantom of deep water.

General Rashood and Ben Badr stared at the charts that marked the long northward journey ahead of them. It was more than 4,000 miles up to the equator, and they knocked off three parts of that with a brisk, constant 15 knots through the cold, lonely southern seas, devoid of U.S. underwater surveillance and largely devoid of the warships of any nation.

They remained 1,000 miles offshore, running 500 feet below the surface up the long Argentinian coast, across the great South American Basin until they were level with the vast 140-mile-wide estuary of the River Plate.

This is the confluence of the Rivers Parana and Uruguay, and the enormous estuary contains some of the busiest shipping lanes in the world, steaming along the merchant ship roads, into the ports of Buenos Aires on the Argentinian side and Montevideo on the Uruguayan.

Ben Badr stayed well offshore here, keeping right of the shallow Rio Grande Rise, and pushing on north, up towards Ascension Island. And long before they arrived in those waters, he cut the speed of his submarine, running through the confused seas above the craggy cliffs of the Mid-Atlantic Ridge on his starboard side, as he made his way silently past the U.S. military base on this British-owned moonscape of an island.

This was probably the only spot in the entire Mid- and South Atlantic they might be detected. And they ran past with the utmost care, slowly, slowly, only six knots, deeper than usual, at 700 feet. The *Barracuda* was deathly quiet on all decks. Lieutenant Commander Shakira huddled in the navigation room; Admiral Badr and the Hamas General were in the control room, listening to the regular pings of the passive sonar.

On Friday, September 18, the *Barracuda* crossed the equator, the unseen divider of north and south in the center of the earth's navigational grid. This was the zero-degree line that slices in, off the Atlantic and through Brazil, a few miles north of the Amazon Delta.

Ahead of the Hamas warship was another 1,000 miles through which they made good speed, covering the distance in a little under three days. By midday on Monday, September 21, they were at their rendezvous point, running slowly at periscope depth, eight miles off the port of Dakar in the for-

mer French colony of Senegal, right on the outermost seaward bulge of northern Africa.

1100 (Local), Same Day
Monday, September 21
Chevy Chase, Maryland.

Arnold Morgan was entertaining an old friend, the new Is-
raeli Ambassador to Washington, sixty-two-year-old General
David Gavron, former head of the most feared international
Intelligence agency in the world, the Mossad.

The two men had met and cooperated at the time David
Gavron had served as military attaché at the Israeli Embassy
seven years previously. They had, by necessity, stayed in
touch during Admiral Morgan's tenure in the White House,
when the General had headed up the Mossad.

Today's was an unorthodox meeting. David Gavron, like
every other high-ranking military Intelligence officer in the
world, knew the Admiral was no longer on the White House
staff. But this certainly had not diminished his towering reputation, nor his encyclopedic knowledge of the ebb and flow
of the world's power struggles.

General Gavron guessed, correctly, that the U.S.A. had a
serious problem. He had for years been a close friend and
confidant not only of Ariel Sharon but also of the former
Yom Kippur War tank-division commander Maj. Gen. Avra-
ham "Bren" Adan. General Gavron was possibly the most
trusted man in Israel.

He was a pure Israeli of the blood, a true Sabra, born a few
miles southwest of the Sea of Galilee near Nazareth. On October 6, 1973, the first day of the Yom Kippur War, as a battalion tank commander, he had driven out into the Sinai right
alongside "Bren" Adan himself. On that most terrible day,
hundreds of young Israelis, stunned by the suddenness of the
onslaught by Egypt's Second Army, fought and died in the
desert.

For two days and nights, David Gavron had served in the front line of the battlefield, as one of Bren Adan's blood-stained young commanders who flung back wave after wave of the Egyptian tank division. Twice wounded, shot in the arm and then blown into the desert sand while trying to save a burning tank crew, David Gavron's personal battle honor was presented to him by Mrs. Meir herself. It was inscribed with the same words as Great Britain's coveted Victoria Cross . . . FOR VALOR.

This was precisely the kind of man Admiral Morgan now needed urgently because only someone like David Gavron, a man who had faced the onslaught of a merciless invading army, could ultimately decide whether his beleaguered little country could comply with America's request to vacate the West Bank of the Jordan River.

So far, in unofficial but probing talks, the signs had not been good. From Tel Aviv, there had been zero enthusiasm. The big hitters in the Israeli military had almost shuddered at the prospect of a Palestinian State. Hard-eyed men from the Knesset, the Mossad, Shin Bet, the interior secret service, had intimated this was too big a favor to ask.

Arnold Morgan stared at the jagged scar on the left side of the Israeli's face. He knew it was a legacy from a far-distant tank battle in the desert. And that scar ran deep. David Gavron's reaction to a polite request for an end to hostilities with the Palestinians would have a major bearing on the next approach by the Americans.

Admiral Morgan did not know precisely how much General Gavron knew, but he suspected Hamas may have informed the Mossad directly of their threat to the United States, and their demand that Israel back up and give their Arabian enemy some living space.

It was a warm autumn day, and they sat outside on the patio surrounding the pool area. Arnold sipped his coffee and gazed into the cool blue eyes of the tall, fit-looking Israeli diplomat, with his close-cropped hair and tanned skin.

"David," he said. "I want you to level with me."

"As always," smiled the General.

"Are you aware of the threat made upon my nation by the high command of Hamas?"

"We are."

"Do you know of the twofold nature of the demands that we vacate the Middle East in its entirety, and that we compel you to agree to the formation of a Palestinian State inside the present borders of Israel?"

"Yes, we are aware of precisely what they threaten."

"Okay. Now, you also know we have begun to make troop and armament movements in our Middle East bases."

"We do."

"And do you think Hamas now believes we intend to comply with their demands?"

"I doubt it."

"Why not?"

"Because you are probably not doing nearly enough. Just playing for time, while you get ready to obliterate your enemy, in the time-honored American way."

"It's damn difficult to obliterate Hamas. Since we can't see them."

"I assure you, there is no need to tell us that. We can see them a lot better than you. And we can't get rid of them either."

"Well, David. We can certainly step up our evacuation plans sufficiently to make us look real. But we plainly need your cooperation, just to demonstrate we have persuaded you to make a lasting peace, with redrawn borders for the West Bank and the Gaza Strip."

David Gavron, somewhat ominously, did not answer.

"So I have two questions to ask you," said the Admiral. "The first because of your known expertise dealing with terrorist enemies of your nation . . . Do you think we should take the Hamas threat seriously?"

"You mean, their assurance that they will cause this giant landslide and then a tidal wave to flood your East Coast?"

"That's the one, David."

"My answer is yes. Because the Hamas have become very

dangerous in the past two or three years. You will have noticed several of their spectacular successes—some at our expense, others at yours . . . ?"

"Of course. We have. And now they are threatening again. Goddamnit, David, they never used to be *that* dangerous."

"Not until they found a new Sandhurst-trained military assault leader."

"You mean the SAS officer who absconded from the Brits?"

"That's the man, Arnold. And I've no doubt you realize he went over the wall in my own country during the battle of the Jerusalem Road in our holy city of Hebron."

"Actually, David, my information was that he went around the wall, not over it."

"Very precise of you," replied General Gavron, smiling. "We do, of course, have the same sources. Anyway, he's never been seen since, and Hamas has never been the same since."

"Don't I know that. But now we're stuck with this volcano bullshit."

"I wonder if you also heard," replied the Israeli, "that he undoubtedly kidnapped and murdered that Professor in London earlier this year, the world authority on volcanoes and earthquakes?"

"We only surmised that very recently."

"We were perhaps quicker in Tel Aviv. But we knew there was an active cell of the Hamas high command in London. Matter of fact, we just missed them. One day earlier might have saved everyone a lot of trouble."

"Or, on the other hand, left you on the short side of a half-dozen assassins . . ."

"Yes, we are always aware of that possibility when dealing with such a man," said General Gavron. "Nonetheless, I should definitely take his threats seriously if I were you . . . We can surmise by his London activities that he is now an expert on volcanoes. And I'm told by our Field Chief in Damascus that they definitely planned to erupt Mount St.

Helens. We've never had confirmation of that, but the coincidence is a little fierce."

"Which leaves our East Coast on the verge of extinction," said Arnold. "I've read up on the subject, and the truth is obvious. He hits the Cumbre Vieja volcano, that mega-tsunami will happen. And that's likely to be *sayonara* New York . . ."

"Of course I see your problem. You are obliged to buy a little time by making moves in the Middle East to look as if you are leaving. But what you are really doing is getting a great battle fleet into operation in the Atlantic in order to find and destroy the submarine, or intercept the missile as it flies into La Palma?"

"How the hell do you know they're in a submarine?"

"Please, Arnold, give us some credit. We know about the missing *Barracuda*s. We know you found one of them, already scuttled. And we know the other one is on the loose. There is plainly no other way to hit the volcano except with a submarine-launched missile. An aircraft is out of the question, so is a surface ship, and a blast from the mainland of black North Africa would be to invite instant detection by the U.S. satellites.

"No, Arnold. They have informed you what they plan to do. And quite obviously, they are going to launch their missile attack from a submarine creeping around, deep, somewhere in the North Atlantic, somewhere off the coast of Africa. And since that *Barracuda* is the only suspect . . . the rest is academic."

"Correct. And if I am *not* able to demonstrate that the nation of Israel is prepared to acquiesce to our instructions, I guess Hamas will open fire, and we'll just have to see if we can stop 'em. I should warn you, however, that if that little scenario should occur, the Knesset ought not to hold its breath for any more help from the U.S.A. . . . finance or weapons."

"I do realize that," said General Gavron. "And quite honestly, I have tried to stay out of the talks. I know there has been nothing formal yet, but these things get around fast. And we are aware that sooner or later we will have to answer a very serious question from the United States."

Admiral Morgan poured them both more coffee. He stood up and walked a few paces, then retraced his steps. "David," he said, "what is your personal reaction to the Hamas demand for immediate recognition of the Independent, Democratic, and Sovereign State of Palestine based on the territories on the West Bank and the Gaza Strip . . . as they say, '*occupied by the forces of Israel since June 4, 1967*'?

"I guess you know that they want all Israeli troops out of these territories, right away?"

"That's what they always demand, Arnold. But they are asking the rulers of Israel to commit political suicide. And you know what your great hero Sir Winston Churchill said about that?"

"Not offhand. What was it?"

"The trouble with committing political suicide is you usually live to regret it . . ."

Arnold Morgan laughed, despite the seriousness of the conversation. He sat back and sipped his coffee thoughtfully.

"Arnold," Gavron said, "there are thousands of families whose relatives died for those new Israeli lands, died defending them against the Arab aggressor. My grandfather was killed in the Sinai in 1967, my beloved and brave grandmother died on a human ammunition line, passing shells up to our tanks on the Golan Heights in 1967. My father's two brothers were killed in the battle for the Sinai in 1967, and my niece, age eleven, was killed by a Palestinian bomb in a supermarket twelve years ago.

"I'm sorry, Arnold, I could never agree to a Palestinian State within our borders. Not one that causes us to surrender the lands we fought for, against overwhelming aggression from the Arab nations. My government might agree if America were to get very rough with us. But would *I*? Never."

Arnold smiled a rueful smile at the old warrior from the Holy Land. "But what about us, David?" he said. "We, who have done so much to keep your nation secure. What about us, in our hour of real need?"

"Well, the East Coast of America is a very long way from Israel. More than 5,000 miles. And just for once, we are not the ones being threatened by an armed enemy.

"In my country, there are vast numbers of young Israelis who were not even born when Egypt split the Bar-Lev line and attacked us on our most holy day of the year. We'd be asking them to support their government giving away great slabs of the only land they have ever known . . . to the Palestinians. Well, Arnold, that's what civil wars are made of . . ."

"You mean Israel is *never* going to agree to the creation of a Democratic Palestinian State, never going to withdraw from the occupied territories?"

"No, I don't mean that. I don't mean *never*. But probably not in the next five weeks. That's just asking the utterly impossible. For a problem that is not even ours. Remember, it's the U.S.A. under threat. Not Israel."

"For an officer and a diplomat, that's a rather shortsighted answer," replied Admiral Morgan.

"Not really. The U.S.A. would find it very difficult to get rough with us. No American President is going to risk losing the massive Jewish vote in New York."

"I was not referring to the U.S.A. getting rough," said Arnold.

"Oh . . . what were you implying . . . ?"

"I was suggesting that if we get jackhammered by this tidal wave, that will somewhat preoccupy us for a while. And since you did nothing to assist us, you'll probably find us too busy to help you."

"But we don't need help, Arnold. We're not threatened."

"If the U.S. Navy and Military are effectively disabled on the East Coast for a period of several months, how long do you think it will take Hamas to turn their thwarted anger on Israel?"

David Gavron was thoughtful. He said nothing for a few moments and then replied, "They are essentially a hit-and-run organization. Terrorists. They do not have our training, our combat readiness. They have no answers to heavy artillery. And we can withstand terrorism. We always have. The Hamas are simply not a big enough force to take down a nation like ours."

"That may have been so three years ago," said Arnold. "But it's not so now. They have a general as accomplished in the field as anyone we've seen for years . . ."

"This damn Kerman character?"

"That's the man, David. That's the man."

**1530 (Local), Monday, September 21
The Atlantic Ocean, 14.43N 17.30W
Speed 5, Course Unconfirmed, PD.**

The *Barracuda* cruised in warm waters out among the bluefin tunas just below the surface, less than 10 miles off the most westerly port in Africa. Dakar, capital city of the old French colony of Senegal, was in the middle of its rainy season, and warm tropical rain lashed the calm waters of the deep Atlantic way out to sea.

They'd been waiting for almost four hours now, and the rain had not let up. Every fifteen minutes, Ben Badr ordered his mast up and scanned the surface picture, looking in vain for the patrol boat from the Senegal Navy, which had been due to arrive at around midday.

When it finally did show up, shortly before 1600, both he and Ravi became extremely jumpy. Running this close to the surface, even in waters in which the U.S. Navy had zero interest, it was still unnerving. Just knowing the U.S. satellites, if correctly focused, could pick them up in moments.

The unrelenting rain reduced visibility, and the Senegalese were more than a mile away when Admiral Badr saw them. Immediately he ordered the *Barracuda* to the surface. With a blast of emptying ballast and an increased hum of the accelerating turbines, the *Barracuda* surged up into the fresh air for the first time for ten weeks. It was the first daylight they had seen since the submarine went deep, just south of the

Japanese island of Yakushima, and headed out into the north Pacific.

The great underwater warship shouldered aside the blue waters of the eastern Atlantic, and the helmsman brought her almost to a halt on the surface, facing south awaiting the Senegalese patrol ship that would pull alongside.

The seas were otherwise deserted and the *Barracuda*'s deck crew waved the incoming ship into position on the starboard side of the hull. They could already see a special long gangway out on the scruffy-looking deck, and they sent over lines to help the two Senegalese crewmen to shove it out between the two ships.

General Ravi, standing on deck with Shakira, gazed in some distaste at the condition of the patrol boat, a U.S.–built Peterson Mark-4 Class 22-tonner, almost twenty years old, black-hulled and in dire need of a coat of paint. The once-white deck was rusted, and further rust marks stained the hull. A couple of black tires were leaned against the super-structure. As a Navy ship, it looked like a Third World fishing smack. But it was the only way to leave unnoticed, and the Senegalese, sharing their Muslim faith, had been willing to help, although Ravi guessed his colleagues in Bandar Abbas had paid expensively for this short Inter-Navy 10-mile voyage, probably as much as the boat was worth.

On board were three smiling seamen, jet black in color, with gleaming white teeth, no uniforms, white T-shirts and jeans. They waved cheerfully and tossed for'ard and aft lines across to the *Barracuda*'s deck crew to make her fast.

"Are we actually going on board this wreck," whispered Shakira.

"'Fraid so," said Ravi. "At the moment, it's all we've got."

They stood on the casing in the rain and said their good-byes to Ben Badr, Shakira's brother Ahmed, and the XO, Capt. Ali Akbar Mohtaj. Everyone had known this was as far as the General and his wife were going, but there was a great deal of sadness in their departure.

Now, however, the task of the *Barracuda* was strictly operational. The mission was laid out, her course set, her missiles loaded, their tracks preplanned. All that was required was a careful command, dead-slow speeds, if they were close to any other ships, and a steady run into deep getaway waters.

There would be satellite signals in and out of Bandar Abbas. There would be possible adjustments in the orders, but the signals coming back to the submarine would be direct from General Rashood. There was comfort in that for all of the *Barracuda*'s executives.

And there was an even greater comfort in knowing that if plans needed to be altered in any way, they would be schemed by the General, the Hamas military leader who would now play satellite poker with the Americans in the final stages of the operation to drive them out of the Middle East forever. On board the *Barracuda*, there was nothing more Ravi could do.

Shakira hugged her brother, kissed Ben Badr on both cheeks, and shook hands with Capt. Ali Akbar. Ravi shook hands with each of them, and then steered his wife towards the gangway. She carried with her a long dark blue seaman's duffel bag, in which was stored her makeup, shirts, spare jeans, underwear, and Kalashnikov AK-47.

General Rashood watched her traverse the little bridge holding the rail with one hand, and then he too stepped off the deck of the *Barracuda* for the first time since they left the Chinese port of Huludao in the Yellow Sea. And he made his way carefully over to the Senegalese Navy's 52-foot-long *Matelot Oumar Ndoye*—whatever the hell that meant.

It took all six of the patrol boat's crew to manhandle the gangway back aboard. The operation was conducted with a great deal of shouting and laughing. Twice it almost went over the side, and by the time they had it safely stowed, the *Barracuda* was gone, sliding beneath the great ocean that divides the African and American continents.

It was heading west, for the moment, out towards the burly shoulders of the Mid-Atlantic Ridge, running effortlessly, 600 feet below the surface, in the gloomy depths of its own netherworld, far away from the prying eyes of the American photographer high in the sky.

Ravi and Shakira sat in a couple of chairs under an ancient awning on the stern, beneath the machine-gun mountings. The Captain, a heavily muscled ex-fisherman, had made a sporting attempt to introduce himself, but he spoke only French in a heavy Wolof vernacular. In the end, they settled for a laugh and a rough understanding that he was Captain Reme, and he'd have them moored in the great port of Dakar within thirty minutes.

So far as he could tell, Captain Reme was restricted to only two speeds—all-stopped and flat-out. Right now they were flat-out, in a ship that shuddered from end to end, as its aged diesels struggled to drive the twin shafts at their maximum possible revs.

Happily the sea was calm all the way, aside from a long Atlantic swell, and the *Matelot* shuddered along at its top speed of 20 knots, towards the great Muslim city of Dakar, where at least one of the towering white mosques rivals the finest in Istanbul and Tehran. Senegal has always had one foot in the Middle East and one in West Africa, similar to Dakar, which has been called the crossroads in which black Africa, Islam, and Christianity have met for centuries, occasionally clashed, yet ultimately blended. The bedrock of the country's subsistence economy is peanut oil and not much is left over for Senegal's Navy budget. The U.S. Government spent more on the Pentagon's cleaning staff than Senegal spent on its Navy.

Captain Reme was as good as his word. They pulled alongside in exactly thirty minutes. The elderly diesels had not shaken the ramshackle craft to pieces, and Ravi and Shakira stepped ashore into a working Naval dockyard. Much of the quayside was stacked with fishing gear and shrimp nets, which made it a somewhat more relaxed operation than the one they left ten weeks ago on the shores of China's Yellow Sea.

But it was a dockyard, no doubt about that. On two adjoining keys, there was a 450-ton French-built Navy patrol craft, twenty-six years old, lightly gunned, named *Njambuur*. Next to it was a Navy coastal patrol craft, a Canadian-built Interceptor-class gunboat, thirty years old. No engines were running. It was plain to Ravi that the Senegalese Navy was not planning to go to war with anyone in the near future.

They were greeted by the head of the Navy, a broad-shouldered black officer, age around forty, Captain Camara, whose teeth were as white as his short-sleeved uniform shirt. He saluted and said, in impeccable English, how pleased he was to welcome them to his humble headquarters. He had spoken to his friend Admiral Badr in Iran only that morning, and everything was ready, as planned.

He would, he said, be driving them personally out to the airport, a short distance of just three miles. But first he was sure they would like some tea. Their aircraft expected them at 1800, so they had half an hour to kill.

Thus, in the now hot late-afternoon sun, General and Mrs. Rashood were ashore at last, strolling along the peaceful African waterfront, through the very heart of the sleepy Senegalese Navy—just a couple of weeks before they were scheduled to eliminate the entire East Coast of the United States of America. The contrast was not lost on either of them.

Tea with Captain Camara was a cheerful interlude. They sat outside and watched little boats crossing the harbor, sipping English tea with sugar but no milk, from tall glasses in silver holders. The Captain asked no questions about the long voyage of the *Barracuda*, though he plainly understood that there was a dark, subversive edge to its mission.

He knew his guests were important, and he knew they had arrived in a submarine, which had then vanished. But he did not think it was his place to pry into the business of his fellow Muslims, who would shortly be flying home across the vast wilderness of the Sahara Desert, which lies to the northeast of Dakar.

He had visited this remote burning landscape only once,

and had recoiled from it, as most black Africans do. But he understood that those endless sands represent the very fabric of the Muslim world. He understood, remotely, that his own tiny coastal community was somehow joined by the swirling dunes of the Arabian desert, to the great Islamic nations of Egypt, Syria, Libya, Iraq, Iran, and the Gulf States. And he knew it was timeless. And that it mattered. And he respected his visitors from the far ends of the Muslim kingdoms.

The Captain observed that General Rashood had an extremely pronounced English accent, and asked if, like himself, the General had attended school in the British Isles.

Ravi, who was desperately tired after a 20,000-mile voyage from communist China, could think of a thousand reasons not to tell anyone of his background. But he smiled and opted for mass confusion. "No, Captain, I did not," he said. "I went to a school in Switzerland. They taught me to speak like this."

"I see," he replied. "But I expect you noticed that I too speak like you, and I did go to school in England. Charterhouse. And from there I went to Oxford University . . . studied engineering at St. Edmund Hall, but my main achievement was to play golf for the University against Cambridge. Twice. Once as Captain."

Ravi, who was almost nodding off in the hazy African heat after the rain, jolted himself back into the conversation and offered, "You're a Carthusian, and you got a Blue for golf? That's impressive."

"I did," said Camara, who was momentarily bewildered by his guest's instant grasp of his elite education, especially the fact that Ravi knew, esoterically, that "Old Boys" of Charterhouse are known as Carthusians.

But he continued, "They taught me to play at school, and when I arrived at Oxford I turned out to be one of the best players. I really enjoyed it . . . very jolly people. It was funny, but they could never get a firm grip on my full name, which is Habib Abdu Camara, and when the team list was posted each week, they used to write me in as 'The Black Man.'"

"Christ, if they did that these days they'd all be in the slammer," said Ravi, smiling.

Captain Camara laughed. "I suppose so, but they meant no harm. And even I thought it was funny. All of them have stayed my good friends."

"You still see them?" asked Ravi.

"Well, I came down from Oxford seventeen years ago. And we did have a reunion for several years at the public schools golf . . . You know, the Halford-Hewitt Tournament down at Royal Cinque Ports in Deal. Of course, we were all playing for different schools, but at Oxford, when we were together, we did beat Cambridge twice, and we're all rather proud of that."

"You stopped going to the Halford-Hewitt?"

"Not entirely. But my Navy career here prevented me from playing for Charterhouse for many years. Matter of fact, I'm going back next year. It's funny, but you see the same chaps, year after year, playing for their old schools. We've been in three semifinals against Harrow and I don't think either team hardly changed."

Ravi stiffened at the mention of his old school, but the chatterbox Captain of the Senegalese Navy had seized the moment to expound on his golfing career to someone who appeared to know what he was talking about.

"Great matches we had against the Harrovians," he said. "Chap called 'Thumper' Johnston was their captain. His real name was Richard Trumper-Johnston, but he was a very fine player. He beat me twice, both times 2 and 1, dropped long putts on the eighteenth . . . he wasn't so good at foursomes."

Again Ravi found himself nodding off. But he jolted back, trying to sound as if he'd been listening. And uncharacteristically he came out with an unguarded sentence, "Thumper Johnston? Yes, he went back to Harrow as a housemaster, taught maths."

"You sure you didn't go to school in England?" asked the Captain. "I know you Middle Eastern officers, very secretive men. Reveal nothing. But many of you went to school in England, especially Harrow . . . Thumper Johnston and King Hussein, eh? Ha, ha, ha."

Captain Camara's wide face split into a huge grin. "I think I catch you, General. But any friend of Thumper's is a very good friend of mine. I keep your secret."

"I didn't say I knew him," said Ravi. "I just know of him. My father knew him."

"Then your father went to Harrow?" said the Captain. "*Someone* must have gone to Harrow . . . to know Thumper. He's never really left the place, except to play golf."

Ravi smiled, and he knew he had to admit something. Anything to shut this idiot up. "My father was English, and I think he played against Johnston in the Halford–Hewitt. I just remember his name."

"Your father played for Harrow?" asked Captain Camara.

This was a critical moment. "No, he played for Bradfield," said Ravi.

The Captain pondered that for a moment, doubtless, thought Ravi, assessing the absurd notion that an Englishman named Rashood was sufficiently impressed by the play of an opponent, Thumper Johnston, in the Halford-Hewitt to regale his son with the man's career as a schoolmaster.

No, I don't think he's going to buy that, Ravi thought.

And sure enough, Captain Camara came back laughing. "Ah-hah," he said. "I think I find you out. You are a highly classified Old Harrovian Submarine Commander . . . You come out of nowhere . . . out of the ocean . . . and I check you out in England next year, maybe with Thumper in person . . . now I give more tea to my friends from deep waters."

Shakira, who was even more tired than Ravi, had actually fallen asleep, and had missed the entire conversation. She awoke just in time to hear Ravi say, "You should have been a detective, Captain, but you have this case wrong . . ."

"Then how come you know Thumper, the Harrovian maths

master!" cried Captain Camara, laughing loudly. "You are rumbled—by the Black Man from Oxford . . . Ha, ha, ha!"

Even Ravi laughed, silently cursing himself for his carelessness. He declined more tea, and asked if they might make their way to the airport. Since Shakira was so tired, she would probably sleep all the way home.

"Of course," said the Captain, jumping energetically to his feet. "Come . . . I'll call Tomas to carry the bags to the car . . . It's parked just over there."

They walked across the quay to a black Mercedes-Benz Naval staff car that carried small flags fluttering in the evening breeze on both front wings—the green, yellow, and red tricolor of Senegal with its single green star in the center.

Captain Camara drove to the airport in a leisurely manner, out to the Atlantic Peninsula north of the dockyard where a Lockheed Orion P-3F in the livery of the Iranian Air Force awaited them. The Captain parked the car and insisted on walking out to the aircraft and carrying Shakira's bag. She climbed up the steps to board and Ravi followed her, now carrying both bags.

They waved good-bye to their escort and watched him stride away towards the car. And quite suddenly, Ravi moved back to the top of the aircraft steps and called out . . . "Captain . . . come back . . . I have a small gift for you in my bag . . . I forgot about it."

Captain Camara grinned broadly and turned back towards the aircraft, as Ravi knew he would. He ran swiftly up the steps. They were agile, nimble strides, the last he would ever make. They were the strides that would end his life.

He entered the cabin and made his way to the rear of the aircraft where Ravi was fumbling in his bag. And with the speed of light, the Hamas assault chief whipped around and slammed the hilt of his combat knife with terrific force into the space between the Captain's eyes, splintering the lower forehead.

Then he rammed the butt of his right hand straight into the nostril end of the Black Man's nose, driving the bone into the brain. Captain Camara had played his last round. He was dead before he hit the floor. Shakira stood staring in amazement at the departed three-handicapper, spread-eagled in the aisle, presumably already on his way to the Greater Fairways.

The pilot, who had not seen all of this action, was fairly astonished too, and he walked down the center aisle in company with his first officer.

"General Rashood?" he said, saluting. No questions. Military discipline.

"Sorry for the mess," said Ravi. "Put his head and shoulders in a garbage bag, will you? We'll throw him out either over the desert or in the Red Sea. I'll let you know."

"Yes, sir."

"Oh, Captain. You'll understand this was a classified operation. This man knew too much about us. He was a menace to Iran, and a danger to Islam. Also he was about to reveal my identity as a Hamas Commanding Officer to the British. That was out of the question. Plainly."

"Yes, sir. I understand. But I'll have to slow down and lose a lot of height if we're going to open the rear door. Just let me know when you're ready. We fly at around 28,000 feet. I have some hot coffee on board, and some sandwiches. We can get something better around 0100 when we refuel at Aswan."

"Thank you, Captain. I think we better get the hell out of here now. Before someone starts looking for the head of the local Navy."

He and Shakira returned to the front of the aircraft and strapped themselves into the deep leather seats usually occupied by observers and computer technicians on the Orion's early warning missions over the Arabian and Persian Gulf areas.

The pilot, Captain Fahad Kani, drove the aircraft swiftly into the takeoff area, scanned the deserted runway in front of him, and shoved open the throttles without even waiting for clearance. The Orion rumbled forward, gained speed, and climbed into the early evening skies, out over the Atlantic.

He banked right, to the north towards Mauritania, then

banked again to a course a few degrees north of due west, aiming the aircraft at the southern Sahara. It was a course that would take them across the hot, poverty-stricken, landlocked African countries of Mali, Niger, and Chad, and then the northern Sudan. An hour later, they would drop down into the green and fertile Nile Valley, way upstream from Cairo at Aswan, home of the High Dam.

Ravi was unable to make up his mind whether to deposit the body of Captain Camara in the burning sands of the Sahara, hoping it would either be devoured by the buzzards or be covered forever by the first sandstorm; or to go for the ocean, where the blood from the Captain's shattered nose would ensure the sharks would do his dirty work on a rather more reliable basis.

Trouble was, he was not sure if there *were* sharks in the Red Sea, and the body might wash up on the shore. Also, he knew that timing was critical in a high-speed aircraft, and that heaving a dead body out of the door would not be easy. He did not relish the prospect of a foul-up, in which the carcass of the former head of the Senegalese Navy landed in the middle of Jeddah. Ravi opted for the buzzards.

He and Shakira were almost too tired to eat anything. But the coffee was good and they each ate a small chicken sandwich with tomato on pita bread, before falling asleep.

Two hours later, Ravi, who never slept longer than that, awoke and checked their whereabouts with the pilot. Right now they had crossed the Mauritania border and were flying over Mali. Ravi had consulted his treasured *Traveler's Atlas,* a small leather-bound pocket edition with pages edged in gold, a gift from Shakira. And he had selected his spot for the Camara heave-ho.

It would take another three and a half hours to get there, and he instructed the first officer to wake him and then prepare to slow the aircraft down, losing height to around 5,000 feet for the ejection.

He went back to the sleeping Shakira and held her hand, but he dozed off only fitfully himself, as they flew above the mountains of northern Chad. A few minutes later, they entered the airspace over the Libyan Desert, one of the loneliest parts of the Sahara, 750,000 square miles, stretching through northwestern Sudan, western Egypt, and eastern Libya.

Ravi had chosen a 100-mile-wide area of unmapped sand dunes between the oases of Ma'tan Bishrah and Ma'tan Sarah. There was not a town for 100 miles in any direction. Down below, in this burning, arid, uninhabitable Al Kufrah district, the temperature hovered around 105 degrees.

Only the GPS could tell the pilot precisely where they were, and Captain Kani was watching it carefully. Ravi, with the first officer, dragged the body to the rear door, as they came down through 10,000 feet and slowed to a just-sustainable 190 knots.

Ravi and the airman were both standing, strapped in harnesses attached to the fuselage. And as they approached the drop zone, they both heard the Captain call out . . . *"ONE MINUTE!"*

The first officer unclipped the door and pulled it sideways to swing it open. The noise was deafening, as the wind rushed into the gap. Both men held on and shoved the body into the doorway with their boots.

"NOW!" yelled the Captain, and with two more good shoves, they rolled the former Oxford University golf captain out into the stratosphere, watched the body fall towards the desert floor, and then hauled the big aircraft door shut, fast.

"Okay, Captain . . . as you were!" called Ravi. And they both felt the surge, as the Orion angled slightly upward, and accelerated towards its cruising height. As a measure of her desperate exhaustion, Shakira never stirred.

As a measure of his profound relief at having eliminated the talkative Senegalese sailor from all contact with the Harrovian Golf Society, Ravi poured himself another cup of coffee.

Captain Kani pressed on across Africa's fourth largest country all the way to the border with Egypt, about 550 miles shy of the Nile Valley. "Little more than an hour to Aswan," called the Captain. "And that'll be the first 3,000 miles behind us."

"How far's that from home?" asked Ravi.

"It's around 1,500 miles from the Nile to Bandar Abbas. 'Bout another three and a half hours. We'll be on the ground in Aswan for about an hour."

Ravi slept while the Orion inched its way across the desert, awakening only when they could see Lake Nasser, the 350-mile-long stretch of water that started backing up against the southside wall of the High Dam when they halted the natural flow of the Nile.

They came in over the 1,600-square-mile artificial lake, dropping down into the flat, barren brown terrain west of the river, and landing at the little airport, which stands 16 miles from Egypt's southernmost city. It was 0100 back in Senegal, but three time zones later, it was 0400 here in the land of the Pharaohs.

Captain Kani had organized food for his distinguished passengers, the Egyptian dish of *kushari*, which a local Air Force orderly brought out to the aircraft on a golf cart. It was still dark, and Ravi and the still-tired Shakira gazed in some alarm at the large plates containing that fabled desert combination of noodles, rice, black lentils, fried onions, and tomato sauce.

It was, after all, still pitch-dark, but they had lost all track of time, and the *kushari* turned out to be delicious. They devoured it with hot pita bread and ice-cold orange juice, and the orderly waited to take everything away, the Iranian Air Force being light on catering in its Lockheed prowlers.

Refueled and refreshed, they set off again shortly after 0500 (local), flying out towards the Red Sea and the Arabian Peninsula. Their halfway point was the western end of the dreaded Rub Al Khali, the "Empty Quarter" in the most inhospitable desert on earth. From there they headed up to Dubai, and crossed the Gulf just west of the Strait of Hormuz, landing at Bandar Abbas at ten o'clock on Tuesday morning, September 22.

A Navy staff car collected General and Mrs. Rashood direct from the runway the moment Captain Kani switched off the Orion's engines. They were driven immediately into the base and delivered to the Iranian Navy's suite for visiting dignitaries. It represented the final word in air-conditioned hotel luxury, from its vast green marble-floored bathroom, redolent with soaps, shampoo, aftershave, and eau de cologne, to its wide four-poster king-size bed.

There were two Naval orderlies dressed immaculately in white uniforms, shirts with epaulettes, and shorts with long white socks. They had already filled the bathtub with scented, oiled water and laid out two soft dark green bathrobes. Black silk pajamas were on the bed.

There was an assortment of clothing in the wardrobe—newly pressed shorts, slacks, navy blue skirts, shirts, socks, underwear, and shoes, for both male and female personnel. Shakira thought she might look like a freshly bathed deckhand when finally she emerged, and Ravi reminded her it was she who had requested permission to join the Navy.

The orderlies had placed a bowl of local fruit salad on the table in the outer room overlooking the harbor. There was fresh coffee, tea, and sweet pastries. The television was tuned to the American news station CNN. Two newspapers—one Arabic, one English—were on a table set between two big comfortable chairs.

One way or the other, it compared very favorably with the General's living quarters in the *Barracuda*.

To Shakira Rashood it looked like paradise, and she languished in the bathtub for almost an hour, washing her hair three times "to stop smelling like a submarine."

The two Iranian assistants left at midday, taking with them all of the two submariners' laundry. They drew down the shades and suggested sleep, since Admiral Badr had convened a meeting in his office at 1630 that afternoon. "You will be collected from here," he said. "The Admiral wishes you both a very pleasant day."

Outside the door, there were four armed Naval guards. At

the base of the stairs there were two more. And a four-man detail was on duty outside in the heat. Admiral Badr was keenly aware of the importance of his guests. He was also keenly aware that half the world would have paid a king's ransom to know where the Hamas assault Commander was at this precise moment.

Ravi and Shakira were awakened by telephone at 1600 and informed they would be collected in thirty minutes. They dressed slowly, poured some coffee from the heated pot, and headed downstairs to the waiting car.

Admiral Badr greeted them both warmly and told them how dramatic it was in the base when news of the eruption of Mount St. Helens came through. "It was a wonderful moment for us," he said, "after all the months of planning. But we have heard no response from the Americans with regard to the new Hamas threat and demands."

"I did not really expect any word from them," said Ravi. "However, I did expect to see some activity in their Middle Eastern bases. And perhaps a general communiqué from the Israelis to the principal Arab and Gulf nations, of which Iran would be one."

"That really is the object of this meeting," replied the Admiral. "We have not been informed of any new initiative with regard to the West Bank. And neither has anyone else. However, I do have a list of movements of U.S. troops and equipment in the bases."

"Perfect," said Ravi. "I would like to consider them, and we can decide immediately what further action to take."

"I think that's correct," replied the Admiral. "I have all the information here . . . but, first . . . How is my son? Is he handling the submarine well?"

"Oh, Ben's great," said Ravi. "He has plainly developed into a first-class nuclear submarine CO, perfectly in command, and trusted by all of his crew. The ship is behaving very well. We've had nothing beyond minor problems, and I expect them to carry out successfully the rest of our plans.

"I also expect them all to make it home safely, eventually.

Though it may be necessary for them to stay deep for a few weeks, should we be compelled to make our final attack."

"As we always planned," said the Admiral. "It is quite apparent to me the *Barracuda* simply cannot be detected during an operation. Even in hostile waters."

"Not if it's being handled by a master, like Ben," said Ravi. "And he has become a master, nothing less. We've moved that ship through dangerous waters, when we knew half the U.S. Navy must be looking for us. But so far as I know, they never got a sniff."

"Those are presumptuous words for a submariner," said the Admiral, smiling. "But I'm delighted to hear them . . . Shall we look at the American evacuation now?"

"Please go right ahead. I'll just take notes as we go."

"Right, first, Bahrain. That's the U.S. Fifth Fleet HQ. Two weeks ago, the *Constellation* Carrier Battle Group was in there, and three days ago it left. Eleven ships, including two submarines. We tracked them down the Gulf to the Strait. Also, we noticed some troop reduction, maybe five hundred Navy personnel flying out to Incirlick in Turkey.

"Second. Kuwait. That's a very big U.S. Army Command and training base. They have upwards of 12,000 military personnel in there. We have observed some movement of U.S. Air Force fighter planes leaving there for Diego Garcia, but no substantial troop movement by sea.

"Third. Saudi Arabia. That's the U.S. Air Force Command base they just reopened. They have 10,000 personnel in there, just like old times. Plus a large but shifting number of reconnaissance and fighter aircraft. We have discerned no appreciable change in anything.

"Fourth. Qatar. There's been a substantial movement of troops from there. We are only seeing two thousand of the original four thousand U.S. personnel. There was a big evacuation of aircraft too. We could tell that because of the huge empty shelters they recently built. We saw no troop movement by sea, but certainly many hundreds of them left by air.

"Fifth. Oman. The docks have always been heavily used

by the U.S. military. So has As-Seeb International Airport. They usually have around four thousand personnel in the country, and we have observed no change whatsoever.

"Sixth. United Arab Emirates. Small U.S. Air Force garrison here. No change.

"Seventh. Djibouti. Busy U.S. Special Forces training area. We've assessed three thousand personnel at various times. No change.

Eighth. Diego Garcia. Navy Base and serious airbase. They have B-52 heavy bombers and stealth bombers. No change in the number of aircraft. And it's a very transitional place for warships. No discernible change."

"They probably think we have a real nerve asking them to vacate Diego Garcia, since it is several thousand miles from the Gulf," said Ravi. "But this list is very disappointing. The United States plainly does not take our threat seriously. They're merely trying to buy time."

"By the way, how many carriers do they now have in the area?"

"One in the northern Arabian Sea, none in the Gulf, and one heading, I believe, to Diego Garcia."

"Is that *Constellation*?"

"Correct."

"They are not really behaving like a nation that is about to have half its business coast obliterated, are they?"

"No, Ravi. They are most certainly not."

"And do we yet have any information as to the attitude of their President McBride?"

"We've heard nothing. Which may mean he is working behind the scenes to destroy us. But more likely he doesn't believe our threat."

"I'd go with the latter, Admiral," said Ravi. "He's a known liberal and pacifist. And those kinds of people usually stick their heads in the sand. The danger to us is when people like Admiral Morgan get into positions of power, because they are likely to lash out. Or at worst, lash back at any perceived enemy."

"So where do you think that leaves us."

"Admiral, I think we're ready to move into the second phase of the plan."

"I thought you might take that view, General. And I agree with you. We have the power right now to make them do what we want. Or at least we should have. Have you decided on your next communiqué?"

"Absolutely. I know precisely what to do. But first I must send Ben on his way. He is well briefed and will not personally be headed into any danger zone. This next step is probably the easiest, and certainly the most likely to get major results."

Admiral Badr smiled. "Go to it, my son. And may Allah go with you."

**1430 (Local), Tuesday, September 22
14.45N 18.00W, Speed 7, Racetrack Pattern.**

The *Barracuda* cruised slowly 600 feet below the surface of the deep Atlantic, 40 miles west of Senegal. As from 1200 (local), the young Rear Admiral Badr had been awaiting instructions via the Chinese Naval satellite. They would be orders direct from Bandar Abbas, where he knew his father and Ravi Rashood were in conference.

Every two hours, out here in these lonely semitropical Atlantic waters, he brought the submarine to periscope depth, put up his ESM mast, and accessed the satellite, requesting a signal. The entire operation took him less than seven seconds, by which time he submerged again. But there had been nothing at 1200, nothing at 1400, which he knew was 1830 on the Strait of Hormuz. And now he was growing anxious.

Another thirty minutes went by, and again he ordered the planesman to blow main ballast and take the *Barracuda* to PD once more. Up went the mast, and again they accessed. And this time, the signal came back from 22,000 miles above the ocean ". . . *Proceed west to 57 degrees (16.50N) . . . Launch 282400SEPT09.*"

At least that's what it meant. What it actually read, coded, was . . . *Proceed east to 157.00–56.50N–launch 300200NOV11*. The time and launch date was plus two all the way. The chart references were coded as agreed—a lunch date in a restaurant on the wrong side of the Kamchatka Peninsula on the shores of the Sea of Okhotsk at end of November 2011.

Ben Badr knew that he had six days for the voyage, a little over 2,100 miles. That meant his father considered an average speed of 12 or 13 knots to be reasonable in these desolate mid-Atlantic seas. Desolate of warships, that is. He would cross the very center of the ocean, deep, at maybe 17 knots, and then slow down within a 1,000 miles of the U.S. Naval Base in Puerto Rico. He was not going that far anyway.

He went down to the navigation office where Lt. Ashtari Mohammed looked lonely without Shakira. She had left the correct charts on her wide desk, and they quickly checked the spot that would be their holding area for the next strike.

The target numbers, 16.45N 62.10W, were already in place in the missile room, preprogrammed into the computers in the nose cones of the Scimitar SL Mark 1s. Ben Badr made a careful note of the holding area, 16.50N 57W, and wrote it down for Lieutenant Ashtari. The selected area was 380 miles east of the target, approximately a half hour from launch to impact. No problem.

Ben Badr returned to the control room and issued his orders: ". . . *Steer course two-seven-two . . . Make your speed 17 . . . depth 600 . . .*"

1130, Thursday, September 24
The Pentagon.

General Tim Scannell knew he had just been dealt the unmistakable bum's rush. He had called the President of the United States on the private line between his second-floor Pentagon HQ and the Oval Office, and for the first time in living memory, a Chairman of the Joint Chiefs had been put through to a White House Chief of Staff instead of the Chief Executive.

Big Bill Hatchard had been polite and accommodating, but that didn't mask the fact that the phone call between the military's executive chief and the C in C of all U.S. armed forces had been intercepted. And worse, Bill Hatchard had wanted to know precisely what the call was about. In the opinion of General Scannell, an unacceptable intrusion, but Hatchard had made it subtly clear that he either was told the reason for the call, or the CJC was not going to speak to President McBride.

And General Scannell, for the only time in a long and distinguished combat career, was forced to surrender. "Tell him it's in relation to the contact from Hamas," he said brusquely, his anger not so far beneath the surface. "And to call me back after he's done with whatever the fuck he's doing."

The General slammed down the phone. On the other end, Bill Hatchard experienced no sense of triumph. Instead he felt a rather unnerving sense of apprehension, knowing that he had just made an enemy of America's most senior and most revered Military Commander, a man who was not afraid in any way of either him or his boss. That was not good.

Bill Hatchard knew the rules. These high-ranking Pentagon guys were extremely powerful, and, more importantly, permanently installed in the White House. General Scannell would be there long after President McBride had departed. So would most of the other gold-braided Generals and Admirals who surrounded him. Quietly, Bill resolved not to mention the bad blood that had so quickly developed between himself and the CJC, to make light of it, as if all was well.

That was all forty-five minutes ago. And General Scannell still hadn't heard anything from the Oval Office. He would undoubtedly have been even more furious had he heard the short, sharp conversation between the Chief and Hatchard

half an hour previously. In essence it proceeded on the following lines:

*"Sir, I wonder if you could return a call to the CJC's
office in the Pentagon?"*
    "What does he want?"
    "Something about that Hamas business?"
    "Have they received something new?"
    *"Don't know, sir. He did not really want to talk to
me, it was you he wanted."*
    *"Call him back and tell him if it's new to try my line
again. If it's not, forget about it. I'm extremely busy."*
    "Yes, sir."

But the mighty nerve that had never deserted the slow-
moving, ponderous Yale defensive lineman in a dozen games
for the Eli's now folded up on him. He simply could not bring
himself to call the Chairman of the Joint Chiefs and make
him look small. This was nothing to do with tact and empa-
thy. This was pure and simple dread. Bill Hatchard was not
about to engage General Tim Scannell in open combat. And
like many would-be executives, operating in waters too deep
and too hot, he elected to do . . . nothing.

Which left an extremely angry General Scannell simmering in the Pentagon, currently on the line to Admiral Arnold
Morgan—*the only person around here who understands precisely what is going on.*

The two men spoke very seriously. According to Admiral
Morgan's guess, the *Barracuda* was probably in the South
Atlantic by now, somewhere in a million square miles of
ocean off the east coast of Argentina.

He listened with interest to the General's report of the
troop movements out of the Middle East and was pleased to
hear that there was no longer a Carrier Battle Group in the
Gulf. Both men believed that the Hamas demand to vacate
the U.S. Navy facility in Diego Garcia was insolent in the ex-

treme. DG was, after all, an official British colony and, in any case, thousands of miles closer to Hindu India than Muslim Iran or Iraq.

But what occupied them most was the knowledge that the terrorist attack had been threatened for October 9. And that was a mere fifteen days away. Arnold was seriously worried about the deployment of one hundred U.S. warships in the Mid-Atlantic, both in terms of logistics and the fact that the C in C of all the U.S. Armed Forces knew nothing of the operation. And that he actively refused to know anything about the operation.

At this point, neither General Scannell nor Admiral Morgan cared one jot for the moral rectitude of the mission. As Arnold put it, "It cannot be right, just because the President says it's right. And it cannot suddenly become wrong, just because the President refuses to consider it. The judgment itself, right or wrong, remains sacrosanct, whatever he thinks."

The fact was that both men sincerely believed the United States to be under threat; a threat in which a million people or more might die, and several of its greatest cities might be destroyed. Unless, that was, the military moved fast and decisively. In General Scannell's opinion, "If there is one chance in twenty this tidal wave might actually happen, we must either stop it, or harness all of our considerable defenses. Any other course of action represents a gross dereliction of duty."

Given the evidence, the General put the chances of this attack on the lethal granite cliff face of La Palma not at one in twenty, but even money. They had to get the President on their side.

0100, Monday, September 28
Communications Center
The Pentagon.

The duty officer stared at the screen, punching the button to download and print. The E-mail signal, unencrypted, was addressed personally to:

THE CHAIRMAN OF THE JOINT CHIEFS,
The Pentagon, Washington, U.S.A.
  Sir, you plainly have not taken our last communiqué
seriously. Pay attention just after midnight tonight,
September 28, and you will see what we can do, and
perhaps change your mind.—Hamas.

Maj. Sam McLean, a veteran infantry officer in the Second
Gulf War, was instantly on full alert. He ordered someone to
trace the E-mail immediately and then, checking his watch,
fired in a call to the senior officer on duty in the United States
Army ops area on the third floor.

Just the word *Hamas,* like *terrorist,* caused him to relay the
message immediately to the CIA in Langley, Virginia, and
the National Security Agency at Fort Meade, Maryland.

It was circulated to the ops-area night staff, with a copy to
the Director's Assistant, Lt. Comdr. Jimmy Ramshawe, who
was still in his office, poring over photographs and signals
that might betray the whereabouts of the elusive *Barracuda*
submarine.

The Army Colonel, holding the fort at 0100 in the Pentagon, did not hesitate. He opened up the hot line to the home
of the CJC and reported the message to General Scannell,
word for word. Jimmy Ramshawe was already on the wire to
Chevy Chase, where Admiral Morgan came out of his sleep
like a Fourth of July mortar shell.

He scribbled a short note and called Tim Scannell who
was still on the line to his office. By 0130, all the key players
were tuned in to the new threat. General Scannell convened a
meeting in the Pentagon for 0700.

Meanwhile, the tracers in the communications center had
come up with a vague solution. The E-mail had originated
somewhere in the Middle East. Either Damascus, Jordan,
Baghdad, or possibly Kuwait. Definitely not to the west of
the Red Sea, nor to the south or east of the Arabian Peninsula. The investigation was so sketchy that Major McLean relayed it only to the CIA, for possible further clarification.

By 0700, there was a pervasive sense of unease throughout the Pentagon. Word had inevitably leaked out that there was a new threat from Hamas. And it had not been specified. It could be anything, even another lunatic driving a passenger aircraft into the building. By the time the meeting began, the entire place was moving to red alert.

In the CJC's private conference room, Admiral Morgan again chaired the meeting, and there was no one who believed that the Hamas writer was not deadly serious.

"I suppose there's nothing on any of the nets that might throw light on the *Barracuda*, is there?" asked Arnold. "I mean, a possible contact anywhere in the world?"

"Nothing, sir," replied Lieutenant Commander Ramshawe. "I've been up all night searching. But there's not a damn squeak. The only item on any Naval network of any interest to anyone came from France. They're saying the C in C of the Senegalese Navy has gone missing."

"Probably been eaten by a fucking lion," growled Admiral Morgan. "Anyway, we're going to find out what these Hamas guys are up to seventeen hours from now. If nothing happens, maybe the President's right. Maybe all of our evidence is just coincidental."

"Not a chance, Arnie," said Admiral Morris. "Something's going to happen, somewhere. And you know it."

"Then we better get the President of the United States of America off his ass, right now," replied Arnold Morgan. "Somebody tell him we're coming over at 0900, and he better be listening."

0900, Monday, September 28
The White House.

GENERAL TIM SCANNELL and General Bart Boyce, accompanied by Admirals Dickson and Morris, arrived unannounced, in two Pentagon Staff cars, at the West Wing entrance to the White House. Three of them were in uniform, as instructed by the CJC. Only the retired Navy Battle Group Commander George Morris wore a formal dark gray suit.

Both Secret Service Agents on duty were somewhat uncertain whether to detain this illustrious military quartet while visitors' badges were issued, or whether to escort them immediately to the reception area outside the Oval Office.

Like all guards, the Secret Service Agents were indoctrinated with a strict code to play every issue by the book. That meant badges. But this was different. The Chairman of the Joint Chiefs, the Supreme Allied Commander of NATO—that's two Four-Star Generals, plus the Chief of U.S. Naval Operations, and the Director of the National Security Agency. Both agents arrived at the same conclusion. Fast. This was no time for visitors' badges.

They escorted the four officers to the Oval Office holding area and informed the secretary precisely who was there to see the President. Within one minute, Bill Hatchard was on the scene and summoned them to his office down the corridor.

"You would like to see the President?" he asked amiably enough.

"Correct," replied General Scannell.

"That's going to be extremely difficult this morning," he said. "President McBride has a very busy schedule."

"That's okay. You've got a full five minutes before we either walk into the Oval Office or instruct the Marine guards to search the place until they find him," said General Scannell. "So hurry up."

"Sir?" said Bill Hatchard, looking desperate. "Is this some kind of a National Emergency?"

"Find the President," said General Scannell. "Now."

Bill Hatchard was not an especially clever man, but he was long on native cunning. And he recognized real trouble when it reared its head. If he continued to defy four of the most senior military figures in the United States, he could very likely be out of a job by lunchtime. Quite frankly, he would not give much for the President's chances either, if this situation was as serious as it looked. *Jesus, guys like this don't just show up en masse unless something very big is happening.*

Bill Hatchard rose. "I'll be right back with some more information," he said quickly.

"Forget the information, soldier," snapped General Scannell, a lifetime of sharp commands to lower ranks suddenly bubbling to the fore. "Come back with the President."

Bill Hatchard bolted out of his office. He was back in three minutes. "The President will see you now," he said.

"Well done, soldier," said General Scannell. "You accomplished that with forty-five seconds to spare, before we relieved you of command."

"Yes, sir," said Bill Hatchard. "Please come this way."

They walked down to the Oval Office, where President McBride awaited them. "Gentlemen," he said, "what a nice surprise. I have ordered you some coffee. Perhaps you'd like to sit down."

All four of them sat down in large wooden captain's

chairs, and General Scannell immediately produced a copy of the communication from Hamas.

"May we assume you have read this short letter, Mr. President?" asked the CJC.

"You may."

"And may I inquire as to your views?"

"Of course. I have taken on board the last communication, allegedly from Hamas, in which someone wrote, one week after the fact, to reveal that he had just exploded Mount St. Helens. It now looks as if the same person may have written again, to suggest he is going to do something else, somewhere, tonight."

"That is correct, sir," replied General Scannell, deferring to the President's rank as Commander in Chief of the U.S. Armed Forces. "And do you have an opinion on what, if any, action, we should take?"

"Yes, I do. Since both letters are plainly the work of a nutcase, my answer is to do nothing. In the great offices of State we can't spend our lives chasing around in pursuit of every damn fool threat that comes our way."

"Sir, there were in fact three communications, as you know . . . suggesting he blew the volcano, demanding we vacate the Middle East or he would blow another volcano in the eastern Atlantic and wreck our East Coast. And reminding us that we are ignoring him at our peril. And that tonight he will show us precisely how dangerous he is."

"Well, we do not have one shred of proof that he's ever done anything. So why should you expect me to turn the world upside down, moving half the U.S. Armed Forces around the world?"

"The answer to that is very simple, Mr. President," replied General Scannell. "Because he might actually be telling the truth. Maybe he did blow Mount St. Helens, maybe he is going to pull off some outrage tonight. And maybe he could cause one of the world's great landslides, and put New York and Washington under 50 feet of water."

"Well, I don't think so. I think we're dealing with a crank."

"Sir. In the military we are taught to think precisely the opposite. What if he did? What if New York was underwater?"

"What if, General. What if, what if?" The cry of the civil servant, the cry of the frightened executive. "What if . . . I would remind you that I did not get to sit in this chair by running scared. I got here, to use your parlance, by facing down the enemy . . . Do you really think that one man could possibly wreak the havoc and destruction you are forecasting?"

"Yes, Mr. President. I do. For a start, we have incontrovertible evidence that cruise missiles may have been fired at Mount St. Helens. And if they were, they came from a submarine."

"From the documents I have read, you were relying almost entirely on a bank manager who appeared to have drunk a half-gallon of Dewars Scotch?"

"The bank manager was actually the President of one of the largest financial institutions in the West," interjected Admiral Dickson. "He will probably run for State Governor at the next election, and the half-gallon of Dewars was unopened. The proof that he heard what he heard is evidenced by the fact that he escaped from the foothills of the mountain, when no one else did."

"All he heard was a couple of gusts of wind, and that's not enough hot air to have me redeploy half the U.S. Army, Navy, and Air Force."

"Sir, we have come to see you to offer advice involving the safety of this country. If our enemy is indeed planning to do something tonight, something quite possibly beyond the scale of 9/11 and Kerman's last attack on our soil, we should be on full alert. I do not need to confirm that the Pentagon is already in a state of readiness. I suggest the White House do the same.

"I also ask your permission to begin deploying the fleet into the eastern Atlantic on a search for the submarine, which might be carrying nuclear missiles, and to begin a substantial troop and aircraft evacuation of our bases in the Middle East.

Essentially I'm trying to buy us some time to locate the Hamas assault ship."

"I'm certain we'd be chasing our tails, General. Permission denied on both counts. Let's just wait till midnight and see what happens."

"I should warn you, sir, that if anything drastic happens at midnight, either to ourselves or to someone else, you will have to consider your position very carefully. Remember, unlike politicians, we in the Military are not trained to lie."

"General, I resent that remark . . ."

"Do you? Then I suggest you spend the next fourteen hours wondering what you'll say . . . if you are proven wrong. Good day to you, sir."

With that, the two Generals, and the two silent Admirals, stood up and took their leave. Alone in the White House, the President shook his head, muttering to himself . . . *Goddamned paranoid military. Nothing's going to happen . . . these guys are crazy . . .* and he hit the button for Bill Hatchard to come in for a sensible chat about the real issues of the day.

2300, Monday, September 28
56.59W 16.45N, Western Atlantic
Speed 6, Course 270, Depth 500.

Admiral Ben Badr's *Barracuda* moved slowly through the outer approaches to the Caribbean. He was due east of the Leeward Isles, and somewhere up ahead, two days' running time at this low speed, were the playgrounds of the rich and famous—St. Kitts and Nevis, Antigua and Barbuda.

Admiral Badr's target was located 25 miles farther into the Caribbean than Antigua. It was much less of a playground than its bigger palm-strewn brothers, since half of it had been obliterated in the ferocious eruption of 1996–97.

Montserrat—battered, dust-choked, grieving, almost

wiped out, workaday Montserrat—tonight slumbered peacefully beneath a Caribbean moon. For those who remained in residence on the island, there was always the hope that the great steaming, smoke-belching heart of the Soufriere Hills would soon calm down and relapse into its dormant state, beneath which generations of islanders had grown up, safe and sheltered.

At least they had until that fateful hour in 1997, when the south part of the island was literally bombarded with massive molten rocks and lava, as the mountain exploded like an atom bomb. Nothing was ever the same, and the islanders have lived ever since in the fear that it would happen again, against the hope that the high-surging magma would finally subside.

Volcanologists had not been so optimistic. People were periodically advised to leave. But too many had nowhere to go. And they merely fled to the north, away from the lethal south side of the volcano. And the Soufriere Hills continued to growl and blast steam, dark smoke, fire, and occasionally lava on an uncomfortably regular basis.

Below its shimmering peak, set to the west, the town of Plymouth, former home to the island's seat of government, lay virtually buried under the ash. One tall British red phone booth is long gone. The high clock on the war memorial juts out almost at ground level above the gray urban landscape of dust and rocks.

As Professor Paul Landon had said to General Rashood in a house in West London, six months previously . . . *"Montserrat! You could probably blow that damn thing sky-high with a hand grenade. It could erupt any day."*

Ravi Rashood's master plan to frighten the Pentagon to death, to scare them into obeying the Hamas demands, was within one hour of execution. The launch time of midnight in the eastern Caribbean was one hour in front of Washington. General Rashood had allowed thirty-five minutes running time for the missile, and maybe twenty-five minutes for the news of the eruption to make it to the networks.

Admiral Badr was confident. His orders were to launch four missiles, the Scimitar SL-1s (nonnuclear warheads), straight at the high crater in the Soufriere Hills. In 1996, the entire island, roughly the form of a pyramid if seen from the sea, had looked like an exploding Roman candle in the night.

Like Mount St. Helens, the Soufriere Hills volcano was not a proud, towering queen, standing like a sentinel over the lush green island.

Instead, like her ugly sister in faraway Washington, she was an unstable, dangerous bitch, rotten to the core, unable to control herself, a lethal pile of shifting black rubble, swollen by mammoth carbuncles that every now and then lanced themselves and released the satanic magma.

Admiral Badr kept the *Barracuda* going forwards to the edge of his launch zone. He checked his watch.

In the past hour, they had made dozens of checks on the prefiring routines and settings. Lieutenant Commander Shakira had personally supervised the numbers that had been punched into the tiny onboard computers in each of the Scimitars' nose cones. They had pored over the little screen that displayed the chart references. All four were the same— *16.45N 62.10W*, the very heart of the volcano high in the Soufriere Hills on the island of Montserrat.

With the competence of the North Korean technicians, and the electronic engineers of Huludao, the quartet of Scimitars could not miss. They would plunge into the crater within 10 feet of each other, each one drilling deeper into the upper layer of rock, all four of them driving substantial fault lines into the flimsy pumice stone crust that held back the deadly fire.

Shakira had selected a southerly route for the missile attack on the grounds of her uncertainty about U.S. tracking stations either in or near the old Roosevelt Roads Naval Base in Puerto Rico.

The Scimitars would swerve 20 degrees off their due-western course and swing through the Guadeloupe Passage, passing five miles to the north of Port Louis on the French island's western headland. They would make their big right-hand turn out over the open water northwest of Guadeloupe, and then come swooping in to Montserrat out of the south-west.

They would flash over the half-buried ghost town of Ply-mouth, and then follow the infamous route of the 1997 magma, two miles at 600 mph over the rising ground, straight up to Chance's Peak, before diving into the crater.

And this time, there would be no Tony Tilton below, no ob-server to hear the eerie swish of the rockets' slipstream through the air. These days, this southern part of Montserrat was deserted. Shakira's plan was for no one to hear, or see, anything. Until the vicious old mountain exploded again.

Ben Badr checked with the sonar room. Then he ordered the submarine to periscope depth for a lightning fast surface picture check. The seas were deserted and nothing was show-ing on the radar—critical factors when launching a missile with a fiery red tail as it cleared the ocean, visible for miles.

He ordered the *Barracuda* deep again. Then he made a fi-nal check with his missile director. And at one minute to mid-night (local), he issued the order to activate the immaculate preprogramming plan. The sequencer was watching his screen. The *Barracuda* was facing west, running slowly, 300 feet below the surface.

"STAND BY TUBES ONE TO FOUR . . ."

"Tubes ready, sir."

"TUBE ONE . . . LAUNCH!"

The first of the Scimitars blew out into the pitch-black wa-ter, angled upwards, and came blasting out of the ocean, and into the warm night air. It left a fiery, crackling wake as it roared into the sky, until it reached its preset cruising height of 500 feet and settled onto a firm course for the Guadeloupe Passage. At this point, the state-of-the-art gas turbines cut in and eliminated the giveaway trails in the sky.

Scimitar SL-1 was on its way, and there was nothing in this lonely part of the western Atlantic that could possibly stop it. And even as it streaked high above the waves, Admiral Badr

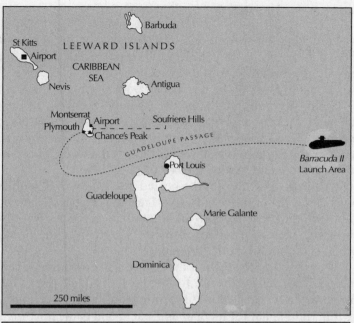

Barbuda

LEEWARD ISLANDS

St Kitts
■ Airport

CARIBBEAN
SEA

Nevis

Antigua

Montserrat
Plymouth Airport   Soufriere Hills
        Chance's Peak

GUADELOUPE PASSAGE

Port Louis

Barracuda II
Launch Area

Guadeloupe

Marie Galante

Dominica

250 miles

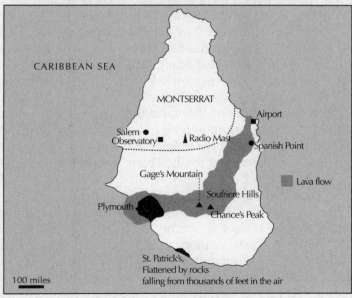

CARIBBEAN SEA

MONTSERRAT

Airport

Salem ●
Observatory ■   ▲ Radio Mast

Spanish Point

Lava flow

Gage's Mountain

Soufriere Hills

Plymouth   ▲
                ▲ Chance's Peak

St. Patrick's,
Flattened by rocks
falling from thousands of feet in the air

100 miles

THE VOLCANIC ISLAND OF MONTSERRAT, BLOWN TO
PIECES IN ITS CARIBBEAN PARADISE

was ordering the second one into the air, then the third, and then, a mere three minutes after the opening launch, the final missile. The volatile, unstable volcano in the Soufriere Hills was about to awaken the Caribbean once more.

Twenty-five minutes after the opening launch sequence, the lead rocket came swishing past the inshore waters of northern Guadeloupe. Four minutes later, it was hammering towards the Plymouth waterfront, deserted now for ten years, beneath the haunted rock face of Chance's Peak.

It ripped over the almost-buried war memorial with its high clock tower, now only five feet above ground level. It shot straight above George Street, with its second-story-only shopping facade, past Government House, over the cricket pitch, and on towards the mountain.

At the back of the town it made a course adjustment, veering right to the northeast, following the inland road down from the east coast airport. One mile from the central crater it swung right again for its final approach, and came hurtling in out of clear skies, straight at Gage's Mountain.

At 0036, on the morning of Tuesday, September 29, General Rashood's Scimitar SL-1, courtesy of the illegal North Korean arms factory, smashed eight-feet deep into the steaming active crater in Montserrat's Soufriere Hills, detonating with barbaric force.

The packed rubble of the volcano gave the blast a dead, muffled, subterranean thumping effect, just as the first missile had done at Mount St. Helens. But less than one minute later, the second Scimitar crashed bang into the middle of the crater and exploded savagely, splitting the already wide bomb-cavern almost in two.

That was plenty for the fragile, cantankerous killer mountain, which seemed to take a deep quivering breath before belching fire and ashes a thousand feet into the air. And then, with an earth-shaking rumble, it erupted with mind-blowing force, sending a thousand white-hot rocks and boulders hundreds of feet into the sky, lighting up the entire eastern stretch of the Leeward Isles.

Admiral Badr did not need missile three, which came arrowing in through the fire and fury of the exploding volcano, and reached its target before detonating in the immeasurable heat of the magma. Missile four melted and blew to pieces in midair, in the raging fires of gas-filled magma that lit up the atmosphere half a mile above the mountain.

A gigantic pyroclastic flow now developed on the southwest side of Gage's, and the dense burning ash began to envelop the entire area, cascading down the upper slopes, heading for farmland that had never recovered from the initial eruption in 1996, and on to the already half-buried town of Plymouth.

If anything, this was a bigger blast than the one seen on Montserrat thirteen years earlier, when the ash plume had blown itself *40,000 feet* into the air and endangered all commercial aircraft. It was not quite so high this time, but by common consensus, the heat and the fire were greater, and the surging lava flow down the mountain was deeper and just as hot.

It took ten minutes for the massive second phase of the explosion. The biggest of the carbuncles to the northeast of Chance's Peak suddenly began to collapse. Later, geological studies surmised that the carbuncle must have shaken and cracked with the upwards surge of the magma, which was unable to exit from the main crater.

It finally gave way, and a new gout of molten rock burst 200 feet into the air in a hurricane of blazing ash, gas, and black rubble. Instantly, the magma began to flow, and it gushed out from the heart of the mountain, rising up from the fires of Hell.

And it rumbled down the northeastern slopes of the Soufriere Hills, down the ghats, down the Tar River Valley towards the airport. Anything it touched burned instantly. It melted the blacktop on the roads, set fire to every tree and hedge in its path, incinerated cottages and barns, mostly abandoned.

Moving at 40 mph, it rolled towards the sea, surging right

to the little town of Spanish Point and then crushing and burning every last vestige of the old airport. The coastal area went completely black, as the burning ash cloud blotted out the moon and stars. The ocean boiled along the shores as the white-hot lava rolled into the light Caribbean surf.

Then, nine minutes after the last square foot of blacktop on the airport runway had melted, Chance's Peak erupted again, this time on the south side. It was a second devastating explosion from the same mountain, and it once more blew rocks and boulders thousands of feet into the air before they crashed down around the remains of the deserted fishing village of St. Patrick's, setting fire to everything within 50 feet of their landing.

Like the other two eruptions, this one broadly followed the lava paths of the 1996–97 blast, the magma pouring south and then splitting near the little village of Great Alps Falls. The main torrent burned its way straight over the road and directly into St. Patrick's, the secondary flow veering left over the same road, a mile to the east and into the sea. There was nothing left to weep for in St. Patrick's. The thriving little seaport had been taken off the face of the earth.

By 0100, there was no one asleep on the entire island. Indeed, almost everyone was awake on the north coast of Guadeloupe, the southwest coast of Antigua around the town of Falmouth, and Charlestown on the neighboring island of Nevis.

The lady who ran the Montserrat radio station was up and broadcasting within seven minutes of the first massive explosion on Gage's Mountain. The transmitter was in a building adjacent to her home on the island's safe area, north of the line that demarked the southern exclusion zone since 1997.

From the studio in the Central Hills, the news was hitting the airwaves by 0048. The giant volcano in the Soufriere Hills had erupted, without warning. In the modern observatory built by the international scientific studies group on a hillside near the western town of Salem, they recorded no pre-eruption activity whatsoever, on either the tiltmeters or the seismographs that constantly monitored the state of the petulant mountain of fire.

In fact the seismographs had given very early and very definite warning of the oncoming catastrophes in 1996–97, their needles almost shaking themselves off the rotating drums, as the onrushing magma rumbled and roared below the earth's crust.

But this time there was absolutely nothing, not one of the observatory's new computer screens registered even the faintest tremor. Nor did the state-of-the-art tiltmeters that the scientists in permanent residence had set to measure, constantly, any earth movement on the mountain slopes around the developing carbuncles, or, in scientific parlance, the domes.

The Montserrat Observatory was the most sought-after study area in the world. Students, professors, and specialist volcanologists traveled from five continents to experience, firsthand, the geophysical hazards of a brooding, threatening mountain, which had already destroyed half of its island.

The detection systems were second to none. Every subterranean shudder, every gout of steam or fire, every ton of escaping lava was meticulously recorded. It was said that the volcano in the Soufriere Hills was the most carefully observed square mile in the world, more so than even Wall Street.

And yet, on this moonlit September night, that volcano had blown out with an unprecedented explosion, without so much as a shudder or a ripple to forecast the cataclysmic eruption. The eruption had come from nowhere, and it would, at least temporarily, baffle volcanologists from the finest geohazard departments of the world's most prestigious universities.

On this September night, the troubleshooters of Montserrat—the police, fire departments, and ambulances—were not even on high alert until the first convulsion of the mountain almost shook the place to pieces. And even then, there was little they could do, although members of the Royal Montserrat Police Force made instantly for the helicopter pads where they ran into scientists already assessing the dangers of flying into an area almost engulfed by smoke and burning ash. The Police Chief himself banned all takeoffs until the air cleared.

This time, there were no instances of farming people being swallowed up in their own fields by the onrushing lava. No one was incinerated in their own homes. This was a clinical no-killing fiery spectacle in the eastern Caribbean lighting up the Leeward Isles and threatening certain members of the United States Military to go into cardiac arrest.

Shortly before midnight EST, reports of the eruption on Montserrat were filtering through to the United States networks. The radio station in Antigua was the first to go on air, describing what could be seen. They managed to hook up with Radio Montserrat, and their signals were picked up by the eastern Caribbean network, which in turn was monitored by one of the U.S. network offices in Puerto Rico.

Moments later, the news was out in Miami, Florida, and three minutes later CNN was on the case in Atlanta. Television pictures from Falmouth, Antigua, were poor and slightly late after the initial blast, but there was truly spectacular footage taken by the scientists' cameras in the Salem observatory.

These were instantly wired electronically to Antigua and Puerto Rico, under the contractual agreement that paid for much of the research undertaken at Salem.

By 12:05 A.M. (EST), thanks to CNN, Atlanta, the sensational pictures of a giant volcano in full cry were on television screens all over the world.

Lt. Comdr. Jimmy Ramshawe was sitting comfortably in an armchair in his parents' pricey Watergate complex when the erupting volcano jumped onto the screen. His fiancée, the surf goddess Jane Peacock, was in bed reading, paying no attention to Jimmy's grave forecast of a big event around midnight.

The first she knew of it was when Jimmy leapt to his feet, stark naked, pointing at the screen and shouting, *"HOLY SHIT!! HE'S DONE IT . . . THAT MONGREL BASTARD WAS NOT JOKING!"*

He grabbed the telephone and dialed Admiral George Morris at home in Fort Meade, as arranged. The Director of the National Security Agency had been to a Naval dinner, and was already snoring like an elephant bull. It took him a couple of minutes to hear the phone and answer, but he was visibly shaken by Jimmy's news.

"How long ago, Jimmy?" he asked.

"I'd guess about half an hour," replied his assistant. "What do we do?"

"Well, we can't do much now. But we'd better schedule a very early start tomorrow. Say, 0600, in my office."

"Okay, sir. You want me to call the Big Man? Or will you do it?"

Just then the Admiral's other line rang angrily—General Scannell. George Morris told Jimmy to speak to Arnold Morgan while he dealt with the CJC and then Admiral Dickson.

Lieutenant Commander Ramshawe, still stark naked, dialed Admiral Morgan's number in Chevy Chase, but Arnold had been watching CNN news.

"Well, sir, that's taken a whole bloody lot of the guess-work out of this conundrum, right?"

"You can say that again, kid," answered the Admiral. "Right now I'm planning to sit here and watch this thing develop . . . Maybe see if there was any warning. And I think that's what we all should do. Then we better meet early . . ."

"Admiral Morris has scheduled a meeting in his office at 0600, which is where I'll be. We can take a look at the CIA stuff, if any. Then I guess we better all meet up somewhere around 0900. My boss is on the line to General Scannell right now . . . Tell you what, sir, I'll leave a message on your machine soon as I know where we're meeting in the morning . . . I guess the Pentagon, but I'll confirm."

"Okay, Jimmy. Keep your eyes and ears open. This bastard's serious. He just hit the fucking mountain with missiles, and that mega-tsunami's getting closer by the minute, no doubt in my mind."

"Nor mine, sir."

"What's happened? Will you please tell me what's going on?" Jane Peacock had lost all interest in her magazine.

"Throw me that notebook, would you?" said Jimmy. "And that pen over there? Now, let me get some pajamas on. I've got to watch the news for at least the next couple of hours."

0230 (Local), September 29.

The *Barracuda* was steaming swiftly away from the datum, 500 feet below the surface. They had been moving for three and a half hours, since the moment the last of the four Scimitars had been launched. They were headed east, making 15 knots through the dark water, a speed that Admiral Badr thought they could sustain for no more than two or three days longer, less because he feared the U.S. Navy hot on their trail than because Shakira had been uncertain where exactly the U.S. SOSUS system became more dense in the North Atlantic.

The men from Hamas were now 50 miles away from Admiral Badr's strike zone, and a total of almost 400 miles from the stricken south coast of Montserrat. He planned to retain speed and keep running at moderate knots towards the disturbed and somewhat noisier waters over the Mid-Atlantic Ridge, where he would be very difficult to trace. Later, when he cut back to 6 or 7 knots, crossing from the Ridge to the Canary Islands in open water, he would be impossible to trace—anywhere in this vast ocean.

They had eleven days in which to make their next launch zone and would spend three of them moving as fast as they dared for thirty-three hours to the Ridge, then forty hours heading north above its rocky underwater cliffs. That would give them eight days to tiptoe over the ultrasensitive SOSUS wires—traps that Shakira had warned Ben were primed to scream the place down if any intruding submarine crossed them. Once they turned east from the Atlantic Ridge, they would be in latitudes around 28 to 29 degrees, 300 nautical miles north of Miami, similar latitudes to places like Daytona Beach, Jacksonville, Cape Canaveral. Finally, they would take up position somewhere east of La Palma, depending on the U.S. defenses that Ben Badr fully expected would be patrolling the area.

In Lieutenant Commander Shakira's opinion, there was no way that the U.S. Navy was going to let foreign submarines go charging around in the Atlantic anywhere north of the 25th parallel without wanting to know a lot about that ship's business.

Admiral Badr, now without his ace-precision missile-direction officer and assistant navigator, was resolved to be excessively careful. He looked forward to his next satellite communication, when someone would doubtlessly tell him whether he had managed to wipe out the island of Montserrat.

0600, September 29
National Security Agency
Fort Meade, Maryland.

The CIA had been on the case all night. And generally speaking, they had drawn a blank as big as that in the newsrooms of the television networks and the American afternoon newspapers: the totally unexplained, and unexpected, eruption of the most volatile volcano in the Western Hemisphere. No reasons. No warnings. No theories.

The CIA was well up to speed with the threats and demands of the Hamas freedom fighters, and even more with the views of the most senior military figures in the nation.

They put twenty different field agents on the project, working through the night, searching and checking for any sign of a missile attack on Montserrat. But so far, they had turned up nothing except for the absolute bafflement of the local scientists, whose equipment had registered zero before the first explosion from Gage's Mountain.

They sent in a preliminary report to the National Security Agency at around 0500, which Lieutenant Commander Ramshawe read with interest. Particularly the last paragraph, written by the senior case officer: . . . *The complete absence of any warning before the eruption is regarded by the professionals as unprecedented. Every volcano betrays the smallest movement of the earth beneath its mountain, and indeed any upwards surge of the magma. This time there was nothing. Which, we think, indicates detonation by a man-made device.*

Jimmy Ramshawe sifted through the reports, and the more he read, the more it became obvious that the *Barracuda* had struck again. Even small eruptions in relatively harmless volcanoes are signaled on their seismographs. And the equipment stationed in the Soufriere Hills was much more sophisticated than most, hooked up to a brand-new computerized system in the observatory.

There were reports of staggering amounts of ash covering Montserrat's buildings, even in the supposedly safe north part of the island. Any building with a flat roof seemed to have a minimum of 12 to 18 inches of the stuff—thick, heavy ash, more like baking flour than the light, airy remnants of a bonfire.

There were reports of ash covering the gardens of Antigua on the southwest coast, especially at Curtain Bluff and Johnsons Point. Guadeloupe awoke to a hot, gray cast over the whole of Port Louis. The southern beaches of Nevis were distinctly off-white. And the southern end of Montserrat was on fire. Miles of green vegetation were still burning from end to end of the exclusion zone. The devastation was almost complete in the south, with even the old disused jetties on fire out over the water.

As the morning wore on, the pictures became more and more graphic. The television networks had helicopter crews up and filming at first light. This was the second mammoth volcano explosion in the Americas within four months, and every news editor in every newsroom in the entire country knew that this was a very big story. Not one of them, however, had any idea precisely *how* big.

Admiral Morris had his 48-inch screen tuned to CNN as soon as he arrived at Fort Meade. There were other home-news items of some interest, but nothing to rival the live pictures from what looked like the detonation of an atomic bomb in a Caribbean island paradise.

He and Lieutenant Commander Ramshawe took only ten minutes to scan the incoming reports, and a lot less to arrive at the inescapable conclusion that Hamas had done exactly what they had threatened.

Pay attention . . . You will see what we can do . . . and perhaps change your mind. The words of the letter were stark in the minds of both men. Dead on time, almost to the minute, they had blown another volcano. Now everything was in place. Tony Tilton's missiles were real. They had exploded Mount St. Helens. Last night had proved it. And now the U.S.A. faced the greatest threat in its long history of wars and battles.

Admiral Morris picked up the telephone and called Arnold Morgan, confirming their meeting in General Scannell's office at 0800. Arnold had been up most of the night, studying charts of the Atlantic, wondering exactly where the *Barracuda* might be, wondering where it was headed, wondering how to catch it. In thirty years, George Morris had never seen him so worried, so utterly anxious.

He and Lieutenant Commander Ramshawe gathered up all relevant charts and documents and climbed into a staff car at 0700, fighting the traffic and arriving at the Pentagon by 0750. Up in the General's office, the pervasive concern of the military had been heightened by the arrival of a new communication from the Middle East. E-mail. Traceable only to either Syria, Jordan, Iraq, or Iran. Useless.

It had arrived at 0415, and it was formal in its tone . . . *To the Chairman of the Joint Chiefs, The Pentagon, Washington, D.C.: We do not, you see, make idle threats. Remove your armed forces from the Middle East now. And bring the Israelis into line. You have exactly eleven days.—Hamas.*

Admiral Morgan was already in his place at the head of General Scannell's conference table. He was flanked by General Bart Boyce and the CJC himself. General Hudson was also in attendance, with Admiral Dickson and the Atlantic Fleet's Commander in Chief, Admiral Frank Doran, former Commanding Officer of the *Lake Erie*, a 10,000-ton guided-missile cruiser out of Norfolk, Virginia.

The other newcomer was General Kenneth Clark, Commandant of the United States Marine Corps, and Admiral Dickson said he had the Commander of Submarine Force (Atlantic Fleet) on standby to fly in from Norfolk, if required.

Admiral Morgan opened the discussions by saying, "Gentlemen, it is perfectly clear now that Hamas have exploded their second volcano. We were 99 percent sure they had erupted Mount St. Helens, and I think we can now make that 100 percent.

"Last night, precisely as they had promised, they blew up Montserrat. I guess that's game set and match to Hamas. With one match still to play . . . I need hardly remind you of the peril we are all in . . . It's a scenario that once seemed remote, then much more likely . . . Now it's a goddamned certainty. Are we broadly agreed on that summation?"

Everyone at the table nodded.

"So that leaves us with three essential tasks—the first of which is to begin the evacuation of Washington, Boston, and New York. The second is to nail the *Barracuda*, if and when it shows. Third is to hit and destroy the missile or missiles, if and when they are launched at the Cumbre Vieja."

"Is there no chance of evacuating the Military in time to

make any difference?" asked Admiral Morris, wanting to explore all options.

"Not in the few days we have left," answered General Scannell firmly. "Not many enough to convince Hamas. And in any case, they want the Israeli peace plan signed and settled by then, with the State of Palestine recognized. We simply cannot get that done. For a start, the Israelis have indicated that they will not cooperate, so it's out of the question, even if we had more time."

"Especially with a President who is not involved in the discussions," said General Scannell.

"And not interested in the defensive measures we must take to avoid this attack taking place on our shores," added Admiral Morgan. "I am therefore proposing that we see him today, explain our aims, and why we believe he should now face up to the problem."

"And if he refuses?"

"Then we will have to remove him from office," replied General Scannell. "I see no alternative. Under the Constitution of the United States, there is no provision for a state of Martial Law being declared without the whole rigmarole going through Congress. And we don't have time for that. I did ask Arnold a few days ago to check out our options. And although I sincerely hope we do not need to realize them, I'm sure he would be glad to outline the alternatives."

Every eye in the room turned towards Admiral Morgan, who said, with neither sentiment nor emotion, "In accordance with Article II, Section I, of the Constitution of the United States of America, the President may be removed from office. It states the reasons for this as his death, resignation, or '*inability to discharge the powers and duties of the said office.*'

"It also says that his powers and duties shall devolve on the Vice President. It's very clear on that, and if both of them need to be unloaded, the Congress has to make a choice."

"Did James Madison actually use the word *unloaded*?" asked Admiral Morris.

"No. He stuck with *removed,*" said Arnold. "I'm just trying to keep it clear."

"Thank you, Admiral," said George Morris. "Just checking."

"That's what you're good at, George. Stay with it."

Even at a moment of such national gravity, Arnold Morgan could still set precisely the tone he wished.

"And, gentlemen," he said. "We have no choice but to get this man out of that damned Oval Office. Since it would plainly suit our purposes to have Vice President Paul Bedford onside, and ready to do as we ask, I have asked him to attend this meeting and he'll be here at any moment. You'll understand, I have undertaken this purely because we have only one week to make our moves effectively to put the East Coast under direct Martial Law with regard to the evacuation—and we don't have time to sit and wait while those damn Congressmen twitter around like a bunch of schoolgirls.

"It's my view that if these Hamas guys fire a couple of nuclear-headed missiles at Cumbre Vieja, the mountain will collapse into the sea and the mega-tsunami will happen. And that's the view of every darned scientist we have consulted. We have to either destroy our enemy or be ready to cope with whatever he throws at us.

"And remember, he's not asking us to *agree* to anything. He's simply asking us to fulfill their demands, now. We've wasted several weeks, thanks to the incumbent in the Oval Office. And right now, time's running out in a big hurry. These guys are almost ready."

Everyone knew that the President had selected a Democratic Senator from the right of the party to help him in the South. It had not done much good, all in all, but Paul Bedford still remained a far less radical liberal than any of Charlie McBride's other acolytes. And he had served as an officer in the U.S. Navy for a five-year term that included the first Gulf War.

He was a fairly worldly man, and was already being sidelined by the strong liberal mainstream of McBride's White

House. In the editorial offices of the *Washington Post* and the *New York Times,* the somewhat sardonic Virginian was regarded almost as an outlaw, thanks to his resolute and sincere support in the Senate for the Republican President who went to war with Iraq in 2003.

His presence in the Pentagon was announced by a young Marine Lieutenant on guard duty outside the CJC's headquarters. And everyone stood up to greet the Vice President when he made his entrance. General Scannell introduced him, then moved back to the long antique sideboard that ran half the length of the main table and poured coffee for everyone. There were no lower ranks in this meeting, no one to take care of menial tasks, except, perhaps, for Lieutenant Commander Ramshawe, who was too busy to even look up from his charts and notes.

When Arnold Morgan inquired exactly how much the VP knew about the problem that faced them, Paul Bedford said flatly, "Nothing." It was a tacit admission that this capable former navigation officer in a guided missile frigate had already slipped out of the Presidential loop.

Admiral Morgan took it upon himself to bring the VP up to speed on the phantom volcano blaster from the Middle East. The men around the table watched Mr. Bedford's eyes grow wider with every sentence. Arnold walked him through the voyage of the missing *Barracuda* submarine, the obvious attack on Mount St. Helens, the threats and demands, the blasting of Montserrat, and the communication that had arrived in the Pentagon a few hours before.

"Are you with us?" asked Admiral Morgan.

"If you mean, do I understand, Admiral, the answer is plainly, yes. But you have not informed me of the reaction of the President of the United States. Does he know?"

"Of course, he knows," said Arnold, without even cracking a smile. "He's now rejected each of three pleas by the highest military officers in the country—pleas to listen, to take some precautions, to make some preparations, or even organize our defenses. He says the letters are from a nutcase, and the whole thing is a figment of our imagination. Needless to say, we did not, do not, and will not agree with that."

"Of course not," replied Vice President Bedford, who was already displaying the built-in respect of a former Navy Lieutenant in the presence of the mighty.

"Have you offered him yet the opportunity to read the latest communication from Hamas?"

"No, sir. We have not," said Arnold. "He sincerely believes that we are all crazy—and if you would like to step up here next to me, I'll show you just how crazy we are."

Paul Bedford moved next to the Admiral. Arnold traced a circle of about eight inches in radius on the Navy chart in front of him. "Somewhere in there, Paul," he said, "is a big nuclear submarine. Russian-built, with one, or probably two, cruise missiles on board containing nuclear warheads, which, as you know, pack a wallop one thousand times bigger than any conventional bomb ever dropped on anyone.

"Eleven days from now, they are going to launch those babies at this range of mountains, right here on this next chart . . . here . . . La Palma in the Canary Islands . . . probably from close range. And that will cause, from a huge height, the biggest landslide this world has seen for around ten thousand years. Straight into the Atlantic.

"The resulting tidal wave, or tsunami, as it is called, will develop into a succession of waves, 150 feet high, which will hit the East Coast of the United States nine hours later."

"How big will the waves be at the point of coastal impact?"

"About 120 to 150 feet."

"You mean, straight over New York?"

"Correct."

"Will the waves break onto the city?"

"No sir. Tsunamis keep right on going. Probably break about ten to fifteen miles inland."

Paul Bedford drew in his breath sharply. "Have you asked top scientists their opinion on this likelihood?"

"Of course."

"How many did you ask?"

"About twenty."

"And how many of them agreed, conclusively, that this will happen?"

"All of 'em."

"Jesus Christ," said the Vice President. "This is going to happen. Unless we can stop it?"

"Precisely. And we cannot stop it by negotiation, or by compliance, because we have two noncooperative parties—Israel and the President of the United States. Anyway, we don't have much more time. Which leaves us with two essential tasks—to evacuate the big East Coast cities and attempt to destroy either the incoming missiles or the submarine, or both."

"And you anticipate having to sideline the President?"

"No. We anticipate the removal of the President."

Bedford looked up abruptly.

"When?"

"This afternoon. Right after lunch."

"You realize I am in office as the Vice President, and I am sworn to support Charles McBride so long as he shall continue to faithfully execute the office of the President, and to the best of his ability, preserve, protect, and defend the Constitution."

Paul Bedford was quoting from the President's sworn oath on the day of his inauguration.

"I guess allowing the Constitution of the United States to go under 50 feet of tidal wave might contravene that preserve-and-protect clause," replied Admiral Morgan.

"Admiral, the whole scenario adds up to a total dereliction of duty. But you have to give President McBride one last opportunity to take this matter seriously. And you have to remember that I am in no position to play any role in the removal of the President from office."

"We understand that, sir," said the CJC. "However, we may have to put you on notice to stand by to *become* the President of the United States, sometime this afternoon." General Scannell at times filled the office of Chairman of the Joint

Chiefs with immense dignity, and this was surely one of those moments.

And he added, "No one in this room wants this to happen. We don't want to be involved in some kind of a Third World junta, removing the President. But this is deadly serious, and only the United States armed forces can avert it, or, in the event of a successful Hamas attack, prepare the populace to deal with it. Remember, the President has already refused, flatly, to grant permission to lay out a Navy submarine trap in the Eastern Atlantic."

"And are you working on that? Moving ships into the area?" Bedford looked from one to the other.

"Of course we are, sir. But we cannot go on like this, operating in defiance of our own Commander in Chief."

"No, you cannot. I understand that." The Vice President was beginning to look more worried than Arnold Morgan, who was frowning right now like General Custer at Little Bighorn.

The former National Security Adviser concluded the outline of the massive task that the military faced. "Paul," he said, "we have to evacuate not only millions of citizens, but also the treasures of this nation, our entire systems of government and business. Right here in Washington, we need to move great works of art, much of the contents of the Smithsonian, not to mention historical papers from the Library of Congress, the White House, and God knows where else.

"In New York, we have to move the art from the great museums. We have to get the entire Stock Exchange—hardware and software—out of range of the ocean. We have to evacuate hospitals, schools, universities, and, most important, people. And we need a strong military presence to prevent looting."

"I understand that," replied the Vice President.

"This operation will involve the military commandeering railroad trains, the New York subway, buses, maybe trucks, and even private cars. This is a national emergency, and we have to be prepared. If this bastard gets those missiles under way, we have to accept the possibility of New York, Boston, and Washington being wrecked as comprehensively as Berlin in World War II."

Paul Bedford was thoughtful, and the room fell silent for a few seconds. "Only the United States military could possibly take care of such a situation," he said at last. "Have you thought of a chain of command?"

General Scannell looked up. "Sir, I am proposing to appoint Admiral Morgan to head up the entire operation. He first alerted us to the problem and, in the course of things, identified the threat as serious. In company with Admiral Morris and Lieutenant Commander Ramshawe, Arnold Morgan has made all the running.

"He is an experienced Naval officer, vastly experienced in politics, and capable of masterminding a plan that may allow us to nail the aggressor. I have no hesitation in appointing him Commander in Chief of Special Op High Tide. And Special Adviser to the President. Above all, every branch of the military, the Intelligence community, and politicians will listen to him.

"Any other course of action would be unacceptable."

"And where do you suggest he works from?" already knowing the answer.

"Oh, the White House, most definitely, since he will have to call the shots.

"Bear in mind—this situation will probably last for only a couple of weeks, *If* we get our act together and catch the *Barracuda*. During that time, speed is of the essence. There can be no arguments, no debates, no reluctance. Everyone must move fast and without hesitation. Admiral Morgan will need instant obedience, and, to tell you the truth, I think he has a better chance of getting it if he's sitting in the Oval Office, as a kind of acting President, before you were to move in, once the operation is complete."

This, more than anything, revealed to Paul Bedford the gravity of the situation—Military Command in the Oval Office. It couldn't be done any other way. He saw that.

"Will you require me to fulfill any duties during the transition period early this afternoon?" he asked simply. A general sigh of relief went through the room. The main hurdle had been passed.

"Better not," said General Scannell. "We intend to ask just once for the President's cooperation, then remove him from office. At which point we shall have an announcement prepared, to the effect that the President has suffered a serious nervous breakdown and has retired, with his family, temporarily, to Camp David. Of course he will be under 'house arrest,' without contact to the outside world whatsoever.

"Right then, we'll have the Judge, appointed by the Supreme Court, to swear you into office in the White House."

"And the great offices of State? Who will you be getting rid of?"

"Not really," replied General Scannell. "Though that idiot Defense Secretary and the National Security Adviser will have to go immediately, before Arnold throttles them both. And you'll probably want to appoint your own Chief of Staff. So that buffoon Hatchard will have to go."

Paul Bedford said, softly, words he never expected to utter: "Correct. Romney and Schlemmer must go immediately. I'll explain to Hatchard that with his boss gone, this is the end of his West Wing tenure."

Scannell spoke for everyone in the room when he said, "Sir, everyone at this table is very grateful for your understanding. We cannot sit here and allow this clown in the Oval Office to stand and watch while our cities are destroyed. We cannot. And will not."

"I understand," said the Virginian. "And I, in turn, am grateful for your foresight, and your confidence in me. Especially Admiral Morgan, of whom, I should confess, I have long been terrified."

"C'mon, Paul," rasped Arnold. "You never even met me before today."

"I assure you, Admiral, your reputation precedes you. And I look forward to working with you . . . er . . . I think."

Everyone laughed, the kind of restrained laughter born of high tension and trepidation. But it would not be long now. And when the Vice President left the room to return to the White House, they all instinctively checked the time. Four minutes past ten, on Tuesday morning, September 29, 2009. It was at this moment that Adm. Arnold Morgan became the de facto leader of the United States of America.

1934 (Local), Same Day, Same Time
Bandar Abbas Navy HQ.

General Rashood and the Commander in Chief of the Iranian Navy, Adm. Mohammed Badr, were trying to decide whether another communication to Washington was necessary. Did the Americans think that the Hamas high command would not carry out their threat because world opinion would most likely turn against them?

In which case, someone needed to put the Pentagon right. Sometime on October 9, young Ben Badr would fire those two Scimitar SL-2s straight at the Cumbre Vieja, no ifs, ands, or buts.

Ravi was working on a draft, and he was nearly through with it. The wording was as follows . . .

To: The Chairman of the Joint Chiefs, The Pentagon, Washington, D.C.:
There is nothing you can do to stop us now. We regret that you have ignored our instructions. You will still be under water when our brothers in Palestine rise again.

They agreed to transmit the letter sometime the following day, Wednesday, September 30.

1005, Tuesday, September 29
The Pentagon.

A minute after Paul Bedford left the office, General Scannell excused himself from the meeting and returned next door to his office. He picked up his private line to the White House and asked to be connected to the President.

"I'm sorry, General. The President is extremely tied up right now. Can I have him call you back?"

"No, you may not," replied the General. "Put him on the line now."

One minute later, the unmistakable voice of President McBride said quietly, "General, I am getting slightly tired of these unannounced interruptions during my working day. However, I understand the priority which your position in the Military grants you, and I am able to give you five minutes . . ."

"Thank you, Mr. President. You will doubtless have noticed that Hamas have carried out their threat, and that at around midnight they did indeed blow up another volcano?"

"Well, I have been told that there was an eruption of Montserrat, if that's what you're referring to, but so far as I can see, it erupts on a kind of monthly basis . . ."

"Not like it did last night, sir. Trust me. That was one of the biggest volcano blasts we've seen for years. Almost as damaging as Mount St. Helens—"

The president interrupted him impatiently. "Well, what do you want me to do about it? It was obviously in no relation to us. It took place 4,000 miles away from here, in a foreign country. I think I advised you when we last spoke on the subject that your theories were a complete waste of time, and there was absolutely no reason to place the Pentagon and the White House on a State of Alert—"

Now it was Scannell who broke in. He could see where this conversation was headed and he wasn't about to waste his breath much longer.

"You did indeed, sir. But they did not threaten to attack us directly, only to show us what they could do, in the hope that we would change our minds and get out of the Middle East. I would say, for the second time in too short a time, they have shown us what they are capable of doing."

"Well, I remain unconvinced. I think that the Mount St. Helens eruption gave some crank the idea to write threatening letters to the U.S. military and by some off chance, they managed to coincide a threat with a very volatile volcano that erupts on a regular basis somewhere down in the Caribbean.

"That is not reason to ask the President of the United States to activate an oceanwide search by the entire U.S. Navy at vast expense, to withdraw all of our forces from the Middle East at even greater expense, and then tell Israel they must evacuate their settlements in the Holy Land by next week.

"Can't you see, General, that these are the actions of a hysteric? They are issues so great, almost impossible, and without any reasonable grounds—no President could possibly tackle them without becoming a laughingstock."

"Sir, I must inform you for the final time that your military high command regards the threat from Hamas as serious. We think they can, and will, explode that volcano in the Canary Islands, which, not for the first time, will unleash a tidal wave. Only this one will flood our entire East Coast.

"I have not spoken to one volcanologist who disagrees with the theory. All these guys need to do is to hit the crater of the Cumbre Vieja with a big missile, probably nuclear, and it will happen. The ensuing landslide is a certainty. And nothing could then stop the tsunami from developing."

"Please," the President said scornfully. "Preserve me from Admirals, Generals, and scientists. Collectively you guys cause more unnecessary trouble than everyone else on this planet combined. You asked me a final question. I give you my final answer. I believe your theories are fairy tales. I have been proved right so far, and I have no doubt I will continue to be right."

He was finished with the discussion, his mind clearly already occupied with other, most important, matters of state.

"As for the overwhelming actions you ask me to take, I must say again, No, General. I deny my permission to sweep the Atlantic for a nonexistent submarine at a cost of about a billion dollars an hour. I will not evacuate our armed forces from the Middle East. And neither will I call the Prime Minister of Israel and demand the creation of an instant independent Palestinian State. Do I make myself clear?"

"I'm afraid you do, sir. I'm afraid you do."

General Scannell replaced his telephone and walked back into the conference room. "I have spoken to the President again. His position has not altered."

Admiral Morgan looked grave but unsurprised. "Then our plan for a transfer of power will have to be put into action. This day," he said. "Gentlemen, I know we must prepare for an evacuation of these cities, but what we *really* need to do is to find and destroy that fucking submarine."

"Arnold," said Admiral Dickson, "do you have a preliminary plan for the Atlantic deployment? I mean this is a huge step involving possibly a hundred ships."

"Alan, I have been giving this a great amount of thought. If this ship is carrying regular cruise missiles, top-of-the-line Russian-built, they have a range of 1,200 nautical miles. In my view, he stands well off, perhaps launching 500 miles, or maybe even 1,000 miles, from his target.

"So let's assume a missile range of 1,000 nautical miles. Initially I suppose we'd have to use SSNs or TAFFs on an area search/patrol."

Admiral Morgan, like all senior Naval officers, spoke to the entire room as if everyone habitually spoke in service jargon. It never occurred to him that not everyone knew an SSN was an attack submarine, or a TAFF was a towed-array frigate, or that the mysteries of the long, sensitive electronic listening device, trailing behind the ship, might not be clearly comprehended by every single person in Washington. Time was too short for explanations, though.

"And remember," he added, "the TA will pick up nothing, unless *Barracuda* makes a mistake or goes unaccountably noisy, which I doubt. But we have to start somewhere. *Something* has to be done, since this is the most serious threat to the United States. *EVER*.

"Now, the Naval commanders at this table will know that the towed-arrays are highly variable. But working from just one at 10 knots, covering a circular area of 10 nautical miles radius . . . that's 300 square miles per hour. We have a search area of 3 million square miles, which means that each towed-array unit needs 10,000 hours to sweep the area once. Fifty units would do it in eight days.

He looked around the room.

"We've got ten days, if we start tomorrow. And that massive sweep would not have covered the inshore areas, which are considerable, and extremely difficult. For that we need a fleet of helicopters with dipping sonars, covering all waters with depths of 15 fathoms, or deeper, to 50 fathoms.

"I suppose one might hope that active sonars might drive the SSN into deeper water, where the TAs have a better chance. But if you are only searching one given spot every eight days . . . Jesus Christ . . . the chances of success are negligible."

He got up and turned to the navigational chart on the wall, indicating the vast body of water they were dealing with.

"And any success depends on us getting there before the *Barracuda*. If we do, and if we are certain of this, we could perhaps form an outer ring through which the fucking *'Cuda* must pass. Total ring length would be 6,000 nautical miles (3.142 X diameter). Fifty TA units would cover 2,000 nautical miles. So to be effective, you'd need to be pretty damn sure from which direction the SSN was making his approach . . . I mean, a sector of less than 120 degrees.

"Gentlemen, not to put too fine a point on it, this is going to be difficult, with the chances of success in the 5 percent bracket at the most. Which, given the effort, is a depressing thought, to say the least. It means a huge deployment of

ASW assets—and even if we had weeks and weeks to continue the search, the likelihood of actually tripping over this little bastard is remote in the extreme. I'm afraid we need to think this out much more carefully."

He sat back down, the worried look on his face deepening.

"Obviously we have to get our warships out of port regardless, unless we want them all crushed or capsized by the tidal wave. But we can't just send them charging out into the Atlantic into the possible teeth of a tsunami.

"I could stand the cost . . . you know, in fuel, food, and personnel . . . but not if I believe we have almost no chance of success. And the prospect of that massive Naval search actually gives me the creeps. Remember, we have not really picked up this damned *Barracuda* in months. Their CO is very good, and we know he's in a very quiet boat. He could creep slowly underneath our frigates and *never* be detected. We've just got to think this out, gentlemen."

"A rather pessimistic speech, Arnold," said Admiral Morris, wryly. "Illuminating, but pessimistic. For Christ's sake, don't repeat it in front of the President this afternoon. He'll think you've become some kind of a fellow liberal traveler."

"George," chuckled Arnold. "That day ever comes, I'll step out of this room with my service revolver, and do the honorable thing, like an officer and a gentleman."

1330 (Local), Tuesday, September 29
The Atlantic Ocean, 18.00N 53.00W.

THE *BARRACUDA* was making 15 knots through deep waters,
east of the Puerto Rican Trench, 600 feet below the surface,
with 2,500 fathoms under her keel. Shortly before first light
that morning, they had come to periscope depth for a seven-
second satellite check, and the signal awaiting them, more
than 20,000 miles above the planet, confirmed their course
and mission . . . *A cruel sea for the songbirds* . . .

   Gen. Ravi Rashood, plotting and planning in faraway Bandar Abbas, did not consider the sin of self-congratulation to
be among his faults but he did harbor one small vanity—he
believed he composed one hell of a military signal . . . and *a
cruel sea for the songbirds* was one of his finest, prearranged
with Ben Badr. It was stuffed with hidden information. *The
Cruel Sea*, the famous book by Nicholas Monsarrat, meant
that the attack on Montserrat had been a total success, the
mention of the songbirds referred to . . . *"Onward! My brave
boys to the Canary Islands."* Three words to explain that the
sensational Scimitar missile attack on the Soufriere Hills had
been accurate, devastating, and world-newsworthy. Three
more to confirm the *Barracuda*'s next mission, and to seal
the fate of the arrogant Satan who dominated the Middle
East. Not to mention most of the world.

Admiral Ben Badr was ecstatic as he and his cohorts crept along towards the destiny Allah had awarded them. Everything was going according to plan.

The *Barracuda* was now 560 miles from Montserrat, steering zero-eight-three, in open water, approximately halfway between the burning Caribbean island and the relative safety of the Mid-Atlantic Ridge.

Admiral Badr and his Chief of Boat, CPO Ali Zahedi, were down in the missile room sipping coffee and inspecting the arsenal they had left—ten Scimitar cruises, eight of them with conventional warheads, plus two Mark-2s, with their 200-kT nuclear warheads. Two hundred kilotons—the explosive equivalent of *200,000 tons of TNT*. Ten conventional warheads (500 pounds each) pack a combined wallop of a couple of tons of TNT.

Ben ran his thumb over the sharp reinforced-steel nose cone of the nearest Mark-2, and he trailed his hand lightly, hesitantly, over the casing, as if stroking a dangerous lion. And he bowed to the golden lettering SCIMITAR SL-2—"It is the will of Allah," he said softly, contemplating the coming thrust to the heart of the Cumbre Vieja.

1500, Tuesday, September 29
The White House.

President Charles McBride had agreed with undisguised irritation to a short meeting with Gen. Tim Scannell and the Chief of Naval Operations, Adm. Alan Dickson. He agreed because he had no choice. Even his Chief of Staff Bill Hatchard had managed to shake his massive head when the President tried to evade seeing the Chairman of the Joint Chiefs . . . "Forget it, sir," he had hissed from across the Oval Office. "You have to see him."

In the following minutes, Big Bill pointed out that no President can avoid his CJC. "It's simple, sir," he said, unnecessarily, because if it had not been simple he would have had trouble with the concept himself. "If he has some really important information for you, and you refuse to see him, and the worst happens, he has it in his power to see you impeached. You *have* to see him, and that's that."

Charles McBride gave General Scannell and the Chief Executive of the United States Navy ten minutes at 3:05 P.M. They arrived five minutes early, in two staff cars because there were rather more of them than the President was expecting.

In the backseat of the first car sat the CJC in company with Adm. Arnold Morgan. In the front passenger seat was Gen. Kenneth Clark, Commandant of the United States Marines.

In the second car was Admiral Dickson, with Adm. Frank Doran, Commander in Chief of the Atlantic Fleet, and Gen. Bart Boyce, NATO's Supreme Allied Commander. With the exception of Admiral Morgan, the rest were in uniform.

They came in through West Executive Avenue, parked in front of the steps leading up to the Diplomatic driveway and the "front" door to the West Wing. Then they strode in tight formation, accompanied by a detail of four Marine guards who had been awaiting their arrival.

They marched to the Marine Guard Station right on the West Wing door, where a tall, polished guardsman in full-dress uniform of red and blue with gold braid, snapped to attention and said crisply, "Good afternoon, sir." The remark was addressed to General Clark, who smiled and nodded as the Marine pulled the brass handle to open the door.

Inside, the White House "greeter," a six-foot-six-inch former Naval Petty Officer, plus one of the resident Secret Agents, were plainly ready for this onslaught of military power. The agent ventured to ask the CJC if he could help.

"Two things," said General Scannell. "A U.S. Navy helicopter from Andrews will be landing on the lawn in less than ten minutes. Make sure the military office knows about it. Inform the main White House telephone executive next to the ops room over in the Old Executive Office Building, we are conducting an emergency exercise, strict security. No further calls for one half hour, incoming or outgoing, as of now."

"Right away, sir," said the agent, a former Army Captain himself. "Oh . . . er . . . Admiral Morgan, sir . . . Will you be requiring a visitor's badge?"

"Sit down, Tommy, I'm busy."

The agent, who had always held an almost hero-worshiping view of the former National Security Adviser, laughed despite himself. And he utilized the Admiral's favorite phrase, one he had heard so many times during his five-year career in the West Wing.

"No bullshit, right, sir?"

"No bullshit, Tommy," replied Arnold.

And with that, all six of them, plus the Marine guard detail, marched along the corridor towards the office of the President of the United States.

Outside the Oval Office, Bill Hatchard was speaking to the President's secretary, who bid General Scannell a polite "good afternoon," curiously looking at the little group. She had not realized there were so many people scheduled for the short meeting, she said, apologetically.

"Don't worry about it." General Clark turned to one of the two Marine guards already on duty outside the Oval Office and ordered him to summon at least eight more to the corridor.

"*SIR! YES, SIR!*" the guard snapped, obeying quickly and instinctively. The secretary now looked vaguely anxious and her alarm deepened when General Clark said to the other guard, "Head down to the main telephone switchboard and ensure that there are no incoming or outgoing calls. The order to suspend all service in and out of the White House has already been issued."

"*SIR! YES, SIR!*" he replied to his Commandant, and set off instantly for the Old Executive Building, where the lines of telephone operators guard the President and his senior people from unwanted calls.

General Scannell now walked straight past the stunned secretary and opened the door to the inner sanctum of the U.S. Government. Charles McBride was at his desk, reading some papers, and he looked up in surprise, as five senior military figures strode in behind the General.

"General, this is unacceptable. I agreed to see two people, not six. Please ask four of them to leave."

The Chairman of the Joint Chiefs simply ignored him. "Mr. President, at 10 A.M. you informed me you would not give permission for the United States Military to take steps either to prevent, or otherwise cope with, a threat from the Middle East terrorist organization Hamas. May I presume you have not changed your mind?"

"You may. It's just a load of nonsense. Now, if that's all you have to say, I'll thank you to leave now."

"Sir. This is by no means all I have to say. I must confirm that the Head of your Navy, the Head of your Army, the Supreme NATO Commander, the Commander in Chief of the Atlantic Fleet, the Commandant of the United States Marine Corps, plus Admiral Morgan are unanimous in their belief that you are wrong.

"Each one of us believes that the East Coast cities of the United States are in mortal danger from a ruthless enemy. You are not just absolving yourself from the responsibility, you are hindering our efforts to protect the citizens and their property. Not to mention the historical documents and treasures of this country, which are held in those important cities."

"Listen, General, these decisions are mine to make . . . not yours, nor any other Military Officers in the Pentagon."

"Sir, I assure you that if we consider this nation to be threatened, and we have an incompetent President in this office, he will go, not us. We are the permanent guardians of this nation. And I think you'll find that the people of the United States trust us more than a politician."

The President stared at him, disbelief on his face.

"How dare you speak to me in that manner? I've had enough of it, do you hear? I have had quite enough. Now get out, all of you, before I have you escorted out by the guards."

"Perhaps I should remind you, sir, that the White House is guarded by the Marine Corps, and their Commandant is standing right next to me . . ."

The President banged his fist on the desk. "We'll see about that," he shouted, picking up the telephone. But the line was dead, as were all lines in the White House. And that was the way they would stay for another twenty-five minutes.

He crashed down the phone, his hands shaking. In short angry bursts, slightly disjointed, and too loud, he hissed "*I've always thought you were all crazy . . . You're asking the impossible . . . I can't just evacuate the East Coast . . . I can't persuade Israel to help . . . I don't even understand deployment of ships . . . Why are you doing this? Why the hell can't you leave me alone? To do what I was elected to do . . .*"

"Sir, it is our opinion that you are not competent to lead this nation in the crisis we now find ourselves in. The President has to talk to the people . . . today . . . and it plainly cannot be you.

"On behalf of the United States Armed Forces, I am relieving you of office. For the next ten minutes, this country will be under a self-imposed Martial Law. By that time, we shall have sworn in the new President . . . As you know, under our Constitution that's Vice President Paul Bedford . . ."

"*YOU CAN DO NO SUCH THING!*" yelled Charles McBride.

"Can't I?" replied the Chairman of the Joint Chiefs. "General Clark, summon a Marine Guard of four men . . ."

"Yes, sir." General Clark walked to the door and ordered four armed Marines into the Oval Office. "Stand on either side of the President's chair and be prepared for him to do something careless," said the Commandant.

"Sir," said General Scannell. "This sheet of paper contains your resignation. You will see it already has the Presidential Seal embossed on it . . . Read and sign . . ."

The President read the sentence . . . "*I hereby resign the office of President of the United States for reasons of failing health. Signed by my own hand on this twenty-ninth day of September 2009.*"

"And if I refuse . . . ?"

"We shall place you under arrest for deliberately, and willfully, endangering the citizens of the United States by refusing to take military precautions in the face of an enemy threat. That would mean, of course, your instant impeachment, and disgrace. Sign it, sir, and sign it now, or we'll carry you out of here. Time, for us at least, is very short."

"But you cannot just appoint a new . . ."

"SHUT UP, McBRIDE!" rasped Admiral Morgan. "You've said plenty."

The President was stunned into silence. With the generals glaring, he signed the resignation paper.

"You will now be escorted to a Navy helicopter out on the lawn and be flown to Camp David, where you will remain under house arrest until we have dealt with the Hamas threat . . . Is the First Lady in residence? Any other members of family?"

"Just the First Lady upstairs in the residence."

"She will be brought to the helicopter immediately. At Camp David neither of you will be permitted any contact with the outside world whatsoever. No phones will be connected. Mobile phones will be confiscated." General Scannell glanced at his watch and muttered, "Have him escorted out right now. We're going straight to the office of the new President. Judge Moore is already in the Old Executive Building, specifically to swear him in."

The operation had been conducted, so far, with immense precision.

The High Command of the United States Armed Forces was trusted implicitly to tell the truth and to operate objectively, free from political or civilian agendas. The members of the Supreme Court understood that perfectly, and the two Supreme Court Judges, required to authorize Judge Moore's powers, had instantly complied to the request from the Pentagon.

The only politician who had been informed of the palace coup was Senator Edward Kennedy, the senior member of the Senate Armed Forces Committee, whose patriotism was unquestioned and whose personal motives to act on behalf of the United States were always impeccable.

In this instance, Admiral Morgan had assured everyone of the Senator's support since, he said, the entire Kennedy compound was situated on the shores of Nantucket Sound, in the direct path of the ensuing tsunami.

"But I know Teddy," he said. "If he lived on top of the goddamned Rockies, he'd still do the right thing about a threat like this. Also, he knows us, and he knows the Navy. He's head of the Subcommittee on Sea Power. And he knows we wouldn't be making this up. He'll trust us, and he'll give us his total support. You can count on it."

And now Charles McBride was on his feet, with a Marine guard on each elbow, being frog-marched to the door of the Oval Office. Upstairs, Mrs. McBride was being escorted more gently along the corridor, carrying only her purse. Their personal possessions would be ferried up to Camp David in the early part of the evening. The announcement of his retirement, to a shocked nation, would be given in a broadcast within the hour, when President Bedford would cite McBride's nervous breakdown.

The six White House visitors walked behind the Marine escort as far as the portico door to the lawn. One hundred yards away they could see the huge rotors of the helicopter already howling. Mrs. McBride emerged from a different door. General Clark remained to watch the U.S. Navy helicopter take off, bearing the President and his First Lady into exile from the seat of Government. The others headed directly to the office of Vice President Paul Bedford. They had agreed to ignore the intricacies of the Twenty-fifth Amendment, which essentially dealt with the transfer of power to the Vice President if a President was incapacitated and unable to carry out his duties. (The Twenty-fifth has only been used twice—once when President Reagan was shot, and once when President Bush underwent general anaesthesia in April 1989.)

In this instance, it was decided that the VP would be immediately sworn in. There was, after all, no possibility of McBride making any kind of a comeback.

Senator Kennedy had already arrived in the VP's office, and Judge Moore intoned the sacred words that all Presidents must recite: "I do solemnly swear that I will faithfully execute the Office of the President of the United States, and will, to the best of my ability, preserve, protect, and defend the Constitution of the United States."

Section 2 of the Constitution made him, at that moment, Commander in Chief of the Army and Navy of the United States.

Within moments, he had signed the prepared document that appointed Adm. Arnold Morgan his Special Adviser for the forthcoming crisis with Hamas. He willingly signed the rider to the document that ensconced the Admiral in the Oval Office, as Supreme Commander of all U.S. military forces involved in Operation High Tide, "with civilian powers as far-reaching as may be necessary for safe evacuation of the citizens of the affected areas."

General Clark, the only person in the room with a working knowledge of a digital camera, photographed the entire scene for the public record, somehow managing to wipe out four pictures taken by Mrs. Bedford the previous week at Camp David in the process. But they had to avoid the intrusion of an official photographer and the endless ramifications of this incredible private ceremony being leaked to the media.

Senator Kennedy observed the formalities and swiftly headed back to the Capitol to brief the heads of Senate Committees on the oncoming political bombshell. The remainder of the House would learn of the shift of power at more or less the same time as the media, and indeed the nation. The Military Chiefs were confident that Teddy would combine his legendary down-home friendliness with the certain tough authority that was his trademark, to convince the elected representatives of the fifty States that the nation stood in mortal danger.

Meanwhile, back in the West Wing of the White House, it was plain that staff members had to be informed and then silenced, until the press had been given the news. Admiral Morgan, standing in the Oval Office with General Scannell, decreed that senior staff should report immediately to President Reagan's specially built Situation Room in the basement of the West Wing. There they would be briefed by the Admiral himself, and there they would watch the television address to the nation by the new President of the United States. A guard of four Marines outside the door would ensure that no one left the room, and all mobile phones would be surrendered to the guards as each senior staffer arrived.

"It's important that Paul tells our story just the way we want it," emphasized Arnold Morgan. "We do not want some newsroom rewrite asshole speculating and jumping to conclusions. This White House already has a reputation for press leaks, and we don't want *anyone* releasing information until we're good and ready, and we have the situation under control."

He glanced at his watch. It showed five minutes before four. He walked out through the Oval Office door and past the ex-President's secretary to tour the building and inform all heads of departments to report to the Situation Room. Since internal communications were down, he ordered one of the Marine guards to walk down to the Press Room and inform those present that there would be a Presidential Address in twenty minutes in the White House Briefing Room.

By now, Admirals Dickson and Doran, in company with Generals Boyce and Clark, had arrived back in the Oval Office. Arnold Morgan, already seated behind the only available desk—that of the former President—was writing fast on a legal pad, on which the former occupant had been drafting a personal speech to the Third World Initiative.

Still scribbling, he spoke without looking up. "Okay, I'll take Frank Doran with me to the Situation Room, where I'll stress the enormous task of the Navy to the senior White House Staff. I think everyone else should go with President

Bedford and stand behind him on his port-and-starboard quarter. General Scannell and General Boyce on his four o'clock, Admiral Dickson and General Clark on his eight. That's the Head of the Pentagon, the Head of NATO, the Head of the Navy, and the Head of the United States Marine Corps. Solid, right?"

Just then, Paul Bedford walked in, and Admiral Morgan immediately stood up, nodded, and said, "Mr. President . . . I'm just drafting a few notes for your address . . . They're only notes . . . but we have no time . . . You'll just have to wing the speech, but it'd be a good idea to stick to the outline here . . .

"Stress the nervous collapse and subsequent resignation of the President, who is currently under medical care at Camp David . . . Tell 'em how shocked we all are . . . then come clean over the Hamas threat, tell 'em the whole story, not in detail, but start with Mount St. Helens, then the demands of the terrorists . . ." His finger ran down the notes on the legal pad. "Then the threat that convinced us of the imminent danger of our country, when they blew Montserrat. Explain the terrible danger, the silent terrorist submarine with its nuclear-warhead guided missiles, the vulnerability of Cumbre Vieja, and the certainty of the tsunami, *if* they hit the volcano."

Paul Bedford nodded as firmly as he was able to. Right now, in his own mind, he was not so much President of the United States as a Naval Lieutenant receiving a briefing of the most staggering importance from one of the most senior Admirals ever to serve his country.

Arnold ripped the page off the writing pad and handed it to the new Chief Executive. He had printed everything in bold capitals, including the first two sentences, then a clear synopsis of the rest.

"Is that it?" asked President Bedford.

"As best as we can do," said Arnold agreeably. "You're on parade in fifteen minutes, and I'm out of here with Frank, right now."

"Okay, sir," said Paul. "I can follow this."

"You can call me anything you like in this room," replied Arnold. "But for Christ's sake don't call me 'sir' in public!"

"No, sir," said Paul Bedford, laughing, despite the gravity of the situation.

"And, Mr. President . . ." said Arnold, as he headed for the door. "Remember one other thing . . . when Sir Winston Churchill demanded an entire reorganization of the Navy fleets in the North Atlantic . . . he told his First Sea Lord if it wouldn't fit on one side of one sheet of paper, it hadn't been properly thought out."

And with that, he was gone, the Commander in Chief of the Atlantic Fleet, with Admiral Frank Doran somewhere in his wake.

"Jesus," President Bedford said to himself. "Is he something, or what?"

And then, to everyone's surprise, Admiral Morgan's head popped back around the door. "Oh, Paul, I forgot. You'd better fire Defense Secretary Schlemmer and NSA Romney right now, and then Hatchard, right after he's released from my briefing. Handwritten notes thanking them for all they have done. One side of one sheet, right?"

"Okay, Arnie, you got it," replied the President of the United States, slipping into the easy informality enjoyed by men under severe stress. "Is it okay if I borrow your desk?"

Still chuckling, Admiral Morgan headed for the West Wing basement, where he found a scene of extraordinary restlessness. The heads of White House Departments had mostly arrived. Protocol, Secret Service, Communications, Catering, the chief Butler, Security, Transportation, the Press Office, the State Department, Speech Writers, Bill Hatchard, and indeed the former President's secretary were crowding into the room. All requesting information, yearning to know what was going on. The four Marine guards had taken up positions outside the door, and two more guarded the exit from the elevator. With the correct credentials, they would let you in, but no one was leaving. Not until the Presidential Address was completed and on television. A small pile of surrendered cell phones occupied a desk behind the principal Marine detail.

Arnold Morgan and Admiral Doran made their way into the soundproof teak-paneled conference room that, aside from its central table, was filled with secretarial desks, computers, and video-conferencing telephones. None of this was currently active, though staff members were hurriedly claiming the desks, since the packed gathering could plainly not fit around the main table.

Admiral Morgan moved into the big chair once occupied by President Reagan. He dragged another seat next to him for the C in C Atlantic Fleet and called the meeting to order by banging his open palm down on the polished surface of the conference table.

"For a very few of you, this may seem a bit like old times. For the rest of you, my name is Arnold Morgan, former Admiral in the United States Navy, former Director of the National Security Agency, former National Security Adviser to the President.

"I'm not precisely sure how fast rumors move around here these days, but I would like you all to know that President Charles McBride resigned within the last hour for health reasons. According to the Constitution, the Vice President has instantly assumed the Oval Office, and he was sworn in by the man appointed to do so by the Supreme Court of the United States, Judge Moore. The ceremony took place in the Old Executive Building, and President Paul Bedford swore to uphold the Constitution of the United States.

"The witnesses present were Senator Edward Kennedy . . . the Chairman of the Joint Chiefs, General Scannell . . . the Chief of Naval Operations, Adm. Alan Dickson . . . the Commander in Chief of the Atlantic Fleet, Adm. Frank Doran, who is seated here beside me . . . the Supreme Allied Commander of NATO, Gen. Bart Boyce . . . the Commandant of the United States Marine Corps, Gen. Kenneth Clark . . . and myself.

"The press will learn of the change in Government inside

the next ten minutes, and you will all see President Bedford's address on the screen in this room shortly.

"There will of course be changes in staff, but none where we are able to rely on the old order. The most important thing that I must tell you, though, is that the East Coast of this country is at present under the most terrible terrorist threat in U.S. history. Worse, immeasurably, than 9/11.

"It was this threat that caused Charles McBride to suffer what his doctors consider to be a nervous breakdown. He willingly and selflessly stepped aside as the pressures on him mounted, aware that he has no military experience and that his Vice President Paul Bedford, who served as a Navigation Officer in a guided missile frigate during a five-year term in the United States Navy, might be a better leader for the U.S. in this time of crisis.

"The former President is resting under medical supervision at Camp David right now. The First Lady is with him and they will not be returning to the White House.

"As to the threat we face, in the simplest terms, there is a Russian-built nuclear submarine, loose in the North Atlantic crewed by a group of Hamas terrorists."

The Situation Room was absolutely silent as Admiral Morgan briefly outlined the situation. He shook his head. "And we know from the events of the last few months," he said, "that Hamas has this capability. They exploded Mount St. Helens, and last night they carried out their second threat, accurate to the minute, by exploding Montserrat down in the Caribbean. Their latest communiqué says they will hit La Palma on October 9.

"We need to find that submarine, most importantly, but we have already started the preliminary stages of an evacuation of the entire East Coast to high ground, just in case we don't find it. By the end of the day, the U.S. Army, National Guard, and the various metropolitan police forces will unobtrusively control the streets to prevent a panic after the President's TV address. From the moment the Cumbre Vieja erupts, it will take nine hours for the tsunami to hit New York Harbor. And those tidal waves don't break . . . They'll just keep rolling.

"Your new President has appointed me Supreme Commander of all the United States forces engaged in this operation for the next two weeks. During this time we will begin evacuating the nation's treasures, its museums, its historic papers, its Stock Exchange in New York, and its schools. I shall be working closely with President Bedford, from the Oval Office, and with the five senior commanders who witnessed the inauguration ceremony an hour ago.

"Right now, I will not be taking questions, and I would like someone to turn on the television sets around the walls and tune in to one of the networks to hear the Presidential Address . . . Admiral Doran and I will remain here to listen with you."

The "Sit Room" remained stunned. No one spoke, but people moved quietly, finding places in front of the television screens.

Meanwhile, upstairs in the Briefing Room, the fifty or sixty members of the White House Press Corps—the journalists Marlin Fitzwater referred to as "The Lions"—were growing more restless by the minute. None of them had a clue what was taking place, and although a few photographers were plainly bored senseless by the whole procedure, dozing in the fourth row, there was an unmistakable growling at the back of the room, where the wire service reporters operated.

This was a most unusual call to a briefing, issued out of the blue at twenty minutes' notice. The reporters were huddled together, discussing possibilities. The favorite forecast was that President McBride had recognized the state of emergency on the island of Montserrat and was sending aid. Big deal.

However, journalists of a more thoughtful nature had noticed the *eight* Marine Corps guards in position in front of the dark wooden dais. That hinted at something more than aid to Montserrat. But it did not suggest the imminent unleashing of the biggest news story of the year.

A few more minutes slipped by and the level of restlessness grew. It was always the same at feeding time. The Lions began to lose their cool if the keeper was late. Actually, it wasn't his lateness that was relevant. It was the pack's perception of lateness that mattered.

Where the hell is he . . . ? Christ, it's getting too late for the afternoon papers . . . Stupid time to call a briefing anyway . . . Who the hell cares if he sends the taxpayers' money to Montserrat?

By 1625, the room was buzzing. And the sudden appearance of Lee Mitchell, Vice President Bedford's spokesman, had no effect on the noise level whatsoever. But when he walked up to the dais, turned on the microphone, and asked for their attention, they gave it reluctantly.

Mr. Mitchell, a tall young former political reporter for the *Atlanta Journal Constitution*, came right to the point. "I am here to announce formally that Charles McBride has resigned from the office of President of the United States less than one hour ago. At seven minutes before four o'clock, under the precise requirements of the Constitution, Vice President Paul Bedford was sworn into office."

The entire room exploded with the shrill, desperate, near-panic-stricken sound of fifty-odd reporters flailing between the quest for more detail and the overriding desire to speak to their newsrooms.

RESIGNED! Whaddya mean resigned? When? . . . Where? . . . Why . . . ? How? . . . Where is he? Is he still in the White House? What caused it?

It took a full two minutes for the row to subside, and only then because it was obvious that Lee Mitchell had not the slightest intention of uttering a single word until there was silence once more from The Lions he was supposed to feed.

"Thank you," he said, carefully. "There will be no questions at this briefing. But I will tell you that former President McBride is resting under medical supervision at Camp David. He has suffered an apparent nervous breakdown and may not recover fully for some weeks. The First Lady is with him. Under the circumstances, he felt he had no options but to resign."

Again, the suppressed pandemonium of The Lions was let loose. Regardless of the "no questions" edict, they stood and roared . . . *This is a national issue . . . The people have a right to know . . . What do you think I'm gonna tell my read-ers . . . What kind of a nervous breakdown . . . ? Has he been ill for long . . . ? This is America not Czarist Russia . . . C'mon Mitchell, you're paid to tell us what the hell is happening to the President of the United States . . .*

The journalists did have some power, and some of them had more than a few brains, but nothing to match the shrewd orchestration masterminded by Morgan, Scannell, and Bed-ford. And at this point the scene shifted. Lee Mitchell moved aside to formally greet the Chairman of the Joint Chiefs, then in quick succession appeared the Head of the Navy, the mili-tary Supreme Commander of NATO, and the Commandant of the United States Marine Corps, who all took up the posi-tions allotted to them by Arnold Morgan, port and starboard quarters to the dais.

And as they did so, the noise from The Lions subsided, to be replaced by a more dignified sound. Through the loud-speaker system came the unmistakably familiar tones of the band of the U.S. Marines playing "Hail to the Chief," loudly, robustly, summoning that overwhelming sense of patriotism within the chest of every American in the room.

By now the White House phone lines were back on, and the place was connected to the outside world by a zillion kilo-watts. The television cameras were rolling, commentators were speaking, the wire service reporters were filing copy from the back of the room. Everyone else, confined to their personal seats by both protocol and tradition, was scribbling.

And into this media feeding frenzy stepped the heavyset, balding Virginian Paul Bedford, making the short walk to the dais in time to the music.

He faced the gathering with outward calm, flanked by the High Command of the U.S. military standing behind the armed Marine guards. He stared at the phalanx of microphones arrayed before him, and then said firmly, "It is my honor to inform you that one hour ago, I became the 45th President of the United States of America. As I believe you have been told, President McBride was compelled to resign at short notice for reasons of health. It was both unexpected, and unfortunate, and we all wish him a swift and full recovery.

"Meanwhile, the business of government must continue, and it is my most unhappy duty to inform you that today we stand in perhaps the worst danger this nation has ever faced. I will not take questions, but I will endeavor to outline the scale of a forthcoming terrorist attack we believe will happen . . ."

"Any connection between the attack and the President's resignation . . . ?" someone yelled.

"I wonder if you'd be kind enough to let my secretary know your native tongue?" replied the President. He was reading off Arnold Morgan's only offering of a riposte to unwanted questions.

The laughter subsided, and Paul Bedford never missed a beat. "Four months ago, we received a communiqué from the Middle East that the terrorist organization Hamas had been responsible for the eruption of Mount St. Helens in Washington State. Our investigations subsequently showed this was likely true.

"We were then informed that we had just a few weeks to completely remove our military presence in the Middle East and to force Israel to vacate the occupied territories on the West Bank. The Administration, needless to say, was skeptical about the validity of this demand, but cautious. We even moved some troops and ships around.

"However, we received another threatening communiqué, and this one contained a further detail—that if we did not comply, they would do the same to a volcano in the Canary Islands as they did to Mount St. Helens."

A deathly hush had fallen over the Briefing Room, as the journalists waited for President Bedford's next words.

He paused for a few moments longer, fervently wishing he had either Winston Churchill or Arnold Morgan passing him notes, never mind the one-side-one-sheet decree.

He soldiered on, outlining briefly the scientific predictions.

"Well, President McBride remained skeptical. He was quite worried, but the military was *seriously* worried. And then came the final communiqué, which said (a) *'we will now show you what we can do, at midnight on Tuesday, September 29,' and (b) 'we will hit the volcano around October 9.'"*

"DO YOU HAVE AMERICAN SCIENTIFIC OPINION ON THIS?"

"Of course not," replied the President, trampling all over his "no questions" ultimatum. "We never thought of that."

This time he reduced the Associated Press reporter to a figure of fun. And once more, he never missed a beat.

"And so, ladies and gentlemen, we are left with two tasks—to track down and kill the submarine, which we believe launched cruise missiles at Montserrat and Mount St. Helens, and to begin to evacuate the East Coast. Just in case we are unable to achieve our Naval objectives."

"SONAR," yelled a reporter, displaying a certain in-depth nautical knowledge. "CAN'T WE CATCH 'EM ON SONAR?"

"Well, we'd prefer trained dolphins, but we may not have enough," shot back President Bedford. "I have asked you not to interrupt me, particularly if you can only shed a glaring light on the obvious." This was the sharp, sardonic turn of mind that would make the press more wary of this new President than they had initially expected to be.

"In any event," Paul Bedford continued, "this defensive operation is 100 percent military. And I have appointed the former National Security Adviser Admiral Arnold Morgan to head up both the search-and-kill submarine operation and the evacuation program. He has the total support of the most Senior Commanders in the U.S. Armed Forces, who are standing behind me.

"That's all I have to say right now, but I hope you will urge

your readers and viewers to cooperate fully at this most difficult time. There is enough time for everyone to leave, but we
have to remain calm and organized. Naturally, you will be informed of the day-to-day operations in the cities, and everyone is advised to move west to higher ground, to camp out
with relatives and friends. If this tidal wave, or tsunami, hits,
there will be no survivors. Everyone must leave the East
Coast, under the guidance of the military . . . Thank you."

President Bedford turned and walked out of the room, accompanied by Generals Clark and Boyce. Admiral Dickson
remained with the Chairman of the Joint Chiefs, who now
stepped up to the dais.

"For anyone who does not know, I'm Gen. Tim Scannell,
and I'm here to support the President. Right now I will be
happy to answer five or six questions regarding the military,
so make them pertinent, since we are very busy, as you may
well imagine."

*"Sir, will there be wholesale changes in key White House
positions, Secretary of State, et cetera . . . ?"*

"That's not military, but I do understand President Bedford
will appoint a new Secretary of Defense tomorrow."

*"Can you describe the scale of the search in the Atlantic
for the submarine?"*

"Not really. But we have decided that a wide search area of
maybe a thousand miles out from the Canaries would be unlikely to succeed. Admiral Dickson, right here, believes a
well-handled nuclear submarine might evade even a hundred
U.S. pursuers on an indefinite basis."

"How do you know it's nuclear?"

"That's our appreciation of the situation."

"If so, how did the terrorists get it?"

"I cannot answer that. But I will say, if it's not nuclear we
would have caught it by now, and will almost certainly catch
it in the next ten days."

*"Can't the sonars pick it up? We're always hearing how
technically advanced the U.S. Navy thinks it is."*

"A modern nuclear submarine is just about silent under 8

knots. And if he's running deep, over 500 feet below the surface, he's dead silent . . . Anyone wants to ask more about the submarine, Admiral Dickson will answer."

"Sir, how will this tsunami develop if the volcano erupts?"

"We're looking at a rock face maybe six cubic miles in volume, crashing hundreds of feet down into the ocean. It will hit the floor, maybe 2,000 feet below the surface, and roll westerwards, building to speeds of over 400 mph, like the ripples on a pond if you drop a big rock into it."

"How long to hit New York?"

"According to the scientists—*all of the scientists*, that is—around nine hours from impact."

"Can the terrorists be stopped?"

"Maybe."

"Can you outline your plan to find and destroy the submarine?"

"No."

"Does that mean you do not have a plan yet?"

"No. It does not. But to tell you is to tell the submarine and its masters."

"Will you be providing us with details of the evacuation plans?"

"Absolutely. We will be on air again shortly to inform the public of evacuation measures and procedures. Thank you for your time. No more questions."

General Scannell and Admiral Dickson left the dais and headed back to the Oval Office, leaving the Fourth Estate to tackle one of the biggest political and military stories of modern times.

They were accompanied by four Marine guards, and on the way, fell into step with Henry Wolfson, press officer to Charles McBride, and one of many senior staffers who would retain their positions in the new Administration.

He offered a handshake to the two officers and introduced himself. "Guess our paths have never crossed before," he said. "But I have a feeling that that's liable to change as from this moment."

"Correct, Henry," replied General Scannell. "We're counting on you to try and keep this situation under control. The object is to prevent an outbreak of public panic without concealing the seriousness of the situation. We'll do a more detailed briefing on this later, but one thing's for certain. Hamas did slam a broadside of big cruise missiles into both Mount St. Helens last May and Montserrat last night.

"It would take something larger to blow the volcano in the Canaries apart. But a nuclear warhead on a medium-range cruise would probably do it. The bastards are firing from a submarine, submerged-launch, and that's real hard to locate. You coming to see the President?"

"Yes, sir. And Admiral Morgan. And that scares the hell out of me."

"Don't worry. His bite's worse than his bark. And he scares the hell out of all of us at times. But I'm glad he's on board for this one."

"That seems to be the general opinion around here, sir," said Henry Wolfson. "Makes everyone feel a little more confident."

"We're supposed to be apolitical in the military," said the CJC. "But things are usually easier for us when the GOP are at the helm."

They reached the Oval Office. Generals Boyce and Clark were just leaving, and General Scannell joined them for the return journey to the Pentagon. Meanwhile, Arnold Morgan had turned the most hallowed room in Western government into a Naval strategy room. He had charts of the Atlantic Ocean all over a central table that he had ordered to be brought up especially from the office of the National Security Adviser. It had a dark polished teak surface and had been in the same place since Admiral Morgan's own years in that office.

Cyrus Romney, the Liberal Arts Professor from Berkeley, had been somewhat irritated by the sudden appearance of White House removal staff and had demanded to know where his table was going.

"Oval Office, orders of Admiral Morgan," was the reply.

Cyrus Romney, who had heard the rumors around the offices, had decided wisely not to pursue the matter on the basis of being certain that he too, in the next couple of hours, would be making a similar, but equally sudden, exit from his office.

In the next thirty minutes, the table became a far busier place than it had been for many months. It now displayed charts of the western Atlantic and the approaches into the Leeward Islands and of the central Atlantic above the Mid-Atlantic Ridge.

There were maps of the western approaches to the Canary Islands, and three different charts of the Canaries themselves—one showing all five islands from Grand Canaria to Hierro, including Tenerife, Gomera, and La Palma; another showing the other two big islands of Lanzarote and Fuerteventura much farther to the east, the latter only 60 nautical miles off Morocco's northwest headland.

The entire seven-island archipelago stretched east to west for 250 miles, and Arnold Morgan had made but one mark on the entire nautical layout—a small circle located at 28.37N 17.50W, the main crater of the great Cumbre Vieja fault line.

Right now he was standing with President Bedford, staring at the depths of water that surrounded the island of La Palma, almost 10,000 feet high, 50 miles to the east, 5,000 feet all around the 1,000-meter line, 200 feet close inshore, and almost 100 feet sloping steeply west right below the cliffs, *almost on the goddamned beach.*

He glanced up as Admiral Dickson came in, the President having retreated to the far end of the room to speak with Henry Wolfson. It was clear already that the Oval Office was about to become Admiral Morgan's ops room, and that an army of possibly five cleaners and tidiers would be required twice a day to keep even a semblance of order.

The former President's secretary, Miss Betty-Ann Jones, the very lady who had been ordered to fire Arnold as soon as the result of the Presidential Election was known, was in the process of clearing her desk and preparing to leave for her home in Alabama. She had given herself no more than two hours to remain at her power desk outside the Oval Office, since it was rumored that Mrs. Arnold Morgan was on her way into the White House, essentially to take charge of her husband's life while he tried to fight off the Hamas threat.

Betty-Ann need not have worried. Arnold Morgan treated everyone the same—Presidents, Admirals, Generals, Ambassadors, Emperors, and waiters. Usually with impatience, occasionally with irritation, but rarely with malice. He would not have remembered the manner of his removal from office—only that he was leaving his beloved nation in the hands of people whom he judged to be incompetent to handle the task. That almost broke his heart. Phone calls from secretaries did not figure in the equation. But he did want his capable wife close at hand in the hours of duress.

"Where the hell's Kathy?" he growled to Admiral Doran.

"Who's Kathy?" replied the Commander in Chief of the Navy's Atlantic Fleet.

Arnold looked up from his charts, surprised. "Oh, Kathy? Sorry Frank, I was talking to myself . . . pretty familiar phrase in my life—they'll probably inscribe it on my grave . . . *'Where the hell's Kathy?'*"

"Is that Mrs. Morgan?"

"That's her. The best secretary I ever had, the best-looking lady who ever even spoke to me, and the best of my three wives, by several miles."

Frank Doran chuckled. "You expecting her, sir?"

"Damn right. I just gave her back her old job, and told her to get right down here to the West Wing, on the double."

"Is she coming?"

"Well, she told me she'd give some thought to working again for the rudest man she ever met. But not to hold my breath."

Admiral Doran laughed out loud at that, and ventured that everyone had to refrain from the impulse to speak to wives and children as if they belonged on the lower deck.

Arnold was about to reply when Kathy Morgan came marching into the office, looking, as ever, radiantly beautiful.

Without looking up, he snapped, "'Bout time. COFFEE! And call the Iranian Ambassador and tell him he's a devious lying son of a bitch."

Admiral Doran was stunned. Admiral Dickson, who had attended this charade before, just shook his head. And Arnold leapt up from his desk and hugged his wife right in front of everyone.

Throughout all her years as Arnold's secretary, she had always been astounded at the commands he gave her . . . Call the head of this, the head of that, ambassadors and diplomats, and say the most frightful things to them. To Arnold Morgan a request for speed of reply from a senior Russian Admiral translated to *Tell Nikolai what's-his-name to get his ass in gear* . . .

The sudden order to lay into the Iranian ambassador was a mere "Welcome Home" to Kathy, who had promised to return to work only if it was for a two-week tenure.

Arnold introduced Frank Doran, and then instructed Kathy to tell that lady outside, Betty Something, that she was welcome to work as Kathy's assistant in the smaller office for a couple of weeks. Failing that, to tell her to go now, and get a replacement.

The former Kathy O'Brien knew the White House routines as well as anyone, but she balked at this. "Darling, I cannot just arrive here and start firing people," she said.

"Okay," said Arnold, returning to his charts of the waters on the eastern Atlantic Ocean. "Get Frank to do it."

"I'm not firing President McBride's secretary!" said Admiral Doran.

"All right, all right," said Arnold. "I'll do it." And with that, he walked out of the door and explained to Betty-Ann that his secretary of many years was now in residence, and that she would be taking over. Betty-Ann should now clear her desk, but she was more than welcome to stay as an assistant in the smaller office, so long as she was sharp and stayed on her toes.

Admiral Morgan did not wait around for a chat. Having established his opening chain of command, he returned to the Oval Office and trusted that matters secretarial would somehow sort themselves out.

He sat at the head of his new table and suggested Admirals Dickson and Doran be seated on either side so they could each look at the Atlantic charts. "We'd better have some coffee, and some cookies," he told Kathy. "None of us had any lunch. And can you make sure I have a pair of dividers, a compass, rulers, calculators, notepads, and pencils?"

"How about a sextant and a telescope, since you appear to be going back to sea?" Mrs. Arnold Morgan had lost none of her edge.

Just then the President himself arrived and Arnold introduced him to his wife. "You were very good on television, sir," she said. "Very neat the way you kept those reporters in line."

"From the wife of Admiral Morgan, I'm taking that as a major compliment," he replied, smiling. "And you're nothing like so stern as he is—and much better looking."

Arnold invited Paul Bedford to sit down and join them. "I'm starting right now with our opening plan to trap that submarine," he said. "We'll finalize our evacuation plans tomorrow. But I want to get some heavy warships into the area we believe he's heading towards. We just might get lucky and trip over him, and I don't want to deny us that chance."

"How many ships, Admiral?"

"I think for the moment we want to send in a dozen frigates. We can use the Oliver Hazard Perry guided missile ships. Then I guess we want to move an aircraft carrier into the area and pack its flight deck with helicopters.

"I think Admiral Dickson and I are agreed we're more likely to catch this bastard from the air, rather than in deep water with submarines. As you know, submarine hunts are very difficult. They usually end up with subs under the same flag shooting at each other by mistake."

"Do we have a CVBG anywhere near?"

"We do. The *Ronald Reagan,* eastern end of the Mediterranean, maybe three days away. The frigates can all be in the area within six days—five of them are halfway there already, and the rest are ready to clear Norfolk tonight, five hours from now."

"Did our departed President know that?"

"The hell he did. If we'd been listening to him, we would not have been ready."

"One thing, Arnold. The communiqués from the terrorists. None of them actually mentioned the Cumbre Vieja, did they? Are we certain we got the right volcano?"

"Sir, you have to get into deep volcanology to find that out," chuckled Arnold. "Hamas mentioned the eastern Atlantic, and when you're talking tidal waves, that means the Canary Islands. Because of the height of the mountains and the depth of the ocean.

"There is nowhere else in the Atlantic where such a tsunami could develop. And when you express that scenario to any volcanologist, they say, before you finish your sentence . . . '*Cumbre Vieja. Canary Islands. It's happened there before, and it will one day happen there again.*'

"It's not even the height of the mountains and the deep ocean that make it unique. It's the enormous volume of underground water, the lakes beneath the volcanic range. That's what will explode the cliffs into the sea . . . if those bastards hit the Cumbre with a nuclear-tipped missile.

"And, Mr. President, we have clear photographs of the Hamas C in C standing on top of the Cumbre Vieja this year with known Iranian volcanologists, studying the terrain. They also kidnapped, interrogated, and then murdered the world's top volcano expert in London last May."

President Bedford nodded. "I guess that's about as decisive as it gets," he said. And Arnold spread out the big chart of the Atlantic in front of them and began a recap on the scale of the problem.

"*Taking a point 400 miles from the island of Montserrat . . . puts him around here at midnight . . . twenty-four hours later, he's probably here if he's steaming through these unpatrolled waters at around 12 to 15 knots . . . That puts him right here tonight and probably here tomorrow night . . . That ship he's in will have to move very slowly over the SO-SUS wires, maybe 6 knots all the way across here . . . That's only 150 miles a day . . . Won't reach the datum until October 9, right? . . . Bang on time, son of a bitch . . .*"

"The question is, sir," said Admiral Dickson, "will he ever get that far? Maybe he'll just stand off and let fly with his missiles from maybe 1,000 nautical miles out?"

"We can't let him, Alan," said Arnold Morgan. "We cannot let him."

"Hard to know how to stop him."

"Hard but not impossible. Question one. How do his missiles get their guidance?"

"They just hook up with the world global navigation system, the GPS," replied Admiral Dickson. "Steers them right in. The satellite does the rest. Punch in the numbers and fire 'n' forget."

"Question two, Alan. Who owns the GPS?"

"Essentially, we do. There's twenty-seven satellites up there orbiting the earth every twelve hours. All American Military, made available to all the world's navigators. They'll guide anyone home, friend or foe."

"Correct. So, Question three. How do we stop this bastard tuning his missiles into our satellites and homing in on the volcano's crater?"

"Well, I guess we could switch 'em all off, so nobody could access them."

"Correct, Alan. And that would do just what I want him to do—drive him inshore. Because when he comes to the surface to check his GPS, his screen will read, '*Satellites nonoperational at this time.*' And that will leave him no option.

He'll have to fire visually, and that'll bring him in to around 25 miles from La Palma. Right there he will be forced to loose off his missiles using visual range and bearing only.

"And that's where we have a chance. Because we'll have our frigates and helos combing the area. When he comes to the surface for a visual fix, we might just pick him up first time. And even if he gets his missiles away, we have two and a half minutes' flying time to locate and kill with a SAM. Failing that, we'll have to rely on ground missiles, probably Patriots, set in a steel ring around the volcano . . . Take 'em out before they hit."

"It's going to take a lot of very brave men to man that missile battery up there on top of the volcano," said the President.

"We got a lot of very brave men," replied Arnold Morgan, sharply.

"Will a nuclear warhead detonate if a Patriot slams into it, in midair?" asked the President.

"Probably not, sir," said Arnold. "These things do not explode on impact. You have to *make* them explode with split-second timing, crashing the two pieces of uranium-235 directly into each other with high explosive and stupendous force, accurate to a hundredth of a second. A couple of hundred pounds of TNT designed to blow the entire rocket to smithereens, on impact, will not fulfill those explicit timing credentials. But it'll sure as hell disable it, and knock the damn thing into the sea."

"What are our chances?"

"They're very good, once we switch off the GPS."

"I was coming to that," replied President Bedford. "I assume we can't just shut it down and leave it at that, can we? I mean, what about all the navigation, all over the world . . . Christ, there'd be ships running aground all over the place, wouldn't there?"

"Sir, if we just shut off the GPS," said Arnold, "I'd say we'd have a couple of dozen supertankers high and dry on various beaches within about five hours. The rest would be turning around in large circles, baffled by that most ancient of skills, or lack of it."

"You're right there," said Admiral Dickson. "Most merchant ship navigators couldn't find their way out of the harbor without GPS. And most of them have grown up with it. We've had military satellites up there since the early 1970s.

"Your average navigator on a big freighter or a tanker knows nothing else. And there are probably four thousand yachtsmen at any one time groping around the oceans entirely dependent on the GPS to find their way home."

"Who runs GPS?" asked the President.

"Fiftieth Space Wing's Second Space Ops Squadron, out at Falcon Air Base, Colorado," said Arnold. "The full name of the system is NAVSTAR GPS. It's really a constellation of satellites orbiting the earth, a space-based radio-positioning and time-transfer system. It provides incredibly accurate data position, velocity, and time. That's PVT in the trade.

"Over the years, it has become a worldwide common grid, easily converted to other local datums, passive, all-weather operational, real-time and continuous information, and survivability in a hostile environment. It's a twenty-four-hour navigation service. And it's all-American, totally controlled from Colorado. We put all the satellites up there, right on the back of a Delta II expendable launch vehicle, out of Cape Canaveral, Florida."

"And we can make the system nonoperational?"

"We can do anything we damn please," said Arnold. "But we will have to give ample warning to the international community, otherwise the consequences might be horrendous."

"It beats the hell out of me why we ever made this military asset available to everyone else," said the President. "Especially since the darn thing is so accurate."

"Left to the military, it would not have happened. But Clinton's Vice President, the great universal do-gooder, insisted. Of course the Military were furious, but Al's boss did not think much of the Military, and that's why we got a bunch of deranged Muslims able to fire accurate missiles anywhere they like."

Even Paul Bedford laughed at this vintage Morganian discourse, despite a certain loyalty to a fellow Democratic President.

"So when do we switch 'em off, Arnold?"

"Well, if the submarine's making 600 miles a day, and he's aiming to arrive and fire instantly, immediately making his getaway, I'd say he'll be within 200 miles of his launch zone by midnight on October 7. He'll probably take a satellite fix in the small hours of the morning of the eighth, and then keep steaming in to his ops area. I guess we better shut the GPS off at midnight on Wednesday the seventh, and keep it off until either we destroy him or he fires his missiles."

"That may be forty-eight hours with the world's navigation system nonoperational?" said Paul Bedford.

"Correct," said Arnold. "But at least they've got eight days to learn how to use a sextant and take a look at the stars and study the positions of the sun, and make their timing from GMT. Do 'em good. Turn 'em into proper sailors."

"No alternative, is there?" replied the President.

"None that I can see. We have to switch off the GPS. Blind him. Drive him inshore. Force him to periscope depth."

"Which side of the island?" asked President Bedford, peering at the charts.

"Oh, he'll come east, right, Alan? Frank?"

"Not much doubt of that," said Admiral Doran. "At least, that's what I'd do. First, because I don't want to get turned over by the tsunami, which I would be if I were west of the impact when the mountain collapses. And second, because I could tuck myself right in here . . ."

Frank pointed at the chart with a pencil, aiming at the waters to the northwest of the island of Gomera. "Right there," he said, "I'm in 1,000 feet of deep water with the land behind me. Sonars are never as good looking into the land, and that's what I'd be thinking—that I was trying to evade other submarines.

"I'd try to make it hard for the guys who were looking for me. I'd run deep and slow. Then I'd make my run in, right through this deep water, 7,000 feet on the chart, still moving slowly. I'd come to PD, take my mark on the island, one of these mountain peaks, get my range and bearing, then go deep again. Right here, 25 miles out I'd give myself a new visual check, then I'd fire two missiles, fast. Then head for shelter, probably behind Gomera or even Tenerife—away from the tidal waves."

"Jesus," said Paul Bedford. "I'm glad you're on our side."

"The only trouble is, Mr. President," said Admiral Morgan, "we have just one slight glitch."

"Lay it on me."

"There is just one other smaller satellite system up there that we do not control. It's the European GPS, the Galileo Project, which is still dwarfed by our own system. But it's there, and it works, and anyone can get into its guidance system. I imagine our Hamas opponents are aware of this. But they must realize we will pull every trick in the book to screw 'em up. Therefore we must be aware of the problem. They might be navigating close in by the European system only."

"We have to use everything in our power to blind our enemy," replied the President.

"Which means, sir, I am about to award you a fairly disagreeable task . . . the central satellite we have to silence is called Helios. It's French and someone has to deal with 'em. And you know how cooperative they're likely to be if they get a call from Washington asking them to switch off their very own GPS . . .

"*Sacré bleu,* and all that Gallic bullshit," added Arnold. "And there is one other irritation that might actually turn out to be of major significance—when the Europeans began work on Galileo six years ago, they rowed in China for a 10 percent share. Cost Beijing $400 million. Gave 'em not only the China-Europe Global Navigation Satellite System, they all agreed the Technical Training and Co-Operation Center would be based in Beijing. We now see China as our geostrategic rival of the future."

"China, always damn China," said the President. "And you mean I have to tackle all of that? Because you know darned well the French will immediately say they have to ask Beijing."

"Well, we'll ask Master Control Station at Falcon Air Base to send a request direct to Paris first," said Arnold. "Then we'll try frightening the French to death by telling 'em the tsunami will also flood their Brittany coastline, which it will. Then we'll have to go President-to-President."

Arnold Morgan paused, somewhat theatrically, then continued.

"And if none of that works, Mr. President, we shall be obliged, on behalf of this great nation, both morally and ethically, under the laws of Almighty God and Man, to shoot the fucker clean out of the stratosphere."

10

MEANWHILE, THE EVACUATION of the East Coast had begun. The Federal Emergency Management Agency (FEMA) had split the mammoth task into five main categories: the general public; State and Federal Government; Culture and Heritage; Commerce and Industry; and Public and Emergency Services.

President Bedford had already put a state of National Emergency in place, and immediately authorized the FEMA to oversee evacuation operations. They had handed over power to the Eastern Seaboard State Governments to mobilize local National Guard troops in all areas under threat. A principal part of the Guard's duties was to patrol urban areas and "maintain control on the ground."

Plainly, as soon as the gravity of the situation had sunk into the mind of the public, a widespread panic would be inevitable, which the criminal element would most likely be swift to exploit. The President warned that in any cases of looting, particularly of federal property, the National Guard was fully empowered to open fire.

A strategic review of the situation, and an assessment of the overall threat, had been under way since earlier that day. Contingency plans were being finalized, and battalions of U.S. Army forces were already rumbling down the highways towards Washington, D.C., and the other three major cities of Boston, New York, and Philadelphia.

The President's next speech, currently being drafted feverishly by Henry Wolfson, would warn of the specific effects of a 150-foot wall of water racing through the coastal shallows and thundering into the streets. It would be similar, he wrote, to the murderous destruction caused by the exploding island of Krakatoa: unstoppable, devastating, and certain death for anyone who remained in its way.

The chaos would be wholesale, the water would level almost anything that stood in its way. Huge waves would continue to pound the coastline after the initial shock. Great tracts of land maybe 15 miles from the beaches would be absolutely wiped out, power supplies damaged, communications severed, and there would be widespread saltwater flooding, fatal to infrastructure equipment and installations, such as power stations and domestic water utilities. Henry Wolfson actually managed to frighten himself.

The drift of this first draft was that every citizen had a duty to his country in the face of the oncoming onslaught from the deep. Every family should attempt to find its own point of refuge, driving to friends or relatives who resided inland on higher ground, but some people should remain in the city for several days, if possible, to assist employers with the packing and removal of all items of value—principally from the Federal Government but also from private commerce. A special department was being set up to record when families vacated their homes and precisely where they would reside during the coming catastrophe.

The evacuation of the poorer areas was an even more pressing dilemma, especially with regard to those under criminal justice supervision. Many did not have their own transportation or a place to go. Local authorities were being instructed to provide both, somehow—buses, trains, and reception areas, utilizing schools and community halls beyond a 20-mile radius. They were already contacting towns and cities in nearby counties to the west and northwest, where the Blue Ridge Mountains leave Virginia and cross the border into Maryland.

The President's seven o'clock speech was dramatic. The East Coast population, already stunned by the resignation of

President McBride, now had to swallow the enormous significance of the mega-tsunami. The entire concept was so outrageous that people seemed unable to grasp this mammoth
intrusion—the specter of the destruction of the entire East
Coast of the United States unacceptable and unimaginable.

People sat transfixed in front of their television screens as
President Bedford outlined the opening steps everyone had to
take in order to survive and preserve what must be preserved.

The first signs of panic began almost as soon as he concluded the address. The White House switchboard was
jammed by thousands of calls. The largest number of viewers
in living memory hit the wires to the television networks, demanding more information. There was a late-night run on
gasoline, lines quickly forming up and down the East Coast
as people prepared to fill up and move inland, right now,
never mind October 9.

On the heels of the President's announcement, the Department of Transportation announced that as of Monday morning, October 5, all ports and airports on the East Coast would
be closed to incoming ships and aircraft—except for those
aircraft specifically designated for evacuation purposes.

The London tabloids, five hours ahead of Washington, set the
tone for the media bonanza, ruthlessly joining together the
two American news stories, and the papers appeared on
the streets by two o'clock, East Coast Time, on Wednesday
morning, September 30.

MAC CRACKS UNDER TERRORIST THREAT, shouted the London *Daily Mail*'s headline, in end-of-the-world type, above a
subhead that read:

> U.S. PRESIDENT MCBRIDE QUITS
> WHITE HOUSE TYRANT MORGAN RECALLED

One single large photograph of the new President was cap-
tioned: PAUL BEDFORD TAKES THE OATH WITH ADMIRAL ARNOLD
MORGAN AT HIS SIDE.

It was in fact a dazzling front page, and all the twenty-four-hour American television news channels were showing it before 3 A.M. The *Mail* devoted six pages to the story, the lead being written by its star political feature writer Tony Pina.

On a bright October afternoon of pure political theater, Charles McBride resigned yesterday as the 44th President of the United States. He left secretly by Navy helicopter from the lawn outside the Oval Office.

Minutes later, Vice President Paul Bedford was sworn into office before a select group of military chiefs, which included the former National Security Adviser Admiral Arnold Morgan, the Chairman of the Joint Chiefs General Tim Scannell, and the heads of the United States Navy and Marine Corps.

Senator Edward Kennedy was also in attendance for the ceremony, which was conducted by Judge David Moore, who had been specially appointed by the Supreme Court.

Fifteen minutes into his Presidency, Paul Bedford summoned the White House Press Corps to the Briefing Room, where he explained that his predecessor had suffered a nervous breakdown and was under medical supervision at Camp David.

He then revealed that the United States has been under a monumental threat from a Middle Eastern terrorist group that has already blown up Mount St. Helens, the giant volcano in Washington State, and then exploded the simmering Caribbean volcano on the island of Montserrat on Monday night.

The threat to the U.S.A. was to erupt the Cumbre Vieja on the Canary Island of La Palma, thus setting off a mega-tsunami across the Atlantic that would wipe out the American East Coast and greatly harm the shores of Western Europe and North Africa—unless the American President agrees to move its entire military force out of the Persian Gulf area, and strong-arm Israel into conceding an Independent State of Palestine, vacating the left bank territories.

So far as we know, the United States has made no effort to

comply with these demands, and is believed to be conducting a massive search in the Atlantic to find a nuclear submarine apparently containing the terrorists and submerge-launch cruise missiles with nuclear warheads.

The terrorists' threat, that horrendous prospect of a mega-tsunami, is believed to have proved too much for President McBride, who was reported to have collapsed on hearing the news that the terrorists had hit Montserrat on Monday, carrying out a previous threat, almost to the minute.

President Bedford has vowed to catch the submarine and destroy it, and has announced plans to evacuate the cities of Boston, New York, and Philadelphia.

Scientists say that from the moment of impact in the seas off La Palma, there would be only nine hours before New York City went under more than 100 feet of water.

On the opposite page was a large picture of Admiral Morgan in Naval uniform, beneath the headline—THE RETURN OF THE IRON MAN. The accompanying story began:

Admiral Arnold Morgan, the former nuclear submarine commander who held the last Republican Administration together, was called yesterday out of retirement and summoned to the White House by the new Democratic President.

The White House confirmed that the Admiral has been appointed Supreme Commander of Operation High Tide, the code name for the massive submarine hunt currently under way in the Atlantic to locate and take out the terrorist warship . . .

Since the Chairman of the Joint Chiefs had been reluctant to admit there was any connection between the McBride resignation and the threat from Hamas, the U.S. television networks had been reluctant to join the two stories. The devil-may-care treatment of the situation by the London papers, however, gave them all the Dutch courage they needed, and by breakfast time, there was no doubt in the minds of Americans: Charles McBride had cracked, and wimped his way out of the Oval Office, afraid to face the personal torment of ordering his fleet into action to destroy an aggressor. Worse yet, he may not have had the courage to order an evacuation of the big cities and coastline communities. And there were several newspaper and television features on Arnold Morgan, "The Man the U.S. Government apparently cannot do without."

There were various headlines on the same drift:

ADMIRAL MORGAN—THE LION OF THE WEST WING
THE DAY ADMIRAL MORGAN FACED DOWN CHINA
ARNOLD MORGAN—A MAN FOR TROUBLED TIMES
ADMIRAL MORGAN—PATRIOT OR A GLOBAL GAMBLER?
MORGAN—THE MAN WHO FLEXES AMERICA'S MUSCLE

What no one wrote, anywhere in the world, was that President McBride had been frog-marched out of the Oval Office by a Detail from the United States Marine Corps, while the Service Chiefs looked on.

It had been a military coup of the kind that usually happens in those restless countries around the world in which economic crises, drug wars, and power-hungry dictators had taken their toll. But with the difference that this was America, Land of the Free, where the coup, if the term even applied, had lasted only ten minutes, after which order was restored and the flag never lowered.

Wednesday morning, September 30, saw a drastic change of pace in Washington. The entire city was dominated by the Military, the National Guard, and the police. All unnecessary business was halted, criminal and civil cases were suspended, arrangements were made to evacuate court officials. In two instances, it was necessary to isolate the juries—certainly for nine days, possibly longer.

Colleges and schools were preparing to close down at the end of the day. Hospitals were canceling planned operations, discharging as many patients as possible, and preparing for the evacuation of the seriously ill.

The Army were already in hospital corridors assisting with the removal of high-value medical equipment. At some of the bigger establishments, there were as many as six 18-wheelers parked outside emergency room entrances, while the troops loaded up and recorded space-age hospital diagnostic machinery in readiness for journeys to U.S. Air Force bases on higher ground.

Hotels and motels all along the East Coast were refusing all new reservations, and guests already in residence were asked to leave as soon as possible. The Hamas threat was not, after all, from a group of reasonable, educated people. It was from a bunch of Middle Eastern brigands who would stop at nothing, and who might even panic and blow the Cumbre Vieja four or five days early, since it was now obvious the U.S.A. could not, or would not, comply with their demands.

If the tsunamis of Krakatoa were anything to go by, any heavy, loose objects, like automobiles, railroad cars, pleasure boats, even light aircraft, would be swept up and hurled around like toys. This applied also to more permanent structures like telegraph poles, statues, billboards, electric pylons, and trees.

Evacuation of the areas was essential for every citizen. FEMA was already drafting plans for removal of such structures, and trucking corporations—even from outside the areas—were to be sequestered by the Government in order to support the evacuation. Railroad stock, both passenger and freight, would be put on standby.

In the meantime, Arnold Morgan pondered the difficult question of how to persuade the awkward and noncooperative French to shut down the European GPS satellite Helios for a couple of days. The question was kicked back and forth in the Oval Office for three entire hours.

Finally, it was decided to make a formal request via the Master Control Station in Colorado, direct to the French Government, to close the satellite down for forty-eight hours, in accordance with the U.S. closure. This would be necessary in order to test significant improvements in the system, which would of course be shared, ultimately, with the Europeans.

All three Admirals agreed this would receive a resounding *non* from their counterparts across the ocean. And at this point, the U.S. would come clean about their real reason for the GPS blackout.

Arnold Morgan had scientific data showing the presumed path of the tsunami, fanning out from the opening landslide all the way to the nine-hour hit zone along the U.S. East Coast. In three hours, the tidal wave would be a wide crescent in the middle of the Atlantic, but also would head north, with gigantic tidal waves already in the Bay of Biscay.

According to the scientists, the tsunami would likely thunder into the French naval headquarters of Brest, three hours and thirty minutes from the initial impact. The tidal waves would not be as great as those crossing the Atlantic, but they would form a 50-foot-high wall of water that would hammer its way onto the rugged western tip of France.

The Americans knew they would have to explain the terrorist threat in some detail to the French, but that was unavoidable if they were to hunt down the *Barracuda* before it wiped out New York.

The sight of Arnold Morgan's tsunami maps was a chilling reminder of the reality of this wave of destruction. The Cumbre Vieja represented a rare geological time bomb, able to ravage countries on the other side of the world. Recent research into the last known mega-tsunami caused scientists to look carefully at the seabed around Hawaii, and they were astounded at what they discovered—the gigantic remains of ancient landslides, millions of years old. The tsunami's first landfall to the west would be the northern coastline of Brazil, six hours after impact, waves 120 feet high. One hour later, the tsunami would swamp the Bahamas and the outer islands of the Caribbean.

Two hours after that, the gigantic wave would roll straight

up Massachusetts Bay, and Boston would be hit by a 150-foot-high wave that would probably sweep away the entire city. The tsunami would then thunder onto the U.S. coast, hitting New York next, then Philadelphia, followed by Washington, and onto the mainly flat coastline of the Carolinas, Georgia, and Florida, all the way to Miami and the Keys.

Arnold Morgan's dossier of recent studies estimated that the first wave could be 2,000 feet high a half-mile west of La Palma, following the mammoth splash caused by maybe a half-trillion tons of rock crashing into the water at 200 mph. Traveling at high speed, 160 miles in the first ten minutes, the wave would weaken as it crossed the ocean, but it would definitely still be 150 feet high when it hit the Eastern Seaboard of the United States.

On the other side of the Atlantic, the shores of the western Sahara would receive waves of 300 feet, from crest to trough, although there would be shelter in the eastern lee of the bigger Canary Islands, Fuerteventura and Lanzarote, depending on where you found yourself as the tidal wave developed.

The scientists were also unanimous that a mega-tsunami off the Canaries, caused by a sudden volcanic eruption, would be the highest wave in recorded history. Even the south coast of Great Britain, though not in its direct path, would still be subject to serious flooding.

In world geohazard opinion, right there, laid out on Arnold Morgan's reclaimed office table, the Cumbre Vieja was an absolute certainty to be next. Everything was ideal for mass destruction—the towering peaks of the mountain range, the colossal height, the depth of the ocean, the sonorous rumbling of the volcanoes. The last explosion, some sixty years ago in the South Crater, proved it was all still active, and that the molten lava was not so very far below the surface. The underground lakes were ready to boil over at the instant of eruption. And of course there was the enormous fracture-line crack in the cliff, which had already caused a 10-foot shift in the rock face high above the ocean.

The newest report pointed out, thoughtfully, that the last

time a volcano erupted with anything like the tsunami potential of Cumbre Vieja was 4,000 years ago on Reunion Island,
a French territory since 1643, situated 420 miles east of
Madagascar in the Indian Ocean.

A report from the Swiss Federal Institute of Technology,
which had high-tech facilities to re-create model waves
created by landslides, stated flatly, "If the Cumbre Vieja
were to collapse as one single block, it would lead to a
mega-tsunami."

So far as the scientists understood, the volcanoes on the
southwest flank of La Palma erupted about every two hundred years. And there was no evidence that one single eruption would cause the landslide. In fact, it might take five
eruptions. There was, of course, no section in the report that
dealt with the probable effects of a couple of 200,000-ton nuclear warheads blowing up in the middle of the Cumbre Vieja
crater.

Admiral Morgan had another fearsome little aid to his
presentation—a two-foot-square, 18-inch-high scale model
of the volcanoes on the southwest corner of La Palma. It
came from the University of California and had been flown
in to Andrews by the U.S. Air Force, arriving at the White
House by helicopter.

The model showed the seabed to the top of the peaks, the
steeply sloping volcanic cliffs falling away from the mountains, way down below the surface of the water. The shoreline
was marked, highlighting the sudden sweep of the land into
the depths. It showed the probable zones of the landslide on
the seabed, and it starkly illustrated the tremendous impact
such an avalanche would create upon the water.

On the top of the model were the great peaks of Caldera de
Taburiente, Cumbre Nueva, and just below them, Cumbre
Vieja, sitting atop a massive craggy rock wall 2,000 feet
above the ocean, which, the model showed, shelved down to
a 4,000-foot depth.

"Jesus Christ," said Admiral Doran. "That puts a pretty
sharp light on it, eh?"

"Just look at the position of the Cumbre Vieja, perched up there on top of the wall," said Arnold. "Just imagine what a nuclear bomb could do . . . Holy Shit! We gotta find this bastard!"

"I've just been reading a damn good book by Simon Winchester about Krakatoa," said Admiral Dickson. "Been meaning to read it for years. That was one hell of an explosion . . . goddamned mountain blew itself to pieces, punched a damn great hole in the ocean, wrecked three hundred towns and villages, and killed 36,000 people. And you know what? Almost all the destruction, and absolutely all of the death, was caused by the tsunami. And the son of a bitch was nothing like the size of the one we're looking at."

"Jesus, Alan. You're making me nervous," said Arnold. "But I guess we have to face the reality, otherwise we'll *all* end up under medical supervision at Camp David."

"Okay," said Alan Dickson. "We've dealt with the President. We've taken care of the French. Nearly. Now we're about ready to sort out the ships. Maybe Frank could give us a rundown on the Atlantic Fleet as it stands."

"Perfect," said Arnold. "Lemme just call the President. He'd better sit in on this. Since he has been C in C of the armed forces for all of four hours."

He called upstairs to the private residence, and within five minutes, Paul Bedford was back in the Oval Office, listening to the rundown of the Navy situation. He had never forgotten his days as a frigate Lieutenant, and he often recalled the excitement of being a young officer, racing through the night at the helm of a U.S. warship.

And predictably, he asked questions no civilian would ever dream of. "Frank, these Oliver Hazard Perry frigates. They were brand-new when I was serving, and I haven't kept up . . . good ships?"

"Excellent, sir . . . 3,600 tons, 41,000 hp . . . couple of big gas turbines, single shaft, 4,500-mile range at 28 knots, need refueling when they reach the ops area. But that's no problem. They pack a pretty good wallop too . . . four McDonnell Douglas Harpoon guided missiles, homing to 70 nautical miles at Mach zero-point-nine . . . plus ASW torpedoes."

"Beautiful," said President Bedford. And he really meant it. "That little son of a bitch comes to the surface, he's history, right?"

"Just so long as we can see him," replied Admiral Doran. "And we are putting a lot of faith in the helicopters . . . You know, each frigate carries two of those excellent Sikorsky SH-60R Seahawks . . . They got state-of-the-art LAMPS Mark III weapons systems. They're just great machines, 100 knots, no sweat, up to 10,000 feet.

"They're exactly what we need . . . airborne platforms for antisubmarine warfare. That *Barracuda* shows up where we think he'll be, we got him. Those helos have outstanding dipping sonar, Hughes AQS-22 low frequency.

"They all have USY-2 acoustic processors, upgraded ESM and Integrated Self-defense. Plus APS-124 search radar . . . and twenty-four sonobuoys. Those helos carry three Mk-50 torpedoes, an AGM-114R/K Hellfire Missile, and one Penguin Mark-2."

"I just hope the French cooperate," said the President.

"They will ultimately not be a problem," said Arnold Morgan. "If they won't shut the damn thing off, we'll shut it off for them. I was not joking when I first said that. We'll shoot it down, because we don't have any choice."

"This means," said the President, "you have entirely abandoned the idea of a wide search out in the Atlantic, west of the islands?"

"Again, no choice," replied Arnold. "With a hundred ships out there in deep water, we could still miss him easily. It's too vast an area, hundreds of thousands of square miles of water.

"So we're sticking to a small force of just twelve frigates, plus the carrier group. Perhaps, Frank, you could let the President know where we are with the fleet right now?"

"Sure," said Admiral Doran, flicking the pages of his notebook. "We just diverted two ships from the Gulf of Maine on a southwest course to the Canaries, that's USS *Elrod*, under the command of Captain CJ Smith, and USS *Taylor*, under the command of Captain Brad Willett.

"The *Kauffman* and the *Nicholas* were both in the North Atlantic, and have been heading south for the past three days. Comdr. Joe Wickman's *Simpson* was off North Carolina, and we sent him east two days ago. Tonight, seven more frigates are due to clear Norfolk by midnight.

"That's the old *Samuel B. Roberts,* commanded by Capt. Clay Timpner—rebuilt, of course, since she hit a mine in the first Gulf War; USS *Hawes* under Comdr. Derek DeCarlo, the *Robert G. Bradley*, under a newly promoted young Commander, John Hardy, from Arizona. Then there's USS *De Wert*, commanded by Capt. Jeff Baisley.

"My old ship, the *Klakring*, will be ready next. She's now commanded by Capt. Clint Sammons, from Georgia, who'll probably make Rear Admiral next year. The *Doyle*'s already on her way under Comdr. Jeff Florentino. And the USS *Underwood*, commanded by Capt. Gary Bakker, will be the last away. She only came in yesterday morning."

"How about the helos for the carrier deck?"

"We're sending the *Truman* out from Norfolk with fifty Seahawks on board—they'll transfer to the *Ronald Reagan* flight deck as soon as possible, then bring the fixed wings home."

"So that'll give us over seventy Seahawks active over the datum?"

"Correct, sir. We'll be flying a lot of patrols around the Islands, as from midnight on October 7. He sticks that mast up for more than a few seconds any time in the next two days, we'll get him. If he doesn't have any satellites, he'll need time to get an accurate range."

"How accurate does his damn missile have to be?"

"If it's nuclear, which we're sure it will be, he can hit within a half-mile of the Cumbre Vieja, and the impact would be terrific. But I think he'll try to bury those babies right in the crater. Remember, he's trying to blow the volcano wide open. He's not trying to knock the cliff down . . . because that won't be enough. He's vowed to erupt the Cumbre Vieja, and he'll need time to set up for an accurate fix. And that's our chance . . . while his periscope's jutting out of the water, and we're sweeping the surface with radar."

"There's a lot riding on this, Frank," said the President. "A whole lot riding on the skill and sharpness of your boys."

"Yes, sir. But if it can be done, they'll do it. Of that I'm in no doubt."

President Bedford and Admiral Morgan refused all requests for interviews via the White House Press Office. There was a hot line established between the National Security Agency and the Oval Office. And Lieutenant Commander Ramshawe was constantly combing the myriad of U.S. intercepts for anything that might give a clue to the whereabouts of the phantom *Barracuda*.

At eleven o'clock on the first morning of Paul Bedford's Presidency, he got one—vague, coded, and not much use to anyone. But the U.S. listening station in the Azores had picked up something that arrived from the satellite of the Chinese Navy's Southern Fleet. A short signal transmitted at 0500 (DST) on Tuesday morning . . . *a cruel sea for the songbirds.*

There was something about it that caught Ramshawe's attention. He stared at it, pondered its possible meaning. *Cruel sea . . . a cruel sea . . . the cruel sea . . . novel about the Navy . . . Nicholas Montserrat! Holy shit! On the day the island volcano blew.*

Lieutenant Commander Ramshawe did not have the slightest idea of the different spelling. This may have been a message from anyone, to anyone. But it was in English, and it was on the Chinese Navy satellite. And it must have meant something to somebody.

So who's the bloody songbirds? He did not waste any

more time thinking. He picked up the phone to his boss, Admiral George Morris, and recounted the signal. George thought slowly. Eventually he spoke. "Jimmy," he said. "That's very interesting. Especially if those songbirds turned out to be canaries."

"Hey! That's a beaut, sir. You got it. Can't be sure what it means, but it surely suggests the bloody *Barracuda* is on its way to La Palma."

Neither of them knew that a new signal had just hit the Chinese satellite. Again brief . . . *RAZORMOUTH 71.30N 96.00E*. General Rashood, operating from Bandar Abbas, did not yet think that the Americans had already cracked the *Barracuda/Razormouth* code many months previously. And in any case, the Americans, who picked up the new signal, would not understand the coded global positions. The code 71.30N 96.00E put the submarine somewhere in the land-locked foothills of the North Siberian Plain.

They should have read 21.30N (*minus 50 degrees*) 48.00W (*divided by 2*). Which put the *Barracuda* precisely where Admiral Badr had her . . . steaming at 15 knots hard above the eastern shoulders of the North Atlantic Ridge, right over the Kane Fracture Zone, more than 900 miles east nor'east of the island of Montserrat. She was making a bee-line for the Canary Islands.

When he went deep again after his transmission, Ben Badr would order a reduction in speed down to nine knots in 600 feet, above the somewhat noisy waters of the Ridge. He would cut it further as they continued eastward, running softly over the quiveringly sensitive underwater wires of SOSUS.

"Well, Admiral," he said, "at least we know where the little bugger is headed. You want to call the Big Man, or will I do it?"

"You go ahead, Jimmy . . . I'm just looking over the comms plan for the command ship . . . We're using the *Coronado*, an old warhorse, newly converted."

He referred to the 17,000-ton Austin-class former Landing Platford Ship, which acted as Flagship Middle East Force in 1980. The *Coronado* was the U.S. Navy's Flagship in the first Gulf War, and Flagship to the Third Fleet in Hawaii in the 1980s.

Commissioned in 1970, she had undergone three major conversions in a long life. A massive rebuild in the late 1990s saw her emerge virtually brand new. They turned her well deck into offices, with a three-deck command facility, and accommodation for four Flag Officers.

She was twin-shafted, driven by a couple of turbines that generated 24,000 hp. All her combat data systems were state-of-the-art, including an automated planning air-control system and wide-band commercial. She used Raytheon SPS-10P plus G-Band for surface search, and carried two helicopters.

After the turn of the century, the *Coronado* became the U.S. Navy's sea-based Battle Lab, to act as test bed for new Information Technology systems.

At nine o'clock that morning, the CNO Adm. Alan Dickson announced from the Pentagon that Rear Adm. George Gillmore, a former hunter-killer nuclear submarine CO, had been appointed Search Group Commander, Task Group 201.1. He would report only to Adm. Frank Doran (CTF 201—CINCLANT), who now represented the Front Line contact, through which Arnold Morgan would remain close to all developments off the Canaries.

Admiral Gillmore had been the outstanding submariner of his year, along with Capt. Cale "Boomer" Dunning, a fellow Commanding Officer from Cape Cod. When he took his first surface ship command aboard the frigate *Rodney M. Davis*, George had quickly proved one of the best ASW officers in the Navy, in a class of his own in almost every exercise.

He had all the right qualities, including the ability to concentrate for hours at a time, the sharpness to react instantly to even a sniff of an underwater contact, and the courage to act decisively when he was sure he'd found one. His long years underwater served him well. Admiral Gillmore could always recollect what he would have done, had he been the hunted rather than the hunter. And he had an almost uncanny knack of being correct in his predictions. Bad news for Admiral Badr and his men.

A tall, bearded disciplinarian, George was based in the Atlantic Fleet, and he had already sailed for the Canaries from Norfolk in the small hours of Wednesday morning two days previously, several hours before President McBride left the White House. It was the fact that such an act of open defiance towards a sitting President had been necessary that had convinced Admiral Morgan and General Scannell that McBride simply had to go.

Admiral Gillmore's overall task would be to coordinate the search frigates, helos, and the Carrier Battle Group ships in an intense and complicated operation that might explode into action at any moment. He would have a staff of more than one hundred men, eighteen officers.

Right now, as the announcement was made, Admiral Gillmore was familiarizing himself with the new systems on board the *Coronado*. He was assisted by two Lieutenant Commanders and three Lieutenants as he toured the ship's ops rooms, checking the comms, the sonar room, the radar, the navigation area, and the GPS, which he alone knew would go dark at midnight on Wednesday, October 7.

The Navy Press Office issued a release to the media announcing the appointment of Admiral Gillmore, but a few doors down the corridor, in the Office of the CNO, there was a major disturbance. They had just received a communiqué from the French. On no account would they close down the European GPS. They cited the consequences to the world's shipping, the obvious hazards to yachtsmen, and the prospect of beached freighters and tankers. They could not, in conscience, agree to such a course of action.

Immediately, Admiral Dickson prepared to go to Plan B,

which would entail Admiral Morgan speaking to—or yelling at—the French Foreign Minister on a direct line to Paris.

Admiral Dickson was quite certain that the American Admiral was capable of frightening the French into submission, which, under the circumstances, would be a wise course of action. There was no question in Alan Dickson's mind that Arnold would blow the Helios satellite clean out of the stratosphere if there was not immediate cooperation from France.

As the evacuation process continued, it quickly emerged that Washington's treasures posed a huge problem, mainly because the capital city was entrusted with the preservation of the national heritage, and all that the nation holds dear. Of the 750,000 residents of Washington, D.C., 70 percent were employed by the Federal Government, which meant that a broad structure was already in existence for easy dissemination of information and execution of the evacuation plans.

The greatest concern by far, in the city itself, was the vast range of fine art, documents, and items of priceless value that record the birth, development, and history of the nation.

Across the Potomac, a Special Ops Room was established inside the Pentagon in the U.S. Navy department. A large computerized screen occupied an entire wall, and two Lieutenant Commanders were marking out the west-nor'westerly direction of the incoming tsunami as it would come driving forward off the Atlantic. So far as they could tell, the one certainty was that the initial impact would be borne by the peninsula of land stretching south from Salisbury.

The path of the tsunami would proceed straight across the outer islands, on to the eastern shore of Maryland, a 150-foot wave taking out Salisbury completely. From there it would roll clean across the flatlands, drowning the Blackwater National Wildlife Refuge, and into the wide estuary of Chesapeake Bay. Speed: approximately 300 mph, causing massive flooding all the way north up the main channel and causing a tidal surge up the Potomac of 120 feet minimum, IF the jutting headland of Pautuxet was able to remove some of the sting from the wave. By now it would have leveled probably fifty small towns and villages.

Minutes later, the great city of Washington, D.C., would go under water. Scientists on the line from the University of California were telling the Pentagon Ops Room they could expect a rise of at least 50 feet throughout the course of the Potomac River as far upstream as Bethesda, where it should begin to decrease to maybe 20 feet, up near Brunswick.

The waters would, of course, recede within a few days, but the damage would be inestimable, and on no account should anything be left to chance. Washington itself was particularly low-lying; indeed, the Lincoln and Jefferson Memorials were built on land that was formerly a swamp. Some of the great city buildings might survive, but not many, and no human being should risk standing in the way of the tidal wave.

The Treasury, the Supreme Court, the Department of Defense, and the FBI were effectively out of action for any new business. The CIA, perilously situated just north of the Georgetown Pike, on the west bank of the Potomac, where the river sweeps downstream to the right, was beginning a massive salvage operation of some of the most sensitive documents in the country, not to mention the kind of high-value equipment and files that could cause a world war, should they wash up in the wrong place.

Like their colleagues in Federal Government offices, the CIA were packing and dispatching computers, hard drives, documents, archive material, and other valuable records. Departmental staff were packing the stuff into military cases, all numbered and recorded, before making the journey under armed guard to Andrews Air Force Base over in Prince George's County. From there they would be flown under guard in the giant C-17 transporters to carefully selected U.S. Air Bases beyond the reach of the floodwaters. Those cases would be stored in Air Force hangars, closely guarded around the clock by Federal troops with orders to shoot intruders on sight.

Over on Independence Avenue there was a major operation in the Library of Congress. Things had been relatively calm in there since they moved into their new building in 1897. But the Library was no stranger to catastrophe, having twice burned down when it was located in the Capitol in the first half of the nineteenth century. Today, the activity was close to frenzied, as troops from the Air Force Base joined the staff, trying to pack up more than 84 million items of information, in 470 languages.

This was the world's largest library; its books, pamphlets, microfilm, folios of sheet music, and maps were all stored in three great stone centers of learning, each one named after three of the Founding Fathers who all were Presidents—the main Thomas Jefferson Building, lavishly decorated in Italian Renaissance style; the James Madison Memorial Building; and the John Adams Building, all located to the rear of the U.S. Supreme Court.

Into big packing cases, the troops and the permanent Library staff were bundling the first volumes of the most priceless sources of information in the entire country—the fountain of knowledge used by Congressmen, Senators, and selected researchers from all over the world.

To complicate the task still further, the U.S. Copyright Office, with its unique store of critical business data, is also located there. It would take twenty-four-hour shifts every day, until the ocean crushed the city, to move even half of the contents of the great buildings on Independence Avenue.

Over on Constitution Avenue, behind the giant stone columns of the National Archives, a more delicate operation was under way. Curators and troops were working in the midst of this ultimate repository for all U.S. Government documents, packing up documents beyond price—the Declaration of Independence, the Constitution, the Bill of Rights—all destined for Andrews Air Force Base, from where they would be flown to secure U.S. military establishments, and guarded night and day.

Up on 14th and C Streets there was a total evacuation from

the U.S. Bureau of Engraving and Printing, where $35 million of U.S. Government banknotes were printed every day, just to replace the old ones. In here they also printed postage stamps, government bonds, licenses, and revenue stamps. There was a U.S. Marine guard of more than one hundred men forming a cordon around this building while the presses were being dismantled and crucial components carried out to the waiting trucks.

All along Washington's imposing Mall, the story was the same. The evacuation was under way. Military trucks lined the avenues, parked two deep outside the Capitol itself, and similarly inside the grounds of the White House. Historic portraits, ornaments, furnishings, and furniture were being loaded by Marines along with Presidential papers and records.

Critical offices of government remained open, and inside the Oval Office, Admiral Morgan and Admiral Frank Doran wrestled with the problem of the United States Navy's warships. They had to be removed, fast, from all dockyards on the East Coast, or else they would surely be smashed to rubble. And they could not be headed east to assist with the submarine operation around the Canaries, not into the jaws of the tsunami. They had to be sent into calmer waters, and the two Admirals pored over the charts. Not even the submarine jetties up in New London, Connecticut, were safe.

And certainly it was too great a risk to send several billion dollars worth of nuclear submarines into deep waters in the hopes that the huge waves of the tsunami would simply roll over them. No one knew the depth of the turbulence that might accompany such a wave, subsurface, and it was clear that the submarines would have to follow the same route as the East Coast–based frigates, destroyers, aircraft carriers, and the like, into a sheltered anchorage.

Frank Doran had considered the possibility of running the ships north, into the 30-mile-wide Bay of Fundy, which divides southern Nova Scotia from the Canadian mainland in New Brunswick.

"There's no problems with ice up there at this time of year," he said. "We could push the fleet north as far as Chignecto Bay . . . That'd put a hilly hunk of land 60 miles wide between the ships and the Atlantic. They'd be safe in there."

But Arnold did not trust the surge of the waves from the southwest, and he was afraid the tsunami might curl around the headland of Fundy, and then roll up the bay, dumping ships on the beach. There would be no possibility of escape in the shallow, confined waters of the Chignecto, and generally speaking, Admiral Morgan preferred to send the fleet south.

"But the Caribbean may be under worse threat than anywhere," said Frank. "This document we have here from the University of California says the tidal wave will hit the coast of Mexico, never mind Florida."

"I know," said Admiral Morgan. "But Florida's a very big chunk of land. It's more than 100 miles wide, even at its narrowest, and the scientists do not expect the tidal wave to last much more than 12 or 15 miles at most, once it hits land. I'm saying we should get the fleet south, around the Keys and then north into the Gulf of Mexico, maybe up as far as Pensacola . . . anywhere there's deep water along that Gulf Coast . . . because there's got to be shelter under the armpit of Florida . . . Are you with me?"

"I am," said Admiral Doran. "And like all sailors, I'd rather go south than north."

"You're not going anywhere," said Arnold Morgan, "except to your office in Norfolk. And you'll be running the show till those missiles come bursting out of the ocean—that is, if your boys don't nail him first. I just wish they were attacking from anywhere else on earth, rather than a nuclear submarine. Anywhere, anything. I'd rather they were attacking from outer space than from a nuclear boat, submerged-launch."

"So would I," replied Admiral Doran. "Meanwhile I'd better get back down to Norfolk. Every time I look at the place I think 'tidal wave,' and the havoc it would cause down there.

That thing could pick up a 100,000-ton carrier, according to the scientific assessments. And if it didn't do that, it would most likely crush the big ships against the jetties.

"I know that the cities are badly threatened, but a tsunami could just about wipe out the Navy on the East Coast. That thing comes in from the southwest, it'll slam straight into Virginia Beach and then take out all three of those bridge/tunnels across the Hampton Roads. And the land's so flat, just a maze of docks, dockyards, creeks, lakes, and rivers all the way in from the Atlantic."

"Don't remind me, Frank. And how about the shipyards, Newport News and Norship, all in the same darned complex. Christ! We got two aircraft carriers half finished in there . . . Couldn't hardly move them if we tried—except with tugs . . . not to mention the West Coast of Florida."

Frank Doran shook his head. "And we have to get Kings Bay, Georgia, evacuated. We got four Ohio boats in there, and God knows how many of those Trident C4 missiles. Probably enough to blow up most of the goddamned universe, and we're prancing around trying to find a bunch of guys dressed in fucking sheets underwater."

Admiral Morgan chuckled. He really liked Frank Doran and his unexpected humor. The task that faced them both was truly overwhelming, and they had to fight against letting it take over. They had a chance to nail the *Barracuda*—both men knew that—if it came to periscope depth. And if it didn't, and just fired straight at the volcano, they had a chance to nail its missiles, surface to air. Failing that, there was one final line of defense—the steel ring of Patriot Missiles around the rim of the Cumbre Vieja, which would hit back. If they had time.

Failing those three options, life would not be the same on the East Coast of the U.S.A. for a very long time.

"Okay, sir, I'm out of here. I'll put the evacuation plan for the Gulf of Mexico into operation right away. If it floats and it steams, that's where every ship is going. I think we better get those ICBMs to sea and headed south as quickly as possible. But we might have to commandeer a few commercial freighters to vacate the submarine support station. There's a million tons of missiles and other material in there. And it's absolutely vulnerable—right on the Atlantic coast, protected by nothing more than a couple of sandbanks."

"Don't tell me, Frank. I used to work there," said Arnold, shaking his head. "Is this a goddamned nightmare or what?"

Admiral Doran walked to the door of the Oval Office. "You coming back tomorrow?" asked Arnold.

"Uh-uh. In the morning. We might have some better news by then."

**1930 (Local), Friday, October 2
Damascus, Syria.**

Ravi and Shakira were back in their home on Sharia Bab Touma. Adm. Mohammed Badr had decided that satellite signals between the Iranian Naval Base at Bandar Abbas and the *Barracuda* were too vulnerable to American interception, so their expertise and advice wasn't needed right now. All they could do was wait.

The Americans could intercept anything, with the National Security Agency's Olympian ability to eavesdrop on anything, anywhere, anytime, and very little was transmitted from the Navy bases of potentially troublesome countries without Fort Meade knowing about it, chapter and verse.

So General and Mrs. Rashood had evacuated their lush guest quarters in Bandar Abbas and flown home to Damascus. And there, high up in the rambling house they had lived in when they first were married, was a state-of-the-art satellite transmitter, and a state-of-the-art receiver. But the path of the signals was Damascus-satellite-Tehran-satellite-Zhanjiang-satellite-*Barracuda*.

On the way back, it was precisely the same in reverse, all coded. Ravi made his way back down the stairs holding the latest message from Ben Badr, which simply read: *72.30N 76.00E*. The Hamas General quickly decoded the true position and marked the spot on his map of the Atlantic.

Ben had made almost 10 knots since Tuesday morning, covering 700 miles across the Mid-Atlantic Ridge. The *Barracuda* was now almost on the line of the Tropic of Cancer, creeping at only five knots over the SOSUS wires. They were roughly 775 miles short of their ops area, which at this speed—120 miles a day—was six and a half days away. Ravi's fingers whipped over the buttons on his calculator. It was now around midday on Friday where the *Barracuda* steamed, and they should arrive at the Canaries firing zone around midnight next Thursday, October 8.

"Right on time for the hit," said Ravi to himself. "Just pray to Allah the Scimitars work again."

"I'm hearing a certain amount of mumbling here," said Shakira, who had just appeared in the doorway to the kitchen. "Would you like some tea, to calm your nerves?"

"Thank you. That would be perfect," said Ravi. "By the way, I've just received a signal from the *Barracuda*, and it's good news. They report no illness or casualties, they're right on time, right on course, in mid-Atlantic, 775 miles short of La Palma."

"I was just watching CNN on the television," said Shakira. "The Americans are very concerned. The President has broadcast twice, and an evacuation of the East Coast is in full swing. They seem to have accepted the reality of our threat."

"Are they saying anything specific about their defensive measures . . . You know, a deployment of ships around the islands?"

"Nothing much, only that they'll be starting an extensive search for the *Barracuda* soon."

"Hmm," replied Ravi. "They'll have a lot of search power out there, but I don't think they'll be able to catch Ben. He's firing from 300 miles out, way to the southeast . . . and so far as I can see, there's no way they'll catch him in that deep water . . . not if he stays slow and deep, and launches from 200 or 300 feet below the surface."

"I don't think we've ever missed anything," said Shakira, thoughtfully. "You think our luck will hold?"

"This isn't luck. It's planning," said Ravi. "Planning over a long period of time."

"You think they know it's definitely a submarine, definitely launching missiles at the volcanoes from below the surface?"

"Hell, yes," said General Rashood. "They know that."

"Well, what would you do, if you were them?"

"Evacuate," said Ravi. "As fast as I could."

"Nothing Military or Naval—no aggressive action?"

"Well, I'd certainly send ships out to hunt for the submarine, but the Atlantic's a big place. I would not hold my breath."

Shakira was still thinking. "You know, my darling," she said, "I spent a lot of time plotting and planning with the missile guidance systems. They do work from the satellites, you know."

"Just on the regular Global Positioning System."

"How about if the Americans somehow interfered with that. Made it nonoperational?"

"Well, I believe there's nearly thirty satellites up there, and I've always thought they were involved in television, telecommunications, and all kinds of things. And every ship in the world is entirely dependent on them for navigation. I don't think even the Americans could somehow turn off the entire communications and navigation system for the whole world. They'd be too afraid of the lawsuits that would probably amount to billions of dollars."

"Let's hope they are," said Shakira, pouring tea into two glasses with little silver holders. "Otherwise, Ben will miss our target."

Midday (Local), Friday, October 2
National Security Agency.

The Fort Meade code breakers had almost done their job. Admiral Morris had taken the first signal off the Chinese Navy's satellite and drawn a large circle on a chart of the North Atlantic.

"That's where we think the *Barracuda* is," he said. "In there somewhere. We are nearly certain this signal with the numbers 71.30N 96.00W is reporting her precise position. Try to come up with something, will you?"

Shortly before noon on the previous day, the code room had come up with a close solution. *"On the first number, we think they just subtracted 50 . . . or maybe 49 or 48. No more. On the second number, the W for West, means E for East. And we are nearly certain they just cut the number 96 in half. Which would give us 21.30N 48.00W, and that's right about in the center of the circle."*

Admiral Morris and his assistant were delighted with that. And they were waiting anxiously for a new signal. At 12:30 P.M. Lieutenant Commander Ramshawe located something on the Chinese satellite . . . *OLD RAZORMOUTH 72.30N 76.00E.*

Jimmy whipped 50 off the first number, and divided the second one in half. He changed the *West* to *East* and came up with 22.30N 38.00W. He checked on his detailed computerized chart of the Central Atlantic, and recorded the precise spot where he believed the *Barracuda* was steaming, probably three hours ago. He checked back with the previous numbers and plotted the submarine 700 miles farther east than they'd been on Tuesday morning.

He calculated the speed, and like the faraway General Rashood, he assessed it at just below 10 knots. *He keeps that up, he'll spring one of those SOSUS wires for sure in the next few hours.* Jimmy Ramshawe's confidence was rising by the minute. The submarine was slightly farther north, maybe 60 miles, but the overall difference was definitely 700 miles. That put her on a direct route to the Canary Islands.

He called Admiral Morris, who guessed it might take four hours to get surveillance ASW aircraft into the area, which would mean the *Barracuda* would be possibly 70 miles farther on. But they had no further guarantee of her course, which could change at any time. And that presented a large surface area—as much as 5,000 square miles to search.

George Morris called Admiral Morgan, who followed the conversation on his wall-sized computer chart, which was now in the Oval Office. He said to put the information on the wire immediately to Admiral Doran in Atlantic Fleet Headquarters, Norfolk, and to the CNO in the Pentagon.

"George," said Arnold. "This comes down to the same thing, as always. A huge area to search, out in the middle of the Atlantic, and almost no chance of catching him if he's deep and quiet. Also, we don't know the timing of the signal from the *Barracuda*.

"I think Jimmy's right. It was probably sent three hours before we picked it up. But it could have been yesterday. This bastard is very smart. Note that there was no time and date on the signal. I guess they know when he's scheduled to transmit, and so long as he says nothing, they know he's on schedule.

"But I continue to think any kind of wide search in the remotest areas of the Atlantic is hopeless. We're not going to find this son of a bitch until we can drive him inshore. Then we have an excellent chance."

Ten minutes later, Admiral Doran was on the line to the Oval Office. His view was the same as Arnold's. "We could waste an enormous amount of time and effort out there. And it's still only about a 5 percent chance we'd catch him," he said. "The value of that signal is it confirms the existence of the *Barracuda*. And it confirms roughly where he is, or was, plus his course and obvious destination. We just have to force him inshore . . . Any luck with the French?"

"I'm speaking to their Foreign Minister in a half hour, Frank. At this stage I'm not hopeful. I think it's going to come down to President-to-President. But I'll be doing my best to scare this little son of a bitch in Paris."

Admiral Doran replaced the receiver. He instructed someone to alert all Atlantic ships as to the perceived whereabouts of the *Barracuda*. And then he returned to the colossal task of evacuating the Norfolk shipyards.

One hour later, thirty minutes late, Kathy got the French Foreign Minister on the telephone. Arnold did not know the man, and decided that politeness was the sensible course to steer. They introduced themselves, formally. The Frenchman spoke good English and the Admiral decided to come straight to the point.

"Minister," he said, "you probably already know why I'm calling. You must have read about the terrorist threat in the newspapers, right?"

The French minister confirmed and impressed his apprehension upon the Admiral.

His government had just received a report from the Swiss Federal Institute of Technology about the likely effects of a tsunami caused by the explosion of the Cumbre Vieja, and were concerned with the apparent seriousness of the situation. However, his Government wasn't yet fully convinced that the threat was actually real. Contrary to the States conviction, they had seen no hard evidence that it would take place.

Arnold asked him to simply accept, on trust, the opinion of the United States military on this matter. "Mind you, we intend to do everything in our power to stop them," added Arnold. "And we're not asking for assistance, though there will be damage to the cities and coastlines of many other nations."

"Yes, the Swiss scientists confirm the damage would be widespread," was the reply.

"And of course your own coast in Brittany may be on the receiving end of a very substantial tidal wave, possibly 80 feet high, straight into your Navy headquarters in Brest. That's almost as much trouble as we'll be in four hours later."

"I understand," said the Frenchman hesitantly. "The issue for us is, firstly, do we believe in the threat? Secondly, do we think it is sufficiently serious for us to dismantle the entire European Global Positioning System? I'm sorry to say that the answer would be no."

"Well, we are not asking for a complete dismantling," said Arnold. "Just a forty-eight-hour shutdown, if we have not already located and destroyed the submarine. You do understand that we will black out our own satellites, which represents a total of 90 percent of all the Global Positioning Systems in space?"

"I imagine you will, Admiral. Given your history with the Middle Eastern nations, I'm afraid the French Government does not approve of anything you do east of the Suez Canal."

"Then I am obliged to inform you of the consequences. First, you will lose your Navy on your west coast. The Atlantic peninsula of Brittany will be catastrophically flooded. Secondly, you will forfeit the goodwill of the United States for a very long time. And should the eruption take place on La Palma, with all that it entails, we will not hesitate to make public the fact that it was France who essentially caused it, refusing even a modicum of cooperation in the cause of preventing a world disaster.

"Thirdly, the President of the United States will ask Congress to approve a bill to level a 100 percent tariff on all French goods entering the United States. And fourthly, we will lock you out of the oil markets of Iraq and Saudi Arabia, both of which we effectively control. Which would seem a pity, for the sake of turning the fucking lights out for a couple of days."

"I will relay your thoughts, and your threats, to my President," replied the French Foreign Minister.

But Arnold had already slammed the phone down. "*Vive la France*, asshole," he growled, to the mild surprise of Kathy,

who had just come through the door with his roast-beef sandwich with mustard, but no mayonnaise.

"Everyone's late today, the French Foreign Minister, the
sandwich . . . I'm being treated like someone who works in
the mail room."

Kathy laughed. "No luck with Paris?"

"None. Can you get the French Ambassador in here right
away. I need to try to get him to understand."

"Now?"

The level of jocularity between the two was at its lowest
level in recent memory. Outside the door, removal men were
carrying priceless tables and lamps along the corridor. Army
trucks were lined up outside. Officers were checking and
recording every treasure every step of the way. The Pentagon had taken over the networks on the East Coast, broadcasting twenty-four hours a day from the Press Briefing
Room four doors from the office of the Chairman of the
Joint Chiefs.

Government spokesmen were already urging families with
no commitment to employers in Washington to leave the city
in order to ease congestion. Traffic was being directed to
state highways to the north and west, leaving Interstate Highways 66 and 270 in the main for Federal convoys and other
official traffic.

It was a little over two miles to the French Embassy, located on Reservoir Road on the northern border of Georgetown University. And Arnold Morgan awaited the arrival of
the ambassador with growing impatience. Finally, Gaston
Jobert showed up at 2:20 P.M. and Kathy ushered him into the
Oval Office, where he was greeted by both Admiral Morgan
and the President.

Kathy brought them some coffee, and M. Jobert sat and lis-
tened to the chronology of events from beginning to end.
Arnold left out nothing, from the missiles identified at Mount
St. Helens to the blasting of Montserrat. He explained the
Hamas demands, the impossibility of complying with them,
and then he explained the strategy of the United States Navy.

Above all, he specified the critical nature of the GPS satellites.

"Generally speaking," said Arnold, "he'll send his missiles in under guidance from our own satellites. If he cannot locate them, he'll search for the European one. And if he locates that, he'll use that.

"If he runs into a blackout situation, he'll have to come inshore for a visual firing. And that's when we'll get him. Needless to say, I am mystified at the attitude of your Government, and I have invited you here essentially in order for you to make them see sense."

"Does my Government know the full history—the submarine, the missiles, and everything?"

"Pretty much."

"Well, I have understood with much . . . er, clarity . . . I see it would be very bad for France . . . if we were seen . . . to, er . . . have stopped you catching this submarine before it destroys your coast, and part of ours as well. That would be absolutely crazy . . ."

"Well, M. Jobert, *we* know that, but I am afraid your Foreign Minister has not understood as well as you have," said the President.

M. Jobert, a debonair man of around fifty, slim, dark, Gallic in attitude, replied, "This was M. Jean Crepeau?"

"That's him," said Arnold. "A very anti-American little man, actually, which is somewhat absurd in the world today. Can you imagine us refusing to help you in this way, if Paris was under threat of a major terrorist attack?"

"No, Admiral Morgan. No. I cannot. But I have lived here for many years. I am very fond of the Americans, and this rather embarrasses me, as it will, in the end, embarrass my government."

M. Jobert paused for a moment and sipped his coffee. "As a diplomat, I am going to speak out of turn. But you have been frank with me. M. Crepeau is a man whose political ambitions are very much greater than his abilities. And our Prime Minister is not much better. But in the President himself, Pierre Dreyfus, you have a man of far greater stature and far more sense . . . a little too proud for his own good. But a man of intelligence and judgment.

"Most people in my government are afraid of him . . . On the other hand, I am not, mainly because he's married to my sister, Janine. I've known him since we were both about fifteen years old.

"I have already discussed this with him. And I think a call direct from President Bedford tomorrow morning will sort this out fairly quickly. In the end, France has no option, because in the end, you would shoot our satellite down, *n'est-ce pas?*"

Admiral Arnold smiled grimly. "You would leave us very little choice," he replied. "The cities of Washington and New York, against your little sputnik Helios? No contest."

M. Jobert stood up to leave. "You may leave it with me, gentlemen," he said. "I will speak to the President at length this evening. I'll tell him it's too much trouble to refuse your request . . . I believe the phrase was *'a pity for the sake of turning out the fucking lights for a couple of days . . .'*"

"Nicely put," said Arnold Morgan.

0800, Saturday, October 3
Mid-Atlantic, 23.00N 38.40W
Depth 600, Speed 6.

ADM. BEN BADR held course zero-six-zero as they moved
across the black depths of the Cape Verde Plain. Young
Ahmed Sabah, Shakira's brother and Hamas officer, had become a trusted confidant of the *Barracuda*'s CO, and the two
men were studying the charts of the eastern Atlantic with Lt.
Ashtari Mohammed, the British-born Iranian navigator.

Nothing is real until it faces you, and what had once looked
like a simple run into the Canary Islands now looked to be
fraught with peril. They both understood that the threat that
General Rashood had issued to the Pentagon had been made
public. Plainly, the United States was taking major steps to
locate and destroy them, and the nearer they crept towards
the Canary Islands, the more dangerous the waters became.

Neither officer had the slightest idea what form the U.S.
defense would take, but Admiral Badr, a former submarine
and surface CO himself, felt confident that they would not resort to a submarine hunt.

"They won't risk firing at each other, Ahmed," he said. "I
think it is much more likely that the Americans will go for
frigates or destroyers with towed arrays. As long as we stay
dead slow and deep, we'll be almost impossible to find. The

one worry I do have is the satellites. We need them for guidance of the Scimitars—and the GPS is just about entirely American.

"If they believe we are going to wipe out their East Coast, they may just shut down the whole system. Which would be pretty bad for us. Because that would leave only the European system and I'm not sure we can log on to it. Whereas everyone has access to the U.S. system."

"Do you think the Americans could persuade the Europeans to shut down at the same time? Well, the Brits would cooperate. But the French might not. My own view is that they will somehow *not* get both systems to shut down at the same time . . ."

"But what if they do?" Ahmed was wide-eyed and very worried.

"Then we have no alternative. We'll go inshore, take a visual range and bearing, and open fire on the Cumbre Vieja. The SL-2 has one advantage . . . Its nuclear warhead does not need the critical accuracy of the SL-1 non-nuclear. We bang that thing in there within a half-mile, we'll split that volcano in half. The burning magma will do the rest."

"How close do we need to be?"

"Around 25 miles. So long as we can see enough through the periscope to get a good visual fix on the volcano."

"Where do we fire from?"

"We'll have to see. If the satellites work, we'll launch from a range of 250 miles . . . from this point here, about 30 miles south of the most easterly island, Fuerteventura. That would put us in very deep water around 30 miles off the coast of the western Sahara.

"The moment we fire, we turn north and make all speed for the eastern coast of Fuerteventura . . . right here, see . . . off the city of Grand Tarajal. That's going to take us one hour from the point of launch. But the missile will take twenty-five minutes to get there. The main explosion causing the landslide will take an estimated ten minutes, and then the tsunami wave will take another 30 minutes to reach the west coast of our island . . . not the east coast where we will be sheltering . . . The wave will go right past us. And we'll just hang around under the surface until everything calms down."

"How about they *do* get the satellites shut off? What do we do then?" Ahmed was fast realizing the enormous risks they were taking.

"Then we would have to come inshore, from the southwest . . . making for this point here." Ben Badr pointed to the chart at a spot 20 miles off La Palma, in very deep water, 8,000 feet. "Right here we take our visual fix, we range these two points here on the chart . . . two lighthouses, Point Fuencaliente, right here on the southermost headland of the island . . . and then, nine miles to the north, Point de Arenas Blancas. We'll see them both clearly through the periscope, right?"

"Yes, sir, Admiral."

"In between those two points is the Cumbre Vieja. We have all the data we need on its precise spot, satellite photographs. We then take a third point, a mountain peak . . . and we take range and bearing . . . it's a regular three-point fix. And even if the satellites are down, we can come back to that exact spot in the ocean, anytime we wish, with just a fast glance through the periscope.

"The next time we come back, we launch the Scimitar SL-2 straight at the volcano, and this missile cannot miss . . . because it doesn't have to be accurate . . . Even allowing for errors caused by wind direction, wind speed, turning circle, height adjustments . . . it still can't miss . . . The warhead is so enormous, even if it is swept a half-mile off course, it will still blow the volcano."

"Admiral, have you given any thought about how we get away afterwards?"

"Yes. I have. So has your brother-in-law. Somewhere in the South Atlantic, somewhere lonely, we bail out and board an Iranian freighter. The submarine will blow itself to pieces a half hour after we all leave. We have to scuttle her in the deepest water we can find. So she'll never be discovered.

Then we sail home on the freighter, disembarking a few men at a time, at various ports, all the way to Iran."

"So right now you want to steer a course more easterly?" interrupted Lieutenant Ashtari. "Presumably we're going to our long-range launch position . . . to see if we can still get a fix on the overheads?"

"Exactly. But we don't need to make much of an adjustment . . . two degrees right rudder. I'll speak to Ali Zahedi . . . just so long as he keeps our speed to 5 knots."

The *Barracuda* was moving quietly beneath the surface, some 540 miles short of its ops area. Sometime in the next three days, Ben Badr expected to pick up the beat of a U.S. warship. But so far, they had been in deserted waters, way south of the much busier North Atlantic shipping lanes.

On this Saturday morning, the nearest U.S. ship to the *Barracuda* was Comdr. Joe Wickman's guided-missile frigate, the *Simpson*, currently steaming southeast towards the northwest point of the Canaries—La Palma.

Capt. Sean Smith had his frigate, the *Elrod*, already in the island area, moving east across the Canary current to a position north of Tenerife. There, he was awaited by Capt. Brad Willett's USS *Taylor*, which had arrived shortly after midnight.

The *Kauffman* and the *Nicholas*, commanded by Capts. Josh Deal and Eric Nielsen, were scheduled to arrive on station sometime in the next two hours, in a holding area 20 miles off Tenerife's jagged northern headland of Los Roques de Anaga.

The seven-frigate fleet out of Norfolk was proceeding in a long convoy across the Atlantic. They were the last to leave and were not expected on station until Sunday night. The *Ronald Reagan* Carrier Battle Group was currently approaching Gibraltar and was expected to arrive at her ops area northeast of Lanzarote by Sunday afternoon.

Adm. George Gillmore, on board the electronic wondership the USS *Coronado*, was already 2,500 miles out from the Norfolk Base, and less than 1,000 miles from his ops area. They were expected to arrive around midnight on Sunday.

The last arrival would be the carrier *Harry S. Truman*, laden with helicopters, and currently pushing through a storm system out over the Atlantic Ridge, escorted by two destroyers and a nuclear submarine, hull 770, the USS *Tucson*.

They were all to the north of the *Barracuda,* unknown to Adm. Ben Badr and his men, who expected trouble but probably not as much as this. *You'll always be safe, if you stay deep and stay slow*. The words of his father rang clearly in Ben's mind. And still, somehow he felt vulnerable without Ravi and Shakira.

This weekend, he was due to open one of the timed safes on board the submarine that held a sealed letter written, but not signed, to him as Commanding Officer from the learned Ayatollah who presently ruled the Islamic Republic of Iran. It had been his father's idea to give Ben a sense of true purpose. It would provide confirmation that he wielded the curved sword of the Prophet Mohammed when he launched his missiles.

Adm. Mohammed Badr had told his son what the envelope would contain. And he was most anxious to read it. He had tried twice already this morning, but the timing device was still locked, and Ben planned to give it another try in just a few hours.

Meanwhile, back in the Oval Office, Admiral Morgan had received another setback from Paris. A communiqué from the President had stated that despite a long conversation with his Ambassador in Washington, he remained undecided about the validity of the Hamas threat and the need to turn off the GPS.

The French President said he would like to "sleep on the problem" and would give his decision on Monday morning. He continued, like his Foreign Minister, to believe that the Americans were exaggerating the importance of a terrorist attack on the volcano. He did not particularly wish to join the

U.S. in alarming the entire world unnecessarily and being responsible for any death that might happen as a result of closing down the world's global navigation system. He could see no merit in providing further fuel to world anti-American opinion, if the threat turned out to be spurious.

Arnold Morgan was furious at the word "spurious." "How could the damned threat be 'spurious'?" he raged. "Who the fuck does this jumped-up fucking despot from some fourth-rate town hall in Normandy think he is? Answer that, someone?"

"I guess he does," said President Bedford, who happened to be the only other person in the room at present. "Does this mean I have to speak to him?"

"It used to," said Arnold. "Not anymore . . . *KATHY! CONNECT THIS OFFICE TO THE PRESIDENT OF FRANCE RIGHT NOW!*"

"For President Bedford?" she inquired, standing in the doorway, and still not absolutely certain why her husband felt the need to yell through closed wooden doors rather than pick up the phone.

"Tell him that," growled Arnold. "Then put the little son of a bitch through to me."

Kathy shook her head and instructed the White House switchboard to make the call to the Palace Elysée in the northwest corner of central Paris, and to stress the urgency of the matter.

Three minutes later, the French President was on the line . . . slightly confused . . . "*Mais je le pense le President Bedford?*"

"Mr. President," said Arnold Morgan. "I am sitting here in the White House right next to the President of the United States of America . . . and for three days now, we have been asking your co-cooperation in stopping what might be the worst terrorist threat this world has ever faced. Am I to understand you are not yet ready to give us your help? That, by the way, is a *oui* or a *non*."

"Well, I have not yet decided as to the merit of the case."

"Is that a *non*, Mr. President?"

"Well, I think we could work something out, possibly in a few days . . ."

"Mr. President, this is a highly charged military action. We do not have time for your vacillation. Either you shut down the satellite when we tell you to shut it down, or that satellite will not even exist this time tomorrow morning . . ."

The line between Washington and Paris froze. "Admiral Morgan, are you threatening me?" asked the President.

"No. I am absolutely promising you. I want that satellite down for forty-eight hours at midnight on Wednesday, your time. And that's what I'm going to have. Either you do it the easy way and have it blacked out. Or you can have it the hard way, and we'll get rid of it for you.

"And, as promised, we'll put an immediate and total ban on French imports into the United States of America. We'll close your embassy, and expel your diplomats from Washington. You have ten seconds to answer."

Morgan felt that the President of France, like so many of his predecessors, was long on posture, short on real principle. The Frenchman thought of the huge expense of renewing the satellite. His mind flashed on the near-total wreckage of the French wine and cheese industries, the colossal damage to Peugeot, Citroën . . . the lockout of France from the many international councils . . . the appalling international publicity . . . the personal hatred of millions of people aimed at him, the man who had refused to help, when the U.S.A., under dire threat—his fellow Permanent Council Members of the United Nations—had asked for what seemed like a comparatively very minor favor. He knew true immortality when he faced it.

"Very well, Admiral Morgan. This time your belligerence has won the day. The European GPS will be blacked out at midnight on Wednesday, October 7, for forty-eight hours. I have not liked your methods. But, as always, my country will do the right thing. Please send your emissaries to my Government with the appropriate documents early on Monday morning."

"That's very good of you, Mr. President. Two things more—don't let there be any delays or foul-ups, and don't forget . . . but for us, you'd be speaking fucking German . . ."

Arnold crashed down the receiver. "I'm not altogether certain that last remark was absolutely vital," said President Bedford, smiling.

"Who gives a damn?" said his C in C High Tide. "The goddamned French satellite is going off, and that's all that matters. We got a GPS total blackout, and that's going to force that *Barracuda* inshore, because his long-range missiles have just gone blind. That's where we want him. That's where we have a real chance."

President Bedford said, "You want me to put the agreement with France into operation? I'll just call the State Department . . ."

"Perfect, sir. Will you also call General Scannell and inform him of the French agreement? He'll get the practical side under control . . . You know, coordinating the satellites, so it all goes blank at the same time."

The President nodded and left the room. And Arnold returned to his huge computerized charts of the Atlantic. "East," he muttered. "It's gotta be East. Anywhere west of those islands is in the direct path of the tsunami as it rolls out. No ship could survive. The *Barracuda*'s CO must have worked that out."

"What's that?" said Kathy, who was trying to beat her way through the piles of paper on the other office table.

"Come over here," said the Admiral. "And I'll show you what I mean . . . See this? These are the Canary Islands . . .

"And the big question is, will the *Barracuda* stay south if he's coming in from somewhere east of the Caribbean? Or will he make a big circle and run north to surprise us?"

"I'm not really sure."

"Well, north is best. We got two nuclear boats up there with the carrier . . . He can't go there without getting caught. My guess is, he'll stay south, come in towards the western Sahara, and then turn in for his launch. He cannot be more than 250 miles out when he launches, satellites or not . . . because if he can't get in behind those islands, fast, the tsunami will dump him right on the goddamned beach in Long Island, upside down with his prop in the air."

Kathy laughed at her incorrigible husband, as she always did.

Back out in the dark waters of the Cape Verde Plain, Adm. Ben Badr held his personal letter from the Ayatollah. It read:

Benjamin, you are a priceless soul in the cause of Allah. And soon you will carry his sword into battle. This letter is to remind you of the responsibility you bear in our crusade against the Great Satan.

Perhaps I should remind you that our Islamic faith came originally from the deserts of Arabia. And it always had overtones of war. For the Prophet was also a Conqueror and a Statesman. There was no precedent for the word of the Prophet. It came directly from God, and within one hundred years, it destroyed the Persian Empire, and conquered great swaths of the Empire of Byzantium

At that time, Arab armies swept through North Africa, obliterating Christianity in Egypt and in Tunisia, the home of their St. Augustine. Those armies ransacked the Iberian Peninsula and drove into France. Ah, yes, my son, from the very beginnings, we have been a warlike people.

Remember too that Islamic science and scholarship were ahead of Europe for centuries. We gave them the idea of universities, which the Crusaders took home with them. We conquered Turkey, captured Constantinople, which became the capital of the Ottoman Empire.

Only in the last three hundred years did the Unbelievers emerge from defeat and total irrelevance to dominate the Middle East. They redrafted our borders, invented new states, divided up our land, stole our wealth, our oil, and divided it up between European Imperialists, forcing upon us Western ways and what they think is culture.

After we had triumphed for so long, the conquest of the entire world by our True Faith seemed inevitable. But it went wrong for us. And now Allah has granted us a way to make a huge stride to correct those three hundred years of Western arrogance and plundering.

You must remember always, this is our endless Jihad, a war both spiritual and violent, and one that would have been blessed by the Prophet. This Jihad should be central to the life of every Muslim. We do not wish to steal what is not ours, but we dream of a wide Islamic Empire, one which is not dominated by the United States of America.

My son, we want them out of the Middle East, and with them, their degenerate, debauched way of life. And if we cannot bend them to our wishes, we will surely make them grow weary of the conflict. I pray for your Holy Mission, and I pray that you and your brave warriors will succeed in this great venture. All Islam will one day understand what you have done. And we wish Godspeed to the Scimitars, and may Allah go with you.

The Ayatollah did not sign the letter, but it was written in his own hand, and Ben Badr folded it and tucked it into the breast pocket of his shirt.

Ben Badr was a consummate Naval professional, at ease with his crew, with his own abilities as a Commanding Officer, and with the rewards of his long training. He did not see himself as a candidate for a suicide mission, but in the deepest recesses of his own soul, unspoken and rarely considered, he knew he was prepared to die, if necessary, a hero, so long as he was fighting for what he and his people believed in. He was honored that he should be in the vanguard of those who were chosen. He would bring the submarine within range of the great volcano, and he would blast it with his tailor-made nuclear missiles. Either that, or he would die in the attempt. He neither sought nor expected death. But if death pressed its hot, fiery fist upon the hull of the *Barracuda* as he drove towards Cumbre Vieja, then he would face it with equanimity, and without fear.

Admiral Badr checked with CPO Ali Zahedi to make sure that their course was correct and the speed still under 6 knots. He then moved down to the bank of computer screens outside the reactor room and talked for a while with CPO Ardeshir Tikku. Everything was still running sweetly after their long, and often slow, journey from the far eastern coast of China. This really was the most impressive ship, Russian engineering at its very best.

The VM-5 PWA, reputed to be Russia's most efficient nuclear reactor ever, was built up on the shores of the White Sea by the renowned engineers in Archangel. So far, deep within the *Barracuda*, it had never faltered and was still effortlessly providing steam for the GT3 A turbine. Ardeshir Tikku could not imagine any ship's propulsion units running with more precision.

The jet-black titanium hull slipped through the water. Every last piece of machinery on board was rubber-mounted, cutting out even the remotest vibration. If you listened carefully you might have heard the soft, distant hum of a computer. But that was no computer. That was the 47,500 hp turbine, driving this 8,000-tonner through the deep waters of the Atlantic.

As each day passed Ben discerned a tightening of nerves among all the key men in the ship. Capt. Ali Akbar Mohtaj was very much within himself, spending much of his spare time with Comdr. Abbas Shafii, the nuclear specialist on board, who would prime the detonators on the Scimitar missiles. They had already decided to launch both the SL-2s at the mountain, especially if there was a problem with the satellites.

Two SL-2s rather than one, the equivalent of *400,000 tons* of TNT, would seem to guarantee the savage destruction of the entire southwestern corner of La Palma. Even if they were detected, even if American warships rained depth charges down upon them, even if the U.S. Navy found them and launched torpedoes, there would *still be time*. Only seconds. But time for the *Barracuda* to launch the two unstoppable missiles that would cause the tidal wave to end all tidal waves. Capt. Ali Akbar Mohtaj and Comdr. Abbas Shafii had thought about that a lot. They'd still have time.

Meanwhile, Washington, D.C., prepared to meet its doom. If Ben Badr's missiles hit the Cumbre, the Presidency of Paul Bedford would be flown en masse, at the last possible hour, direct from the White House to the new secret base of the Administration, at the northern end of the Shenandoah Mountains, out near Mountain Falls.

The base, with all of its high-tech communication systems and direct lines to the Pentagon and various foreign governments, was constructed inside a heavily patrolled military base. It was a vast complex built almost entirely underground, fortuitously in the rolling hills to the west of the Shenandoah Valley, several hundred feet above sea level.

Known in Washington circles as Camp Goliath—as opposed to Camp David—it was always envisaged as a refuge for the Government *and* the Military if the U.S. ever came under nuclear attack and Washington, D.C., was threatened. It took three days to activate all the communications, and it now stood in isolated, secret splendor, a five-star hotel with offices, situation rooms, every secretarial facility, every possible element of twenty-first-century technology required to keep the world moving.

The President, along with his principal staff members and their assistants, would fly to Camp Goliath in one of the huge U.S. Marine Super Stallions, a three-engined Sikorsky CH-53E helicopter capable of airlifting fifty-five Marines into trouble zones.

Just in case Hamas proved even more ambitious than it seemed so far, the helo was equipped with three 12.7mm machine guns. It would rendezvous in the skies above Washington with four cruising F-15 Tomcat fighter bombers to escort it to the American heartland beyond the Shenandoah River.

Camp Goliath was located 15 miles southwest of Winchester, in the wooded hills above the valley where "Stonewall" Jackson's iron-souled Southern regulars had held sway over the Union Army for so many months in the 1860s, and when Maj. Gen. Nathaniel Banks and his 8,000 troops were driven right back across the river—Harpers Ferry at the confluence of the Shenandoah and the Potomac. Here, General Jackson's men captured 13,000 Northern troops; it was the site of Fort Royal, Cedar Ridge, and a little farther north, the bitter killing fields of Antietam.

Camp Goliath stood above those historic Civil War farmlands on the Virginia-Maryland border, where the two great rivers met. And if the missiles hit the mountain in La Palma, and that great complex was activated, Hamas would surely feel the wrath of another generation of ruthless American fighting men.

Meanwhile, the Washington evacuation continued. And by Sunday morning, the thousands of National Guardsmen who had joined the troops in the city were concentrating on a task equally as important as moving the Federal Government and its possessions out of harm's way. They were now trying to safeguard the thousands of artifacts, documents, books, and pictures that recorded and illustrated the founding of the Nation and its subsequent development.

Much of this priceless hoard is contained within the Smithsonian Institution—another great sprawling complex, which embraces fourteen museums—the collective custodians of literally millions of priceless exhibits, ranging from centuries-old masterpieces to modern spacecraft. In the gigantic National Air and Space Museum alone, there are twenty-three galleries displaying 240 aircraft and 50 missiles, a planetarium, and a theater with a five-story screen.

Already, some of the museums understood they were not going to get this done, with thousands of items packed and in storage, not even on display. All of the staff had called the White House for guidance. Admiral Morgan was impatient: *Priorities. Establish priorities, hear me? Concentrate on objects of true historic value. Forget all about those special exhibits. Abandon all mock-ups and models. Get photographs, copies of drawings. But concentrate on what's real. And keep it moving over there . . .*

National museum curators are unaccustomed to such brusque and decisive tones. In some of the art galleries, there were so many pictures, it was impossible to crate and ship them all. Decisions had to be made to leave some in the upper floors of the buildings intact in the hope they might survive the initial force of the tsunami, and the subsequent flooding would not reach the top story.

Chain gangs of troops and employees were moving up and down the massive staircases of the National Gallery of Art, trying to lift masterpieces, some of them from the thirteenth, fourteenth, and fifteenth centuries, either down to awaiting trucks or up to the higher galleries, please God, above the incoming waters.

There were some tasks too onerous to even contemplate. The warships, submarines, and aircraft displayed in the 10,000-foot-long Memorial Museum in the Washington Navy Yard would have to take their chances. So would the massive collection of historic machinery, the heavy-duty engines that drove America's industrial past, all located on the first floor of the National Museum of American History.

An even more difficult task was the National Zoological Park. The Madison Bank took a special interest in the animals' safety and set up an ops room in their Dupont Circle branch. Twenty people spent the day in a frenzy of activity, contacting other zoos inside a 100-mile radius, checking their spare capacity, trying to find temporary homes and suitable habitat for the creatures, in the limited time available.

They hired cages from Ringling Brothers and trucks from U-Haul. They even commandeered a couple of freight trains from the Norfolk Southern Railroad. Everyone wanted to help the animals, though the Baltimore baseball management balked when a young Madison Bank zealot demanded they turn the 48,000-seat Oriole Park at Camden Yards into a bear pit.

By the afternoon, the evacuation of the Zoological Park was well under way. And all over the city there were even more poignant reminders of the horrors to come. The historic statues, by special order of Admiral Morgan, were being removed and shipped out to the Maryland hills.

This had caused the first real friction of the entire operation, because the National Parks official, who administers to the historic sculptures and their upkeep, decreed the task to be utterly impossible.

"What do you mean impossible?" rasped the voice from the Oval Office. "Get the Army Corps of Engineers in here with heavy lifting gear, cranes, and trucks."

"It simply will not work, sir. The sculptures, in almost every instance, are too heavy."

"Well, somebody put 'em up, didn't they? Someone lifted them."

"Well, yes, sir. But I imagine those people are all dead. And you can't fax the dead, can you?"

Arnold did not have the time for "smartass remarks from fucking bureaucrats." "Guess not," he replied. "You better try E-mail. But get the statues moved at all costs." At which point he banged down the telephone.

Within hours, the Army Corps of Engineers was on its way from Craney Island, at the head of the Norfolk shipyards, up the Potomac with barges full of the necessary hardware. By dusk, the great Theodore Roosevelt Memorial was being lifted from its island in the middle of the Potomac.

And the 78-foot-high Iwo Jima Marine Corps Memorial, one of the largest sculptures ever cast, was being raised by crane, together with its black marble plinth, 500 yards from the Potomac at the north end of Arlington National Cemetery. The sight of the memorial being removed attracted a large, sorrowful crowd, watching the apparent conclusion of

America's most touching tribute to the courage of the U.S. Marines.

"Don't worry about it," called one young soldier. "We'll have this baby right back here by the end of the month."

Officers from the Engineering Corps were already inside the classic domed rotunda of the Jefferson Memorial, which houses the 19-foot-high statue of America's third President, gazing out towards the Tidal Basin. It was a difficult task, but not impossible. Outside, there were four different-sized cranes and fifty troops to do the job, all experts in their trade.

A young Lieutenant, under strict orders, used his mobile phone to call the White House.

"We got it, sir. The Jefferson will be on a truck by midnight."

"That's my boy . . . How about the Oriental cherry trees around the outside?" replied Admiral Morgan.

"Gardeners say no, sir. They'll die if we move 'em."

"They'll sure as hell die if they get hit by a fucking tidal wave," said Arnold.

"Yes, sir. I did mention that to the gardeners. Well, words to that effect. But they said the trees could be replaced. It was a waste of time."

"Glad to see those gardeners are thinking, right Lieutenant?"

"Right, sir."

The Lincoln Memorial, Arnold's favorite, presented an even bigger challenge. Another 19-foot sculpture, this one of solid marble—Abraham Lincoln, the sixteenth President, seated on a high chair, overlooking the Reflecting Pool of the mall, surrounded by his own immortal words carved in stone.

It was considerably heavier than the sculpture of Thomas Jefferson, but the Engineering Corps was undaunted. As darkness fell, they began moving two cranes through the twelve towering white colonnades along the front of the building.

There were dozens of others, some of which would be designated to take their chances, while others would be lifted and moved, like the Ulysses Grant Memorial and the bronze casting of Andrew Jackson on horseback, made from British cannons captured at the Battle of Pensacola in 1812.

The eternal flame, which burned in a bronze font at the grave of the thirty-fifth President, John F. Kennedy, in Arlington National Cemetery, could not be extinguished, and Admiral Morgan and Senator Teddy decreed that a new flame would be lit from the original and transported to another military cemetery.

They ordered the flame, which had burned without interruption since the President was laid to rest in 1963, to be extinguished the moment that the new one was relocated in consecrated ground. The entire grave site and Memorial were then to be sealed immediately in steel and concrete, in readiness for the relighting when the floodwaters subsided.

Senator Kennedy was uncharacteristically shy and reserved about his late brother's memory. But Arnold said precisely what was on his mind . . . "I'm not having some goddamned terrorist snuffing out the Eternal Flame at the grave of a truly great man. If it's going to be extinguished, the Navy will attend to it. And the Navy will relight it at the proper time. Just so its light never dies, right here on American soil. And Teddy's with me on that."

America was a nation that honored its heroes, and one of the largest memorials to be removed was the solemn 500-foot-long gleaming black marble wall that immortalizes the men who died, or remain missing, in the Vietnam War. Thousands of pilgrims visited here each year, just to reach out and touch the stone, just to see a name. Arnold Morgan ordered it to be removed *"by strong men wearing velvet gloves."* "I do not want to see one scratch on that surface when we return it," he said.

And there was already a company of Army Engineers in Constitution Gardens, carefully wrapping the long line of angular black marble tablets that bear the names of every last one of the 58,156 soldiers who were lost. The Memorial was set less than 300 yards from the stern, giant figure of Abraham Lincoln, who, perhaps above all other Americans, would have understood the cruel perversity of that distant battlefield.

Admiral Morgan ordered an evacuation of the Peace Memorial erected to honor Navy personnel lost at sea during the Civil War and he asked someone to remove and store the statue of Benjamin Franklin, which depicts the old statesman in his long coat, holding the 18th-century Treaty of Alliance between the United States and France.

"He probably could've got the goddamned satellite shut down a helluva lot quicker than us," added Arnold.

Cranes, the armies of workers, the endless roar of the huge evacuation trucks made up the steady stream of traffic bearing its citizens to the high ground of the northwest. The University was now closed and the streets in Georgetown were thinning out.

Fortunately, the nation's capital wasn't home to much large-scale commercial business and industry, but at the banks, there was intense activity, with customer records, cash, and safety deposit boxes being shipped to outlying branches.

On this Sunday, the banks were open until 10 P.M., allowing customers preparing to flee the city at first light Monday morning to withdraw funds or remove valuables. Many law firms, lobbying companies, and stock brokers were moving one large truckload of documents apiece out of the offices and generally heading for the hills.

Almost all other commercial operations not involved in transportation or in assisting the government with emergency procedures were already closed down, having removed as much stock and hardware as possible. Theaters and cinemas too had locked their doors.

But Washington's local television and radio stations were instructed to keep transmitting for as long as possible, under the control of the Pentagon, and, from time to time, they were watched with a beady eye by Admiral Morgan. They would turn off the power only upon the certain information

that the Cumbre Vieja volcano had blown itself into the Atlantic Ocean. That was the official time to leave. Nine hours.

The evacuation of the hospitals was a long and laborious
operation. Every ambulance in the city had been running
nonstop since Friday, ferrying not-too-sick patients home to
leave the city with their families, and driving very sick patients to other hospitals inland, wherever beds could be located. No new patients were being admitted, except for
victims of accidents, and other emergencies. The situation
was getting extremely difficult, because so much of the best
medical equipment had already gone into military storage for
safekeeping.

Any hospital with any spare capacity within 100 miles of
Washington was accepting patients from the city. No one
wanted to move very sick patients any farther than was absolutely necessary, but the Pentagon had ordered all patients
to be out of all hospitals by Wednesday evening. That would
entail every ambulance driving well outside the city at the
time Ben Badr launched his SL-2s. Admiral Morgan had
made it clear he did not intend to lose any ambulances whatsoever, no matter how great the flood.

For the final forty-eight hours, the Military would provide
reserve medical units, out of Fort Belvoir, the gigantic military base south of Alexandria, right on the severely threatened west bank of the Potomac. Emergency treatment
centers, staffed by the Army, were already operational in
Whitehaven Park, Constitution Gardens, and the Washington
Hospital Center.

A small fleet of U.S. Marine helicopters was on standby to
ferry serious cases to a brand-new military field hospital set
up in a safe area out near Dulles Airport. Treatment centers in
the city would remain open until they received the message
that the Hamas missiles had hit home on the faraway island
of La Palma. At which point the Marines' Super Stallion helicopters would evacuate everything and everyone directly to
the Dulles area.

The Police Department in downtown Washington was possibly the busiest place in the city. All leave was canceled, officers were working around the clock, mainly on the streets, patrolling in groups of three and four, especially in areas where widespread evacuation had already taken place. This was not confined just to shops and department stores; the police were vigilantly patrolling and checking on all private homes. The Oval Office, backed by the Pentagon, had made it clear to the public that looters would be shot, if need be.

"Otherwise this whole damn thing could get right out of hand. We've got a bastard of an enemy out there, certainly we do not deserve to fight enemies within. If it comes to that, they can expect no mercy . . ." Arnold Morgan was not joking.

And, of course, the hard-pressed police department knew that as the evacuation gained momentum, the traffic problems would multiply. They were already providing information and advice, and escorts for large convoys. Overhead, police helicopters were constantly reporting and issuing a general overview of traffic movement within the city, and helping to direct resources to where they were most needed.

They were already getting support from thousands of National Guardsmen, who were out on the streets not only assisting with logistics, transportation, and vehicle recovery, but also watching the streets and observing the movements of Washington's citizens closely. This was, one way or another, a bad time to be an American criminal working the nation's capital.

The various fire departments were under orders to stay open and active, providing cover until the very last moment, but reducing their manpower wherever possible. All fire-fighting vehicles were already in working order, so the whole fleet could be withdrawn en masse down the specially cleared highway at the first news that Ben Badr had struck the volcano.

By far, the most troublesome point of the Pentagon's evacuation plan was the prisons and the moving of highly dangerous criminals elsewhere in the country. General Scannell had detailed three companies of National Guardsmen—three hundred men—to assist in preparing a disused military base in West Virginia.

Right now, working under newly installed security lights, they were building high perimeter fences and fitting out accommodation huts. This part of the camp was for prisoners judged to be a menace to the public, and they would be under constant surveillance by armed Army personnel.

Other less dangerous prisoners would be moved to normal jails with spare capacity, but there was little room for brutal convicted killers, and no one had yet taken Admiral Morgan's advice to *"put the whole lot of them in front of a goddamned firing squad and have done with it."* He'd said it only half-jokingly.

Meanwhile, out in the real battleground, U.S. warships were arriving on station, and by midnight, the USS *Coronado* had steamed into her holding area 40 miles northwest of the coast of Lanzarote. Admiral Gillmore immediately opened communications with the *Elrod* and the *Taylor*, which were positioned north of Tenerife, some 60 miles to the west of the *Coronado*. The first orders issued by the new Task Group Commander were for these two frigates to patrol close inshore around the islands at first light—tomorrow, that is. Monday, October 5, four days before H-Hour—*H* for Hit.

Admiral Gillmore did not expect to stumble across the *Barracuda* by accident. Indeed, he did not believe the Hamas submarine to be in the area yet. But in the next day or so, they needed to familiarize themselves with the local charts. The Admiral wanted more reliable underwater fixings. They needed to identify anomalies and problem spots among the permanent characteristics of this part of the eastern Atlantic basin—areas of water swirl, thermal layering, fish concentrations, rocks, reefs, and ridges—all the myriad subsurface elements that can confuse a sonar operator.

Nonsubmarine contacts do one of two things: vanish completely, if they are, for instance, fish shoals, or, if they are rocks, remain solidly in place. Submarines are apt to get moving, giving strong signals with marked Doppler effects.

The initial task of the inshore group was to conduct a comprehensive search of the whole area, mapping the ocean floor as they went. They would use depth charges if anything suspicious came up, and even if no contact was located, their active sonar, sweeping through the depths, would almost certainly drive a marauding submarine out into deeper water, possibly at speed.

And out into that deeper water, Admiral Gillmore was sending six towed-array frigates, ultrasensitive to the slightest movement, the merest hint of an engine. Their task was to prowl the surface, probing the depths, waiting, listening. This offshore group, effectively a second line of attack, would be working in 30 fathoms or more, 25 miles out from the island beaches.

The USS *Samuel B. Roberts,* USS *Hawes,* the *Robert G. Bradley,* the *De Wert,* the *Doyle,* and the *Underwood.* These were the six submarine hunters designated by Admiral Gillmore to guard the offshore areas, and at the same time watch for the *Barracuda* if it tried to run in from out of the west.

The *Kauffman* and the *Nicholas,* two of the earliest arrivals in the Canary Islands from the North Atlantic, would take the western half of the inshore patrol, moving into the waters close to the islands of Tenerife, Gomera, tiny Hierro, and, to the north, La Palma itself.

Because Admiral Gillmore believed the *Barracuda* was most likely to take a southerly route into its ops area, he felt it was most likely to be detected east of the big islands closest to the shores of North Africa—Lanzarote and Fuerteventura. That's where he wanted his two first-choice ships, the *Elrod* and the *Taylor.*

These frigates were commanded by two very senior Captains he had known well for many years, Sean Smith and Brad Willett, both dedicated ASW men, sub-hunting specialists like himself, with months of service in the still suspect Atlantic waters up by the GRIUK Gap.

Like Admiral Morgan, and his immediate boss, Adm. Frank Doran, George Gillmore had arrived at an irrevocable conclusion . . . the terrorist submarine would have to launch its missiles from a point where it could rush for cover from the tsunami. Before the *Barracuda*'s comms room discovered the satellites were down, they would surely try the area off the western Sahara for a long-distance launch, and then race for the cover of the eastern shore of Fuerteventura.

When they did discover there were no GPS satellite coordinates, they would need to creep to the south of Grand Canaria, in the area the *Elrod* and the *Taylor* patrolled, before running toward the south coast of Tenerife, and then into the inshore waters around Gomera. From there they would need to regroup, then get a good visual fix and then move in towards La Palma for the launch.

The *Elrod* and the *Taylor* had a chance of detecting the *Barracuda* as it made its way in from the open ocean, running south of all the islands towards the North African shore. They definitely had a shot at an early detection while the men from Hamas had a mast up while trying to access the GPS. And there would be another opportunity if and when the *Barracuda* began a move west towards Gomera.

The U.S. sea operation consisted of four ships inshore, and six standing off, 25 miles out. Admiral Gillmore had done his geometry. Each TA frigate would need to patrol in a radius of 10 to 20 nautical miles . . . the area measured from the volcano itself to cover the entire band out to 25 miles from the work of the inshore group. The distance around such a circle is about 150 nautical miles. And this would allow the six frigates to cover the entire area continuously. If the *Barracuda* somehow strayed into those waters, life could quickly become extremely tense for Ben Badr and his men.

This left Admiral Gillmore with two other frigates, Capt. Clint Sammons's *Klakring* and Comdr. Joe Wickman's *Simpson*. He would use these to extend the search area whenever it might become necessary, or to prosecute nearby towed-array contacts, or even to thicken up radar coverage inshore.

In such a complex operation, George Gillmore knew better than to leave himself without flexibility. At this stage, his task orders were, of course, extremely narrow—sink the *Barracuda*, however, wherever, whenever, but soon.

Situated 20 miles to his east was the *Ronald Reagan* CVBG. The massive aircraft carrier was preparing to rendezvous with the *Harry S. Truman*, and essentially exchange its fixed-wing aircraft for ASW helicopters. The Battle Group arrived with two LA-class nuclear submarines, but Frank Doran was not anxious to use them in any kind of an underwater hunt.

Admiral Gillmore was aware of that, and both men felt the destruction of the *Barracuda* would be achieved by the ASW helicopters. The *Truman* was expected to arrive on Monday morning, and the exchange operation would begin immediately. As the sun came blazing out of the clear African skies to the east, there was still no sign of the second carrier, but they knew it was under 100 miles away. And the *Elröd* and the *Taylor* were already on their way to their inshore search areas.

By 0900, the *Truman* had made its Atlantic crossing and was 30 miles off the northwest coast of La Palma, steaming east towards the rendezvous with the *Ronald Reagan*. The sea was calm, and a brisk, warm southeast wind blew off the coast of Africa. In the next three hours, this was forecast to shift southwest and bring in a succession of rainsqualls throughout the afternoon. Which was not perfect for the large-scale carrier-to-carrier transfer of aircraft, scheduled to begin at 1400.

Shortly before 1030, Admiral Gillmore completed his deployment of ships for the offshore operation, and, led by USS *Hawes*, under Comdr. Derek DeCarlo, the six frigates set off for their respective search circles in the wide band of ocean between the islands of La Palma and Hierro and the 25-mile outer limit of their operations area.

The *Kauffman* and the *Nicholas* made their way into the inshore waters of La Palma and Hierro, where they would move slowly around the coastlines, mapping the ocean bottom and recording the appearance of sudden shoals of fish or the perfectly stationary sea ridges. Then they would move on to Gomera and Tenerife, always watching the computer screen, which would betray a creeping nuclear submarine.

0800, Monday, October 5
Mid-Atlantic, 27.30N 24.50W.

The *Barracuda* still ran slowly, at just under six knots, still 500 feet under the surface, transmitting nothing. Adm. Ben Badr checked their position and noted that they were 240 miles out from the most westerly Canary Islands, La Palma and Hierro, around 18.50W. They were on a due easterly course, which would take them 20 miles south of the seven volcanic islands that jutted up separately from the ocean bed.

So far, they had heard no searching submarines, no warships. They had twice ventured to periscope depth to make certain the GPS was in sound working order, and found no problems. They had two more days to run before they slid quietly into the area that Admiral Gillmore's ships were currently combing.

As soon as the *Barracuda* slipped by its first landfall, the island of Hierro, it would be within 19 miles of the *Nicholas*, unless Capt. Eric Nielsen had already moved on to the southern coast of Tenerife, into the waters once scanned so thoroughly by the honeymooning Admiral Arnold Morgan.

If the *Nicholas* moved, the chances of the *Barracuda* remaining undetected were doubled, because even the south shore of Tenerife lay 25 miles farther north than Hierro. This would put the *Barracuda* 44 miles south of the nearest U.S. warship, but the day, and the game, were both still young.

Three and a half thousand miles away on the U.S. East Coast, the sun was battling its way out of the Atlantic into cloudy skies. And it was not just the big cities that were trying to empty themselves, but all along the seaboard, rural communities were frantically making their preparations to escape the wrath of the coming tidal wave.

It was cold on the rocky, tree-lined islands off the coast of Maine, and most of the summer people had stored their boats and vanished south to escape the notoriously chilly Maine fall. Inland, the cold was, if anything, worse. There's usually snow in the outfield by the first week of November at the University of Maine baseball park, home of the Black Bears.

The islands were effectively left to the Maine lobstermen, one of the most intrepid breed of cold-water fishermen in the world. Yet there was not a single safe harbor along this coast.

It was essential to either haul the lobster boats and get them to higher ground or, more daringly, anchor them in the western lee of one of the 3,000 islands that guard the downeast coast. These rocky, spruce-darkened islands are mostly hilly—great granite rises from the ocean, which may not stop a tidal wave but would definitely give it a mild jolt. On the sheltered side it was just about possible that the tsunami might roll right by, perhaps leaving a high surge in its wake, but not dumping and smashing large boats on beaches 10 miles away.

The seamen of the Maine islands were accustomed, more than any other fishermen on the East Coast, to terrible weather. And for three days now, they had been moving the endlessly scattered fleet of lobster boats to anchorages out of harm's way.

Boats from Monhegan, North Haven, Vinalhaven, Port Clyde, Tennants Harbor, Carver's Harbor, Frenchboro, Isleboro, and Mount Desert headed inshore, their owners praying that if the giant wave came, the islands, with their huge granite ramparts, would somehow reduce the power of the waves.

Similar prayers on precisely the same subject were almost certainly being offered by somewhat less robust people—librarians, politicians, and accountants, 600 miles south in Washington, D.C. The Library of Congress was also made out of granite from the Mount Desert area. So was the House of Representatives and the Treasury Building.

Out in the deep water, 15 miles from the coast, the three great seaward guardians of Maine's stern and mighty shoreline—the remote and lonely lighthouses of Matinicus Rock, Mount Desert Rock, and Machias Seal Island—were left to face the coming onslaught single-handedly. According to local scientists, the mega-tsunami would sweep more than 100 feet above them. Whether they would still be there when the water flattened out was anyone's guess.

Meanwhile, the fishermen and their families were being ferried on to the mainland, where relatives, friends, and volunteers were lined in packed parking lots, waiting to drive them to safety. Maine is a tight-knit, insular community offseason, with fewer than one million residents. At a time like this, they were all brothers and sisters.

In far, far greater danger was Provincetown, the outermost town on Cape Cod, 120 miles to the south across the Gulf of Maine. This small artistic community, set in the huge lefthand sweep of the Cape, is protected strictly by low sand dunes and grass. By that Monday afternoon, it was a ghost town. Those who could, towed their boats down the mid-Cape highway and onto the mainland. The rest just hit the road west and hoped their homes and boats would somehow survive. Lloyds of London was not hugely looking forward to future correspondence with regard to Cape Cod.

All along the narrow land, every resident had to leave. Massachusetts State Police were already supervising the evacuation. All roads leading from all the little cape towns to Route 6A were designated one-way systems—Wellfleet, Truro, Orleans, Chatham, Brewster, Denisport, Yarmouth, Hyannis, Osterville, Cotuit, and Falmouth. No one was to come back until the danger had cleared.

The evacuation, all the way down that historic coastline, was total. The whaling port of New Bedford was deserted by Monday evening, and the flat eastern lowlands of Rhode Island, a myriad of bay shores and islands, were going to be a write-off, if Admiral Badr's missiles made it to the volcano.

In the shadow of the towering edifice of Newport Bridge, the little sailing town was on the verge of a collective nervous breakdown. Some of the most expensive yachts ever built were home here for the autumn, and many of them had not yet been hauled or had not yet departed for the Caribbean or Florida.

The New York Yacht Club's headquarters, gazing out onto the harbor, would probably be the first to go if the tidal wave came rolling in past Brenton Point. Offshore, Block Island had been evacuated completely by Sunday night, and whether Newport Bridge itself could survive was touch-and-go.

Farther up the coast, there were obvious areas of impending disaster in the long, narrow New England state of Connecticut. The shoreline was beset by wealthy little seaports, the closer they were to New York, the more plutocratic. Bridgeport, Norwalk, Stamford, Darien, and Greenwich— Connecticut's Golden Suburbs, all along the narrowing waters of Long Island Sound. Billions of dollars' worth of manicured property and people, all hoping against hope that central Long Island itself, around 15 miles wide, would bear the brunt of the tsunami.

But it was the northern seaport of New London that was causing the most concern in the state of Connecticut. This is one of the United States Navy's great submarine bases, and home of the Electric Boat Company, which builds them. It is a traditional Navy town, and there had been ferocious activity since before the weekend, all along the jetties, preparing the big nuclear boats to make all speed south to the west coast of Florida. Unfinished ships were being towed 10 miles up-river—anywhere that might be beyond the reach of the tsunami after it hit the helpless north shore of Long Island Sound.

South of New York, the flat sweep of the Jersey shore, with its miles and miles of vacation homes, was defenseless. So

was the entire eastern shore of Maryland, which was nothing
but a flat coastal plain on both sides of the Chesapeake Estuary, with no elevation higher than 100 feet and nothing to
stop the thunderous tidal wave but the flimsiest of outer islands, not much higher than sand bars beyond the long waters
of Chincoteague Bay.

By Monday afternoon, the entire area was almost deserted, hundreds of cars still heading north, joined by another huge convoy from neighboring Delaware, which
shared the same long shoreline and was equally defenseless.

South of Virginia, the coastal plain of North Carolina was,
if anything, even more vulnerable than Maryland. The Tide-
water area was flat, poorly drained, and marshy, meandering
out to a chain of low barrier islands—the Outer Banks—separated from the mainland by lagoons and salt marshes. Out
on the peninsula of Beaufort, Pamlico, and Cateret Counties,
which lie between the two wide rivers the Neuse and the
Pamlico, the issue was not whether the giant tsunami would
hit and flood, but whether the little seaports would ever stick
their heads above the Atlantic again.

Myrtle Beach Air Force Station, right on the coast of
South Carolina, was playing a huge role in the evacuation of
the coastal region, with a fleet of helicopters in the skies assisting the police with traffic. Hundreds of Air Force personnel were helping evacuate the beautiful city of Charleston,
one of the most historic ports in the United States and home
of Fort Sumter, where the Civil War began.

Right on the border lies the oldest city in Georgia, the port
of Savannah. There were 10,000 troops assisting in the evacuation there, and no one even dared think about the wreckage of this perfect colonial city, so carefully preserved over
the centuries, yet so unprotected from the ravages of the
ocean.

Florida was, of course, another story, with its 400-mile-
long east coast open to the Atlantic, largely devoid of hills
and of mountains, all the way south to Miami, Fernandina
Beach in the north, then Jacksonville Beach, Daytona and

Cocoa Beach, Indian Harbor, Vero Beach, Hobe Sound, Palm Beach, Boca Raton, Fort Lauderdale, and Miami.

Stretching out to the south were the low-lying resorts of the Florida Keys, all the way across the Everglades, right down to the yachtsmen's paradise of Key West. Although every one of the Keys had borne the wrath of Atlantic hurricanes before, they hadn't seen a tsunami since long before the Pharaohs ruled Egypt.

The East Coast of the U.S. was absolutely powerless in the face of such a threat. General Rashood had thought out and prepared his attack with immense skill, giving the U.S. population no option but to pack up and run, taking only what little they could carry.

Unless Adm. George Gillmore and his men could find that submarine.

1700, Monday, October 5
Atlantic Ocean, 29.48N 13.35W.

OPERATION HIGH TIDE was one of the most complex and large cross-decking operations in recent memory. The *Harry S. Truman* stood a half-mile off the port bow of the *Ronald Reagan*, and it was pouring like the devil, a gusting sou'wester that swept sheets of rain across the carriers' flight decks.

On paper, the preparations looked simple: to transfer fifty Sikorsky Seahawk helicopters from the deck of the *Truman* onto the deck of the *Ronald Reagan*. Trouble was, the deck of the *Reagan* was already full with the bigger part of its eighty-four embarked aircraft, most of them being flown by four of the most famous fighter squadrons in the United States Air Force.

The new F-14D Tomcat fighter bombers were controlled by the fabled fliers of the VF-2 Bounty Hunters. Three large groups of F/A 18C Hornets were flown by the VMFA 323 Death Rattlers, the VFA-151 Vigilantes, and the VFA-137 Kestrels. In addition, there were the Prowlers and the Vikings, but these were parked carefully away from the main runways.

And then there were the mighty E-2C Group II Hawkeyes, the biggest and most expensive aircraft on any carrier. The early-warning radar and control aircraft, the quarterback of the squadron, first to get in the air, and always parked right below the island, wings folded, ready to head for the stern catapult. No U.S. carrier would leave port without at least three onboard.

Aside from the Prowlers, Vikings, and Hawkeyes, the rest were ready for takeoff from the rainswept deck of their long-time home—the 100,000-ton Nimitz-class carrier, the *Ronald Reagan.*

Over on the just-arrived *Harry S. Truman,* fifty Sikorsky Seahawk helicopters, the latest in modern submarine hunting, were lined up alongside the main runway, blades folded, with six just preparing to leave. The U.S. Navy had three hundred of these hovering state-of-the-art ASW specialists, but not one of them had ever been under more steel-edged orders than those received in the Norfolk yards last week.

Admiral Gillmore had left it to the carrier COs to carry out the aircraft exchange, and both Captains had decided on six at a time as the safest method, especially in this weather.

The helicopter maintenance crews were ferried across separately in a Sikorsky CH-53D Sea Stallion assault and support helicopter, transported from Norfolk especially for this phase of the operation. The Sea Stallion was designed to carry thirty-eight Marines, but today, it was to move back and forth between the carriers, laden with spare parts for the Seahawks plus the Navy experts who knew how to fit them. They would also be ferrying the fixed-wing maintenance crews that were returning to the U.S. with the Tomcats and Hornets.

And now the Seahawks were ready. The *Truman*'s flight-deck controller signaled them away, and one by one their screaming rotors bore them almost vertically into the sky, banking out over the port side of the carrier to form a long convoy that made a wide, slow circular route toward the *Reagan.*

With six airborne, there was now an open deck for the first of the *Reagan*'s Tomcats to land. And over on the Battle

Group's flagship there was intense activity. The red light on the island signaled . . . *Four minutes to launch.*

The first Tomcat was in position at the head of the runway, the visual checks completed. Two minutes later, the light flicked to amber, and a crewman moved forwards to the catapult and attached it to the launch bar. The light turned green, Lt. Jack Snyder, the "shooter," raised his right hand and pointed it directly at the pilot. Then he raised his left hand and pointed two fingers . . . *Go to full power* . . .

Then he extended his palm straight out . . . *Hit the afterburners* . . . Immediately, the pilot saluted, and leaned slightly forward, tensing for the impact of the catapult shot.

Lieutenant Snyder, still staring directly at the cockpit, saluted, then bent his knees, extended two fingers on his left hand, then touched the deck. He gestured: *FORWARD!* And a crewman, kneeling on the narrow catwalk next to the fighter jet, hit the button on catapult one, and ducked low, as the stupendous force of the hydraulic mechanism hurled the jet on its way.

Engines howling, flat-out, it left a blast of hot air in its wake. And, as always, every heart on that deck, every heart in the island control centers, stopped dead. For just a couple of seconds, no one was breathing, as the Tomcat hurtled towards the bow, up the ramp, and out over the water, climbing away, dead ahead, ready to start its 25-mile circle to the flight deck of the *Harry S. Truman*, which would bear it home to the United States.

Five more times, the flight-deck crew of the *Ronald Reagan* sent the Tomcats away, up into the lashing rain, before the flight controller, in his fluorescent waterproof yellow gear, signaled that the Seahawks were on their way in.

Back on the *Truman*, the flight-deck crew anticipated the first of the F-14 Tomcats, which had broken off from the stack of six and circled at 8,000 feet, 20 miles out, heading their way.

It was a 22-ton brute of an aircraft that didn't just glide in, flaring out elegantly just above a mile-long runway like a big passenger jet, but came bucking in, lurching along in all weathers, at 160 knots, damn near out of gas, and then slamming down onto the deck, the pilot praying for the arresting wire to grab and hold.

If it missed, he would have approximately one-twentieth of a second to ram the throttles wide open and thunder off the flight deck . . . before $40 million worth of aircraft would hurtle over the side and punch a hole in the ocean's choppy surface. And there was always the possibility of an outright catastrophe—the hook missing, the pilot's reaction a shade slow, and the aircraft slewing around, piling into forty others, all within yards of millions of gallons of jet fuel.

However many times a pilot had done it, the exercise of landing a fighter bomber on the heaving deck of a carrier would remain a life-or-death test of nerve and skill.

Right now, on the rain-lashed stern of the *Harry S. Truman*, the Landing Signals Officer, tall, lanky Texan Eugene "Geeno" Espineli, was in contact with the incoming Tomcat's pilot, Lt. J. R. Crowell from West Virginia. Geeno's binoculars were focused as well as they could be in this weather, trying to track the aircraft's incoming path.

Ensign Junior Grade Taylor Cobb, the Arresting Gear Officer, was calling the shots, bellowing down the phone, above the howl of the wind, to the hydraulics team working below. He was out on the stern in his bright yellow waterproofs, earphones on, his eyes scanning the deck, checking for even the slightest speck of litter, which could suck into the Tomcat's engine and blow it right out. He was checking for the fourth or fifth time for a broken arrester wire, which could lash back and kill a dozen people, not to mention the absolute certainty of sending the aircraft straight over the bow.

"STAND BY FOR THE TOMCAT . . . TWO MINUTES!"

The massive hydraulic piston was set to withstand the controlled collision between fighter jet and deck. And now everyone could see J. R. Crowell fighting to hold the Tomcat steady, 2 degrees above the horizontal against the driving rain and unpredictable gusts.

The *Truman* was pitching through 3 degrees in the long swells, dead into the wind, at 18 knots. She was rising and falling one and a half degrees on either side of the horizontal, which put the bow and stern through 60 feet every 30 seconds—conditions to challenge the deftness and fortitude of any pilot.

"*GROOVE!*" bawled Ensign Cobb, code for "*She's close, stand by . . .*"

Then, 20 seconds later, "*SHORT!*"—the critical command, everyone away from the machinery.

Out on the deck, all LSOs edged towards the big padded pit into which they would jump if young JR misjudged and piled into the stern. They could see the aircraft now, screaming in through the rain, engines howling.

"*RAMP!*" bellowed Ensign Cobb. And with every eye upon it, JR slammed the Tomcat down on the landing surface, and the flight-deck crew breathed again as the cable grabbed the hook, then rose up from the deck into a *V*. One second later, the Tomcat stopped dead in its tracks, almost invisible in the swirling mist of rain and spray in its wake.

The deck crews came out of the starting blocks like Olympic sprinters, racing towards the aircraft to haul it into its designated parking spot. And out there on the stern, Ensign Cobb, the rain beating off his hood, had already made contact with the second incoming Tomcat . . . "*Okay one-zero-eight . . . wind gusting at 38 . . . Check your approach line . . . Looking good from here . . . flaps down . . . hook down . . . Gotcha visual . . . You're all set . . . C'mon in . . .*"

One by one, they repeated the procedure. Then six more Seahawks took off in the failing light. Then six more Tomcats blasted off the deck of the *Reagan* and headed for the stack 20 miles astern of the *Truman*. Six at a time. Then the Hornets, six more groups, all going through the same death-defying combat procedures, slamming the jets down on the deck, the aces of the Death Rattler squadron, the Vigilantes, and the Kestrels.

These unsung heroes of the U.S. Navy displayed the lunatic, rarefied skills of their profession almost always in private, out here in the Atlantic, away from the celebrity-obsessed society they were trying to protect.

It took six hours to complete the transfer of the aircraft, and it was almost midnight when the final Hornet made its landing. By now, the rain had stopped, and the weary flight-deck crews were heading for their bunks. The fighter pilots were going home with the *Truman* and their aircraft.

The Seahawk crews, now safely on board the *Ronald Reagan*, were mostly asleep. Their task, their ceaseless, intensive mission, to find the *Barracuda*, would begin at first light on Tuesday morning, October 6. And there would be little rest until the submarine was detected. If it would be.

Another twenty-four-hour-a-day operation had been taking place simultaneously, 2,700 miles away to the west in the concrete canyons of New York City.

Ten times more vulnerable than Washington, D.C., New York would take the full might of the tidal wave head-on, straight off the ocean. And although the great towers of Wall Street would probably be the most resolute barrier the tidal wave would hit, they could not possibly stop a force that would probably have swept the Verrazzano Narrows Bridge clean off its foundations seven miles earlier, planted the Coney Island fairground on top of Brooklyn Heights, and dumped the Statue of Liberty into the bottom of upper New York Harbor.

Whether the skyscrapers of downtown Manhattan would still be standing after the opening surge was a subject currently being assessed by a team of eighteen scientists working everywhere, from basements to the city's skies. Opinion ranged high and the only thing they could agree on was that none of them thought more than a half-dozen buildings at best could survive in any shape whatsoever.

Midtown, with its close, tight grid of towers, stretching high into the sky, was an even worse prospect. The breakwater of Wall Street would have reduced the first two waves significantly, but nonetheless, like a house of cards, Midtown would fall. Several of the scientists believed that if two or three high-rises crumbled before the onslaught of the ocean, they would cause a chain reaction and bring down others until the city was leveled.

The most dangerous part was the two wide rivers that flowed past, east and west of Manhattan—the Hudson and the East River. The tsunami would have lost none of its power when it rampaged up these ship-going seaways, and both rivers could rise, initially, by around 100 feet, with millions of tons of ocean water crashing through the city's cross streets. The tides of east and west would probably collide somewhere in the middle, around Park Avenue, moments before the main surge smashed with mind-blowing force into the old Pan-American building, somewhere around the 15th floor.

New York City was no place to be these two weeks. And the same went for Staten Island, Brooklyn, Queens, and the Bronx. The flatlands of New Jersey were even more exposed, and places like Bayonne, Jersey City, Hoboken, and Union City were utterly defenseless. So was Newark, with its flat, wide sea-level airport, right where the Passaic River widens into Newark Bay. That was tsunami country, with a vengeance.

New York City's evacuation operation had begun the previous Wednesday, but the city's biggest problem wasn't so much historic documents, books, and artifacts. It was people. New York City received more visitors every day than the combined permanent population of Washington, D.C., and its environs. In addition to its eight million residents, who lived and worked in the crowded urban sprawl of New York and its greater area, 800,000 visitors took in the sights below the world's most famous skyline every day.

It was a colorful, vibrant melee of races, religions, and nationalities, a volatile mix in a time of crisis. Immigrants from the Far East, India, and Mexico had been pouring in for years, and most of them had few contacts outside their ethnic neighborhoods. Now they had no way of moving themselves, their families, and their few possessions out of the city to higher ground. A couple of days after the President's TV address, Tammany Hall had accepted the responsibility of evacuating two million residents of New York City, providing food and shelter for those who had nothing and those who would most likely have nothing to go back to.

The exodus from New York had already begun, and thus far there had been monumental problems, due to the sheer volume of people who had to be moved westward. Most of them were terrified, panicked, and shocked. Rumors coursed wildly; crowds were alternately lining up for cars and gas masks or hitting the highway in a rush, sitting for hours on congested roads. Everyone was up in arms, and the Army and National Guard could just barely control the mobbed streets, anxiety and fear flaring on every corner, spreading slowly across the city, simmering. Hundreds of National Guardsmen were drafted in from all over New York State to prevent the breaking out of riots.

The Police Department had by now issued instructions for the more affluent members of society to drive out of the area. They designated highways as strictly one-way systems, and decreed which roads could be used to get away, no matter who you were. If you lived in Brooklyn or Long Island, the way out was across the Verrazzano Bridge to Staten Island, and then through the Outerbridge toll, wide-open now, crossing onto highways running west and southwest.

Residents of Queens and Manhattan were ordered to use the Lincoln and Holland Tunnels and then pick up the westward highways. The great span of the George Washington Bridge was off-limits both ways, for the use of the Police, Army, and Government Officials only. The great convoys of trucks evacuating the city were nonstop, both ways, twenty-four hours a day.

During the weekend, a brand-new worry cropped up. Thousands of people, many of whom hardly spoke English, were too afraid to wait for their transportation slots from the Army, the National Guard, or the New York City Police Department. Some were more afraid of those than of the incoming tidal wave. Many took matters into their own hands, buying and temporarily fixing up an entire armada of ancient car wrecks, not only unfit to be on the road but a danger to anyone in or near them.

This clapped-out procession of backfiring, brakeless rattletraps was moving like a mobile junkyard out into the mainstream of the traffic, which was now already crowding the roads and highways.

By Sunday evening, the traffic jams had escalated, the likes of which had rarely, if ever, been seen in the free world. People were sitting on the roadside beside vehicles that were filled to overflowing with humanity and possessions. Cars edged slowly towards the west, coming to a complete standstill as soon as an ordinarily harmless, flat battery felled a vehicle in front of it. On the Triboro Bridge and the 59th Street Bridge, both levels of each were throbbing with cars. Cars jammed the Whitestone, clogged the Throg's Neck, and brought the West Side Highway to a standstill. The Lincoln and Holland Tunnels and the Harlem River Drive were simply parking lots.

By Monday morning, the Mayor had signed an edict giving the New York Police Department emergency powers to sequester every broken-down truck in the city and hand it over to the National Guard. The authorities could designate instant scrapyards; under raised highways and under bridges, they beat down wire fencing to free up space on outdoor basketball courts. They dragged vehicles off the bridges and out of the tunnels and dumped them in the nearest available space.

The Mayor had already declared New York City a potential disaster area, and now he had the army move in and take over the subway and all of its trains, as well as Amtrak and the entire Long Island Rail Road.

The trains were for transportation out of Manhattan and Long Island only. But the going was slow. Vast lines of travelers had been formed along Seventh and Eighth Avenues around 33rd Street, waiting for hours to enter Penn Station.

The trains were efficient and available to move people out of the city on a continuing basis, and the executives of Amtrak and the major New York bus corporations were summoned to City Hall to coordinate and manage the operations.

A massive complex—a refugee camp of sorts—was set up in the hills of New Jersey, west of the horse country around Far Hills. It was a former Army base and the huts were still waterproof. By Monday evening, 100,000 Guards and Troops were on duty, assisting with the evacuation from New York City.

The nearest New York came to full-blooded riots was, curiously, at truck hire corporations, which were attempting to quadruple the usual prices. The companies had no way of knowing if they would ever see their trucks or vans again in the face of the oncoming disaster, but locals saw it as naked price-gouging, a cynical exercise in ripping off frightened citizens. Three hooligans actually set fire to one rental operation on the Lower East Side, torching the office and three vans. The fire department didn't make it in time to salvage them, and the National Guardsmen who arrived quickly on the spot had little sympathy for the owners.

The Police Chief and the Mayor moved in immediately and made price increases illegal, adding that if van rental corporations no longer wished to conduct business, that was fine too, empowering the National Guard, in the same breath, to sequester all trucks in the city.

They came a few hours too late for a more serious riot on the lower West Side when hundreds of fleeing people became enraged at the asking price of $1,000 a day for a compact-sized van. They stormed the office, overpowered the four assistants, smashed the windows, seized the keys hanging on a cork board at the rear of the counter, and made off with twenty-six vans.

Again, there was nothing much the Police could—or would—do. They were working in squadrons with the Army, systematically clearing out residential blocks, helping people with their possessions, issuing exit instructions from the city. More and more National Guardsmen were being ferried in from Upstate New York to help with the compulsory evacuation.

And their task was mammoth, especially in Midtown and the Upper East Side where so many residential apartment blocks were crowded close together, on all streets from 57th Street, north to Sutton Place, First, Second, and Third Avenues. Not so much the more commercial strips of Lexington and Madison, but on the densely residential Park Avenue, and, of course, the east side of Fifth Avenue.

Almost all visitors to the city were either gone or on their way, having been advised at the end of the previous week to leave without delay. The Mayor ordered the Police and the Army to seize the bus corporations in order to ferry thousands of tourists out to the airports.

Officials alerted foreign governments to the imminent disaster, and informed every U.S. embassy, worldwide, that all visitors were now banned from flying to any airport on the East Coast. They requested foreign airlines to bring in extra aircraft, empty, to assist with the transportation of tourists out of JFK, Newark, and La Guardia. Inbound aircraft with passengers were diverted to Toronto to refuel and return home.

The Port of New York was closed, except to outgoing ships, which were redirected south—unless you particularly wanted your big cruise liner or freighter to end up in Times Square.

All businesses not directly involved in transportation were closed—commercial or retail, the service industry, tourist attractions and places of entertainment. Schools, colleges, and universities.

The objective was partly to drastically reduce the amount of routine traffic on the streets of the city in order to provide space for the Army and Police, who were dispatching truck-loads of important government and commercial documents stored in Manhattan by the big corporations.

The closing of shops and stores caused another specter to rear its snarling head in the planning offices of Tammany Hall: the chilling recollection of the Big Blackout in the summer of 1977 when a massive power failure plunged the city into almost total darkness. It had taken the criminal element about ten minutes to realize all the lights were out and the burglar alarms silenced, and several thousand looters and rioters went into immediate action. By first light, they had broken into stores citywide and stolen millions of dollars worth of merchandise.

The situation at hand was not quite that serious. There was plenty of electric power, and many extra thousands of Police and National Guard on duty. And looters themselves had to fear for their lives. Nonetheless, the great empty neighborhoods of New York City and stores full of merchandise would be standing unattended, tempting nefarious characters far and wide.

The police presence tended to gather in full force in certain areas, moving as one large unit from block to block, leaving desolate areas in their wake. Two serious break-ins along West 34th Street near Macy's department store alerted the authorities, and the armed National Guard were moved into the silent areas the moment they arrived in the city.

Police cars drove slowly along the streets, loudly informing anyone who was listening that this was now a designated no-go area, closed to pedestrians and private cars, unless on official business. The cold-blooded warning was loud and clear: *LOOTERS WILL BE SHOT.* This was as close to martial law as it was possible to get, but the Service Chiefs had been adamant—there is only one way to run an operation like this . . . *rigid rules, and ruthless application of those rules. Citizens must learn to do precisely as they are told. Instantly. And not to step out of line. That's the only way we can get this done.*

The guidelines on the desk of the New York City Mayor had come directly from the White House, from the all-powerful Adm. Arnold Morgan, and refined by the Chiefs of Army Staff in the Pentagon. There was to be no arguing, no discussion, no interruptions, no alternative plan. This was strictly military. These were orders, not suggestions . . . *DO IT! AND DO IT NOW!*

Generally speaking, it was working. There had been some dissent and attempted robberies at first, but the sight of the perpetrators who were caught, bundled into the back of an Army truck, and driven off to God knows where had a steadying effect on anyone else with similar ambitions.

The police worked around the clock, aiding, protecting, urging people along the way. On the Upper East Side, elderly former chief executives and various New York dowagers found it was too much to ask to be separated from a precious painting or valuable items of furniture, and refused to leave without them. Most New York cops were understanding, the more so since these people usually had two or three automobiles at their disposal, plus chauffeurs, and were more than happy to make them available to help with the evacuation.

An acute problem was the number of prisoners and guards under supervision of the New York City Department of Corrections, which was currently holding 19,000 inmates, plus a staff of just over 10,000 uniformed officers, and 1,500 civilians. The City Department ran ten holding facilities on Rikers Island—a building around the size of the Kremlin, which sat in the middle of the East River—including two floating detention centers docked off the northern tip of Rikers in an old converted Staten Island ferry. This was, of course, a site unlikely to have much of a long-term future once Admiral Badr drew a bead on the Cumbre Vieja—it stood an outstanding chance of being flattened and simply swept away by the tidal wave.

There were six other jails run by the Department, one in Manhattan and one in Queens, two in Brooklyn, and two more in the Bronx, one of which was an 800-bed barge moored on the south side. The New York City Chief of Police had immediately decided on the early release of those detainees that he judged unlikely to represent much of a future danger to the public, and those unable to post bail. The rest were being transferred to jails in Upstate New York, New Jersey, Pennsylvania, Connecticut, and Massachusetts, under armed guard, on trains in which security was somehow more manageable than on the open highway.

Back in Manhattan, the trenches of Wall Street had been in a state of near-pandemonium for five days. After September 11, many corporations—the headquarters of multinationals, general commerce, manufacturing, service industries, and financial institutions—had been jolted into reviewing and updating their crisis-management procedures. They had already put disaster recovery strategies into operation to get the businesses back up and running in the event of a catastrophe, and thought of backup facilities and systems that could be activated fast if the head office were struck or disabled.

But not many of them had thought it through quite well enough, and many of the same old problems that had haunted so many U.S. corporations in the aftermath of 9/11 were still present.

Several corporations, devastated by the fall of the twin towers, did have backup systems, but in neighboring streets of Manhattan, which obviously rendered them utterly useless in this case.

There were other corporations that had tried to save money by sharing facilities through third-party providers, outfits that had reasonable storage for information technology facilities, but almost no desk space for employees, and were trying to salvage the business from calamity.

The tsunami suddenly brought into prominence the looming potential for a systematic failure that might put several of the world's largest financial institutions out of operation for a significant time. On this early October Monday, the financial capital of New York City was staring down the gun barrel of the most terrible domino effect that could very easily lead to the total collapse of the world's financial system.

A stern warning, in the aftermath of 9/11, had been issued by the regulatory body, the Security and Exchange Commission. In one section of the consultative document, the SEC had imposed specific requirements on major financial institutions, stipulating precisely the acceptable recovery periods and minimum distances between backup facilities.

Some corporations, like International Business Machines, had put these hugely expensive plans onto a fast track, probably fast enough to stay ahead of the tsunami. IBM had scoured the Kittatinny Mountains area out in western New Jersey, looking for a site to install a complete new complex that would enable them to provide, in corporate parlance, "full IT resilience" plus duplicate live data centers.

Finally, they had settled on Sterling Hill and invested heavily in setting up their Business and Continuity Recovery Center in a maze of great office complexes 35 miles northwest of Wall Street—some of them underground, in old disused mines, others in the hills and forests. And there, many of their clients had paid a monthly rental for several years, in return for secure office space with computers and desks, plus entire computer backup if ever required.

IBM's foresight caused several other Manhattan corporations to head for the New Jersey hills as well. For five days now, there had been a steady stream of executives—bankers, financial officers, and an army of backup operators—moving out to New Jersey. A gigantic electronic surge in the local power stations signaled their arrival, as the alternative offices came on stream, operating parallel to their headquarters in nerve-racked Manhattan.

Still battling away, in the almost-deserted ops rooms of Wall Street, was a battalion of computer technicians retrieving hardcopy material, main servers, and ancillary equipment, sending truckload after truckload of high-tech data out to the crowded highways towards to the mountain ranges east of the Poconos.

Morgan Stanley, the securities giant, had been forced to relocate 3,700 employees when the World Trade Center was destroyed. In the ensuing years, that corporation had been committed, more than most, to building a state-of-the-art backup trading facility. They selected their site and were up and running, 18 miles outside of Manhattan, by 2007. The only problem: the complex was located in Harrison, less than two miles from Mamaroneck Harbor, along the flat northern shore of Long Island Sound, where the tidal surge was estimated at about 80 feet. Not ideal for Morgan Stanley.

Alas, very few stockbrokers were among the exodus. The New York Stock Exchange had made a strategic misjudgment. In response to the edict laid down by the SEC, they had built an alternative trading facility to serve as backup in the event of a disaster in lower Manhattan. It could be put into full operation within twenty-four hours, a turnaround time superior to even the one laid down by the SEC. Problem here: the NYSE's backup facility was in New York City.

Its unfortunate location was causing anxieties, from Wall Street to the White House. The sudden closure of the main world market, possibly for several weeks, would likely have catastrophic effects.

The NYSE listed more than 2,800 companies (both foreign and multinationals) that had a global market capitalization of around $15 trillion between them. Its daily functioning was absolutely fundamental to the continued stability of the world markets. Almost all stock exchanges, major and regional, had been agonizing in recent years over disaster recovery facilities. Three thousand business personnel supported trading on the NYSE floor every day, using 8,000 telephone lines and 5,500 handheld electronic devices. A backup trading floor, with full equipment, cost $50 million.

And it's not as if everything neatly kept together. The NYSE has historically spread itself all over the place. They had started enlarging and remodeling as long ago as 1870, beginning with their original five-story building at 10 Broad Street. Over the years, more buildings opened, finishing with a fifth trading room located at 30 Broad Street in 2000, which featured the most up-to-date display technology on earth.

All of this was no easy operation to pack up, and it was almost impossible to imagine duplicating everything somewhere else, under one roof. The exodus of the Stock Exchange was a permanent preoccupation for many high-ranking government officials, the irony being that the tsunami would most likely rub out the backup before it even hit the main Exchange. It looked like they would have to head for Chicago. Philadelphia was out of the question, since the City of Brotherly Love was sited on a peninsula, where the broad Schuylkill River ran into the even broader Delaware. The Philadelphia Navy Base had already evacuated both ships and personnel, since scientists from the University of Pennsylvania thought the rivers might rise up to 25 feet.

The third and biggest issue, after the evacuation of the big businesses, was the removal of the city's art treasures. As one of the world centers of art and culture, New York City contained seventy-five notable museums, plus scores and scores of art galleries. The Metropolitan Museum of Art, the Museum of Modern Art, the Guggenheim, the Whitney, and the Museum of Natural History, known locally as "the Big Five," were world-class institutions. The dozens of others, if they were located in a smaller city, would be star attractions in their own right.

The Metropolitan, for example—or the "Met," as they say in the Big Apple—is tantamount to a universal culture zone, all on its own, with wing after wing, labyrinths of corridors and galleries, containing three million objects in all . . . paintings and sculpture, ceramics, glass, furniture, the armor of medieval knights, bronzes, and the rarest of musical instruments. Each item, historic, genuine, and coveted by curators the world over.

For days now, a great convoy of military trucks had been evacuating the building designated by the U.S. a National Historical Landmark. Already, they had removed 36,000 treasures of Ancient Egypt, from dynastic and pre-dynastic times. Everything was on its way to a U.S. Air Force Base in Upstate New York, where it would be guarded, 24/7, by upwards of 300 military personnel.

Statues, carvings, and sculptures from the land of the pharaohs were packed and shipped, each truck occupied by museum staff, plus a minimum of a dozen armed soldiers. An absolutely priceless life-sized, limestone sculpture of Queen Hatshepsut enthroned, who ruled during the fabled Eighteenth Dynasty (1570–1342 B.C.), was transported in an Air Force truck all on its own, save for the stern attendance of twelve unsmiling bodyguards from the National Guard. It must have been like old times for the Queen, as she roared over the Triboro Bridge, not even considering the possibility of the tolls. The entire Temple of Dendur, a gift from the people of Egypt, had been dismantled and trucked out. The massive stones dating from the Roman period, and depicting Caesar Augustus making offerings to the Egyptian and Nubian gods, had been presented to the U.S. for helping to save ancient monuments during the 1960s, after the construction of the dam at Aswan, which flooded the Nile and formed Lake Nasser.

Roman and Greek statues and sculptures—some up to 5,000 years old, even a bronze chariot worth millions—had been packed and sent north to the enormous Fort Drum Military Base, far upstate in the Watertown area, where the St. Lawrence River runs into Lake Ontario.

Paintings were in the process of being removed by a special detachment of United States Marines, an entire battalion of six hundred men, working around the clock. By special order of the Pentagon, one of the greatest collections the world has ever seen was being removed to West Point Military Academy, 50 miles up the Hudson. Thus, from the moment they were taken down from the walls, the paintings were under guard in the hands of some of the most trusted men in the United States.

During the weekend, they had packed and trucked away

almost the entire collection of Florentine and Venetian masters—works by Raphael, Tintoretto, Titian, Veronese, and Tiepolo, plus some of El Greco's greatest work. The $100 million *Juan de Pareja*, painted by Diego Velázquez in the mid-seventeenth century, was already being guarded at the U.S. Army's stronghold on the Hudson.

And one of the most famous paintings in the world, *Aristotle Contemplating a Bust of Homer,* by Rembrandt, was due to leave at the end of the afternoon, in company with the artist's several other works owned by the Met. The shimmering waters of Claude Monet, Van Gogh's cypresses, the dancers of Degas, the works of Paul Gauguin, Auguste Renoir, Manet, Rodin, and every other renowned artist who has ever lived, were also on their way north.

The Met's collection of drawings alone, by Leonardo da Vinci, Michelangelo, Rembrandt, Dürer, Rubens, and Goya, were worth sufficient money on the world market to operate the annual budgets of every African country south of the Blue Nile.

Master Sergeants prowled the corridors of the museums, while Privates and Corporals sweated and heaved the huge wooden packing cases. Officers supervised the convoys. Inside the Met there were two U.S. Marine Brigadier Generals.

Two hundred miles to the north, the city of Boston, though less than a quarter the size of Brooklyn, was in as great a danger as New York, its downtown district being surrounded by open water. The tsunami would roll in from the southeast, heading northwest, and although the island of Nantucket, the shoals of Nantucket Sound, and the narrow sandy land of Cape Cod just might offer some kind of shield, expert opinion nonetheless forecast that the wave that would come seething up Massachusetts Bay and smash into the downtown area would still be over 100 feet high.

There were only 550,000 people resident in the city, 250,000 of them students at sixty different colleges and universities, all of which had been closed, similar to the 3,000 software and Internet corporations, which sprouted around the city during the high-tech revolution of the '80s and '90s.

Of greatest concern were the famous education centers: the Harvard School of Business, situated three miles upstream, right on the west bank of the Charles River. The Massachusetts Institute of Technology (MIT) sprawled across 150 acres downstream near Harvard Bridge, one mile on the Cambridge side of the wide Charles River Basin, right on the water.

Boston University, the third largest university in the United States, had a vast waterfront campus west of downtown Boston, on the opposite bank of the river from MIT. Dr. Martin Luther King's old alma mater had 30,000 students from fifty states and 135 other countries, most of whom had returned home or to friends for the week.

The evacuation of the universities and the museums was identical in procedure to the other great East Coast cities, but little Boston was somehow more vulnerable than the others. It lacked the granite muscle of New York and Washington's shelter from the ocean. There was a feeling of genuine terror all around the historic New England seaport.

0600, Tuesday, October 6
La Palma Airport, Canary Islands.

The runway of La Palma Airport, newly extended, was now a mile long, almost as if the arrival of the four giant U.S. Air Force C-17 Globemaster III freighters that were now making their approach from the west—six miles apart, line astern—had been anticipated. The cargo leviathans, with their 170-foot wingspans, stood 55 feet high on the ground, with a cargo compartment three times longer than a Greyhound bus and over 12 feet high.

Right now, all four were full, as they came in over the Atlantic, circled around to the north, and headed directly into the southwest wind gusting over the runway. One by one, they touched down at the little airport seven miles south of the main town of Santa Cruz, 20 miles northeast of the yawning crater of the Cumbre Vieja volcano.

Each of the aircraft taxied to a special holding area where its massive rear doors were opened and lowered. There, over the next two hours, they were unloaded by U.S. Army personnel who had traveled all the way from Air Mobility Command, Charleston Air Force Base, South Carolina, 437th Airlift Wing.

The first Globemaster contained the front ends of four army trucks, which were driven out and then backed up the ramps of the other three. When they drove back down and onto the blacktop, they looked more complete, with the long bed of the truck now attached.

And fitted to those flatbeds were the mobile truck-loaded Patriot Missile Launchers, eight of them, the super-high-tech platform for the state-of-the-art MIM-104E guidance-enhanced missiles, the only SAM that has ever intercepted ballistic missiles in combat.

Each launcher came complete with four of these MIM-104E Patriots, the sensational long-range, all-altitude, all-weather defense system designed to counter tactical ballistic missiles, cruise missiles, and advanced aircraft. The thirty-two, already fitted inside the launchers on La Palma, were built by Raytheon in Massachusetts and by Lockheed Martin Missiles and Fire Control in Florida.

Their theoretical objective was relatively simple—to seek out and destroy incoming missiles. The reality, though, was rather more complicated. These things traveled at Mach 5, close to 4,000 mph, which pretty much guaranteed that whatever enemy missile might be on its way would have zero time to get out of the path.

The U.S. military spent all of the 1990s trying to perfect the Patriot after it missed too many of Saddam's SCUDs over Israel in the first Gulf War. Months and months were spent in the Pacific, ironing out problems. The new, updated, improved Patriot had an uplink from its ground-radar control unit with which to feed it final course-correction target-acquisition orders, and possessed a downlink to feed back information on the target's position. These had to be transmitted pretty sharply, since the Patriot was traveling as close to the speed of light as possible.

The system is known as TVM-track-via-missile guidance system and is fitted to the new low-noise front end, which had dramatically increased seeker sensitivity to low radar cross-section targets. The Patriot MIM-104E was a completely new missile, a variant of the Lockheed Martin ERINT (Extended Range Interceptor). It's the last word in advanced hit-to-kill technology, carrying a warhead consisting of 200 pounds of TNT—enough to knock down Yankee Stadium.

Admiral Badr's Scimitar missiles were fast, reliable, and accurate. But in the devastating new Patriot they had a ferocious opponent. The main asset of the Hamas attack was the element of surprise, enjoyed by all submerged-launched missiles. No one would know where it was coming from. You had to see it, and you had to move very fast.

Your Patriot would nail it, but you'd have to get it away in split seconds. Not minutes. The soldiers working on the La Palma airfield knew that. The first four launch trucks moved off now, down towards Atlantic Highway 1. They were heading south to begin with, but would soon swing up the west coast of the island towards the volcanoes and the rugged rim of the Cumbre Vieja, where they would set up their missile battery in readiness, perhaps, for their last stand, against a lethal enemy.

There were sixteen young soldiers in this first group, four of them officers. Each of them knew that if the system acquired their 600-mph incoming target and they missed, it would be their last act on this earth. It would spear in at them from a high trajectory, and the Scimitar would blast the great mountain peak to smithereens, sounding a violent death knell not only for them but for the whole of the East Coast of the U.S.

Maj. Blake Gill was in overall command. Age thirty-five, he was a career officer trained at West Point. Back home, in Clarksville, Tennessee, his wife and two sons, ages five and eight, were waiting. As one of the U.S. Army's top missile experts, he was stationed, along with the 101st Air Assault Division, at one of the biggest military bases in the country—Fort Campbell, Kentucky, hard on the Tennessee border.

Blake Gill had been in an army missile team seconded to the U.S. Navy's cruisers during the Patriot testing programs off Hawaii. He was an acknowledged aficionado of the Patriot system, and a glittering career awaited him with either Raytheon or Lockheed Martin, if and when he ever finished with the Army.

But Blake Gill was like his missile, a Patriot. He was a man cut in the mold of Adm. Arnold Morgan himself, a sworn enemy of his country's foes, a man to whom personal gain was a total stranger. The heavyset Southerner, with his scorched-earth haircut, was plainly headed for the highest possible rank his branch of the Service had to offer. If anyone was going to slam the Scimitar, it was Blake Gill, husband of Louisa, father of Charlie and Harry. Missile man.

He rode in the lead truck in front of the launcher, the four hunter-killer Patriots towering behind him. He carried with him three different ground elevations of the Cumbre Vieja site—one, a satellite photograph of the entire area, taking in the coastlines; another, a map drawn from much closer in; and the last one, a detailed map of the undulating terrain directly around the crater.

Since no one had an exact estimate as to which direction the incoming missiles were to be fired, Blake Gill was relying on the facts presented to him at the Pentagon on his way to the Charleston Air Force Base. He knew he must cover the westerly approach and the more unlikely north, but he had been carefully briefed by both Adm. Frank Doran and the Chairman of the Joint Chiefs himself, Gen. Tim Scannell, that the biggest threat was from the east and southeast.

The *Barracuda* ultimately had to get out of the way of the

tsunami or it too would be destroyed. And that meant it had to seek cover on the eastern side of La Palma or Gomera if it launched at close range.

Major Gill had penciled in one of his mobile launchers to face outwards from the eight principal points of the compass. Any preprogrammed cruise missile could be directed on the most circuitous route into any target, but not without GPS. Therefore a major detour around the volcano, and then a route in from the north or west, seemed utterly unlikely.

Yes, the Pentagon was nearly certain that the missiles would come straight in, out of the east or southeast, simply to give the submarine a chance to save itself. Major Gill knew he must place launcher number five to the southeast. The problem of the northeast occupied him, however. There would be no course correction to the incoming weapons, and no cover out there in open water, nor any place the submarine could reach to find shelter before the tidal wave slung it straight onto the sandy beaches of Western Sahara.

And yet . . . he knew these suicide bastards from the Middle East . . . Maybe sacrificing himself was the master plan . . . Maybe they just did not care . . . They would fire and forget from any spot they pleased and let Allah do his worst. Paradise, perhaps, beckoned. It was not, after all, particularly unusual for the young braves of Hamas to terminate their lives willingly in the Jihad against the West.

Major Gill was thoughtful. Clearly, the *Barracuda* was on its final mission. They were never going to take it home. To where? It could never again come to the surface, never again fire a missile. The forthcoming launch would betray its position, and the odds of it evading a strike force like the U.S. Navy currently had at sea were close to zero.

No, the Hamas terrorists almost certainly knew the game was up the moment they opened fire within a very few miles of ASW warships and helicopters. So they just might launch from anywhere. And he, Blake Gill, had to be ready for a threat from any direction with plenty of overlap.

He would position his mobile launchers, evenly spaced

around the compass, facing out from the crater, in all directions. His maps showed the ground to be extremely rough and uneven, once the end of the road had been reached, and he was grateful for the huge U.S. Marine Chinook helicopter awaiting him up at the summit, which he knew would place the launchers with effortless efficiency precisely where he wanted them.

They drove on down to the village of Los Canarios de Fuencaliente, where hot springs had once bubbled but, long buried by the eruptions of various volcanoes, now formed part of the deadly, roughly 10-mile-long cauldron beneath the mountain.

Major Gill studied his maps. To the south, he knew, was the Volcan San Antonio. A signpost directed visitors to a pathway and a visitors' center around its gaping black crater. Even farther south was the Volcan Teneguia, which is off the beaten track and where only a few adventurers could struggle up its slopes and peer in over the shattered rim.

The convoy of launchers was headed the other way, north, up towards the Cumbre Vieja, glowering under the crystal-blue arc of the sky above the islands. As they drove on in a cloud of black dust, the Major could see the Chinook parked up ahead, about 200 yards off the main road.

It took about twenty minutes to secure the cables that would take the weight of the launcher. Major Gill and the missile crew climbed aboard for the short ride to the summit, and under his direction, the Navy pilot put the launch truck exactly into position, facing due east, overlooking the Atlantic and the distant shores of Gomera and Tenerife.

The giant helo had already deposited all the equipment needed for the Engagement Control Station farther up the escarpment, to a slightly higher peak to the north. Twelve more technicians who had traveled across the Atlantic in the *Truman* had already begun to erect the station, ensuring it had views in all directions overlooking the Atlantic to the east and west, where the frigates were patrolling. And, of course, overlooking the Patriot batteries around the crater to the south, with clear radar range at every point of the compass.

The Engagement Control Station was the only manned station in a Patriot Fire Unit. It could communicate with any M901 Launching Station and with other Patriot batteries, and it also had direct communications to the higher command facilities, in this case Admiral Gillmore's *Coronado*.

Three operators had two consoles and a Communication Station with three radio-relay terminals. The digital Weapon Control Computer was located next to the VHF Data Link terminals.

One of the C-17 Globemasters had brought in the trailer-mounted Raytheon MPQ-53 phased-array Army radar unit, a band-tracking radar capable of identifying one hundred targets at a time. It was a superb component of any top-of-the-line shore missile batteries, and it would carry out search, target detection, track and identification, missile tracking and guidance, plus electronic counter-countermeasures (ECCM) functions.

Its radar was automatically controlled, via a cable link, by the digital weapons control computer in the Engagement Control Center sited farther up the hill. The radar had a range of up to 55 miles, and could provide guidance data for up to nine missiles at any one time. Its wideband capability provided target discrimination never before achieved.

In normal circumstances, this overwhelming piece of electronic equipment might have been considered overkill in the search for one or possibly two incoming "birds." However, in this case, by express orders of Admiral Morgan, there was no such thing as overkill.

As the Patriot missile came flashing into its target, the TVM guidance system would be activated, and the weapon could scarcely miss. And it would not require a midair collision to blow Admiral Badr's Scimitar clean out of the sky. The Patriot just needed to be close enough for a proximity fuse to detonate the high-explosive warhead, in this case, an M248 91kg—200 pounds—TNT blast fragmentation.

The MIM-104E was over 17 feet long, 16 inches in diameter, and weighed 2,000 pounds. At Mach 5, its range was 43 miles and, if necessary, it could fly to a ceiling of 80,000 feet. Arnold Morgan had estimated a very high trajectory from the *Barracuda*'s missiles, which, he thought, would aim to lance down very steeply at the crater of the Cumbre Vieja.

Major Gill had a copy of that shrewd assessment from the Supreme Commander folded neatly in his breast pocket, as he prepared the U.S. Army's ring of steel around the volcano's black heart. As he watched the mighty Chinook flying the Patriot launcher trucks right over the crater and into position, he knew that if the frigate's batteries were not in time, out in the open ocean, his own guided missiles would be the United States' last line of defense.

2330, Tuesday, October 6
The Atlantic Ocean, 27.25N 20.50W.

Five hundred feet below the surface, the *Barracuda* had cut its speed from six knots to five, after a very slight swing to the south. Its course would take it 14 miles south of the flashing light on Point Restinga, the southernmost headland of the Canary Island of Hierro. Right now they were a little under 40 miles to the west, and several days out of satellite contact with General Rashood.

Ben Badr was in the submarine's control room with his XO, Capt. Ali Akbar Mohtaj, who was coming to the end of the First Watch.

The Admiral ordered the submarine to periscope depth for a swift GPS check and a visual look at the surface picture.

In the clear autumn night skies they could see that the ocean around them was devoid of shipping. The GPS numbers were accurate, according to their own navigation charts meticulously kept by Lt. Ashtari Mohammed, Shakira's old colleague.

"*DOWN PERISCOPE . . . MAKE YOUR DEPTH 500 . . . SPEED FIVE . . .*" Admiral Badr wore a soft smile as he felt the ship go, bow down, 10 degrees. He felt safe—so far as he could see—no U.S. Navy dragnet was trying to hunt him down.

The time was 11:30 and 15 seconds. What he didn't know, as the *Barracuda* glided back towards the ocean floor, was that in precisely 24 hours, 29 minutes, and 45 seconds, the world's GPS systems, U.S. and European, were shutting down. Ben Badr was proceeding to a long-range launching, which could not work. First blood to the United States.

He and Captain Mohtaj sipped hot tea with sugar and lemon and stared meditatively at the charts. They would be inside the grid of the seven islands shortly after dawn, and he would now head east, according to their original plan, to launch 30 miles south of Fuerteventura, 30 miles off the coast of Western Sahara.

"If we can launch long-range," said Ben, "we're bound to hit. The missile takes longer to get there. We have longer to get into shelter, and our chances of being detected are close to zero. So far, I like it very much."

By the time they finished their tea, and Captain Mohtaj had retired to his bunk, the GPS was still transmitting. But in twenty-four hours, there would be a mind-blowing change to their plan.

Worse yet, the U.S. guided missile frigate the *Nicholas* was still in the area, and Captain Nielsen's ops room had very nearly picked them up when they put up a mast for that last GPS check. The U.S. frigate was less than 20 miles away, and it caught a slight paint on two sweeps of the radar. It had disappeared on the third, but the ops room of the *Nicholas* was very sharp, and the young seaman watching the screen had called it immediately. His supervisor had logged and given it a numbered track. It was now on the nets, circulating to the rest of the fleet. Of course, it could have been anything—a flock of birds, a rainsquall, a breaching whale or a dolphin. But the operator was not so sure, and the *Nicholas* hung around for an hour, wondering if the "paint" would return.

But nothing unusual occurred, and Captain Nielsen proceeded on slowly through the night down the coast of Hierro, before making for Tenerife. He was steaming only a little faster than the *Barracuda*, which was traveling in the same direction, 20 miles off their starboard quarter, deep beneath the waves.

Wednesday, October 7
The Eastern Atlantic.

THE *BARRACUDA*, still making only 6 knots, steamed quietly past the flashing light on the stark southern headland of Hierro's Point Restingo shortly after 0700. They remained 500 feet below the surface, 14 miles south of the lighthouse, on a bright, sunlit morning.

Twenty miles to the north, moving slowly south, four miles off the rust-red volcanic eastern coastline of the island, was the gunmetal-gray 3,600-ton U.S. frigate the *Nicholas*. She was on a near-interception course with the *Barracuda*, but Capt. Eric Nielsen would turn east for Tenerife 10 miles north of the submarine.

On the west coast of the island, Capt. Josh Deal's *Kauffman* was combing the Atlantic depths electronically, searching, searching for the telltale whispers that may betray the presence of the lethal underwater marauder.

If Captain Deal held his course, he too would eventually reach the submarine's track, but he was also under orders to swing east for Tenerife. Both ships were proceeding with caution, not too fast to miss anything, but with enough speed to cover the wide patch of ocean allotted them by Admiral Gillmore.

The tiny island Hierro, only 15 miles wide, used to be

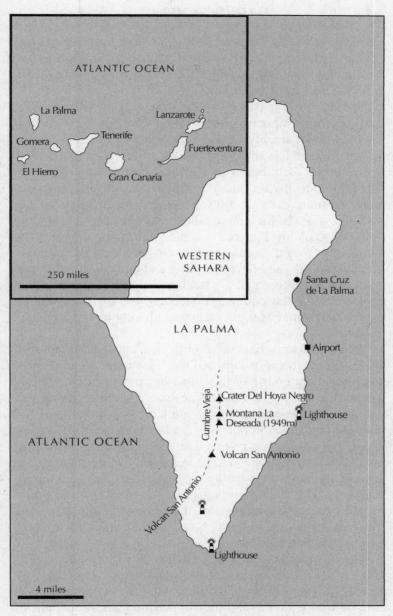

THE LINE OF VOLCANOES IN THE CUMBRE VIEJA RANGES
MAKES LA PALMA'S SOUTH A THREATENING PLACE

about three times the size. But a massive eruption around 50,000 years ago blew it asunder and, according to modern volcanologists, dumped about 100 square miles of solid rock onto the bottom of the Atlantic.

The shape of the island conformed precisely to the geological pattern of a great volcano rising up from the seabed. It shoaled down steeply to 850 feet right off the rock-strewn beach, then, in less than seven miles, plummeted to a narrow plateau 5,000 feet below the surface. From there, the ocean floor dove steeply for one mile and a half, straight down to a depth of more than 12,000 feet. Almost identical ocean statistics to those of La Palma, 50 miles to the north.

At 0800, Adm. Ben Badr ordered the *Barracuda* to creep up slowly from these massive depths to access the satellite, check the GPS, and to report course and position to the private satellite receiver above the house on Sharia Bab Touma in Damascus, the command headquarters of the operation where the former Maj. Ray Kerman already lurked, awaiting the signal.

Admiral Badr's Executive Officer, Capt. Ali Akbar Mohtaj, ordered the periscope and the ESM mast up. There was no threat radar on the surface, and the comms room instantly retrieved a message off the Chinese navy satellite. It revealed the wave-band numbers of the French GPS, should the U.S. take the precaution of blacking out the main access channels. General Rashood had received intelligence of possible "limited GPS interruption," but the Pentagon had been cagey, releasing the news only on the restricted shipping and airline channels. The Arab newspapers hardly mentioned it, and it would be several hours before the General could access the *Wall Street Journal*, since he was operating eight hours ahead of the U.S. East Coast.

The *Barracuda*'s comms staff checked French and American GPS wave bands. Both were onstream. Suddenly they heard U.S. Navy radar. Captain Mohtaj quickly ordered mast and periscope down, and the submarine back to a depth of 500 feet. Too late. Eric Nielsen's *Nicholas* had picked up a suspect at extreme range with three sweeps, 12 miles north of the jutting periscope.

The frigate's computers flashed into action, bringing up the previous "paint," seven hours previously at 40 miles to the west. If the same ship had caused both sightings, they were looking at a transient contact, making around six knots, bearing zero-nine-zero, due east, along latitude 27.25N.

Within seconds, the computerized deductions hit the comms room in the *Coronado* up to the northwest of Lanzarote, and Admiral Gillmore immediately appreciated the situation. For the moment, the *Elrod* and the *Nicholas* were slightly behind the eight ball, but on standby. Right off the northeast headland of Tenerife, he had Capt. Clint Sammons's *Klakring* and Comdr. Joe Wickman's *Simpson*. He ordered them to make good speed south for 100 miles and to begin their search as they crossed latitude 27.30N. ETA *Barracuda*: 2200 hours.

So far as Admiral Gillmore could see, he had the submarine strapped between his four frigates. But he also knew that the *Barracuda* was so quiet, it could creep 500 feet beneath them, at a silent 5 to 6 knots, and not be detected by passive sonar, though it might be "active."

Admiral Gillmore fired off a signal to Adm. Frank Doran, who was still in the command center at Atlantic Fleet Headquarters in Norfolk . . . *"070800OCT09 Possible detection* Barracuda, *course zero-nine-zero, 14 miles south of Hierro Island. Course and speed correlates possible six-knot transient submarine detected 070100OCT09.* Elrod *and* Nicholas *tracking,* Klakring *and* Simpson *running south to intercept. Gillmore.*

Eight minutes later, Arnold Morgan leapt to his feet from his desk in the sparsely furnished Oval Office, punched the air, and gritted . . . *"Come on, guys . . . let's tighten the fucking screws, put that little bastard on the seabed . . ."*

"You're not beginning to take this personally, by any chance, are you Arnold?" asked President Bedford, disarmingly.

"Christ no, sir. I just love chasing boatloads of underwater terrorists around the oceans—I just get a little edgy after the first year . . .”

Meanwhile, back in the eastern Atlantic, Admiral Gillmore ordered the carrier the *Ronald Reagan* southwest towards the coast of Gran Canaria, from its holding position 15 miles north of Lanzarote.

The U.S. Navy's dragnet was closing in, but Admiral Gillmore was taking a calculated risk that the transient contacts were indeed the *Barracuda*. If they were not, and the Hamas terrorists were coming in from farther north, he would be heavily dependent on the steel cordon of guided-missile frigates out of Norfolk, which currently circled La Palma, inshore and offshore.

Right now, a carrier was flying two continuous patrols between the west coast of La Palma and the towering coast of the island of Gomera, where the precipitous cliffs crash headlong into the ocean, just 35 miles northeast of Hierro.

All of the Navy's assessments claimed that the submarine, if it was to fire its missiles visually, *must* come in towards the Cumbre Vieja from either Gomera's southwest or northeast coast. The *Barracuda* might ultimately duck back behind this rocky fortress for shelter in the moments before the megatsunami surged outwards into its horrendous reality.

Oblivious of the bear trap closing in around them, the *Barracuda* had somewhat carelessly failed to detect the closeness of USS *Nicholas,* and now the Russian-built nuclear boat proceeded deep along her easterly course, slowly and quietly.

Down in the Navigation area, Lt. Ashtari Mohammed estimated that by midnight, they would reach a point 24 miles southwest of Playa de Ingles, the seething gay Mecca of the island of Gran Canaria, winter headquarters of Sodomites International, and a place likely to be crushed beneath a 50-foot tidal wave one hour after impact. Still, death by drowning would probably arrive on fleeting wings, which would doubtless beat the hell out of being turned to stone.

That particular point on the chart would be critical for the submarine, because they would arrive there just as the world GPS was scheduled to crash. And the precise moment that Admiral Badr ordered his ship to the surface would determine how swiftly he would know that a long-range launch was out of the question.

And they ran quietly and silently all day, without the U.S. frigates locating them. At 0030 on that moonlit Thursday morning, Admiral Badr ordered the *Barracuda* to PD, and her periscope came thrusting out of the water, alongside her mighty ESM mast, which was almost as thick as a telegraph pole. The two steel poles jutted right into the path of the radar sweeping across the water from all four of the trailing U.S. frigates.

The *Barracuda* sucked down a signal from General Rashood in the couple of seconds before the submarine's ops room picked up the frigates on their ESM. Continuous sweeps. Captain Mohtaj simply said, "We're surrounded, sir."

"I understand that," replied Ben Badr. "But they're six miles away and we're not finished by any means . . . *10 BOW DOWN 600 . . . MAKE YOUR SPEED TEN . . . COME RIGHT TWENTY DEGREES . . .*"

At that moment, young Ahmed Sabah came bursting out of the comms room with the communication from Damascus . . . *U.S. GPS satellite communications crashed at midnight . . . Zhanjiang naval base making no contact with French version . . . world GPS black. Abort long-range launch. Repeat abort long-range launch . . . Change course northwest and proceed to coast of Gomera . . . Then head into La Palma launch zone 25 miles off the east coast, for visual setup. Allah goes with you. Rashood.*

All four U.S. frigates picked up the radar contact, and all four had solid contact. Both previous detections had been along the 27.25 line of latitude, and so was this third one. Each of the four Commanding Officers—Eric Nielsen, C. J.

Smith, Clint Sammons, and Joe Wickman—was now certain
that they had their quarry under surveillance. And they all
knew, of course, that the GPS was down, and that the *Barracuda* was almost certain to change course right here at
27.25N 16.06W.

Admiral Badr's navigation room had not immediately understood the extent of the GPS blackout. Lt. Ashtari Mohammed had observed that they were receiving nothing from
the satellites on their screens, but he was looking for a tech-
nical fault at first. It was not until Ahmed Sabah read out the
signal from General Ravi that Ashtari fully realized the implications of his blank screen. There was no GPS, and there
was not going to be any. The U.S. Air Force's 50th Space
Wing, out in Colorado, had placed a four-minute transmission delay on their formal announcement:

No GPS signal before 0100 Saturday October 10.

That had been Admiral Morgan's order, on the grounds
that four minutes would be too long for the *Barracuda* to
leave a mast up, and it might just run on for several more
miles before they realized the GPS was down permanently.

General Ravi had dealt with that, however, and now Ben
Badr ordered an immediate course change . . . *"COME
RIGHT ONE HUNDRED NINETY DEGREES . . . STEER
COURSE THREE-ZERO-ZERO . . . MAKE YOUR SPEED
FIVE . . . DEPTH 600."*

Captain Mohtaj, at the helm of the *Barracuda,* now making course west-nor'west, handed the ship over to the CPO,
Chief Ali Zahedi, at 0100. There was a 90-mile deepwater
run to the shelter of the eastern shore of Gomera, and there
was no problem staying "below the layer," 600 feet under the
surface, since the Atlantic all around the Canary Islands was
nearly two miles deep.

But the sudden course change had unnerved the crew.
Even though just a few of the senior command were aware
that they were surrounded by U.S. warships, and their long-
range launch plan had been scuppered, everyone quickly
knew there was something amiss.

They were headed into the jaws of the United States Navy, which was not a great place to be. But General Rashood had made no mention of aborting the mission. Rather he had urged them forwards, as the soldiers of Allah, to strike the fateful blow against the Great Satan.

Admiral Badr called a briefing meeting in his small private office. In attendance were Captain Mohtaj, Comdr. Abbas Shafii, the nuclear specialist, Comdr. Hamidi Abdolrahim, the chief nuclear engineer, Lieutenant Ashtari, the navigator, and Ahmed Sabah.

"Gentlemen," said Ben Badr. "I am no longer able to say with any certainty that any of us will survive this mission. However, my orders are that it must be completed, and it will be completed."

He poured tea for them all from a silver pot into the little glass cups with their silver holders. And he paused carefully, to allow his words to sink in. It was the first time in two underwater missions that anyone had ever suggested martyrdom.

But the anticipation of death is not so very far from the minds of any Islamic freedom fighter, and the fear of imminent death was less among these men than it might have been among those of another religious persuasion. Nonetheless, Ben Badr was surrounded by grave faces, and he was aware of the need to hold their attention.

"In many ways," he said, "nothing very much has altered. Of course it would have been preferable to fire our missiles from two or three hundred miles out, but as we now know, that will no longer be possible. However, our target has not moved, and we are perfectly capable of creeping in, to a 25-mile range, taking our visual bearings, and launching our Scimitar missiles straight at the volcano.

"The only change in our attack pattern is a need to be nearer the target, but the computerized missile will still obey our command. We just have to aim it straight and true. A nuclear missile doesn't need to be dead accurate, as long as it hits within a couple of hundred yards of the target. The blast will do the rest."

"But there are two changes, Admiral," said Ahmed Sabah. "One is the length of time we shall be on the surface, the other is our departure."

"Of course," said Ben Badr. "We will most certainly be detected by the American warships, but I believe we will have a few precious minutes to get deep after the two launches. And no matter how good they are, it remains extremely difficult to locate and attack a quiet submarine that is running very slow, hundreds of feet below the surface."

"How deep, sir?" asked Commander Shafii.

"One thousand feet, minimum. If they are using depth charges we will go to twelve hundred. It's blind chance, and terrible bad luck to get hit at that depth. Especially if we have a 5- or 10-minute start on them. And we'll try to make our missile launch at least two miles from the nearest warship."

"Will they launch missiles at us the moment they catch a sight of it?" asked Ahmed.

"I'm hoping they'll concentrate their energies on trying to shoot down the Scimitar," replied Admiral Badr. "They may get a couple of ASROC away, but even then we still have a few minutes to get deep. They'd be very lucky to hit us, especially if they were hell-bent on shooting down the Scimitar at the same time."

"I think we've got a serious chance of escape," said Ahmed Sabah.

"Yes," replied the Hamas Admiral. "An excellent chance."

"Sir, how about an attack from the air? I mean, torpedoes launched from helicopters?" said Commander Abdolrahim.

"That, Hamidi, is a game of cat-and-mouse. We will put up a mast for our fix. Then go deep again and stay there, before we run up to our ranged launch point, take our bearings, and fire, twice. The helicopter may be close, but it is unlikely to be close enough in my view. And again, all U.S. energies will be concentrated on the Scimitars. We still have a great chance, believe me. And we have one other huge advantage . . . Allah goes with us, not with the Infidels."

And with that, Ben Badr called the entire ship's company

to prayer, using, expertly, the words of the muezzins that echoed from a thousand Middle Eastern mosques four times a day:

> *Allahu Akbar* . . . (God is most great.)
> *Ash hadu an la ilaha Allah* . . . (I bear witness
>   that there is none worthy of worship but God.)
> *Ash hadu an-an Muhammadar rasulul-lah* . . . (I bear
>   witness that Mohammed is the Prophet of God.)
> *La ilaha ill Allah* . . . (There is no Deity but God.)

Each man, with the exception of the helmsman and the sonar chief, made his declaration of intent and enacted the twelve positions of prayer, making two prostrations in which their foreheads touched the steel of the deck.

The second salam signified "Peace and Mercy to You," and Admiral Badr, aware of the men's fear of the next few hours, began by quoting from the Koran . . . *"Never think those slain in the way of God are dead. They are alive and well provided for by their Lord."*

And he reminded them that the Prophet Mohammed, close to despair, once cried out to God . . . *"O Lord, I make my complaint upon thee of my helplessness and my insignificance before mankind. But thou art the Lord of the poor and the feeble. And thou art my Lord. Into whose hands wilt thou abandon me?"*

And Ben Badr, summoning all of the emotion of the 1,400-year-old worldwide brotherhood of Muslims, quoted again from the Koran, from God . . . *"Remember me. I shall remember you! Thank me. Do not be ungrateful to me. You who believe, seek help through patience and prayer."*

Each member of the crew, now standing, palms outstretched to God, now wiped them across his face to symbolize the receipt of God's blessing.

Admiral Badr prayed silently, then he too wiped his face, and indicated that prayers were concluded. He once more confirmed to the helmsman the course of west nor'west and ordered his senior staff to the missile room, where they would begin the task of checking the nuclear warheads on the two great Scimitars.

By this time, Admiral Gillmore was in receipt of the data from all four of the tracking frigates. Their data showed the precise position of the submarine's periscope, which all four of the U.S. radars had swept, at 0030, 24 miles off the most promiscuous area in the North Atlantic outside of the rutting stags, breeding on Scotland's Isle of Skye.

U.S. Navy Commanders are accustomed to keeping accurate charts and would cope with the downed world GPS system better than anyone else. And George Gillmore studied his screen carefully . . . *Now this character understands he can't fire long range . . . Therefore he'll turn in toward his target . . . Maybe west nor'west . . . Maybe due west back along his old course . . . But no other direction is any good to him . . .*

He immediately ordered the *Elrod* and *Nicholas* to take the west-nor'west track, with the *Klakring* and the *Simpson* proceeding more westerly. He also ordered the carrier to alter course, bringing its formidable air power from the northwest coastline of Tenerife westward into the 80-mile-wide open seaway that divides that island from La Palma.

But the *Barracuda* kept moving forward, slowly, softly, through the dark ocean depths, unseen, unheard, her transmissions shut down. She made no sound through the water. Her great turbines were doing little more than idling, betraying no vibration lines. The Russians had spent years and years building their two state-of-the-art underwater hunter-killers, and thus far, no one had detected either of the Hamas *Barracuda*s with any real certainty or accuracy.

Admiral Gillmore thought he knew damn well where the *Barracuda* was, and so did his four frontline frigate Commanders. At least they did one hour ago. But no one could prove the submarine's direction, and until the Americans locked on to a new surface radar paint, or obtained an active radar contact, that submarine would remain elusive.

And all through the next fifteen hours it ran on undetected. Despite the constant Seahawk helicopter patrols across every yard of water between the seven islands, despite the probing searches of the ASW specialist S-3B Viking aircraft. Despite the quivering sensitivity of the frigates' electronic towed arrays, and the high-powered blasts of their active sonars. And despite two serious attempts to trap the submarine between highly alert electronic sonobuoys, dropped into the water from the helos.

Not all the probing of the dipping low-frequency sonars could locate the *Barracuda*, as it steamed silently west nor'west, way below the thunder of the noise above the surface, where the distinctive howl of the Viking's GE turbofans were sufficient to waken the dead.

Only twice, towards the end the long journey up to the coast of Gomera, did Ben Badr risk a fleeting five-second thrust of his ESM mast, and both times they picked up radar transmissions from the Vikings that were operating beyond the 25-mile circle around the volcano. Each time, the ESM computerized accurate bearing and classification. By the time they came into the inshore waters, "behind" the east coast of Gomera, Admiral Badr privately thought that this had rapidly begun to turn into a suicide mission.

Again he called his most trusted men into his office— Mohtaj, Shafii, Ali Zahedi, and Ahmed Sabah.

Did they still have a chance? At getting away, that is, not firing the Scimitars. Answer, probably not. They were driving forward into the very teeth of the U.S. Navy's steel ring of defense. And right now they each understood that they would need several separate sorties to periscope depth. To try to achieve their mission with just one, or even two, extended visits to the waters right below the surface would be tantamount to blowing their own brains out.

Their only chance of success and escape was to come to PD fleetingly to make their visual setup to get a fix on the land and the high peaks of the Cumbre Vieja mountains. And then to vanish, to return for a final fleeting range check, then to fire the two missiles in quick succession. At no time should they spend more than seven seconds above the surface. Not if they hoped to live.

By 1600 on that Thursday afternoon, they were in relatively shallow water, 2,500 feet, running 600 feet below the surface, four miles off the east coast of Gomera. Captain Mohtaj was in the navigation room assisting Lt. Ashtari Mohammed as he plotted a northerly course to a point 6 miles off Point del Organo. From there it was a straight 16-mile run-in to the proposed launch zone, 25 miles off the volcanic coast of La Palma. Subject to enemy intervention, they aimed to fire from 28.22N 17.28W.

Every man in the ship knew that the U.S. defenses would grow tighter and tighter with every mile they traveled. But no one had ever put a firm fix on the *Barracuda*, as far as they knew. Its crew was now generally aware of the prospect of imminent death, but they also felt a sense of security in their deepwater environment. They had just journeyed several hundred miles under the brutal surveillance of the U.S. Navy, and no one had located them yet. They still had a chance.

By 1800, it was still broad daylight as they crept along the Gomera coast, and Lieutenant Ashtari advised they now had a clear range in front of them, straight to La Palma. Admiral Badr had already rolled the dice in his own mind. He was determined to accomplish the mission, determined to get a correct fix on the Cumbre Vieja, determined to fire his two missiles straight into the crater, or as near as he possibly could. For the escape, everything was in the hands of Allah. But Admiral Badr knew that the odds heavily favored the Americans.

Lieutenant Ashtari checked the ship's inertial navigation system (SINS), a device beyond the purse of most commercial shipping lines and, in the end, way beyond the purse of Russia's cash-strapped Navy. But the *Barracuda* had one, and it had measured course, speed, and direction every yard of the way since they had left the submarine jetties in Huludao in the northern Yellow Sea three months ago.

The system was developed especially for submarines in the 1950s, and had been progressively refined in the years that followed. It had one objective: to inform navigators precisely where they were in the earth's oceans, even after not having seen the sun, moon, or stars for weeks on end. Both U.S. nuclear boats, the *Nautilus* and the *Skate,* had used the system when they navigated under the polar ice cap in 1958.

The *Barracuda*'s SINS was vastly improved from those days—and phenomenally accurate—calculating regular accelerations but discarding those caused by gravitational attraction, pitching, and rolling. All the way across the North Pacific, all the way down the endless west coast of Canada and the U.S.A., around South America and up the Atlantic, the SINS had provided a continuous picture of the submarine's precise position. Given the pinpoint certainty of their start point, the system would be accurate to between 100 and 200 yards at the completion of a round-the-world voyage.

In recent years, the ease and brilliance of the GPS had somewhat overshadowed the old inertial navigation processes, but every submarine navigation officer kept one quietly onstream. Indeed, most senior Navy navigators instinctively checked one against the other at all times.

Lt. Ashtari Mohammed knew precisely where he was, despite the best efforts of the U.S. Air Force in Colorado to confuse the life out of him. The SINS screen now put him at 26.17N 17.12W. They were off the north coast of Gomera in 125 fathoms, still 500 feet below the surface.

This would be the final visual fix before they headed into the firing zone, and Lieutenant Mohammed requested a 7-second look through the periscope to take a range and bearing on the towering basalt cliffs of Les Organos, a little over 5 miles to their southwest, and still visible in the late afternoon light, now a little after 1830.

Ben Badr agreed to head for the surface at slow speed, and he did so knowing their target above the coast of La Palma was dead ahead, 41 miles, west nor'west. The periscope of the *Barracuda* slid onto the azure surface of the water on a calm afternoon. The Admiral was staring at a stopwatch ticking off the seconds. He heard them call out the fix on two points of Gomera's coastline—Les Organos and the great curved headland north of the village of Agula.

> *"UP PERISCOPE!"*
> *"All round look . . ."*
> *"DOWN!"*
> *"UP! Right-hand edge—MARK! DOWN!"*
> *"Two-four-zero."*
> *"UP PERISCOPE! Left-hand edge—MARK! DOWN!"*
> *"One-eight-zero."*
> *"UP!"*
> *"Organo anchorage light . . . two-two-zero . . ."*
> *"DOWN!* How does that look, Captain Mohtaj?"
> "Excellent fix, sir. Course for launch position . . . two-nine-zero . . . distance 16 miles."

Admiral Badr heard the comms room accept a signal from the Chinese naval satellite, and then he snapped: *"Okay, that's it, five down . . . 600 feet . . . Make your speed 7 knots. Make a racetrack pattern when you're on depth . . ."*

Ben Badr knew there was little point making a three-hour low-speed run through the night into the launch zone, and then hanging around until daybreak right on the 25-mile line from La Palma's east coast. The place would be jumping with U.S. warships, helicopters, and fixed-wing aircraft.

Right here, off Gomera, no one was looking quite so intensely. Generally speaking, Ben Badr preferred to run in silently, arriving at first light and setting up his visual fix with the sun rising to the east directly behind him. That way he could come to PD, essentially out of nowhere, and he'd surely be able nail down his fix without detection, 7 seconds at a time.

He called for the satellite message, which he knew was from General Ravi. *Ben, the thoughts of both Shakira and myself are with you at this time. If Allah is listening, as He surely must, His humble warriors will be safe. The prayers of all Muslims right now are only for you . . . to wish you the safest journey home after the Scimitars have done their holy work. Ravi.*

2300, Thursday, October 8
The White House, Washington, D.C.

Admiral Morgan and President Bedford were gathered with senior Naval Commanders in the Situation Room in the lower floor of the West Wing. A huge, backlit computer screen showed a chart of the Canary Islands, a sharp red cross in a circle signifying the last two sightings that the Navy believed were of the *Barracuda*. A brighter white cross in a circle showed the spot Adm. Frank Doran on the Norfolk link now believed the *Barracuda* to be.

He had it already on the 25-mile radius line from the La Palma coast. Which was slightly jumping the gun. Admiral Badr had not yet made his final commitment to the run-in to the launch zone. And would not do so for another half hour. The U.S. Admirals' estimates were about 16 miles ahead of themselves, which is a fair long way in a remote and deserted ocean.

Admiral Morgan was personally bracing himself to read a report from a hastily convened meeting in London of the International Convention for the Safety of Life at Sea. This august gathering meets only about every twelve to fifteen years, explicitly to draw up the International Regulations for the Prevention of Collisions at Sea, more generally known as the Rules of the Road.

Before him was the Convention's first report of a day without GPS. And the opening instance of disaster, the very first serious wreck, astounded him. A Liberian-registered crude carrier of some 300,000 tons had somehow mistaken the southern shores of the entrance to the Strait of Magellan for the Isla de la Estada, turned sharp right making 20 knots, and driven the tanker straight onto the beach at Punta Delgada.

"Five hundred miles off course! In a calm, nearly land-locked bay, and he thought he was on his way through the roughest goddamned ocean waters in the world, on his way to Cape Horn!

"Jesus Christ!" said Arnold. "Jesus H. Christ."

The second item did even less to restore his equilibrium. A Panama-registered freighter out of Indonesia had completely missed Japan's huge southern island of Kyushu, never mind the port of Kagoshima, her final destination.

The freighter headed straight for the tip of the South Korean peninsula, but never made that either, charging straight into the seaport of Seowipo on the lush subtropical island of Jejudo and ramming into the evening ferry from Busan.

Arnold could hardly believe his eyes. The third item was equally appalling. The master of a 200,000-tonner, carrying crude oil to Rotterdam, slammed into the Goodwin Sands at low tide, six miles off the east coast of Kent at the north end of the English Channel, and was still jammed tight in about four feet of water.

There was another huge tanker on the beach in northern Nigeria, a chartered yacht parked 300 miles adrift off the wrong island in the West Indies, and the captain of a large cruise ship out of Naples was wondering why no one was speaking Italian on the island of Corsica.

Lloyds of London was apoplectic. Every fifteen minutes, there was another report from some remote corner of the globe where an expensive ship had lost its way and floundered ashore. Admiral Morgan was just beginning to see a glimmer of humor in all this, but the consequences of massive lawsuits directed at the United States for switching off the GPS prevented him from actually laughing out loud.

"The legal ramifications are clearly a nightmare," offered Adm. Alan Dickson. "Lloyds might see it as an opportunity to get back at us after all these years—you know, that nutcase U.S. judge who nearly bankrupted them twenty years ago, holding Lloyds responsible for all those asbestos cases that happened years before anyone even dreamed the stuff was a health hazard."

"They might at that," said Arnold. "But they'll have to do it here. And since it was essentially the Military that switched the GPS off for military reasons, we'll probably refuse to submit to the judgment of civilians."

"Good idea," replied Admiral Dickson. "Meanwhile the world's beaches are filling up with shipwrecks."

"Driven and piloted by incompetents," said Arnold. "Guys who should not hold licenses to navigate in open waters. And we gave all shipping corporations ample warnings of a forty-eight-hour break in GPS service. They put monkeys at the helm of their own ships, that's their goddamned problem, right?"

"Absolutely, sir," said the CNO. "Guess there's no change in the eastern Atlantic. No sight nor sound of the submarine, for what? Almost a day?"

"Almost," replied Arnold. "And right now we're coming up to midnight. Just a few minutes and it's October 9. D-day. I just hope the little bastard comes to the surface real soon. George Gillmore's got the entire area surrounded."

"Well, the only good thing about not seeing him is that he can't fire without coming to PD. Just as long as he stays submerged, he ain't firing. And that pleases me no end."

"Me too," said Arnold.

Lt. Comdr. Jimmy Ramshawe, sitting thoughtfully in the corner with his laptop, spoke suddenly. "You know, sir. I wouldn't be the least surprised if we were way off in our assessment of the *Barracuda*'s position right now. I can't imagine why he'd run right up to the most heavily patrolled spot in the area and then hang around. If you ask me, he's still lurking off Gomera. And he won't close in till he's good and ready to launch."

"As a matter of fact, that's what I'd do," said Arnold. "I'd stay somewhere quiet and then run in at first light."

"How long's that, Arnold?" asked the President.

"Well, they're four hours in front of us, so I'd say another couple of hours."

"Not me, sir," said Lieutenant Commander Ramshawe. "I'd go while it was still bloody dark. And I'd go damn slow, so the minute I got there, I could get the periscope up and make my visual fix."

"Have you ever been in a submarine, Ramshawe?" said Admiral Morgan, sternly.

"No, sir."

"Well, you shoulda been. Got the right instincts. And I think you might be correct. Let's get Frank on the line in Norfolk. See what he thinks. Then we'll get a signal on the satellite to George Gillmore."

Meanwhile, beyond the White House, the East Coast prepared for the final stages of evacuation, which, by Presidential decree, would begin at midnight. The streets were busier now than they had been for several hours. The lights were beginning to go out in several government buildings as skeleton staffs headed for the cars and the roads to the northwest.

The Police were scheduled to make the Beltway around the city one-way, counterclockwise, and designate the main Highway 279 "North Only" starting at midnight. This would enable all members of Government to head for the Camp Goliath area, fast.

President Bedford insisted on being among the very last to leave the deserted capital city. "Not until we know that the volcano has been blown," he said. "Not until the tsunami is within 500 miles of our shores. That's when we go."

Over at the Pentagon, the Special Ops Room staff intended to remain functional until the very last moment before flying up to Goliath. The U.S. Marines had two Super Stallions ready to take off from the Pentagon, and two more on the White House lawn. Between them, they could airlift 220 key personnel from the teeth of danger.

As the clocks ticked into the small hours of the morning, the vast evacuation of the East Coast was almost complete. It was now October 9, and all the small towns from Maine to south Florida were very nearly depleted.

Places like Boston, Newport, and Providence, Rhode Island, the Long Island suburbs, New Jersey, and the Carolina coastal plains were all but deserted. The one city still writhing in desperate last-moment agonies was the Big Apple—New York City—where the traffic snarls were still appalling, and the railroads were still packed with thousands of people trying to make it to safety, west of the city. But their journeys were much longer than those of the short-haul Washington evacuees and the New Englanders fleeing Boston for the relative closeness of the Massachusetts hills.

Trains took twice as long to return to New York, across the vast New Jersey flatlands, most of which were about six inches above sea level. And there were so many more thousands of people with nowhere to go. The Army was coping valiantly, bringing in hundreds upon hundreds of trucks, and commandeering just about every gallon of gas in the state. But the evacuation was just swamped with the massive throng of people trying to get out of the city, and the Army Commanders began to think that there were not enough trucks, buses, and trains in the entire world to sort them all out, before the whole goddamned place went underwater.

The Ops Room in the Pentagon received a new and heartfelt request from New York every hour. More transportation, more manpower, more helicopters. The last request read by Gen. Tim Scannell was from a Gulf War veteran, a high-ranking Colonel, and it ended thus . . . *"Sir, you have absolutely no idea what it's like up here. I never saw so many frightened people. Terrified people, that is. They don't know what's going to happen to them. I implore you to get another hundred trucks into Midtown Manhattan. Or I'm afraid we'll just go under."*

Admiral Morgan was well aware of the crisis facing the Big Apple, and he conferred with General Scannell on an hourly basis. They banned any form of crisis coverage by the media, shut down the New York newspapers, and took over the television networks, using them strictly to broadcast Military information and instructions to the population. Coverage of any kind of confusion, or of human-interest stories that might spread panic, was absolutely banned.

Admiral Morgan told all corporate media managements that if one of them dared to transgress his guidelines, their building would be instantly shut down and then barred by the heavy guns of the tanks that roamed the New York City streets.

General Scannell actually appeared on the screen in a closed-circuit television linkup to all broadcasting stations on the East Coast to confirm the Martial Law threat made by the Supreme Commander of Operation High Tide. "We can cope with damn near anything," he said. "Except for mass panic. Do not even consider stepping out of line."

So far, no one had.

And now it was 0100 on the morning of October 9, D-day for the Hamas hit men. With exception of the churning cauldron of New York City, the East Coast evacuation was winding down. Millions of people had made their way to higher ground and now waited in the western hills from Maine to the Carolinas and beyond.

Military spokesmen occupied every television and radio channel, and their words were professionally calming, assuring the population that the front line of the United States Navy still stood between the terrorists and the execution of their attack on the great volcano in the eastern Atlantic.

Admiral Morgan had instructed the military broadcasters to sign off each one-hour bulletin after midnight with the reassuring, morale-boosting words . . . "We have the power, the technology, and the bravest of men to carry out the Pentagon's defensive plan—and always remember the words of the great American sportswriter Damon Runyon, *The race is not always to the swift, nor the battle to the strong—but that's the way to bet!*"

0905, October 9
Eastern Atlantic
Barracuda, **28.21N 17.24W**
Speed 5, Depth 600, Course 290.

The waters were still dark above the *Barracuda* as it ran silently along its west-nor'west course. They were three miles short of their launch position, running well below the layers, transmitting nothing, still undetected.

At 0530 local time, Admiral Badr slid up to periscope depth, and inside his seven-second exposure limit he was immediately aware that the entire area was "lousy" with antisubmarine units, active and therefore probably passive too. But the "layers" had protected him well, and he threaded his way deep again, into the great underwater caverns, which so distort and confuse probing sonars from the surface.

Ben had enough time to assess that there were almost certainly Viking aircraft combing the surface above him, but few ships. As they continued forward, however, he could hear active transmissions from helicopters and frigates inshore of him. All in all, he concluded there was a highly active layer of U.S. defense from about 12 miles off the towering eastern shores of La Palma.

For the fifth time in the early morning journey, he ordered a major course change, just to check that there was no one trailing behind him. Then he corrected it back to two-nine-zero, and slowly, making scarcely a ripple, he once more brought the ship to periscope depth for his final "fix." And as the submarine slid gently into the now-brightening surface waters, he made one single order:

"PREPARE MISSILES FOR LAUNCH!"

They detected no close-active transmissions, and Admiral Badr nodded curtly to the helmsman, CPO Ali Zahedi, who cut their speed to just three knots.

"UP PERISCOPE, ALL-ROUND LOOK!"
Twenty seconds later—"DOWN!"

Ahmed Sabah, keenly aware of the seven-second rule drummed into him by Admiral Badr, knew the mast had been up too long. And he stared at the CO, trying to read either "rattled," "desperate," or "confused" into his leader's facial expression. But he saw nothing, apart from a certain bland acceptance. And he did not like what he saw. Not one bit.

Allah! thought the brother of Mrs. Ravi Rashood. *He's given up, he thinks we're trapped.*

"Sir?" he said, questioningly.

And Ben Badr, apparently unhearing, said mechanically, "The place is swarming with helicopters. And I thought I saw a frigate inshore." And then:

"STAND BY FOR FINAL FIX AND LAUNCH! UP!"

"Point Fuencaliente Lighthouse. Bearing. MARK! DOWN!"

"Two-eight-six."

"UP! Point de Arenas Blancas Lighthouse. Bearing. MARK! DOWN!"

"Three-zero-seven."

The planesmen held the submarine at PD. And the seconds ticked away before Ben Badr again ordered:

"UP! High Peak, Cumbre Vieja Mountains. Bearing. MARK! DOWN!"

Lt. Ashtari Mohammed, drawing swift, straight pencil lines on his chart, connected the final *X* that marked the High Peak and the launch point, then called clearly:

"TWO-NINE-SEVEN . . . range 26.2 miles."

"Plot that pilot—and get the positions into the computer right away—for launch."

**0556 (Local), U.S. Army Patriot Station
Cumbre Vieja Volcano Summit.**

To the east, the American guided-missile men, manning the ring of Patriot rockets, had a sensational view of the Atlantic

Ocean, beyond which the sun was shimmering dark red as it eased its way above the horizon. The rose curtain of dawn reflected the burning west coast of Africa, and it seemed to illuminate their battleground.

The Americans stared down-range towards the waters that shielded their enemy. They were out there somewhere, but hidden, an unseen force waiting to strike at them from out of the blue. But the men of the Patriot batteries were ready, and many of them stood, fists clenched tight, watching the tireless Navy helicopters and Vikings clatter over the distant ocean wilderness, sonars probing.

Maj. Blake Gill had snatched some sleep late the previous afternoon, but had been wide awake ever since, patrolling his eight missile batteries ranged around the crater. He made his patrols on foot, accompanied by four Special Forces bodyguards. At each one, he stopped and stared at the looming launch platforms above his head, as if probing for a mistake, a wrong angle, a wrong electronic connection. But he found nothing.

The MIM-104E-enhanced guidance Patriots, the only SAM that had ever knocked a ballistic missile out of the sky in combat, were immaculately deployed on all points of the compass. All thirty-two of them were in place, ready to go at a split second's notice. Blake knew he was looking at the greatest interceptor ever built, a steel hit-to-kill weapon.

He had towering pride in the equipment he controlled, and he told each and every team as they gathered around him up there in the dark, on the summit of the volcano . . . "I been in the ole missile game a long time. And I seen a lot of guys come and go. But if I had to name the one team I ever met who would damn-and-for-sure knock this bastard out of the sky, it would be you guys. And hot damn! I mean that with all of my heart."

He left them all feeling 10 feet tall, ready to operate at the absolute top of their game. And now he was watching the screens inside the Engagement Control Center, just a little higher up the hill from the eight batteries, and he was demanding a last-minute check on communications, ensuring they were in constant touch with the missile launch and tracking stations on the four frigates in the immediate area, the *Elrod,* the *Nicholas,* the *Klakring,* and the *Simpson.*

Major Gill opened up the lines and checked with Admiral Gillmore's ops room in the *Coronado.* He checked the computer lines and the comms to the patrolling airborne helicopters. Blake left nothing to chance. Any one of those guys out on the water—radar men, lookouts, sonar rooms, pilots, or navigators—anyone who saw anything was just two touches of a button from instant contact with the Patriot Engagement Control Center.

They needed to move fast. But they still had time. In Major Gill's opinion, the U.S. defense forces were heavy odds-on to win. Just as long as everyone stayed on top of their game.

The big 17-foot-long Patriots would do the rest. At least the 200 pounds of TNT jammed inside the warheads would, as they streaked in towards the Scimitars at MACH 5. The Hamas missiles had the element of surprise in their favor, but the U.S. Patriot was six times as fast, and well proven over the course.

Major Gill spoke to Admiral Gillmore, and the two men once more checked their entire comms systems. The new Patriot could cope with bad weather—a long, 40-mile-plus range, any altitude, and it did not need to collide with the incoming missile. The Patriot's state-of-the-art proximity fuse would detonate when it came close, which would blast the Scimitar to bits without even hitting it.

0635 (Local), *Barracuda*
28.22N 17.28W, Launch Zone.

"UP! Better all-round look . . ."

Ben Badr looked and felt relaxed. He marked a helo in the dip three miles to the west, and another in transit two miles to the north. He noted the class of the Oliver Hazard Perry frigate inshore of him, and its bearing.

It was a rather leisured survey of the waters around the submarine, conducted by a man who believed he had all the time in the world, but knew, in his heart, that there would be no escape in the end. They couldn't stop him firing, and they probably would not have time to stop the Scimitars. But whatever happened, they would not let him out of the waters around the Canary Islands. This had become, most definitely, a suicide mission.

The *Barracuda*'s periscope was jutting out of the water for all of sixty seconds—too long, too hopelessly long. And the U.S. helicopter in transit, piloted by Lt. Don Brickle, caught it on radar, at 0635.

He swerved towards it for a dip on the last known position, and instantly alerted the ops room in the *Nicholas*, plus any other helicopter in the vicinity.

Three minutes later, the *Barracuda*'s sonar room reported the helo's hydrophone effect (HE) and sonar transmissions from close astern.

Simultaneously Lieutenant Ashtari called out the positions inserted into the Scimitar's fire-control computer.

"MISSILES READY TO LAUNCH!"

Lieutenant Brickle banked his Seahawk hard to starboard and spotted the great black shadow of the *Barracuda* just below the surface as he overflew. It was holding its two-nine-seven course, and over his right shoulder he saw the *Nicholas*'s second helo, piloted by Lt. Ian Holman and hurtling in from the southeast.

And at that precise moment, Ben Badr ordered his missiles away.

"STAND BY!"
"READY!"
"FIRE!"

The big Russian submarine shuddered gently as the first of the mighty Scimitars ripped out of its tube and broke the surface, roaring skyward in a cloud of fire and spray. Its rear wings snapped out sharply, and it cleaved its way up through the clear early morning air, growling and echoing with malevolence, just as it had been programmed to do by the secret rocket engineers beneath the North Korean mountain of Kwanmo-bong.

Admiral Badr watched it through the periscope. He stood staring at the lenses as the Mark-2 nuclear-headed weapon made a high, steep trajectory, 600 mph on an unswerving course, straight at the crater of the Cumbre Vieja, 26 miles away. Two minutes and thirty-six seconds' flying time. It was headed straight into the path of the USS *Elrod*, under the command of Capt. C. J. Smith.

Ben Badr wished with all of his heart that Ravi and Shakira could have been with him to share the moment. He would not, however, have wished the next half hour on his worst enemy.

And he stepped away to give what he believed correctly might be his last command.

"STAND BY MISSILE TWO!"

High above them, Lieutenant Brickle was hard at work vectoring Lieutenant Holman on to their target.

"Firm contact active, classified CERTSUB bearing two-nine-seven range, 600 yards, opening slow. Vectoring Dipper Delta Three into immediate attack, using lightweight torpedo."

"Delta Three, this is Bravo Two, vector 225, stand by weapon launch . . ."

"Delta Three, roger—out."

"STAND BY—STAND BY! MARK DROP! Now! Now! NOW!"

Lieutenant Holman hit the button with his right hand, and

the Mark-50 torpedo flashed away from his undercarriage, diving steeply toward the water.

"Bravo Two—this is Delta Three. Weapon in water. I can see his periscope still headed west nor'west. Intend taking dip station three miles ahead."

"Roger that, Delta Three. Target speeding up—Jesus Christ! He's launched another missile!"

On board the *Barracuda*, everyone heard the explosion and they felt the massive impact of the torpedo as it slammed into their starboard quarter 30 feet astern of the fin. The blast almost spun the submarine over, rolling it onto its portside.

Aft in the reactor control, Comdr. Abbas Shafii and Comdr. Hamidi Abdolrahim were hurled with terrific force into the bulkhead. But the roll was too great for the reactor, which automatically "scrammed," the rods dropping in and shutting it down completely.

The main lights went out instantly, and water cascaded onto the decks, but the compartments were sealed, and though Admiral Badr knew that the ship was damaged, probably severely, it wasn't sinking. He ordered the crew to reduce speed down to 5 knots, on battery power only. And he made a course change to the south, bow down 10, trying to get deep.

The battered Commanders in the reactor control room regained their feet. CPO Ardeshir Tikku came away from the screens and tried to assist. Every alarm in the ship was sounding, and Captain Mohtaj took over the conn while Ben Badr and CPO Ali Zahedi made their way for'ard.

"SHAFII . . . we need to get that reactor up and running fast . . . Start pulling the rods, otherwise we're beaten."

Chief Tikku's fingers flew over the keyboard, unaware that high above, Lt. Ian Holman and Lt. Don Brickle were preparing to strike again.

The two Seahawks were clattering directly above the wallowing *Barracuda*, communicating calmly, with a new arrival, Delta Four, the helicopter from the *Elrod*, piloted by Lt. Paul Lubrano.

"This is Bravo Two. Explosion on bearing two-nine-six. Delta Four stand by second weapon drop. Delta Three interrogative hot?"

"Delta Three Hot, bearing three-five-six, range two thousand five hundred yards. Explosion on bearing, still closing. Explosion on bearing. Delta Four stand by."

"Delta Four."

"Delta Four, Delta Three, vector 065, stand by."

"Delta Four, this is Delta Three, MARK DROP! Now, now, NOW!"

"Delta Four, weapon away!"

The second torpedo dropped away from the pursuing Seahawk and split the waves with its impact, powering hard towards the stricken *Barracuda*, which now limped along 50 feet below the surface. The torpedo smashed into the casing for'ard of the fin and blew a hole almost 30 feet wide. Water thundered into the submarine.

No one knew exactly what had hit them. In precisely thirty-two seconds, the submarine had been slammed twice, and now she made her last dive. Through the sonars, the U.S. Navy operators heard the strange metallic tinkling sound that signifies a big warship was breaking up on its way to the ocean floor.

The reactor control room staff managed to seal off their section of the boat with seconds to spare. And they may have lived one minute longer than the rest of the ship's company. But at 2,000 feet, the pressure could not but crush the remnants of the hull. And now it sliced down in several large pieces, still clanking, like the bells of hell.

Meanwhile, on board the *Elrod*, the lookouts saw the missile launch and watched it climb to the west. Inside the ops room, the McDonnell Douglas Harpoon radar system acquired the target immediately and locked on.

The Officer of the Deck reported to the CO, "Captain, sir,

subsurface missile-launch green 65, four miles opening arcs for SAM."

"Very well, Missile Control . . . you have permission to shoot—WEAPONS FREE!"

The first ASROC lanced into the air in a huge cloud of smoke, making Mach 0.9, straight at the Scimitar hurtling, high overhead. Seconds later, there was a huge puff of smoke, way up in the stratosphere, as the heat-seeking U.S. missile smacked into North Korea's finest, reducing it to high-altitude rubble.

In the same split second, the next Harpoon was launched at the same target, but in the absence of a Scimitar it locked onto the nearest Seahawk, Bravo Two, swerved towards it, and was just cut down in time by the *Elrod*'s fire control center.

Bravo Two's pilot, Lt. Don Brickle, nearly had a heart attack when he saw the Harpoon scything through the sky, coming straight at him. And even when it blew apart a mile and a half out, he was still aggrieved.

"Jesus, you guys. Are you out of control? I'm on your side . . . You think I was wearing a fucking turban!"

There was a semblance of mass confusion, and a slight amount of shaky laughter interspersed with one report stating that the second Harpoon had been cut down and splashed into the water, another confirming the hit on the first Scimitar. A third confirmed two major explosions from the submarine. Yet another announced the second of the *Barracuda*'s missiles was on its way.

The high-octane chatter on the helicopter frequencies was now baffling the life out of everyone. Capt. C. J. Smith ordered, "WEAPONS TIGHT!" before someone else tried to shoot down a Seahawk.

And then it became crystal clear. The second Scimitar was well on its way, making a steep trajectory, straight down the bearing towards the Cumbre Vieja. It had been running a full forty seconds, and was still climbing after six miles. C. J. Smith himself snapped out the critical order:

"*Patriot Boss—frigate* Foxtrot Charlie. *Missile inbound one-one-three. All yours, over.*"

Major Gill, up on the heights in the Engagement Control Center, watched the automatic system instantly activate the band-tracking radar, the radar beams that could locate and track one hundred targets at a time, if necessary.

The search, target detection, track and identification, missile tracking, and guidance took four and a half seconds to lock on . . . "*Got it, sir!*"

"*This is Patriot Boss. We have it. Are you expecting more?*"

"*Unknown, Patriot Boss. We have problems out here, but launch vehicle is under heavy attack. Further launches possible but unlikely.*"

"*Patriot Boss, roger that.*"

At which moment, the first of the most sophisticated guided missiles ever built howled into the sky above the crater, its radar being controlled automatically by the digital weapons control computer right next to Major Gill in the ECC.

The Patriot thundered up its course, bearing 113, seeking its target, which was now headed downwards from an altitude of 30,000 feet, about 10 miles out from the crater.

Major Gill ordered missiles two, three, and four to launch. But there was scarcely a need. Patriot One, making over 3,000 miles an hour, screamed through the air towards the Scimitar. Twelve seconds from launch, it blasted with staggering force less than 50 feet from the Hamas missile. Two hundred pounds of TNT—almost enough to make a dent in the island of Gomera—cast a bright but smoky glow in the azure skies.

The second Scimitar was blown apart, its burning fuel falling colorfully over a wide area, nine miles out from the volcano. Its nuclear warhead never ignited but simply dropped into the Atlantic. And the cheer that went up from Major Gill's missile men would not have disgraced Yankee Stadium.

"Foxtrot Charlie. *This is Patriot Boss. Missile splashed.*"

"Foxtrot Charlie. *Thank Christ for that.*"

Admiral George Gillmore sent in the official report to the Pentagon . . . *090652OCT09.* Barracuda *submarine fired two submerged-launch guided missiles at the Cumbre Vieja volcano east of La Palma from 25-mile range. Submarine destroyed and sunk by two helo-launched torpedoes. Both missiles splashed. Harpoon from USS* Elrod. *Patriot from the summit. God Bless America. Gillmore.*

EPILOGUE

OPERATION HIGH TIDE was declared at an end in the small hours of October 9. Americans awakened to learn that the danger had passed. The threat had been real. The U.S. Military had destroyed it, and it was a weary Adm. and Mrs. Arnold Morgan who left the Oval Office at four o'clock that morning.

They climbed aboard the new Hummer 2A, with its bulletproof darkened windows, and were driven out through the northern suburbs of Washington to the big Colonial house in Chevy Chase, followed by a Secret Service detail of four guards.

It was almost 5:45 when Kathy produced poached eggs, English muffins, grilled bacon, and sausage. It may have seemed like a banquet, but neither the Supreme Commander of High Tide nor his wife had eaten anything since the previous Wednesday's breakfast of fruit salad.

Admiral Morgan, calling the shots from the Oval Office, may have looked like what the media called him—the Consummate Military Hardman. But the Hamas threat to the U.S.A. had taken a seven-week toll on him.

Personally, Kathy blamed Charles McBride. "If that damn fool had listened," she said, sipping her coffee. "If he'd just taken the advice of his Intelligence Officers and the Military, half the pressure would have been removed from this Operation. The people who knew how to handle things could have just got on with it."

"You're right there," muttered Arnold. "We've got to keep our guard up. Always. Because there's a lot of enemies out there. But the biggest danger to the United States of America is when you get some comedian in short pants in the Oval Office."

"Do you think it will all come out—the military coup in the White House, the removal of the President, and . . . everything?" asked Kathy.

"I sure as hell hope not," replied Arnold. "I hate to see the country tearing itself apart. And I'm just hoping that that jackass McBride feels suitably ashamed. At least too ashamed to write his goddamned memoirs."

"Did Alan Dickson tell you how close that last missile was when the Patriot blew it up?"

"Oh, that wasn't a problem. The guys had a ton of time once they got the bird away."

"Yes, but how long would it have been before it hit the crater?"

"Forty seconds."

"Mother of God."

President Paul Bedford made a broadcast to the nation at 7 A.M. He announced an end to the emergency, and an end to the effective martial law that had been in place for the past ten days.

He appealed for a calm return to normal life and assured everyone the Armed Forces would do everything in their power to help restore order in the big cities.

He congratulated the media on their restraint and cooperation, without ever referring to the fact that Admiral Morgan had threatened to blow up their buildings if they stepped out of line.

He regretted all of the inconvenience and huge amount of federal money that had been spent on the civilian and government operations.

"However," said President Bedford, "I was sworn into this great office, not just to protect the Constitution, but to protect the citizens of the United States of America. Each and every one of you. It was an unwritten promise, but one that I took most seriously."

He outlined with brevity, and a certain coolness, the scale of the threat from a group of Middle Eastern terrorists.

"I could take no chances," he said. "Five hours ago, the United States Armed Forces destroyed the terrorists and their missiles, and their submarine. The danger is passed.

"However, we have opened up consultations with the Government of Spain to place a U.S. missile shield on permanent guard on the summit of the Cumbre Vieja. We have also begun negotiations to form a coalition of interested parties to build an engineering system that will drain the underground lakes beneath the volcano.

"And with these initiatives, we issued a warning to Hamas, and to other organizations like them—*WE ARE NOT YET FINISHED WITH THIS—WE WILL COME AFTER YOU WHEREVER YOU MAY BE HIDING."*

Same Day
Damascus, Syria.

Ravi and Shakira Rashood, watching the CNN satellite news broadcast in the big house on Sharia Bab Touma, were stunned at the announcement, slowly grasping the fact that Ben Badr and Ahmed Sabah, together with the rest of the crew, were dead.

They had believed their mission to be impregnable, that even the mighty U.S.A. was powerless to locate a marauding nuclear boat.

Still in shock, they walked to the great Umayyad Mosque before the citadel and prayed for their fallen comrades. Each of them had known of the massive danger. And each of them had realized that Allah might call their colleagues to Paradise at any moment.

However, when close friends, comrades, and relatives are

involved, death always comes on ravens' wings. And the General and his wife were unable to speak for a long time.

Same Time
The White House.

Meanwhile, President Bedford concluded his address to the nation . . . "Once again," he said, "the men of the United States Army and Navy have come through for all of us with their customary bravery and efficiency. And I thank them all, in particular their outstanding Commanders.

"I thank also the Supreme Commander of this operation, both civilian and military—Admiral Arnold Morgan—who most of you will remember from the last Administration. The Admiral, as always, stepped up to the plate when the nation was threatened.

"He scarcely left the White House for the past eight days, and yet, when our combat troops fought that short and vicious engagement out there in the eastern Atlantic this morning . . . well . . . I guess we had an extra man on every missile battery, at sea and on land . . . in every helicopter . . . in every ops room . . . A man who was, in a sense, with them, every yard of the way.

"Admiral Morgan is just that kind of guy, and every man in the Armed Services knows it. And I do not quite know how we would have gotten along without him.

"And I am sure you will join with me in now wishing him a long and happy retirement."

Same Time
Chevy Chase.

Arnold took another king-size bite of sausage, and Kathy blew him a kiss from across the room.

"Hear that, my darling?" she said. "Retirement."

"That's right," said Arnold, munching away cheerfully. "That's what I'm doing."

"Right," replied Kathy Morgan, a little uneasily. "It's just that I darn well know, when something diabolical happens, they'll summon you again. And when the bugle sounds, you'll still come out fighting."

Acknowledgments

MY LONG TRANSGLOBAL JOURNEY in a Russian-built nuclear submarine was masterminded by Adm. Sir John "Sandy" Woodward, former nuclear boat commander, former Flag Officer Submarines, Royal Navy. The Admiral is the last man to fight a full-scale modern Naval action at sea—as Task Force Commander, Royal Navy, in the battle for the Falkland Islands, 1982.

He also advised me, with endless patience, on the complexities of nuclear propulsion, without demonstrating even a glimmer of frustration . . . Well, not that many. In the decisive Naval action of the book, it was his decision to strike from the air rather than underwater. He also helped me plan the U.S. Navy's search-and-kill strategy in the eastern Atlantic. And, as ever, he has my gratitude.

The former Special Forces officers, who tend to be in constant attendance while I write these "techno-thrillers," never wish to be identified, for obvious reasons. But I thank them, all the same. And they each know how grateful I am.

I consulted, on both sides of the Atlantic, with three eminent scientists on the causes and effects of tsunamis. On two or three critical issues there was a slight variance of opinion. I thus name none of them, since to do so might cause a certain amount of friction in the geophysical community. Worse yet, I should almost certainly get the blame for tampering, albeit lightly, with sincerely held opinions!

—*Patrick Robinson*